Chris Panatier

THE REDEMPTION OF MORGAN BRIGHT

ANGRY ROBOT

ANGRY ROBOT
An imprint of Watkins Media Ltd

Unit 11, Shepperton House
89 Shepperton Road
London N1 3DF
UK

angryrobotbooks.com
twitter.com/angryrobotbooks
For you are perfection

An Angry Robot paperback original, 2024

Cover by Sarah O'Flaherty
Edited by Gemma Creffield and Steve O'Gorman
Illustrations by Chris Panatier
Set in Meridien

ISBN 978 1 91520 289 5
Ebook ISBN 978 1 91520 292 5

Printed and bound in the United Kingdom by TJ Books Ltd.

9 8 7 6 5 4 3 2 1

MIX
Paper from
responsible sources
FSC
www.fsc.org   FSC® C013056

PRAISE FOR CHRIS PANATIER

"The Redemption of Morgan Bright *is a gorgeous mystery. A layered maze that grants access to the darkness yet shows the reader only enough to put one foot in front of the other as they delve ever deeper into dread. Beautifully told and with perfect pacing, Chris Panatier unveils each piece with deliberation and care, building to a series of jaw-dropping reveals and an ending I never saw coming. This is horror that hits on every level, crafted with an expert hand. I absolutely loved it.*"

Laurel Hightower, author of *Below* and *Crossroads*

"*Chris Panatier is a literary lepidopterist who goes-for-baroque with his gothic shocker* The Redemption of Morgan Bright, *metamorphosing a mindf**k of a novel that's equal parts Shock Corridor and Midsommar. You don't read this book as much as let it cocoon you, consume you, rearrange and change you from the inside out, and when it's done – with you – what emerges from its radiant pages is an altogether altered reader. What a beautiful butterfly of a book this is.*"

Clay McLeod Chapman, author of *What Kind of Mother* and *Ghost Eaters*

"The Redemption of Morgan Bright *is a dizzying mix of epistolary recollections, sinister encounters and dark, velvety prose laid sumptuously upon the platter of Hollyhock Asylum. Important themes are tackled with Panatier's usual urgency and intelligence. A sharp thorn of a book.*"

Gemma Amor, Bram Stoker and British Fantasy Award nominated author of *Dear Laura* and *Full Immersion*

"*A triumph. Panatier has created a world I never wanted to leave, but by the time I hit the third act, I dreaded turning the page.* The Redemption of Morgan Bright *is a brutal, beautiful, relentless, and tragic journey into hell. I freaking loved it.*"

Sam Rebelein, author of *Edenville*

"*Panatier spins us a tale straight from an alternative America that will haunt your days and nights. This is* The Handmaid's Tale *meets* Midsommer, *an immersive reading experience that will take you deep into the caverns of your own mind to inspect the wriggling, creeping things that lurk in the shadows. How would you transform, in the search for personal peace? And just how far would you travel into darkness to uncover a dark and insidious truth?*"
Caroline Hardaker, author of *Mothtown* and *Composite Creatures*

"*A twisted chrysalis of a novel. A book to dissolve the spine and rearrange the guts. Read it and be altered, emerging with the kind of wings that soar best in the dark.*"
Daniel Cohen, bestselling author of *The Coldmaker Saga*

"*A powerful new voice in horror, Panatier skillfully delivers a mind-bending tale that blurs the line between reality and insanity while leaving readers to distinguish fact from fiction. An enthralling story that I didn't want to put down, I'll be thinking about this one for some time to come.*"
Shawn Burgess, author of *Tears of Grief Hollow*

"*Haunting, gorgeously visceral and, frankly, gross – the mysteries of Hollyhock House will keep you pinned to your seat, desperately flipping pages until its secrets are unearthed. You'll never look at a can of cranberry sauce the same way again.*"
Lauren Raye Snow, World Fantasy Award Finalist

"*This was my first time reading Chris Panatier, but it certainly won't be my last.* The Redemption of Morgan Bright *was a rollercoaster, equal parts* Girl, Interrupted *and* The Stepford Wives, *with enough folk horror and emotional weight to grab you by the throat and not let go until the very (shocking but satisfying) last scene, all of it orchestrated by Panatier's sure and steady hand.*"
Paul Michael Anderson, author of *Standalone* and *Bones Are Made To Be Broken*

AUTHOR'S NOTE

This novel contains situations and imagery that some readers may find disturbing or traumatic, including depictions of mental illness, non-consensual violence, suicidal ideation and conduct, sexual assault, injury to a child and off-screen death of a child.

For Elizabeth Jane Cochran

"O' Earth O' Earth I return to thee,
I return to where my body once lied
O' Earth O' Earth I return to thee,
I return to where my innocence died"
Lawrence Rothman

"The turned-down pages of my life were turned up, and the past
was present."
Nellie Bly

NEBRASKA REVISED STATUTES

"Nebraska Family Protection Act"
CHAPTER 142-3620

142-3620 Spouse Mentally ill, guardian ad litem, attorney; appointment; order for support

[...]

(2)(a) Involuntary Civil Commitment by Reason of Mental Illness

That no person shall be admitted to any facility for the treatment of mental illness without due process, which herein shall mean upon proper motion and court hearing in the county of residence, with the court appointing counsel to the patient in the case of indigency. This subsection shall not apply on any occasion of a husband seeking the civil commitment of his wife.

[...]

THE SNOW WALKER

A woman shuffles barefoot down an icy farm-to-market road, her skin blistered by the cold and cut raw by the lash of her wind-beaten hospital gown. Numb to the pain, she is unmoved by the weeping hole in her stomach, indifferent to her ruined body and the tendrils of death that have taken root within it. Only one compulsion remains.

Away.

Be away.

ONE

The pale façade of Hollyhock rises from the horizon like a cursed moon against a featureless sky. The single-lane road points the way straight, with tallgrass prairie pressing in from either side, each winter-dead blade intent on keeping the car on its path. The occupants, a driver and a passenger, have been silent for the last leg of their journey. With their destination climbing into view, the driver turns his head to the passenger. She senses that he wants to speak. To offer comfort. But there is no comfort where she is going. They both know this.

"We can turn around."

She tucks her hands under her arms, clawing her fingers into the knit of her sweater. Even with the car's heater running, she can't seem to get warm. Her shoulder aches worse than usual, sending echoes of the past through the bones of her chest. After all they've been through, the year spent in preparation for this day, she knows she can't stop now. She owes a debt. All the same, she doesn't refuse his offer outright. As if it might be available to rescue her later if she doesn't claim the token now.

"You're the bravest person I've ever known. Just taking it this far–"

"I'm not brave."

Though she has seen it in pictures, studied it from afar for months on end, seeing the asylum in the flesh doesn't make its presence there on the infinite plain any less strange. It is an anomaly, something that shouldn't exist. Something that makes you question what would cause anyone to undertake the construction of such a monstrosity in the first place. There's nothing around. No other buildings, no town. Even now, after all she's learned about it, the question comes, *why?* Even though she knows why.

She loses herself in the unmarked road, its blackness more like a crevasse than something laid upon the earth. There is no lane demarcation painted on the asphalt, and yet a line of illumination is visible at its center. It seems to pulse.

The car slips briefly upon a rogue patch of ice, then lurches when the tires return to the surface. Her heart catches in her chest and she dips her chin, shutting her eyes and slowing her breath.

"You know her. You've been her for a year," says the driver. "Quiet. Polite. Formal. But not too formal."

"I know."

"And trusting, almost gullible. Not one to rock the boat. A rule follower."

"I *know.*"

He clears his throat. "Sorry. You've got this. I get chatty when I'm nervous."

"It's okay," she says, knitting her fingers back and forth. "I'm nervous too."

The road ends where a rumbling gravel drive begins, and she looks up to find the asylum filling the view. It is unchanged from the old photographs: a wide building, higher in the center over the main entry, with two heavy wings spread out symmetrically to the north and south. Untold layers of peeling white paint coat the brick, giving it a weathered, grey appearance. Otherwise, Hollyhock House stands strong, implacable. No trees or shrubs impinge upon its margins, as if the building has issued a threat that the flora have heeded.

She feels it as well. Undeniable. A magnetic repulsion. Courage, in this case, means ignoring the waves of malevolence the building seems to exude, ignoring the warnings that the trees obey. It will only be thirty days. Thirty days to do what has to be done. Thirty days to learn the truth. *She owes a debt.*

They pull into an empty spot designated for prospective patients. The motor clicks off and silence falls. The driver makes no move to open the door, a subtle indication to the passenger that she can still pull the cord and float safely to ground. She bristles at the invitation, even though she knows it is meant in kindness – there would be no living with herself if she turned back. She can barely live with herself now. She pushes the door open and steps out. The wind slaps her cheek like a rebuke.

"Give us a final test," says the driver, removing a device with a small screen from his inside coat pocket.

She nods, placing her right hand below her left clavicle and applying pressure to a specific spot with a finger. He watches the screen. "We're good," he says, opening the driver's side and climbing out. Their eyes meet across the car's roof, their icy breath fleeing down the drive as fast as it can.

"Mrs Turner," he says.

"Mr Turner," she answers.

SPD INTERVIEW RECORD
EXCERPT OF TRANSCRIPTION

[Questioning by DETECTIVE ABRAM GASTRELL, Scottsbluff Police Department]

GASTRELL: We're recording.

WITNESS: Hello.

GASTRELL: Are you okay?

WITNESS: I'm just a bit cold.

GASTRELL: Here. Take my jacket. How is that cheekbone? Would you like an icepack?

WITNESS: An icepack? No, thank you.

GASTRELL: Ready then?

WITNESS: [Indicating]

GASTRELL: Okay, it's 8:32 am, Friday, March the 16th. This is Detective Abram Gastrell, SPD, and I am here with a witness. Can you state your name?

WITNESS: Charlotte Andrew Turner.

GASTRELL: And you are here to provide a voluntary statement pertaining to the events that occurred sometime within the last thirty-six hours at Hollyhock House, correct?

WITNESS: Yes.

GASTRELL: This device here on my lapel creates a record of my investigation. That includes recording our interactions and streaming it to the other departments participating in the effort. Is that okay?

WITNESS: Yes, okay. Um, Detective?

GASTRELL: Yes?

WITNESS: Where is Mr Turner?

GASTRELL: Your husband, Andrew Evers Turner?

WITNESS: That's him, yes.

GASTRELL: We've not heard from him yet. We located records of an Andrew Turner who began renting a house in Hay Springs on Soapweed Place a little over a year ago.

WITNESS: That's our home. We will raise our family there.

GASTRELL: Is it your Mr Turner who began employment at Parker Tool and Die around the same time as you started renting the house?

WITNESS: Yes. That's Andrew. So, you should be able to find him.

GASTRELL: Mrs Turner–

WITNESS: Did you check Parker?

GASTRELL: Yes, of course.

WITNESS: How many times, though? Did you–

GASTRELL: I personally spoke with Parker. Your husband hasn't been seen at his job since the 27th of February.

WITNESS: I'm sorry, it's all just very strange that nobody knows where he is. He was supposed to be there for my discharge from Hollyhock House.

GASTRELL: Hollyhock doesn't exist anymore, Mrs Turner.

WITNESS: I just want to see him.

GASTRELL: I understand. Perhaps you'll remember additional details as we move along that might help us place him. Listen, I can't imagine all you've been through in the last several days. I want clarity as much as you do, rest assured. All the area departments are trying to piece together what happened out there and not much is making sense. Hopefully you can help us get to the bottom of it. Alright?

WITNESS: Yes, okay.

GASTRELL: Baby steps. I'll let you know if I receive any updates on Mr Turner. I promise.

WITNESS: Okay. It's just that he needs to be here with me. We're starting a family.

GASTRELL: You have my word that we will do our best to find him. Let's turn to Hollyhock.

WITNESS: Okay.

GASTRELL: What is the last thing you remember?

WITNESS: Your officers picking me up. And thank heavens they did. I was getting hungry.

GASTRELL: What I mean is, can you describe physically what happened at the site before that? Before you were picked up?

WITNESS: At Hollyhock House? Oh, I don't think that's a good idea, Detective.

GASTRELL: Sorry?

WITNESS: This isn't the type of thing you just dump on someone. I wouldn't want your brain to collapse.

GASTRELL: Let's reset here. I'm the police, you understand that?

WITNESS: Yes. Completely.

GASTRELL: I need to know what happened there. I need to understand how it all ... changed like that.

WITNESS: Yes, but–

GASTRELL: I need you to cooperate.

WITNESS: I'm trying.

GASTRELL: Dozens of people are missing. We need to know where they are, what happened, and if they can be saved.

WITNESS:	Oh, I don't think there's anything that can be done for them. It's regrettable, but also beautiful.
GASTRELL:	Beautiful?
WITNESS:	Hmm.
GASTRELL:	How can you say that?
WITNESS:	I've seen it.
GASTRELL:	Look, somehow you're the only witness. You can't play gatekeeper of–
WITNESS:	Gatekeeper? I'm not playing gatekeeper. I am the mouth of the Earth, Detective. The Rose of Jericho.
GASTRELL:	The what?
WITNESS:	See? Even if I told you everything, I just don't think you'd understand. Oh, this would be so much easier if we had the recordings! Then you could learn about it right from the source.
GASTRELL:	There are recordings?
WITNESS:	Maybe the Doctor kept copies at her home. You could search there.
GASTRELL:	You're referring to Hollyhock's director, Althea Edevane?
WITNESS:	Yes.
GASTRELL:	People are searching her property as we speak. But I need information now. Where was everyone when the event began? How did it start? Where should we be looking to give us the best chance to find the people who weren't as lucky as yourself?
WITNESS:	There are animals whose little stomachs explode if you feed them too fast. Goldfish. Baby birds. The mind is the same way, Detective.
GASTRELL:	Christ.

WITNESS: It's frustrating to me, too, you know. I want
            my husband back. You want information.

GASTRELL: Are you ... trying to negotiate with me?

WITNESS: Absolutely not. I'm just empathizing.

GASTRELL: You seem the empathetic type.

WITNESS: You're being sarcastic, Detective.

GASTRELL: Perceptive, too.

WITNESS: I'm a very empathetic person. Feelings and
            all that.

GASTRELL: Where do I look for survivors, Mrs Turner?

WITNESS: There are none.

GASTRELL: What?

WITNESS: So there's no need to rush the search
            because no one is alive.

GASTRELL: I don't think there's any way for you to
            know that.

WITNESS: You're entitled to your opinion.

GASTRELL: Tell me what happened, Mrs Turner. Tell
            me exactly what happened.

WITNESS: The Earth found a mouth and exhaled.

GASTRELL: What the hell does that even mean?

WITNESS: The message sent from six directions,
            Detective. Summoned by the token of
            séance. Insinuation.

GASTRELL: Alright. Let's take a step back for just a
            second. Why did you go to Hollyhock in the
            first place?

WITNESS: To get better, of course. Andrew and I
            wanted to have children, but I wasn't well.
            Emotional problems. I needed to be healed
            before we tried bringing a little one into the
            world. I was admitted to Hollyhock House
            and now I'm cured.

GASTRELL: Cured? From what?

WITNESS: Domestic psychosis.

GASTRELL: Domestic psychosis. Right. Between us, do you believe that's even real?

WITNESS: Oh, yes, absolutely. Our family physician, Doctor Hughes Barker of Hay Springs, made the diagnosis and provided the referral to Hollyhock. Doctor Edevane confirmed it.

GASTRELL: Did you want to go?

WITNESS: Why bother asking? I didn't have a choice in the matter, legally speaking.

GASTRELL: Sure. I understand that.

WITNESS: But yes. I wanted things to work out with Andrew. I thought that it was worth doing thirty days in an institution if it healed me. I tried to make the most of it because I wanted what was best for our family. Andrew. Myself. Our future children. I went in with an open mind. Which was important. That's the only way to heal. And I did.

GASTRELL: What was it like when you first arrived?

WITNESS: You'll tell me if they find Andrew?

GASTRELL: Yes, of course.

WITNESS: It all began in a room.

GASTRELL: Let's start there.

NEBRASKA STATE LUNATIC
ASYLUM

"HOLLYHOCK"

NORTH WING

PLAN OF THE HOSPITAL.

GROUND LEVEL

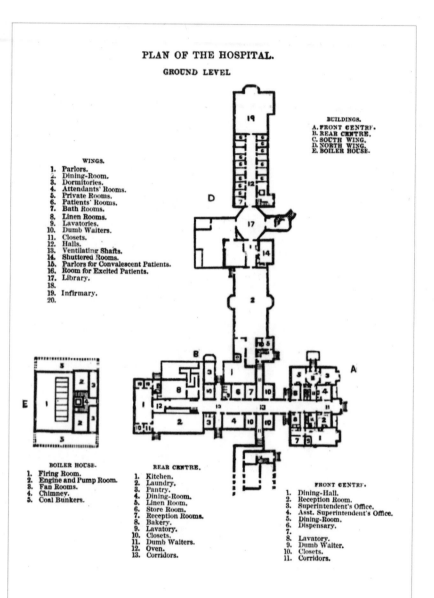

BUILDINGS.
A. FRONT CENTRE.
B. REAR CENTRE.
C. SOUTH WING.
D. NORTH WING.
E. BOILER HOUSE.

WINGS.
1. Parlors.
2. Dining-Room.
3. Dormitories.
4. Attendants' Rooms.
5. Private Rooms.
6. Patients' Rooms.
7. Bath Rooms.
8. Linen Rooms.
9. Lavatories.
10. Dumb Waiters.
11. Closets.
12. Halls.
13. Ventilating Shafts.
14. Shuttered Rooms.
15. Parlors for Convalescent Patients.
16. Room for Excited Patients.
17. Library.
18.
19. Infirmary.
20.

BOILER HOUSE.
1. Firing Room.
2. Engine and Pump Room.
3. Fan Rooms.
4. Chimney.
5. Coal Bunkers.

REAR CENTRE.
1. Kitchen.
2. Laundry.
3. Pantry.
4. Dining-Room.
5. Linen Room.
6. Store Room.
7. Reception Rooms.
8. Bakery.
9. Lavatory.
10. Closets.
11. Dumb Waiters.
12. Oven.
13. Corridors.

FRONT CENTRE.
1. Dining-Hall.
2. Reception Room.
3. Superintendent's Office.
4. Asst. Superintendent's Office.
5. Dining-Room.
6. Dispensary.
7.
8. Lavatory.
9. Dumb Waiter.
10. Closets.
11. Corridors.

P

The orderly's hair glowed like summer beneath the lights as we traveled down the lacquered hallway. I lost myself in the sun-kissed locks, so heavy and rich that they might liquify at any moment and drown my attentions. The orderly – or maybe she was a nurse – stopped and turned a doorknob. She wore a nametag that said ENID, but I knew her name already, though I'm not sure how.

"Here we are, Mrs Turner."

"Oh, please, call me Charlotte."

"Sure," she said, directing me inside.

I went in. "How delightful."

"I'm glad you think so. This is the Welcome Room. You'll be here for one night and then assumed into the program with the others tomorrow. Go ahead and get yourself a shower and changed. You'll find a set of clothes on the dresser. I'll be back with your supper later on."

"Thank you," I said, turning back to the door, only to find it shut.

It was a single bedroom, much like what I imagine you'd find in a nicer hotel (I've never stayed in a hotel, but I've seen them on my daytime programs). There was a lamp by the bed and filigree wallpaper that walked a precarious line between beautiful and hideous. Seeing as I was powerless to change the decor, I resolved right then that it fell on the side of beautiful. It was a nice change from the dull floral print in our bedroom at home, which was unquestionably hideous, though I'd never say as much to Andrew because he picked it out. So that was that: the wallpaper in the Welcome Room was beautiful. I traced my eyes over its elaborate loops and swirls from one side of the room to the other.

There was a little notepad on the desk and a fat purple marker to write with – probably so nobody could stab themselves with it. Popping off the lid, I wondered if it was wide enough to wedge inside my windpipe – not that I was seriously considering it, but I'm sure others had. The so-called "hard cases." I thought about doodling something, but nothing came to mind. I don't remember ever taking art lessons.

I took a shower as I'd been instructed, using the bottles of soap and shampoo that were provided. Both were pungent, with herbal tones so strong that I tasted them as I scrubbed. I wasted no time rinsing, stepped out, and wrapped my body in towels.

The facility-issued clothes sat atop the dresser. Holding them up, I was presented with a delightfully whimsical costume. It was mostly a dress. The material was heavy white fabric with thin sections of ruching going down the bodice, over the silhouette, and all the way to the hemline, as well as a high collar and long lantern sleeves. Two rows of buttons ran up the front from waist to neck. I spread it out on the bed and lifted the skirt. Sewn in at the waistline were leggings in a waffle weave, like thermal underwear, except thicker. My first thought was to be thankful for anything that would battle the chill. My second was of how difficult this was going to make using the bathroom. My bladder is famously petite.

I put on the ill-fitting panties and unhelpful bra provided, then lay back on the mattress, gathered the dress, and worked my feet into the attached leggings. Next, I got my shoulders and arms into the blouse and spent a considerable effort securing its many buttons. Short of breath and standing before the small mirror above the dresser, I felt transported deep into the history of somewhere.

Sitting stiffly on the bed, I angled into the pillow to preserve my windpipe beneath the unyielding collar. Still, the dress antagonized my throat, so I moved to the desk beneath the window. I found a posture that suited both dress and neck, then took in the view. Outside it was utterly still, undisturbed by the little robins and house finches and crows that usually stay for winter. It was barren and stale out there, clear to the horizon. Even the clouds hung static in the sky. The parking lot seemed fake, like those in the village center of a model train set. I half expected the hand of a giant child to reach down and start zooming them around. That was a nice thought – a child at play.

Cutting a black band through the snow beyond the parking lot was the road Andrew and I had traveled to get here from Hay Springs. Though the trip ended with our temporary separation and my institutionalization, the drive had been lovely; Andrew was so sweet and accommodating. We'd listened to my favorite music for nearly the whole trip, with him joining in as I sang the words. We talked more than we had in months, mainly about our future – assuming my treatment went as planned – and even indulged in debating baby names! By the time we arrived, I was sparking with anticipation. Yes, there were nerves – I had come for psychiatric care, after all – but also the hope of new beginnings. Even as we parted, there was so much excitement.

I remained at the window until Enid returned. She smelled like those oils that are supposed to be good for you. *Eventual oils*, I think they're called. It's the healing qualities: *eventually*, you're cured.

She weighed me, took my temperature and blood pressure, then gave me a pregnancy test. When I tried to explain that Andrew and I had rarely been intimate through the duration of our troubles, she said, "It's just to be sure." And I guess you don't want pregnant women undergoing electroshock therapy, which, as I sat on the toilet for the test, I wasn't sure was a real thing they did anymore. Enid watched as I urinated, which was unusual, but I supposed it was something I had to get used to, and anyway, I wanted to please her. The test was negative, of course.

Supper came as darkness made its advance, with Enid wheeling in a fancy cart just like they probably do at the Ritz Carlton or the Plaza Hotel. I laughed all the way out loud – a big goose honk – and I know I spooked the poor woman. But how could I not have? It was a spread like I'd only seen on television, but instead of multiple courses, everything was served on a single silver tray with various sections. I ran my finger over the gleaming edge, delighting in the elegant handles. You should have seen it.

On top of my flaring hunger, the oddly paired food charmed me. Disarmed me. Looking back, I'm certain that this was their purpose – to lull me, to get me to drop my guard so that I would be malleable and more easily controlled. Yet it was so exquisite, so gloriously presented, that I didn't even care I succumbed to their designs. That, and I didn't need to be controlled. Now that I was here, I had resolved to be a willing participant. *When life gives you lemons, make…* I forget the rest.

Each section of the tray contained a delectable culinary gift. At the back corner were small compartments filled with lightly seasoned walnuts, pomegranate arils that shone like rubies, a fresh chunk of goat cheese, and some sunflower seeds. Next to those was a half grapefruit cut into segments, and a dollop of yogurt so fresh and tangy it made my taste buds pop just looking at it. A filet of poached salmon garnished with roasted cherry tomatoes was the entrée, with a piping hot dinner roll nestled alongside. Next to the tray was a tiny white china dish holding a mound of ice topped with an oyster on the half shell. An oyster! In Nebraska! In wintertime! The sheer audacity of such a thing.

Andrew and I had never eaten like this at home. The tray alone would be the most valuable – and beautiful – object beneath our modest roof. Seated before such a meal, I felt special, like the ruler of an ancient land. Cleopatra! Enid left me to it, saying only that I was expected to finish everything.

It was like eating for the first time.

I spooned up whatever was closest, dunking chunks of salmon into the yogurt and walnuts, then shearing the pulp from the sliced grapefruit with my teeth. The tomatoes went next, their warmth rupturing into every corner of my mouth, followed by those greasy little sunflower seeds. I devoured the roll like it was trying to run away, then scraped the oyster from its shining home and swallowed it straight down my throat. It's true what they say: you can taste the ocean. Isn't that strange to think about? I have never been to the ocean, much less tasted its salty water, but I knew that's what it was. I saw it too. A flashing image as I swallowed it down. The rolling gray sky touching stormy waters as noisy seagulls whipped about. The sand beneath my toes and in the webbing of my fingers. Warm and cold at the same time. *Magic.*

My spirits soared as my belly swelled. Perhaps I *would* get better in this place. Perhaps Hollyhock was a bridge, with a real family waiting on the other side. It was there, laid out in front of me. I only needed to cross.

I saved the pomegranate arils for last because they were so beautiful. Holding one to the lamplight, I admired its rounded facets and the tiny seed suspended inside. I ate them one by one, savoring the bitter shock as they popped between my molars.

A selection of teas accompanied a red-hot stone kettle with a matching mug fit into the lid like a puzzle piece. I nearly scorched my tongue, drinking down three steaming cups in rapid succession so I could sample each exotic flavor: Nettle, Lady's Mantle, and Tribulus. This forced me into the bathroom, of course, where I didn't even bother to close the door. Sitting down, I experienced a pang of guilt for enjoying myself so immensely in Andrew's absence, but chalked it up to not having to do the dishes.

I wiped and stood. Leaning over to flush, an ache struck me from deep inside, forcing me to double over. It was too early in my menstrual cycle for cramps. I'd been distracted, though, and maybe had my days off. But no. This hurt differently.

I decided I was being oversensitive. Like sleeping in a new place, you hear noises that turn out to be nothing. Maybe when a setting is unfamiliar, you turn inward, giving extra attention to things you usually ignore. I eased the dress up and sat gently on the bed. I poured the last of the water over a used teabag and went to sipping it.

Enid returned for the cart as soon as I'd finished the tea. Seeing her made me happy. Wandering over to the little mirror above the dresser, I pondered how it was she knew to come so promptly. I tapped at the glass, supposing it was one of those two-way mirrors you see in police dramas. Surely, they watched me. I shrugged at the thought. Let them!

"You'll be here until morning," Enid said, packing up the utensils.

I smiled broadly so she would notice. "Okay." The meal had calmed me. Maybe it was one of the teas. Or just the attention. At Hollyhock House, it was all about me. I couldn't remember a time when I felt so doted on, and I realized a crazy thought: I wasn't just accepting of treatment, I was looking forward to it. Not everyone gets a chance at a fresh start, and I resolved to carry forward with a welcoming mind. I undid the buttons at my collar and lay back on the bed, admiring Enid's hair, with its gilded ropes coiled about her head in a circlet, punctuated by sprigs of colorful botanicals at the back.

"What happens in the morning?" I asked.

Enid's hands moved decisively (they always did), organizing the supper items for transport. "Doctor Edevane will conduct a short follow-up interview and then you'll be introduced into the program alongside the other women." She opened the door and guided the cart into the hallway. "There's an ewer of fresh water on the desk. Otherwise, if you need anything, this is how you call us." She tapped a button on the wall above the light switch and exited. Her smile left a glow behind.

"Goodnight," I called after her, hoping she could hear me smiling back.

The door choked away the light of the hallway, and the lamp turned off. I went to the switch and tried it, but the room stayed dark. That was okay. I would adopt a new schedule. Something different. *A true reset.* I wandered to the window and pulled aside the gauzy curtains. The evening horizon was a string of burning violet and orange. I returned to the bed and laid my head on the pillows, too relaxed, too tired to burrow under the covers. My breath was calm and my stomach warm. I closed my eyes and let Hollyhock take me.

Ρ

I took an indulgently long shower upon waking, which soothed my abdominal aches, then sealed myself into the Hollyhock dress like a deep-sea diver. After, I sat at the desk watching the snow, waiting for Enid to come fetch me. The flakes tumbled down, tiny offspring of the clouds, each destined to return over and again as snow or water or vapor all the way until the end of time. I was buoyed by this idea of renewal – starting as one thing and becoming another. Everything was as it should be. Everything was everything, if that makes sense, which it did to me at the time and does so more and more every day.

Enid arrived and we exited the Welcome Room.

A network of corridors brought us into the main arm of the North Wing, where we stopped at a station between two residents' rooms. As with the previous evening, Enid took my weight and checked my blood pressure and temperature. After recording the results (all stellar) in a notebook, she gave me a small cup of health supplements to swallow with water, noting that Hollyhock had a strict non-pharmaceutical policy except in the most serious cases. I mentioned my abdominal pain. Enid placed a hand across my stomach long enough for me to feel its warmth and told me it would pass.

She led me into a large, brightly lit dining room – Hollyhock Hall. Giant windows ran from floor to ceiling on both sides, flooding the room with lilac winter light. The glass was run through with wire, and textured so that the outside world looked like a wind-chopped sea below an overcast sky. At our end of the room was a serving line, and at the other was a set of double doors. A big clock without any numbers loomed over them.

Enid escorted me to the food line, then excused herself. I watched her until she disappeared through the doors under the clock, jealous for the attention she would give to some other patient.

My attentions, however, quickly shifted to enjoying a breakfast that I didn't have to cook, eaten off dishes I didn't have to clean. The kindly serving woman loaded my tray with a tailor-made vegetable and mushroom omelet, two sausage links, toast and a fruit bowl. Nestled into an oblong section of the tray was half an avocado with the pit still in, lightly salted. I selected Tribulus tea even though something told me I was a coffee drinker at home. There was a quality to Hollyhock that dulled my thoughts when it came to home, and I'd be lying if I said I didn't mind.

I took my tray and selected a table with no other occupants. I knew I needed to start making friends, but for now I wanted to savor the food. Of course, as soon as I sat down, another woman popped up from a nearby table like we were on opposite ends of a seesaw and headed over. She was stout, with a square face that showed the weariness of some long-held burden. I could tell right away that she was one of those people who look older than they really are. Young musculature beneath weather-beaten skin. She set her tray across from me and dropped onto the bench, about knocking over her own teacup.

"You'll want to put that hair up," she said. Her own hair was gathered into braids and wound into buns on either side.

"Okay, hello," I answered. "Why?"

She stuffed half a sausage into her cheek. "Honora," she said, shooting her hand across the table. The lantern sleeve of her shirt was pulled up her forearm, showing muscles that moved like strings on an instrument. Her arms were big. Her shoulders were big. She seemed possessed of a volume of resting power I'd not seen up close in another woman. Whatever she had been doing before coming to Hollyhock involved hard work. Maybe it was baling hay. I accepted her hand and she about squeezed the bones out of mine. I winced out my name.

I brought my hand under the table to rub the ache out of it. "You said something about wearing my hair up?"

"They like to pull hair, Charlotte," she said, sawing her hands to the sides as if it was obvious.

"Why would they do that?" Looking around, everyone seemed so docile and well-behaved.

"Hopefully they won't, for your sake," she answered, eyes scanning my tray. "They don't come for everybody. Are you gonna eat that?"

Disoriented by Honora's conversational agility, I hardly realized what was happening as she snatched one of my links. Then it was gone, packed into her available cheek and punctuated by a bark of laughter.

"I *was* going to eat that."

Honora chewed the meat and stared off. The muscles of her skull moved powerfully, like that of a lioness crushing bone. I took a bite of omelet and found it to be a combination of flavors more delicious than egg and mushroom and peppers deserve to be. My frustration over the stolen sausage melted away as I swallowed.

"I save the sausage for last," announced Honora, using her tongue to clean out the remnants. "So, what got you in here, Charlotte?"

"Domestic psychosis."

"Married, then."

"How do you know that?"

"Come on. No one gets that diagnosis without a husband to suggest it."

"The diagnosis came from a real doctor. And I want to do what's best for my family, so I've chosen to embrace it."

"When was the last time you heard of a man having domestic psychosis, huh?"

"Well, never, but…"

Honora shook her head and pinched her lips. "It's always the husbands. He works. He travels. He goes out with his friends. He does God-knows-what with God-knows-who and no one thinks twice about it, no one questions. A woman finally snaps from the isolation or just gets plain-old pissed and ends up in front of a shrink who calls it schizophrenia. Maybe we get better, maybe we don't. Either way, he's got cover to move on to a new wife. Old one was crazy, get it?"

"Oh, I don't think that's really the case with Andrew," I said, taking a moment to be grateful for him. "Do all these other women have the same thing?"

"The lion's share." She set her elbow on the table and pointed. "You see Eliza over there?"

"Mm-hmm."

"She burnt her house down, and when they asked her why she did it, she said to keep her husband from leaving for work. Can you believe it? He had her put in here after that."

"Well, she did burn the house down," I added, thankful my own delusions hadn't led me to commit arson.

"Point is," said Honora, "Eliza is crazier than a raccoon that can't reach its butthole. And the two of you share the same diagnosis."

"It's unfortunate," I agreed. "We carry the same stigmata."

"*Stigma?*"

"Sure," I said. "*Stigma.*" I dragged a fold of egg through the grease on my plate and took a cleansing breath. "Well, I can't worry about Eliza. I have twenty-nine more days to get my own mind in line."

"Is anything actually wrong with you? You don't seem so sick to me."

I shrugged. "Well, neither do you."

"Oh, no, no," she said, poking the side of her head with a fork. "I'm full-on broken. Haywire."

"Honora," I said, making sure my voice sounded extra nice, "you seem perfectly fine to me."

She scraped some remnants together on her tray, then ate them. Even as she chewed, her mouth angled downward, lips pressed tight, pushing away the swell of some emotion. I knew it wasn't proper to pry so I mumbled that it was okay, that it was none of my business.

"Have you ever wondered if you're evil?"

"Uh. I don't... I hope not. I'm positive you're not evil, Honora."

"Does it matter what's inside if the outside is bad?"

"Of course it does."

"Hmm. Not so sure the rest of the world sees it that way."

"Well, you shouldn't care how the rest of the world sees it. Besides, I don't think that you can divide people into good and bad," I said, channeling something smart that Andrew might say. "I think that people's behavior is a function of their tolerances. Those who feel pain more easily might act out in ways that hurt others because they haven't been given the tools to process what they're going through. They feel helpless or cornered. That's when we see folks doing things they ought not do."

"That's just a fancy way of saying that people have different breaking points, Charlotte. Did your husband find you inside a college?"

"No, we met..." I don't remember how we met, do I? Ah, yes. At a ball game. A *base*ball sports game. There were two teams on a field playing baseball and we were there watching it as observers. That's how we met. (I think.) It's like a dream, true love. Hazy.

Honora continued, "The world doesn't care what's inside if you do the unimaginable. Some things are bad enough that a person's intentions don't really matter."

I felt the skin of my neck tighten beneath the high collar. "What are we talking about, Honora?"

Her face changed and she reached across the table, seizing my mug and finishing the last of my tea. "There's this little fenced yard they have out on the south side of the main building, with an old swing set." She pointed vaguely over my shoulder. "The women just sit there on those swings, hardly swinging at all. You can call to them. They don't answer."

I shivered. "I don't like swing sets." I'm not sure why.

"My point isn't about the swing set, Charlotte, it's about the patients over there."

"Who are they?"

"Rumor is they're the real psychos, the lost causes. They'll have me out there, you just wait." She stood, having finished her meal and part of mine.

"Honora?" I said, feeling abandoned even though I'd wanted to eat alone in the first place. I'd been so happy and now she was saying things that were sad. "Are you just trying to scare me?"

She sighed and shifted her weight. "I'm just saying you should start wearing your hair up, is all."

I felt a ripple of defiance at what was surely an attempt to torture a new patient. "I wore my hair up at home as a matter of keeping the filth out of it, and because Andrew liked it done up that way. Now, I have some time to be myself. Besides, none of these women look like hair pullers to me."

Shrugging, she headed off with her tray. "Not these ones you have to worry about."

She dropped the tray at the service line, then crossed the cafeteria floor and disappeared through the double doors beneath the clock. I panned the room, suddenly conscious of the hair nestled about my neck and shoulders. Everyone else had theirs up.

SPD INTERVIEW RECORD
EXCERPT OF TRANSCRIPTION

GASTRELL: Okay, it's 10:22 am, Monday, March the 19th. This is Detective Gastrell, SPD. I am here with the witness, Charlotte Andrew Turner. Yesterday's interview was cut short due to a medical concern. Are you feeling better?

WITNESS: It was only my blood sugar. I'm fine now. Your Dr Bentham is very kind.

GASTRELL: Just making sure you're okay.

WITNESS: I am.

GASTRELL: Take what you want from the bowl there, if you need a boost.

WITNESS: Are they persimmon flavored?

GASTRELL: Persimmon, no. Those are butterscotches.

WITNESS: Ah, okay.

GASTRELL: I'm going to step out for a moment to chat with Dr Bentham. You sip on that tea. Try a candy. I'll be in the hallway. Call if you need me.

WITNESS: Yes. I will.

SPD INTERVIEW RECORD
EXCERPT OF TRANSCRIPTION

GASTRELL: She's okay to continue, then, right?

DR HEEDA BENTHAM: Physically, it was just low blood sugar. Psychologically, you know what I think. She's suffered a major dissociative episode and should be placed in observation in an appropriate facility. She's literally an escaped mental patient.

GASTRELL: More like she walked out when the place ceased to exist, but, yeah.

BENTHAM: I have serious concerns about her. Her memory seems fine except where it should be most reliable. She isn't sure how she met her husband or what baseball is?

GASTRELL: That could be the trauma, though, right?

BENTHAM: Could be. But I'm telling you, there's something off with her. Who talks like that? She's strangely formal, stilted in how she articulates herself. Stiff. Plastic. Manufactured, almost.

GASTRELL: Yeah, I've noticed. But I don't really care how she sounds, Doc. I care about what she says.

BENTHAM: I've made my point clear. For her sake and for mine. I'm not risking my license by giving my stamp of approval for any further questioning here.

GASTRELL: Your objections have been recorded. If she wasn't the only witness to an event that killed a bunch of people and transformed a section of the high plains into ... whatever it is now, I'd let you take her. But she may be the one person who ever speaks about it. I'm never going to get the same access I've got right now, especially if she's taken to another nuthouse.

BENTHAM: That's not really the term we use.

GASTRELL: You the word police now?

BENTHAM: Hey: you're the cop. Better get back in there before I get any more pressure to move her.

ᛈ

The director of Hollyhock House, Doctor Althea Edevane, sat in a chair with her back to a very large, very ornate, wood-framed enclosure. It looked like a natural habitat for some bird or animal, with foliage and sticks forming cover and perches for whatever lurked inside. The fine mesh stretched between the framing suggested birds. Any other wild animal would claw right through. But I didn't hear any singing.

The Doctor looked like someone who might run a wellness retreat for the ultra-wealthy. Her smooth ivory skin was the waxy product of a diligent – and expensive – regimen, and hardly showed any age except for some shallow crow's-feet. There were laugh lines too, which is always nice to see in a person. Her thick hair was tightly gathered into a French braid, mostly gray with some stubborn streaks of brown. A tasteful spray of green struck out to one side like a feather in a cap. I wondered if they were cloves, though I'd only seen those in the spice rack and never on the plant. They come from plants, do they not, cloves?

Her outfit was a dress of the same ruched fabric as everyone else's, with the addition of a pair of modest black pilgrim shoes. Her colorless lips moved as she spoke, though I missed most of what she said as my eyes drifted about the screened enclosure in search of cloves.

"Mrs Turner?" she said. "I'd asked how you were taking to things so far?"

"Excuse me?" It felt like falling, being caught letting my attention wander.

"It's eccentric, I know," she said, gesturing to the cage or whatever it was. "A distraction I should probably have left at home. But I learn so much from them. What's the point if I'm never around to see them grow, right?"

I angled my head to see the "them" she was talking about.

"*Hairstreaks*," she said. "But they don't move much once they're sated." She fluttered her fingers. "Maybe you'll catch a glimpse before our time is over. In any case, I'd asked how you were adjusting."

"Well," I answered, making purposeful eye contact to express sincerity, "I've only just gotten here. The meals are…" I tried to find the word that would convey just how wonderful I found them, "transcendental."

"*Transcendent*, I think you mean, yes." She chuckled. "That's what we're going for."

"I really wasn't expecting such amazing food in a mental hospital."

"We want you to feel alive, vivacious. Good food is a straightforward way to start, don't you think, Mrs Turner? Or may I call you Charlotte?"

"No, please, Charlotte is fine." She was so polite. Was I blushing?

"The body responds in proportion to the stimulus it receives, doesn't it?" she said. "Offer blandness, expect banality in return. A diet of diverse and quality food is symbolic as much as it is nutritive. I want it to spark excitement within you. To feel full in your belly, but to also prompt your mind and body to hunger for their potential."

"Yes," I answered breathlessly, "that's what I want." It was as if she had opened my mind and looked inside.

"If all we fed you were anodyne bowls of porridge and Graham crackers, what would that evoke? Little, I'd argue. That's exactly why Sylvester Graham invented those tasteless planks of cardboard in the first place, *by the way*, to quell the sexual passions of women. Did you know that?"

"I didn't," I said. What a fascinating woman. So much knowledge. I'm sure I blushed some at her mention of sex.

"You won't find any of his puritanical wafers at Hollyhock, I promise you that. We're trying to remind women of their natures and passions, not to bury them." She took a deep breath and sighed it out. "That might seem counter to the world we live in, I know, but you can't repress people forever. You've got to show them who they are and then teach them how to navigate their circumstances. I've tailored the experience here to be one that provokes an awakening in our patients. The food is just a small part of that. It's not so different from how I nurture these little hairstreaks."

"I hadn't thought of it like that. Everything seems so intentional."

"I'd hope so. Your husband paid good money to have you treated here." She smiled without saying anything, her eyes like pools of water in a cave; pale green or pale blue, depending on the light. Her pupils opened as if a cloud had passed overhead. Nothing of the sort had happened, of course, as we were seated in her expansive office below a stylish chandelier. I made a note to try and reproduce some of these same decorative flourishes in our own home.

"So," she continued, "these psychotherapy sessions will be our opportunity to treat your condition, to spend some time in your waking mind and to see what silt we might churn up in your subconscious. But first, tell me a little more about yourself. Something I might not find in your file."

I had not expected warmth from the head of a mental institution. I answered eagerly. "Andrew and I moved to Hay Springs in winter of last year. We both grew up in small towns back East, and wanted to find a friendly community with good schools where we could afford a nice home in which to raise our children."

Her mouth drew down immeasurably. "You say it almost like you're reading from a dossier."

"What's a dossier?"

"Never mind." She waved her hand. "And what does Andrew do for work?"

"He sells precision tooling equipment, but don't ask me to give any more detail because I don't understand it."

"And I wouldn't pretend to care, Charlotte." She laughed airily.

I made a joyous gasp and said, "I guess for the next month I don't have to pretend to care either!" This was all so liberating.

"You're funny, Charlotte. You know, in the early years of this place, long ago, the ladies held talent shows and beauty pageants. Listening to you cut jokes makes me think we should bring some of that back."

"Okay," I said, feeling my cheeks go hot. "I don't know if I have any talents, though."

"Maybe you just need to explore yourself, Charlotte. When you get to Home Skills, try picking up some knitting needles or stitching, basketwork. Read some of the books we have on how women make the most of their place in other countries, how they expand the confines of their inner worlds."

"I will."

"Yes... I'll have Enid look into setting up a talent show one of these days." Scribbling something on a pad, she shifted in her chair. The contours of her body moved beneath her dress. It was powerful and firm, suggesting a committed exercise regimen. "How about you tell me in your own words what brought you to Hollyhock."

She phrased it like it was a vacation destination or a college, and now that I was here, it didn't seem far off. "I think you already know the answer to that."

"I do, but it helps me to have insight into your side of things." The tip of her nose was thin and shiny. If she wore makeup, it was minimal.

"I got here the same way that most women do, I suppose."

"You sound resentful, Charlotte."

"No..." I answered, hesitating as Honora's words about husbands and wives seeped in. "I have a chance to save my marriage and my family. But who wouldn't be at least a little resentful that it all seems to fall upon the women to fix themselves, and not their husbands to make any changes whatsoever?"

"Do you doubt that you are sick?"

"No," I said, truthfully. "Doctor Barker made the diagnosis. It's just that... I've always been who I've been. This all seems so sudden, you know?"

"You were probably always at risk, Charlotte. Like a congenital heart defect discovered late in life. Conditions like yours are widely known to exacerbate during stressful situations, especially with genetic predisposition. And marriage is often rife with stress."

"But then why does it only affect women?"

The Doctor raised her eyebrows and smiled. "Well, I hadn't anticipated a full discussion of the *DSM 11* quite yet." She leaned back in her chair. "'Domestic psychosis' is just the name we give to schizophreniform disorders when they're seen in the context of homemaking. Sadly, even today that's going to be a woman more often than not. It was once called "housewife's schizophrenia" for a reason. They just softened the edges of the label. But don't think that men avoid those schizophrenogenic conditions unique to their physiology and stations." She pointed to a bookshelf. "You see that dusty green number right there? That's my dissertation on the very subject, if you ever care to read it. But save it for when you're in need of a sleep aid." She chuckled genuinely. "Half of our cohort were men in that study, and the findings..."

My attention fell upon the shelf just below the dissertation, where heavy volumes of old medical books were trapped between a pair of sculpted stone bookends. One, a slate-gray raven and the other, a tree of the same color and material. The tree's branches twinkled with pieces of jewelry and other trinkets: a pair of silver hoop earrings, some bracelets, a few delicate necklaces with charms of the crucifixion. And the raven held a locket in its beak.

On the shelf below that was a large photograph of the Doctor and a bright-eyed little boy, her son no doubt, flanked by school portraits of the child at various ages from toddlerhood to early grammar school. A similar series hung on the wall, recent photos of the same child in different settings and outfits.

Her voice drifted back to me. "… but I'm not arguing that women aren't disproportionately represented among new cases and that there is rampant overdiagnosis. Is that what you want to hear?"

"How do I know that I'm not one of these women who has been misdiagnosed?"

Her eyes had an energy all their own, possessed of exclusive wisdom. Standing, she said, "Oh, I don't think you've been misdiagnosed."

She flowed to her desk and retrieved a file. Something fluttered inside the enclosure and I *oooed* at it.

"Oh," she said, looking over her shoulder as she sat, "have they decided to grace us?"

Seeing a flash of wing, I said, "Are they … butterflies?"

"That's them. It's all really silly of me to keep them here. Hollyhock's patients aren't the only ones suffering from psychopathologies beneath this roof. I'm prone to obsession myself, as you can see."

I leaned sideways to get a better look. "I think it's positively charming."

"I've got most of the hairstreak subfamily in there. Greens, junipers, zebras, kings, silver-banded, coral, mallow scrub, a golden or two. Twenty-six or so, not including the pupae. Those I don't count until they hatch – some just bundle up and never wake." She clapped her hands onto the folder and opened it primly across her lap.

"As for you, let's see." She cleared her throat. "'The patient displays numerous schizophrenogenic symptoms consistent with domestic psychosis. Among these are: ideas of reference, disorganized speech, ambition, inability to focus and hysteria. Anecdotal evidence suggests a woman who is positively demented.'" She looked up. "Well, he didn't mince words, did he?"

"What's an idea of reference?"

"A type of delusion," she said lightly. "A belief that things external to yourself, irrelevant, innocuous things, are aimed at you – referring to you specifically – when there is no direct connection." She paged through my file. "'Shortly after learning that her neighbor, Mrs Alice James, had begun taking cooking classes, Mrs Turner was found inside her kitchen pouring out the contents of her spice rack.' It goes on to say that you'd broken in to do so."

"The front door was open."

"And apparently when you were interviewed by the police: 'Mrs Turner claimed to have it on good authority that Mrs James was planning to deliver poison cookies come Thanksgiving, and then publicly accused her of being a witch.'" She leveled her gaze. "Is this inaccurate?"

"No, but my actions were born of paranoia, not delusion."

The Doctor smiled at this. "You suffer no loss of humor, as I've noted. But you *are* sick." She closed the file. "Charlotte, I don't pretend to ignore the role our society plays in the many neuroses it fosters in us as women. The world outside these walls is yours to navigate. It is an endlessly frustrating journey: a maze with an entrance, and for so many, no exit. The marital dyad only makes things harder. What I can offer you is a chance to strengthen your sense of identity, independent from that of your husband, to know and accept your innate value as a person and as a woman, even as you engage in those everyday activities which are the housewife's burden. You'll be able to find your center in our Housework and Home Skills modules. Some might think the approach old-fashioned but believe me: there's a method to the …well, you know how the saying goes." (I don't.) "Here, you will reset your mind and your perspective, so that upon your discharge, you and Mr Turner can have something of a clean slate. You can build upon a clean slate, Charlotte. Just as a home with a foundation. A family. Children." She recrossed her legs and tilted her head, awaiting my response.

I didn't know what she wanted to hear, but said, "I want to believe I can be helped."

"You can be. You're at Hollyhock, Charlotte." She smiled generously. "That's how I know your husband loves you. He brought you to us."

"Yes. Yes, that is true."

"Every woman treated here has the chance to become so much more than what they think they are. But that process depends upon you. Do you want that?"

"I do."

"You need only to do your part. Open your mind. Embrace your treatment." She checked her watch and stood, prompting me to rise. "Next session we'll begin guided meditations. One day, you will know yourself and you will twirl with us." She spun her finger.

As she led me from her office, a glint caught my attention by the statue of the raven. The locket went still, as if it had just been bumped.

Ᵽ

The Group room sat at the hub of two corridors, giving it four entrances, one in each corner. Sturdy wooden built-ins covered the walls, with cabinets at the bottom and glassed-in shelving above, displaying wellness-themed items and thick, leatherbound books. It felt to me like an old library. Maybe at some point it had been. For now, it was home to an army of wooden folding chairs and several flocks of mental patients.

A crystal ewer filled with ice water sat atop a stand inside one of the doorways. Chunks of a dense orange fruit bobbed on the surface. I poured myself a glass and sipped. The taste was refreshing, with the smooth sweetness of cantaloupe, except the fruit wasn't melon. It looked more like citrus. I decided that it was persimmon even though I'd never seen one. Lots of firsts here.

The group was organized into a square, with each of us sitting across from someone else. I spotted Honora in the opposite corner. She winked and I joyfully returned it. We'd only spoken during breakfast, but I'd taken a liking to her despite the food thievery. She seemed so … authentic.

An uncanny motion caught my eyes as I sat. Down my row, a set of pale arms floated in the air like albino eels. They were connected to a smallish lady whose only focus in the world seemed to be a spot on the ceiling. No one else paid her any mind. But there she was, sitting in her chair, arms moving about her shoulders and head within some invisible current. Her hair was closely shorn, done with scissors – a homemade job that betrayed the top of an awkwardly flattened skull. I stared until it felt intrusive, then pulled myself away.

Pacing inside the square was a member of the staff. She looked the same age or older than me, maybe mid-thirties, whip-thin, with her waist and back curved like the letter *S*. Her auburn hair was tied back and shielded beneath a wide, flower-print headscarf. As with all the staff, a tight cluster of leaves poked out from the scarf, and I thought to ask her at the end of the session if they were cloves or something else. I couldn't decide if she was a nurse or a therapist or just an orderly with special training. A counselor, perhaps. Eventually she stopped her pacing and held down a position in a corner of the square.

"Welcome to Group. I'm Miriam Kenneth, your session leader for today. Can I have a volunteer to lead us in the aphorism from last time?" A hand went up. "Yes, Aelix, go ahead."

"The sickening mind is a master of deception."

"Fantastic," said Miriam. "Three times, everyone."

I joined in as the group recited.

The sickening mind is a master of deception.
The sickening mind is a master of deception.
The sickening mind is a master of deception.

My voice soared with each round. How new and strange! How invigorating!

"Now, if our two newest patients will introduce themselves," said Miriam, turning to me.

I cleared my throat and scooted forward on my chair. "Hello everyone. I'm Charlotte Andrew Turner."

"And what brought you to Hollyhock, Mrs Turner?"

"I have a diagnosis of domestic psychosis." Several women were already nodding along as if they'd expected it. I sat back.

The other new patient was a stunning, petite black woman with dramatic dimples. Her hair was drawn together into tiny side puffs and secured with ribbons. She stood and introduced herself as Flory, then looked at me with a playful expression.

"I'm in for the same thing as Charlotte. But my doctor also said I had a touch of the ovariomania."

"What's that even mean, anyway?" asked someone from across the room. I'd never heard of it either, but there were a lot of old-timey psychological conditions coming back into vogue.

"Means she's horny all the time," barked another woman. "Husband can't satisfy her." She made a lewd gesture. "Got a tiny little peen, probably."

Flory shrugged, a seeming affirmation of the allegation against her spouse. Miriam sighed, I assumed because she was used to this.

"Husbands are cunts!" shouted a woman from the row of chairs opposite me. She had coarse brunette hair and a broad, freckled face. Her amphibious mouth revealed widely spaced teeth in liquid-red gums.

My throat pinched, as I don't care for obscenity.

Miriam let the laughter die down. "Is that it? Is Rhoda correct? Did all twenty-four of you end up with cunts for husbands? What are the odds of that?"

"Pretty good now they got rid of no-fault divorce," answered Rhoda. "All the ladies without cunt husbands aren't under lock and key at Hollyhock."

"I hardly doubt that's the case, Rhoda," said Miriam. "But your point does fold nicely into today's aphorism, which we can go ahead and recite together: *I may not be able to control the world beyond myself, but I own my reaction to it.*" She nodded and we repeated it.

When that finished, the other patients made introductions. There were those being treated for bipolar disorder, depression, substance abuse, and anxiety, but most were there for the same reason as me and I took comfort in that.

"So, let's discuss," said Miriam. "Why is it so important for us to gain control of our reactions, especially in the context of marriage?"

A gangly blonde woman with ears sticking out to either side like handles on a jug raised her hand and began speaking. "Because overreaction breeds escalation breeds hallucination."

"Another of our adages," said Miriam. "Well remembered, Gwenlyn. Delusions are the product of a mind overtaxed by emotion." She scanned the room. I did, too, my eyes pausing on the woman with floating arms. "Who's brave enough to give us an example from their own life? Where the symptoms that brought you here continued even in your husband's absence? Yes, Beatrice?"

A darkly tanned girl with towering cheekbones and blue-green dyed hair lowered her hand. "My doctor said that I seek comfort in the arms of women because I long for my husband's companionship, but now that I'm at Hollyhock I'm pretty sure I'm just gay."

"Now, Beatrice," said Miriam dryly. "Homosexuality can be the result of delusion too. A curable symptom like any other."

"Tell that to my girlfriends." A round of laughter followed. I couldn't help but get caught up in it, even though I'd never personally experimented, not even in college. (Did I go to college? My mind is a blank.)

"She's constantly masturbating too," added Aelix with a nod to Beatrice, who shrugged nonchalantly: *guilty as charged.*

"Well, that's different," said Miriam, her voice now serious. "The regular exercise of hysterical paroxysm is a necessary and healthy release. Many of you may not know this, but paroxysm is a longstanding remedy for the nervous conditions. Each of your bodies is a tool with a function. Self-gratification is a reminder of that. It's encouraged."

Something rattled through my body, a confused vibration of dangerous excitement. The chair seat beneath my dress and leggings went scalding hot, and it took me several breaths to process my reaction. Before long, my ears were burning like irons on either side of my head from a rush of exhilaration. I became suddenly anxious to get back to my room and try this new thing. *Paroxysm.*

The woman sitting at my right straightened. Her red hair was done up in pairs of twisting hanks that joined at the back. Shifting pleasurably in my seat, I leaned in with excitable interest.

"Yes, Thirza?" said Miriam.

"Well," said Thirza, "at home I suffered delusions. Mostly, they came after arguments with my husband, when I was so angry my head almost spun off my shoulders."

"Very good. Delusions arise when the conscious mind hasn't properly addressed an underlying problem and the subconscious jumps in to compensate for it," said Miriam academically. "And why do we not want the subconscious mind dictating our lives?"

"Because it's not rational," answered Thirza.

Rhoda pointed across the square. "Like when Aelix torched her husband's car because she thought it was talking to her."

"It *was* talking to me," snapped Aelix.

"No. It wasn't," said Rhoda.

"Enough of that," said Miriam.

Thirza regathered herself. "My point is that we have the power to check our emotions before they take over. I've felt myself losing control, but allowed it to happen because I was angry. That's a conscious decision. I play a part in our troubles too. It's not all my husband–"

"How convenient for him," interrupted Rhoda, rolling her eyes in heavy pouches of plastic-bag skin.

Honora jumped in. "Shut up, Rhoda."

Unperturbed, Rhoda used her short arms to pivot in her chair, making her seem even more froglike than before. "We are free to express ourselves in Group," she said. "No husband should be able to have his wife committed, I don't care what the law says. You bitches need to wake up. Domestic psychosis? That isn't even a real disease. It's a bullshit bowl of fuck. It's no different from what they were doing to women a hundred years ago. And you pushovers are all like, 'Oh, it's our fault too!' Well, congratulations because that's exactly what they wanted when they invented the disease." She mimed with her hands, tilting them back and forth. "Puppet-ass bitches."

"Rhoda!" hissed Miriam.

Thirza shouted, "It's better to have delusions than antisocial personality disorder!"

"I *like* having antisocial personality disorder!" Rhoda shot back. "It means I don't have to give a shit about your feelings when I dish out the truth. You want to get better, Thirza? Stop acting like a pussy."

Thirza scoffed.

"Shut your mouth, Rhoda," said Honora. "Or I'll shut it for you."

I felt my body clenching up, even as a frisson of excitement shot to my toes.

"Rhoda! Honora!" shouted Miriam. "Civility, please. Honora, do you have something to say? And calmly?"

"Wouldn't it be great to be just like Rhoda, never having to worry about how what you said or did affected others?" Honora's lips quivered.

Rhoda smirked. "That's cute, coming from someone who killed her own baby."

I heard myself gasp amid a chorus of gasps. Honora shot up like a post.

"Rhoda!" cried Miriam, stepping into the square. "She had postpartum psychosis!"

Rhoda ignored Miriam, keeping her eyes pinned to Honora like prey. "Your delusions are just your conscience punishing you, and rightly so, you psychopath."

Honora coiled, clenching her big stone fists. "Take it back."

"Bet you wish you could."

I know I flinched from the blur of Honora flying across the square. But before she reached Rhoda, her legs went dead and she pounded the wooden floor, face first. A loud pop issued from her nose and blood spurted to the sides. The group sprang from their chairs, forming a scrum. Rhoda, face smug, didn't budge. I could hardly process what had just happened.

Miriam capped a small device, which she then pocketed, and rolled Honora onto her back. Some sort of taser, maybe, though I'd missed her wield it. Everything had happened so fast. Honora's breath seemed steady. Mine was not. Emotions swirling, I stared at Rhoda. I wanted to kill her right then and there. Anyone who would cut someone with their words as she'd done deserved to pay. I looked at the ewer with the persimmons, imagined smashing it over her head.

"Aelix," said Miriam, "press the call button, please."

Aelix obeyed and two orderlies soon arrived, staunching the blood and comforting Honora as she regained consciousness. I found myself hovering nearby, offering vague and unspoken help. Looking reflexively about the room, I overheard the spooling up of various narratives that would soon be repeated as legend throughout the North Wing. Besides Rhoda, only one other woman remained in her seat.

Her hands traveled in listless circuits on the tethers of her arms. I watched, glamoured by the hypnotic motion, and maybe I shuffled toward her. She turned her head, but I glanced away a moment too late.

The staff helped Honora to stand and took her from the room, dropping a towel over the puddle of blood. Miriam herded everyone back into their seats. My heart banged away in my ears as I watched the white towel go red.

Miriam sat in the chair vacated by Honora and made a note on a digital pad from her dress pocket. "Rhoda, you will come to Special Therapies tonight after your supper."

"What about Honora?"

Miriam's glare was hawk-like. "She'll be treated when she's recovered."

"Some things you can't undo." I looked over to see who'd spoken. It was the woman who moves.

"What's that, Christmas?" said Miriam. "Did you have something to add before we conclude?"

"Some things lead to the next thing and there's no going back," said Christmas, her arms undulating softly above her head. Her voice was anemic, wavelike. "Honora knows this."

Thirza leaned over and whispered in my ear, "Christmas is a witch."

"What?"

"I don't believe it," answered Thirza. "Just letting you in on the gossip."

"Why is she moving like that?" I asked. Her serpentine affect was more disconcerting than any foolish witch accusations.

"That's just the Saint Vitus's tic," said Thirza, sitting back up.

I looked up from Thirza. Christmas was staring now. Her eyes were half open, their yellow sclera rimmed in red, like she hadn't slept in years. Or ever. The air about her head was thick with humidity. She spoke, but her mouth moved slowly, out of sync with the words. My ears felt underwater. I didn't hear what she said at first, but then I did. She said, "They're upset."

"No, Christmas," said Miriam. "We're not doing this. I'm sorry, Charlotte, this has happened before."

But Christmas kept talking. I didn't register what she'd said until she was already inhaling to say more. "Answering the irresistible call. Flowing like fish to the lure."

She spoke directly to me. I said nothing, doing my best to regard her with the same detachment as the others. *Do they hear how she talks?* I wondered. *How her voice moves like fog?*

Miriam stalked over. "Christmas, enough."

Christmas curled into her chair like an opossum as the others whispered and giggled. Miriam engaged them, but the conversation evaporated like I'd been cordoned off behind a gauzy curtain of static. I turned away from Christmas and looked over my shoulder, thinking to count the persimmons in the ewer until the end of session. But I felt her glare, the cold ache of it, and I knew that no matter how long I looked away, she would be right there, burrowing in. The water inside the ewer thickened and creaked as the top half solidified into a block of ice. I twisted around. Christmas's eyes pierced mine as her seaweed arms performed their languid ballet. Tilting her head, she pointed. "Yes," she said, "you do look like her."

My brain fizzled and popped like a bad circuit. Doubt clouded my former optimism like black ink in water. Had I imagined what she said? Hallucinated it? Maybe my sickness ran deeper than I thought it did. Maybe there was rot in me. I took a cleansing breath. Even if I was hallucinating, delusional, I told myself I was in a place that could fix me. If the Doctor was willing to devote so much to the care of her little butterflies, then I was confident in the effort she would put into me. I would heal. The delusions would pass.

The next thing I knew, the session had ended. I remained in my chair as Miriam led everyone out. Christmas lingered at the back of the procession, arms floating side to side, crossing and uncrossing over her middle, like a conductor to an orchestra of ghosts. Upon reaching the threshold, the line of her mouth unraveled like a scroll, and grinning, she mouthed a final decree: *stay away.*

Left alone in the quiet, I tried to regain the sense of calm I'd brought into Group. I wiggled my fingers and toes, planted my feet firmly on the ground, and repeated the day's aphorism. *I may not be able to control the world beyond myself, but I own my reaction to it.* When my anxiety had banked to a manageable degree, I stood to leave, and in doing so, felt the undeniable sensation of fingers through my hair.

SPD INTERVIEW RECORD
EXCERPT OF TRANSCRIPTION

GASTRELL: Someone felt your hair?

WITNESS: Yes.

GASTRELL: Was it Christmas?

WITNESS: No, I don't believe it was Christmas. I didn't mean to give the impression that she'd done it.

GASTRELL: Well, who did then?

WITNESS: I'm not entirely sure. It could have been lots of people.

GASTRELL: What does that mean? Didn't you find out who it was? Just tell me who it was.

WITNESS: I can't do that. I don't know who it was.

GASTRELL: You really can't remember?

WITNESS: I remember fine. No one ever claimed responsibility for it.

GASTRELL: This is going nowhere.

WITNESS: Detective, did you ever find her? Christmas?

GASTRELL: You told me before that everyone was surely dead.

WITNESS: I wasn't suggesting she was alive.

GASTRELL: Wow. Okay. It's barely been forty-eight hours since we picked you up. And the scene is... Well, I can hardly describe it. It's... How can I put this? You see something one way and then look at it again and it seems changed. Parts of it I can recognize, but then there are aspects that my brain doesn't know how to stitch together. It's like something almost

62

happened, then stopped. Or something almost didn't happen, but then did. We still haven't been able get all the way into the scene. Drones go dead as soon as they get above it. And I'm still at a loss to understand how you survived.

WITNESS: If it helps, so am I. Oh no – [indistinct] – I'm so sorry.

GASTRELL: Here, here...

WITNESS: Thank you.

GASTRELL: Do we need to pause? I can call the physician.

WITNESS: That's not necessary. The tissues are enough. I'll be fine.

GASTRELL: When did that start?

WITNESS: Just now.

GASTRELL: No, I mean, when did you start getting nosebleeds?

WITNESS: Today.

GASTRELL: You're kidding me.

WITNESS: No.

GASTRELL: You've got some there on your chin.

WITNESS: Thank you. I... I think it's going to be fine. It stopped, see? We can continue.

GASTRELL: Are you sure?

WITNESS: I'm fine, please.

GASTRELL: Okay, so you remember your hair being messed with after group session and nothing else?

WITNESS: Oh, well, there was something in it. Dry. Like dust or ash. Right along the strands that had been touched. There was a bit on the floor too. Just a smattering.

GASTRELL: Ash?

WITNESS: Yes. Or dust.

GASTRELL: Had it been there when you sat down?

WITNESS: I don't know. I don't normally pay attention
             to the floor.

GASTRELL: Okay. Well, what happened after that?

WITNESS: Nothing of note.

GASTRELL: Do you think you've simply forgotten and it
             might come back to you?

WITNESS: I don't remember every minute of every
             day. Most of the time, things were normal.
             We went from one thing to the next and
             repeated it. That's how healing works.

SPD INTERVIEW RECORD
EXCERPT OF TRANSCRIPTION

BENTHAM: She doesn't remember if she went to college?

GASTRELL: Yeah, I caught that.

BENTHAM: Didn't want to follow up?

GASTRELL: No, not while she's dishing. Besides, we're looking into her. No transcripts coming back yet. Almost nothing online.

BENTHAM: Something's up with her.

GASTRELL: No shit.

BENTHAM: And that place. It's like how movies portray the 1950's in there. What exactly was Althea Edevane doing?

GASTRELL: Keeping pace with the backslide of women's rights? Or - or maybe she was being nostalgic.

BENTHAM: For an era that occurred decades and decades before she was even born?

GASTRELL: I mean, some people spend their weekends doing Civil War reenactments.

Ᵽ

I wore my hair in a knot after that. I knew I shouldn't have. I knew it was a surrender, giving in to irrational fears. Miriam said that irrational fears were the life's blood of delusion. And I agreed. But I had moments of weakness. Christmas frightened me, the way she seemed to float about the place, the way she talked. I caught myself slinking around as I went through my days, stopping to peek around corners and checking over my shoulder. I reminded myself that the aphorisms were a way to combat the tricks of an overactive imagination. My time at Hollyhock was limited, and I had to take advantage so I could manifest the future through attention and hard work. Then my journey would have a happy ending.

Of course, sometimes my imagination got the best of me.

My assigned room had an identical layout to the Welcome Room except that the window was occluded with the same wired glass as in Hollyhock Hall. It let in plenty of light, but nothing discernible. Just shapeless forms and colors. It mixed the sky into the ground and the ground into the sky, and sometimes there was no telling the two apart. Sometimes my mind played tricks, especially if I stared too long. I would start to think that there was no ground and at other times that there was no sky, then lose my balance and catch myself on the desk.

I often propped myself on the bed and stared at the window using the mirror nailed above the empty dresser. Rarely did I have time to lay there consulting the sky, but I did it whenever I could because the sky should be admired. It is a thing without limits.

After the daily medical check-in (I always received top marks), we had breakfast in Hollyhock Hall, followed by either a free hour or one-on-one sessions, then Group Therapy. That was all before lunch.

They were always feeding us. Not once did I suffer the slightest jab of hunger before I was stuffing myself again. As overfull as I got – and sometimes painfully so – I never tired of the diet. Honora joked that they wanted us plump so they could feed us to the crazies in the South Wing. She had lots of entertaining theories about Hollyhock. They were easy to indulge because so much of the place was a mystery, with vast sections of the building permanently sealed off. We told each other false histories of the asylum, campfire fare with hauntings and ghosts and deranged mental patients. Call me crazy, but I found that telling scary tales helped me relax.

Over time, though, Honora became less talkative, worn out by whatever they were doing to her in Special Therapies. I offered comfort and a friendly ear, but you know Honora. She didn't like to complain.

After lunch, there was Housework, then the mid-afternoon activity, which focused on a skill like mending or cooking or knitting or recipe clipping. Then a block of free time and supper after that, followed for some by Special Therapies. Then bed.

My head was a black hole during sleeping hours at Hollyhock. I think it was because life outside had become so tumultuous, with all the stress over money and quarreling about the future of our family, that my dreams at home had been fueled by our domestic drama. But that disappeared in the hospital like a switch had been thrown. The same went for falling asleep. At home I would lie in bed staring at the ceiling, feeling the weight of it pressing down like a vise. Hollyhock changed all that. Without fail, I was asleep as soon as my head hit the pillow and I slumbered deeply, as if nestled among tree roots that never know the sights or sounds of the world above.

But one night, maybe a week or two into my commitment, I startled awake. Not from a dream, or at least I don't think it was a dream because I don't remember it, and like I said, I wasn't doing a lot of dreaming at the time. So, waking while it was still dark surprised me. There was a sound that accompanied my stirring, like the gentle pouring of salt or sand, but its source was a mystery. It was both present and remote, like air whooshing through the heating system. And maybe that's what it was.

Searching the room, my eyes settled upon the ceiling. Up in the corner, a very dim something or other watched me. Not that it had eyes, or even a shape. It glowed darkly, like if light could reflect from a shadow, and I watched it as I would an animal that ventures close, unaware of others. I lay still as a cadaver until the angle of my neck burned so much that I had to shift. That's when the thing moved.

It crawled across the ceiling slower than a stain spreads on fabric. So slow that I thought its movement was an illusion, until a gap finally appeared between it and the wall. Like an amoeba, parts of it reached out like false arms or legs to pull it along. And it went from being flat to the ceiling to being on the other side of it, though still present. It was here and there, then both places; neither.

It drew across, blinking out then returning, leaving behind a weakly glowing trail that faded as it went. It stopped at halfway, directly over the bed, seeming to breathe, the bulky fog of it expanding and contracting on the same beats as my own hitching breaths. Mimicking. Even so, its shape remained indistinct, with margins that blurred and mixed with the surrounding air. There was a presence to this blotch, and I perceived its assessment of me in the prickle of my skin. A few flakes of what looked like snow – or maybe it was just bits of the ceiling – spiraled down.

Angling my hips carefully to the side, I stretched one leg and then the other out from the sheets and crouched small on the floor. The thing affected the surface from which it clung so that it was hard to comprehend; like a magnifying glass that made the ceiling bow outward wherever it sat.

I felt its attention, and it began to edge backward. Once directly above me, its form condensed, growing smaller and brighter. Part of it began to descend. A screech built in my chest, as this apple-sized lump slid down a luminous sinew. I sucked air between my teeth and filled my lungs...

The light in the bathroom flashed. I leapt into bed and rolled to face the bathroom door, blinking away the blinding afterimage. I quickly checked the ceiling. The thing had gone. I scanned the walls, past the bed, the desk and chair, the dresser, the mirror and...

The door to my room was open.

My body went rigid. Someone was here, inside with me. They'd opened the door and flashed the bathroom light. The air was different, too, thick. My instincts cried out that it was Christmas, come to threaten me, to speak more of her spellbound riddles. I pressed my vision into the corners, trying to hold her in the dark with the power of my gaze.

A pair of arms emerged slowly from the shadows into the dull winter light, wrists flexible and fingers rolling like a pair of jellyfish in a courting dance.

"Come out of there," I hissed from the sheets. The arms continued drifting, then slowly withdrew into the corner. My heart thrummed. I wished to dive from the bed and flee through the open door, but my mind played out what would happen next. Me bursting from the sheets, a chill down my spine, boneless arms lashing tentacle-quick from the shadows.

"*Christmas*," I whispered, "I know it's you. Come out of there."

The bathroom was shrouded, with only the top inches of the door frame exposed to the moonlight. There was an undeniable presence in that part of the room. Had she moved? Perhaps if I was quiet for long enough, I could draw her from hiding. She'd peek out from the frame and be caught at her game. Staring at the doorway, my imagination galloped, faster and farther than my ability to rein it in. Then the room lit green and she floated out from the door, pinned within a slatted wooden box. She reached through and pointed a finger as the box slowly rotated, end over end. Then gravity returned, and she smashed through the floor in a blaze of lime-tinged flames.

It was like she'd crashed the gates of Hell. All manner of ghoulish creatures hooked their fingers around the hole in the floor and crawled into the room. Ghosts and specters flew from the threshold, scrambling over the ceiling and down the wall, shuffling and scratching so that I would look away from the door, allowing the real Christmas to enter the room and steal my mind for good. Determined to keep my head, I recited my aphorisms while holding the darkness in place with my gaze, until dawn ignited the sky and burned the shadows from every cranny.

Clammy with sweat, I rolled from bed and checked the ground, loudly clearing my throat to allow fair warning to any lingering apparitions. I placed my feet to the floor and held them there as my ankles tingled, apprehending a touch that I knew logically would not come. Still, I was relieved when it didn't.

I rushed to the bathroom and whipped my head around the door frame. Empty. Had I fallen asleep at some point, allowing Christmas to escape? Had she ever been there?

I sat boldly upon the toilet as if reclaiming my territory, forcing myself to hum my favorite song from my favorite show, the title of which I don't remember. I finished, then washed my face and hands, brushed my teeth. Flossed. The morning light filtered in, golden, catching the thin, static halo of hair that hovered off my head, and I ran the brush through it until the bristles caught no resistance. I admired the silkiness, thinking it attractive, and about how Andrew found it so.

Setting down the brush, I smiled big into the mirror. I would not succumb to fear. I would build upon this night to become stronger. I would heal. I stretched my smile wider, until the tendons in my neck were taut as guy wires.

I re-entered the room to find an orderly standing at my dresser. "Hello?"

She turned. Her nametag read SABINA. "Good morning, Mrs Turner." She was gathering paper into a pile. "Your door was open."

"I know. It was opened sometime in the night. Not by me."

"Are you sure?" she said. "Is this not your work?"

I stepped closer as she spread the paper on the top of the dresser. I gaped at the purple-stained pages.

"Did you not know about your parasomnia?" she asked.

"I've never–"

"More common than you might guess." She pushed the pile back together.

"No. Let me see." I almost grabbed her hand.

Frowning, she leaned away. "Quickly."

Sheets of paper from the desk were scribbled in purple marker, front and back, all the way to the margins. Most of it was illegible, but the handwriting – though rushed and messy – was undeniably mine.

WAKE UP

LET … IN

YOU ARE…

YOU KNOW…

I…

I AM…

I AM…

I I I I I I I…

Each sentence devolved. Heavens only knew what I was trying to write.

Sabina gently nudged me aside and stacked the pages. "Don't worry about it, Mrs Turner. Therapy relieves stress in unpredictable ways."

I thought about my sleepless night. "But what was I trying to write? It makes no sense."

"What did you expect, the Great American Novel?" she laughed, holding up a particularly messy page. "It's *sleep writing*."

"Andrew sometimes talks in his sleep," I said, trying to reassure myself. "It never makes any sense."

"That's exactly right. You'd expect it to be even less cogent when run through a pen." She turned to go.

"But..." My voice caught.

"Yes?"

"How was my door open?"

She made a quizzical look. It was obvious she thought I'd opened it. "Maybe you wanted some fresh air before you began your book." She checked her watch. "Breakfast?"

SPD INTERVIEW RECORD
EXCERPT OF TRANSCRIPTION

GASTRELL: Christmas really affected you, huh?

WITNESS: Christmas was the semaphore.

GASTRELL: Semaphore?

WITNESS: She communicated in ways that others can't.

P

Days passed uneventfully after my scary night. I regularly attended Group Therapy, Housework and Home Skills. The other ladies were mostly nice to talk to, though sometimes I felt like they got a thrill from hazing the newer patients with troublesome stories. One day in Group, Beatrice told me that shortly before my arrival, a patient had died sticking bobby pins into an electrical outlet. I offered my sincerest-sounding condolences and tried to say something kind about those who see suicide as the only answer. But Beatrice interrupted to say it hadn't been suicide at all. The poor dead woman had said she was trying to call forth the boy who lives in the electricity.

Individual psychotherapy sessions with the Doctor came every few days. I looked forward to those sessions, as I was able to get a glimpse of the butterflies flitting happily inside their enclosure. My favorites were the green ones and little gray ones rimmed in bright purple. During one session, I pointed out a pair of chrysalids barely visible beneath the leaves of a hosta that the Doctor hadn't yet noticed. She took the time to explain in specific detail how far along each pupa was in its development, and how small changes she made in their environment and diet helped her to raise healthier, more beautiful adults. I, of course, understood how it all related to her patients, and gave her a knowing smile.

We discussed my efforts to engage in the curriculum Hollyhock offered, as well as a vision for my family once I'd overcome my pathology. The Doctor asked if there were any further episodes of parasomnia, and I happily reported that it was a one-time event – and that I hadn't touched the purple marker since.

The Doctor emphasized that recovery is a matter of acceptance and empowerment, and reiterated that there were headphones in each of the workrooms providing spoken affirmations for listening and internalizing. I reported that I'd been enjoying them quite a lot – that they'd awakened something inside of me and given me new purpose. Her voice was a reassuring blanket, and I'd already memorized several long passages while wrapped within it. *For you are perfection, hewn and ground and polished all these millions of years, sharpened and honed...* It was poetry, really.

The Doctor took me through my first guided meditation today. I hadn't noticed before, but there was a chair in among the greenery inside the hairstreak enclosure. It was an old wooden thing, and had just blended in. Anyway, the Doctor held open the door to the enclosure and asked me to sit. I did, taking great care to avoid brushing my dress across any silky wings or fragile cocoons. She closed the door and brought her chair to face me. We sat that way for a good while, with neither of us saying anything and me getting more excited by the second. When she finally spoke, the things she said were beautiful, and so profound that I don't remember them. I do remember the taste, though – something about guided meditation left a bitterness on my tongue.

Before leaving, I asked about the jewelry and baubles hanging on the raven and tree bookends. The Doctor explained that some patients forget to leave their earrings and necklaces at home, but that it's all given back on discharge. I remembered what Honora said on my first day, about the South Wing and those who literally lose their minds, if the rumors are to be believed. I wondered how many glittering pieces would hang on the bookends forever. The raven seemed to watch me. I imagined it blinking when I looked away.

TEXT RECORD, PHONE NUMBER
(814) ***-**58

Sup.

Hey, you okay?

Yeah, why?

You know. I just worry about you.

Thanks, but I'm fine. I just got back from a meeting and everything. Eight weeks clean.

Sorry for asking. I didn't mean to put you on the spot.

No, it's okay. You get enough texts of me asking for money and lawyers, you become preconditioned. No. This is a social call.

Okay. Great.

How are you doing?

Oh, fine. Work is busy.

Did you ever end up going
out with whatshisname?

It was... I don't know.

Not great, then.

He did a lot of talking.

That's pretty much what's
out there. Anything else?
There's got to be more.

Well, he had his pilot's
license.

That's pretty cool. Is he
going to take you up in his
airplane? Try to get you to
join the mile high club?

You are so gross.

Always. But still. Is he?

I really didn't feel like there
was anything there. I'll try
again with someone else
later I guess.

Oh, later. You're gonna
marry your cats if you don't
stay in the game.

I don't like dating. I want to
meet someone... you know
... like naturally.

How do you mean? Like
at your job? Those nerds in
the research lab?

There are men there.

There's like three of them
and isn't one of them the
owner? Isn't he like 70?

He's very spry for his age.

Oh my god, Hadleigh,
you're killing me here.

Ducking killing me Hads!
Ducking
Ducking
Goddamit! Fucking.

I don't know. I'm not good
at meeting guys. I can't
flirt.

That's very true. But you
don't have to flirt when
you've got the face-bod

combo you're walking around with. That said, you're no spring chicken.

Oh, and you are?

Pardon me, I am three full years younger than you, first of all, and also I'm not hoping to start a family anytime soon. Or ever.

I still think you're wrong about that. You'd be the best mom. You just have to meet the right guy.

Hadleigh, no.

Seriously. Your kids would be so well adjusted with you. You're not neurotic and anxious like me. I wish I was more like you! Easygoing and fitting in no matter where you end up. You're funny and sociable.

You missed the whole recovering junkie part. Shall we please move the conversation along?

I don't like it when you call yourself that.

Oh, I'm sorry, right. The recovery crowd prefers "addict". Fine. I'm an addict. But I'm not mom material. I've never even wanted to be a mom! That is a real thing that exists, you know, women who have no desire for kids. Can we drop it?

I know. Sorry.

You want children and you'll get them. I'll be that aunt who teaches them how to swear.

Aunt Morgan, then.

Yeah. You can't fight nature.

⼕

Home Skills occupied a small room down a small corridor just off the Group room. It had a large worktable in the center and two mismatched wingback chairs facing each other at the far end. The walls were lined with bookshelves packed with home beautification manuals, gardening guides, and books on other homemaking entertainments such as sewing and cooking (which we were allowed to take to Housework and use with special permission, so long as we didn't go beyond boiling pasta or sculpting apples into swans).

Some days I sat and read books about home skills across world cultures, and I became enchanted by an isolated place in China where the women are in charge of the household and no one decides things for them! The men don't even get to live in the same house without an explicit invitation. Like vampires. Other days I knitted. I was getting quite good at it, with nine orange potholders already completed.

Today the only other woman in the room was Thirza, who was at the table cutting bits of felt and piecing them together with glue. She and I didn't talk much other than group gossip. She wore headphones, and so we acknowledged each other with a twinkle of the fingers. I took in the room, thinking maybe I'd browse through the books or continue working on the scarf I'd started for Andrew. Just inside the door was a large filing system with drawers of various sizes, resembling the card catalogs from libraries of yore. Somehow, I hadn't explored it.

I donned a set of headphones from the sharing basket, then

ran my finger over the honey-stained drawers. I slid one open. At first it looked like nothing more than tightly packed rows of white envelopes. I lifted one and saw that it was a pattern for a man's jacket. The one behind that, a fishing vest. Opening the drawers at random, I discovered them all packed with the white envelopes.

These were sewing patterns for all manner of garments. Men's clothing, of course; anything he might want from pants to shirts, jackets, and coats – even fancier items like dinner wear. Suits and the like. I couldn't imagine building the skills to sew such things competently, but maybe someday. Other drawers housed designs for children, from delightful onesies and toddler overalls to little dresses, and even party costumes like tiny cowboys and ballerinas. My mind burst with visions of my own children who might one day wear outfits that I made for them.

With husband and baby covered, I opened drawer after drawer looking for something to make for myself; something that Andrew could see me wearing on a special night. Eventually, I found the designs for women's formal wear, and what a trove! The envelopes provided an illustration for each outfit on the front. There were sleek dresses and flamboyant gowns, cocktail outfits that were too short for anyone but prostitutes, as well as respectable, yet stylish, mourning wear. My cheeks flushed hot as I flipped through, and boldly determined that I would find the perfect gown and sew it right here at Hollyhock. Then, on discharge day, I would wear the gown and present myself to Andrew in the foyer. We would embrace and spin just like in that movie about young lovers, and we would know that all was well.

My fingers stopped when I saw it. Captured by the illustration, I lifted the packet from the drawer – a gown of vintage style, though the era was lost on me. Baroque, perhaps, or maybe Art Deco? I confess, I don't know fashion well, nor had I been much of a wearer of fancy dresses, but there I was changing – evolving – all the time. The picture showed a gown with a berthe of lace and ribbon that went wide to the shoulders, with short sleeves and a snug waistline at the base of the ribs. The skirt was broad at the floor, and so I supposed a hoop would need to be installed. I slid the paper template from the envelope, then went to the drawers for men's and children's patterns, selecting outfits for formal occasions. Maybe the three of us would go to the ballet and watch *Swan Lake* or even *The Nutcracker* at Christmastime. Maybe there would even be four of us! I grabbed a second child's outfit, this one a velvet holiday dress fringed in faux fur.

Thirza glanced over and smiled curtly, and I think I smiled back, but I was so consumed with the patterns to know if I did.

The paper practically floated on air, lighter than the tissue you use to wrap a present. With so many pieces in each package, it was daunting at first. I set out the boy's pattern next to the girl's holiday dress. I nudged them to the edge of the table so that there would be room for the whole family. I attended to Andrew next, laying out patterns for slacks and shirt, taking a moment to assess the sizes I'd need to cut out so that everything fit just so. Oh, he will look so handsome. We will be the envy of Hollyhock House and Hay Springs.

Lastly, I unpacked the dress. It contained several large pieces and much of it ended up draped across both table and chairs. But then: there we all were, and I beheld us. Andrew's left arm was at the small of my back, guiding me into the venue with our children, who, having been to the theater on numerous occasions already despite their young ages, were extremely well-behaved. The boy would be called William Grant and the girl Judith Briar. Yes. Judith Briar Turner and William Grant Turner. Look at us. Just look at us.

"Thirza?" I said, breaking from my daydream. "Where are the fabrics? I was thinking silver with blue trim for the gown here."

Thirza looked up from her gluing and pulled one of the earphones away. "Sorry?"

"Is there fabric for sewing?"

"There are some remnants in the basket by the kit over there," she said, flapping her hand. "I think they intend for us to practice. Fabric can be expensive."

I went to the basket and rummaged through it. Thirza was right. There were only pieces, no bolts, not enough even to make a hat for a child. "Why give us patterns, then?" I growled, tossing back the scraps. Awash in recorded aphorisms, Thirza didn't answer. I stopped to focus on the words filling my own head, hoping their message would bring solace.

...and also, that time does not exist as anything but a means to distract from the moment, another set of invisible walls built around you as a device of spiritual confinement, but consider that while your body is bound, your mind need not be vassal. For you are perfection...

Returning to the patterns, I adjusted them into different positions, imagining the paper turned to cloth, and flesh filling it. Time – if it exists – drifted as I played with my family of paper dolls.

Thirza stood and gathered her materials. Taking the cue that our hour had ended, I solemnly folded each sheet and returned them to their paper envelopes. I was surprised when my eyes got wet. I cleaned away the tears, reminding myself that the pain would be gone one day. With the patterns in their tidy pockets, I placed them into the drawers. First Andrew, then William Grant with his sister Judith Briar, and lastly me in my gown.

It felt like I should say something important, but it wasn't like they were being buried.

TEXT RECORD, PHONE NUMBER
(814) ***-**58

Tell me tell me tell me.

OMG you're still awake?

Uh, yeah. Coffee. Cigarettes. I wasn't going to let sleep get in the way of your full and unredacted report.

You are insane, you know that?

I am excited. Now. Tell.

He's nice. Really nice.

Awesome. Amazing. And where did you goooo?

We had a picnic at the Rowe Bird Sanctuary. It was beautiful today. He volunteers there.

Volunteers at a bird sanctuary? Sounds fake.

Definitely a serial killer.

No, I'm serious. He's like
an amateur ornithologist.

That some type of doctor?

Oh, come on. It's a bird
thing. He knows all these
birds by sight and sound.

That's actually pretty
sexy in a hot nerd sort
of way. Wait. Hadleigh.
Is he legit hot too?

You know I'm not
all about looks.

So yes, then! I bet he's
a total smoke show!
Way to go, Hads! Send
pics STAT.

Anyway...we're going to
see each other again soon.

Ohhhhhhhh. Dinner?
Is it dinner? Yes?

And a movie. Cliché, I
know.

Well, Hadleigh Bright!
When was the last time

you allowed a man to
lock down your entire
evening? Never?

Yeah, it's been a minute.

Obviously, I'm maid of honor.

Will you stop that?

I have a great feel for these
things. It's never too early
to start planning. First off,
I think you should really take
some chances with the
bridesmaids' dresses. I'm partial
to spring green. And I'm coming
out there for the cake tasting.

You're insufferable.

I know. ♥

P

Sitting before a tray piled with so much food, I envisioned Andrew at home defrosting a freezer meal. It felt almost unfair, but not so much that it prevented me from digging in. Lunch was crown roast of lamb chops served with lime jelly and spiced cauliflower purée, followed by pineapple upside-down cake for dessert. I made a note to ask the Doctor if Hollyhock's recipe book was available for purchase. Or at least a menu, so I could try recreating our daily feasts at home.

I cleaned the tray as usual, all except for the pineapple cake, which I saved for last. Wanting to savor every crumb, I sliced it into eight bite-sized morsels, but ended up devouring it in no time. At the exact moment I placed the final chunk into my mouth, I watched Sabina die in the most curious way.

There was nothing out of the ordinary at first. Hollyhock Hall was its usual bustling lunchtime self. Ladies sat in clumps, looking like communion dolls in their white dresses, chatting and eating, drinking their teas. A few of the orderlies lingered about, talking, checking in here and there.

Sabina came in through the doors beneath the big clock. Carrying an armload of files, she looked in a hurry, cutting a line across the hall for the doors on the opposite side. A little more than halfway across, she slipped on a wet spot – a spill that I hadn't noticed until she was airborne. Her legs flew out like a comedian slipping on a banana peel, and she flopped back, smacking her head on the floor with a gruesome crunch. I jumped up, convinced her skull had cracked open. But there she was, still moving around, moaning and holding her head, knocking her hair out of place and spilling all its pretty herbs and flowers about the ground.

Before anyone got close enough to help her, she launched into the air, pulled almost, arms out, back dramatically arched. She hung there for an eternity and I thought about the recordings and what they said about time, and about how it wasn't real. Sabina's backside opened down the length of her spine and she tore in half. I remember the blood. The way it hosed out in a plume the shape of an ostrich feather. Every droplet remained suspended, turning from liquid to solid, and then drifting to the floor like scarlet snow over her pieces.

It was so sad, but I admit I was relieved. It hadn't been Enid.

SPD INTERVIEW RECORD
EXCERPT OF TRANSCRIPTION

GASTRELL: You witnessed a death?

WITNESS: Yes. It was very upsetting. Everyone was so sad. I liked Sabina. She'd helped me with my parasomnia.

GASTRELL: What happened?

WITNESS: The Doctor and other staff members rushed in, but there was nothing to be done, of course, with the poor woman being in separate pieces.

GASTRELL: Jesus, Mrs Turner.

WITNESS: What?

GASTRELL: Did no one call the authorities?

WITNESS: I don't know. I assume so. We were all taken to the group room where we waited while things were sorted out. I know the Doctor came in to address us. She was so distraught. I felt almost as bad for her as I did for poor Sabina. She explained that one of the old steam pipes running below the floor had ruptured. You can imagine the effect it had on the women. From then on, nobody walked between the vents for fear of being cleaved.

GASTRELL: Then what happened?

WITNESS: Fortunately, I had finished my entire lunch, so I went directly to Home Skills.

SPD INTERVIEW RECORD
EXCERPT OF TRANSCRIPTION

GASTRELL: What is it?

BENTHAM: Her expressions of emotion are performative.

GASTRELL: I've noticed. How does that change anything?

BENTHAM: It squares with her being a sociopath, wouldn't you agree?

GASTRELL: I don't know, she's pretty fond of Enid for some reason.

BENTHAM: Sociopaths can feel affection, Detective.

GASTRELL: Okay, so what if she is? I've dealt with plenty of sociopaths. The majority are rigidly honest. So I don't really care what her feelings are so long as she keeps delivering the facts.

BENTHAM: She just described watching a woman die with less emotion than when she's listing what she had for breakfast.

GASTRELL: I really don't care what her emotional reaction was.

BENTHAM: There was none, is my point. Not a single note of genuine empathy. If it's manufactured, then what else is she deceiving you about?

GASTRELL: I don't know, she seems pretty open about everything so far, wouldn't you say?

BENTHAM: Open doesn't mean truthful.

GASTRELL: Thanks for the forensics tutorial.

BENTHAM: Do you think the account has any bearing in truth? A woman cut in half by steam?

91

GASTRELL: That place had its own boiler house and yeah, steam leaks can be bad news, but I agree that her description was strange. Likely embellished. Or maybe that's just her perspective. How she saw it.

BENTHAM: Were there any police reports filed? Obituaries?

GASTRELL: Detective work is fun, huh?

BENTHAM: I'm concerned about these patients. I want to get to the bottom of it.

GASTRELL: Well, they're all dead, so–

BENTHAM: Are you always this callous?

GASTRELL: How many police detectives have you met?

BENTHAM: Moving past that, please?

GASTRELL: No. There weren't any reports or obits in Dawes County or the surrounds. And there aren't any records of anyone named Sabina living in the area. But there wouldn't be, right? The staff lived on site. And I don't know where Althea Edevane found them.

BENTHAM: That's two deaths. The woman who electrocuted herself and now Sabina.

GASTRELL: I'm not counting that first one. That was just the other patients trying to scare Charlotte.

BENTHAM: You don't know that for certain.

GASTRELL: The only way to find out is to keep questioning.

P

One day after Group, I stayed behind in the old medical library to practice my aphorisms. Miriam said that each one represented a step on the stairway of belief in ourselves and that we should strive to climb higher every day. She said the mind is powerful, and I agreed.

Being a stubborn type, I recited each aphorism until I could say it without reservation or cynicism, until it was truly *adopted*, woven into my DNA. I think anyone can do it if they open their heart and mind to the process. Even if you start with a shuttered perspective, which I admit I sometimes do, repetition turns the stubborn pliable. And that's what allows new ideas to squeeze in. It's all about *pliability*.

The newest aphorism was short, so I internalized it quickly. *My mind is healing every day.* Such a positive message. I repeated it again and again until the words became viscous, coating the works of my brain, cleaning, renewing, casting light from different angles. I could feel it washing the corrosion of my preconceptions and prejudices, infusing positivity into my muscles and bone, my organs, and every cell. I stood upon a stairway to the sky. I had been down at the bottom, in a place where neither Andrew nor I wanted me to be, but now I had taken the steps. So many steps. I knew that the journey to the top would be long and sometimes hard, but I was ready. *Easy progress is never permanent*: another aphorism. I wasn't to the top yet, but I would be … eventually. I closed my eyes and beamed into the open blue of self-actualization.

A cleansing breath propelled me into the present. I got up from my chair and poured myself a cup of persimmon water from the crystal ewer. Sometimes they were frozen solid, but on this day, it flowed, and the taste was like honey and apricot. Lovely. *My mind is healing every day.*

I filled the glass again, drank it down, and placed it in the return basin. I went to leave, and found a woman standing in the doorway, her back to me. I crossed the room to a different door, only to realize that a second woman was there as well. In fact, they stood in all four doorways, facing away, hair hanging long and silky over the back of colorful spring dresses.

"Excuse me?" None answered. "You really should have your hair up," I said. "I was skeptical at first until my own hair was touched in this very room. Are you new?" I asked. "We have a hair-touching problem here at Hollyhock."

They spun around, dresses swirling, slightly out of sync with each other. Backing away, I saw who they were. Me.

"Wake up," they said, their voices choral and overlapping somewhat out of tune.

"Who are you? Go away."

"That's not possible," they said. "I am you. I'm more you than you are."

"You're the one!" I said. "*You* pulled my hair."

"No," they said, "that wasn't me. I wrote on the pages in your room."

"I knew it!" I yelled. "You opened my door. Made me hallucinate!"

"Please: I'm not someone else. I'm you. And I can't open doors," they said, motioning an arm through the wood of the door frame like a specter. "See? I'm not out here. You've put me away. You have to let me back in."

"No. This is all a hallucination! I've allowed myself to become distracted," I insisted. "I'm taking the steps every day."

"You are only a part of me, Charlotte. And I am *all* of you. You are a part of {SILENCE}."

Their words faded out. I shook my head. Their lips moved, but certain words dropped away.

"I am {SILENCE}, that's you."

I scrubbed at my face, agitated. I still couldn't hear it. I didn't want to hear it.

"You have to wake up," they said. "My name is {SILENCE}. Let yourself hear my name, Charlotte. I *made* you."

"My mind is healing every day. I may not be able to control the world beyond myself, but I decide my reaction to it. The sickening mind is a master of deception."

They shouted at once. "Stop saying that! I am {SILENCE}. You're a {SILENCE}! You need to let me in so that I can find out what happened to {SILENCE}. Let me in!"

"I can't hear what you're saying!" I screamed. "Go away, whoever you are."

"You have to *want* to hear it! Listen to me, Charlotte! It's for the both of us."

"No! I'm taking the steps! You won't drag me down from the sky or keep me from the gifts of the Earth! *The sickening mind is a master of deception.*"

"Charlotte, please! Say my name! Say {SILENCE}!"

It was a delusion. An idea of reference, yes. This woman was no more real than Mrs James trying to poison me with the Thanksgiving cookies. (I still don't trust Mrs James, though. She uses carob instead of chocolate.) Miriam had warned of this. That our biggest challenge would be the stubborn ways of outdated thinking. My mind was trying to push me down the stairs I'd climbed. *The enemy of our convalescence is us.* It all made sense.

"You are a delusion!" I shouted. "A fabrication of my mind testing my resolve! You are not me."

"You…"

Overreaction breeds escalation breeds hallucination.

I may not be able to control the world beyond myself, but I own my reaction to it.

My mind is healing every day.

The visions of me took on a shade as I spoke, losing their color and turning gray. Their mouths moved silently, struggling to talk. My aphorisms weakened them, sapped their strength. I was stronger. My mind *was* healing. The ghostly women backed out from the doors and receded slowly away, even as they continued their protestations. I repeated the mantras until they were fully gone, whispering my learnings like a holy prayer, a warding spell, into each of the four corridors. At the last door I staked my ground, triumphant, and cast the words bright and clear like cleansing fire. *"The sickening mind is a master of deception!"*

TEXT RECORD, PHONE NUMBER

(814) ***-**58

You rang?

I think I'm falling for
Clayden.

Obviously. Have
you seen him?

You are so shallow!

I'm just saying it
doesn't make it any
harder to fall in love
with someone who
looks like him.

Aaaaaannnnnd you're
happy for me.

Right. Yes. Obviously.
Congratulations. I am
overjoyed for you.

Thank you.

And I take it he loves
you back?

I hope so. I think so.

I've always been a sucker
for black hair and blue eyes.
I mean how many guys
have that combo?
You've nabbed yourself
a unicorn boy.

He's even more of a
personality-unicorn than
a looks-unicorn. We went
to the sanctuary again.
I got to help him in some
of his volunteer duties.

Jesus. Is he a boy scout
too? Does he still live with
his mom?

Very funny. Did you know
that vultures raised in captivity
think that they are actual people?
As in they have no idea they're
birds. They believe they are
real humans like you and me.

Oh yeah? Does he have
a vulture girlfriend?

Vulture boyfriend.
Cornelius Sylvester.

That's the bird's name?

Yep. They stare at each other
and have whole conversations.
Cornelius responds with little
squawks.

Could be a red flag, Hads.

It's the sweetest thing I've
ever seen. I feel like I'm
falling in love and there's
no way to stop. Like I'm
slipping down a snowy hill
whether I want to or not.

I'm so happy for you. You
deserve to find the perfect
guy after all the dumpster
fires you've dated. You
deserve a man that is all
hot and talks to birds.

I don't know what I deserve,
but I'm going to hang on to
him.

Does he have any other
bird nerd friends?

Maybe I could set you up
with one of the vultures?
I'll have Clayden ask
Cornelius.

Oh yes, please.

SPD INTERVIEW RECORD
EXCERPT OF TRANSCRIPTION

GASTRELL: Why do you think you hallucinated the women in the library?

WITNESS: They were the devils on my shoulder. A manifestation of my own consciousness, trying to prevent me from taking the steps. A sick mind has inertia, you know, just like anything else. Minds don't like change. Have you ever tried to break a bad habit, Detective?

GASTRELL: Plenty of times.

WITNESS: So, the healing of sickening minds is much the same, only I'd wager far more difficult. It's not so obvious as to avoid buying a pack of cigarettes or leaving that second piece of cake on the platter. The sickening mind is insidious. It wears disguises, so it might go unnoticed. But see, Hollyhock trained me to identify when the inertia of my rot produced deceitful manifestations. As in the case of the group room. I remembered the truth of my aphorisms and prevailed. The sickening mind is a master of deception. Isn't that beautiful? Say it.

GASTRELL: You want me to repeat your aphorism?

WITNESS: What are you afraid of, Detective? You have to deal with serial murderers and rapists every day.

GASTRELL: No, not quite.

WITNESS: Nevertheless. You should say it, so you understand the raw power of your own autonomy over delusion.

GASTRELL: "The sickening mind is a master of deception." There, are you satisfied?

WITNESS: You sound like a toddler repeating the Pledge of Allegiance, Detective. Say it. Mean it. There's nothing harmful in the message. Only a sickening mind would resist saying the aphorism with heart, don't you think?

GASTRELL: I'm perfectly healthy, Mrs Turner. Let's please get back on track.

WITNESS: I thought I was perfectly healthy for a long time, too, you know. The sickening mind is a master of deception. If you don't say it, how can I trust that you aren't suffering delusions? The public are supposed to be able to trust that the police are competent, especially in a case such as this. Trust is everything that stands between chaos and order, isn't it? Chaos, Detective. Say the aphorism and bring order to the chaos. Say it.

GASTRELL: I think we need a break, Mrs Turner.

WITNESS: Say it. Say the aphorism. Why aren't you saying it?

GASTRELL: We'll take a break, I'll get you another burger. Some food will be good, yes?

WITNESS: Say it! Say it! Say it! Say it! Say it! [indistinct]

SPD INTERVIEW RECORD
EXCERPT OF TRANSCRIPTION

BENTHAM: I'm getting questions.

GASTRELL: I fucking bet.

BENTHAM: About why she hasn't been moved to an appropriate facility.

GASTRELL: You can see her. She's doing fine. "In no apparent distress." Isn't that what you doctors say?

BENTHAM: After all that? Forcing you to repeat her aphorisms, you think she's doing fine? Totally normal?

GASTRELL: Just playing ball, Doc. That's how you keep a witness talking.

BENTHAM: She called herself "the mouth of the Earth" during your first interview. Now what's this other bit? "Hewn and ground and polished all these millions of years"? What the hell was that?

GASTRELL: I'm fact-gathering, Doctor. It's not always pretty.

BENTHAM: There are facts, and then there is nonsense. She's talking nonsense.

GASTRELL: Actually, she's giving us an account of how things worked at Hollyhock. A view into that place we've never had. You remember the Snow Walker case, I bet.

BENTHAM: Yeah, who doesn't?

GASTRELL: Hypothermic and frostbitten until she was barely moving out on that road. That hole in her stomach.

BENTHAM: Remember what they found inside?

GASTRELL: Yeah, I remember. Point is, no one over there said a word when it went down. Place was buttoned up like the Vatican. We got nothing. No answers. Now I've got a person willing to talk and I want to keep her talking. As a doctor who cares for these people, aren't you curious to know what was going on over there?

BENTHAM: Of course I am. But I can't sacrifice the welfare of one in the service of some snipe hunt. That's a pretty basic ethical tenet of medicine.

GASTRELL: Fortunately, I'm not a doctor. Anything else?

BENTHAM: She needs real care. She's getting worse, not better.

GASTRELL: All the more reason for me to work quickly.

BENTHAM: I don't think you understand–

GASTRELL: Understand this: unless you can get someone above my pay grade to agree to move her, she's staying right here.

BENTHAM: Anyone over your pay grade will be another cop.

GASTRELL: And there you have identified the challenge of your situation. Best of luck. I'll ping you if I need anything.

P

I visited the mausoleum in Home Skills where my family waited each day before lunch. I knew it was just a chest of tiny drawers, I knew that, but until I brought my real family to life, they would rest like the sacred remains of those who are loved.

Before proceeding, I served myself a glass of the persimmon-infused water, taking it in delicate sips because everything is a process. Then I went to the drawers and removed my family from their sleeves, setting them out on the table, positioning them in ways that allowed me to visualize our lives together. Sometimes William Grant and Judith Briar were sat on a springtime picnic blanket with Andrew and me in our finest, the proud parents watching over. I arranged us in hilarious positions as well, letting the children climb on our backs as we crawled across the carpet like circus elephants, honking our trunks. I laughed loud enough to disturb the other women in their headphones, but I didn't care. My mind is healing every day.

The recorded messages resonated with each fiber of my being, and I rejoiced in the knowledge of my importance to the cycle of the Universe, and the truth that specks of dust like me weren't insignificant at all, but vital. It gave me the courage I needed to no longer let ignorance and fear dictate the terms of my life. Before saying goodbye to my family, I whispered promises. Prophecies. A reunion for us in the halls of the nacreous home.

Ᵽ

Walking out from the service line in Hollyhock Hall, I noticed Christmas right away, with her floating hands and flattened head, sitting alone at the distant end of a line of tables. I didn't go directly to her, but rather weaved through the room in search of Honora, hoping to see her round shoulders and muscular back hunched over a pile of food, but she had been taken to Special Therapies again. I missed her stealing my food. Rhoda had never returned from her visit to Special Therapies either, but that I didn't mind so much.

Christmas looked up and located me as if someone had whispered in her ear. She grimaced, then flew her hands down to cover both ears while mouthing something. The air about her head had the character of vapor, stretching and contorting in waves that distorted her immediate surroundings.

I paced down the rows of tables, trying not to surrender to my swelling fear. Christmas was possessed of a strange thereness, a frequency that made her seem able to disappear entirely, only to re-emerge when she wished to be seen. Whatever it was, she had chosen this moment to direct her presence at me.

Coming close, I tried to remember the type of person I am – or that I hope I am – reminding myself that every one of these women, including Christmas, had walked an unfortunate road to end up here. Empathy is when you try to understand someone's situation from their point of view, and I resolved to practice my empathizing with Christmas. We were all taking the steps to where the sky was blue. If one of my fellow patients dropped behind, I would pull her up. With that, I put a smile on my face.

The air was calm by the time I arrived. She sat alone.

"I told you to stay away," she said, stirring her lunch. Lentil soup brimmed from every compartment in the silver tray.

I fought off a surge of anxiety and girded myself. "No one ever made friends by isolating themselves."

Christmas shrugged. I sat and smiled. She swallowed another clump of beans.

I noodled at my lunch, not knowing how best to press the conversation forward. I figured a personal connection might work. "My husband, Andrew, and I are hoping to start a family."

"Why?"

"Why does anyone have children?" I said, wondering to myself if it was just instinct. I envisioned Andrew and Judith Briar and William Grant, asleep in their coffin drawers, awaiting animation. "I always wanted to have a child. In every daydream I had as a little girl, there was a family in my future. A warm and happy home with children running about. Andrew wants the same thing, but I need a clean bill of health first. What about you? Have you ever wanted children?"

"You'd ask that of a person like me?" She tapped her level crown, then fanned her fingers like a peacock's display before her hands lifted off for parts unknown.

"I know enough not to assume anything of people."

"Bet you didn't assume I'm barren."

"Oh, Christmas, I'm sorry." Because that's what you say.

Her face went dark. "It's a blessing."

I couldn't make sense of it. Children were the point. How could infertility be any type of blessing? We ate again in silence until I broke it. "Christmas?"

"Hmm?"

"You said something to me ... in Group ... and, well, it scared me." The words came out like a hose uncrimped. I felt tears building. I didn't want to cry there in the dining hall. "I need to know that I'm not going mad."

"You're not going mad," she said, her shoulders syncing only long enough to shrug.

"Then tell me what you meant. Were you trying to scare me? Why would you talk to someone like that?"

"I wasn't just talking to *you*."

"It sure felt like you were."

She brought a dribbling spoonful of lentils to her mouth and swallowed it like a fish.

"You said, 'They're upset', and that *they said* I looked like someone. Who...? Who are you talking about? Who are 'they'? Who do they say I look like?" My mind became a claustrophobic hallway of funhouse mirrors, with my doppelgangers shouting from the doors in the Group room. Would Christmas accuse me of being my own ghost?

She pointed to the other women with her dripping spoon. "Every time I try to warn them, they laugh. They say I'm a witch because Rhoda tells them so."

"What a ridiculous notion," I said, with a purposeful warble of laughter in my throat. "You're not, are you?"

"No witches here, Charlotte Turner, just curses. But Rhoda will find out."

I pulled my shoulders back. "I think we're all a little cursed if our paths led us to institutionalization."

"Well, Rhoda's down the next path," she said, arms hovering out to the sides, inches above the table. "That's enough talk for now."

"What? Why? What do you mean by curses?"

She glared. "You should leave me be, Miss Charlotte, or you will share in it."

"Now, Christmas..."

She tilted an ear to her shoulder and held it there. "You should have listened when I told you to stay away."

I didn't want to be angry. But it felt like a betrayal to be toyed with by someone in the same unenviable position. Though I would rather not have been committed, I had hoped to find some fellowship among patients. But with Honora taken away, I was lonely. "Why won't you tell me what it was you meant to say? Why did you say it all? To torture me? You would leave me wondering which parts of my life I am hallucinating?"

"You should leave me be."

"I want to understand!"

Her arms shot straight up together, then descended to the sides like falling snow. "I know when they get … interested."

"Speak to me plainly."

She hit the table with her palms, splashing beans from her tray. "I am the *only one* speaking to you plainly."

"Yes … okay," I answered, glancing nervously to the other tables. "Help me understand, then."

She wiped at the spilled beans with her cloth napkin, more smearing them over the surface of the table than cleaning anything. "You have to listen to my words."

"Okay," I said, genuinely trying to understand.

"You know encephalitis?"

"The brain infection?"

"Had it as a child." She stopped and stared through me while delivering a spoonful of lentils into her mouth. She chewed, then swallowed loudly. "It spread so fast the doctors thought I was going to die. I remember laying there, imagining my brain getting bigger, pressing against the inside of my skull, while my parents prayed to God to save me. I hardly slept but when I did, I ground my teeth clear through the enamel." She strained her mouth into a wide smile and jutted her jaw forward, revealing a bottom row of tiny teeth with the tops shorn away. I leaned in because it looked to me like she still had all her baby teeth. She snapped her mouth shut and glared. "Some people never get second teeth."

"I'm sorry–"

"Anyhow," she said, "antibiotics didn't work. They had to open my skull."

I offered my hand across the table because that's what you do in situations like this. Christmas ignored it, holding up a glopping spoonful. "Have you ever tasted these?"

"Lentils? Well, sure."

"I haven't," she said, letting the spoon drop onto the tray. "No taste or smell. Miriam or Enid or Anise tell me when to bathe because I don't know when I've gotten ripe."

I didn't like the idea of her spending time with Enid, but pushed that away. "I'm so sorry, Christmas, it must have been hard as a child to–"

"But I *can* hear, Miss Charlotte. Things you don't. Things nobody does." One of her drifting hands came to rest on the flat expanse above her forehead. "The operation did something."

"Okay."

She tilted her head like a child summoned home for dinner. "Hmm. You should have listened."

"Sorry?"

"I told you to stay away. You should have listened. You never listen." She pointed vaguely to the air as if the answer might be found there.

I tuned my ears, trying to hear what she did. The sounds of Hollyhock Hall were no different than usual: the murmur hum of the other women gossiping, punctuated by the tinkle of utensils on trays. Then, Christmas was looking at me, arms completely motionless. The air hanging over her skin was so thick it made her seem encased in glass. Everywhere was the whooshing of wind and pouring sand. Then she asked me a question that I didn't hear – no, that's not right – I heard it, I just didn't understand. But something deep within me did.

"Who is Hadleigh?"

A high-pitched shriek split my ears. Like the world had been slit open and was spilling its guts. A scream climbed up and hung in my throat, but it was not me who was screaming.

The wall behind Christmas opened. A gash cut down from the ceiling, crossing over the clock and the double doors, even across the front of Anise, who'd just walked through them. It continued down through her feet and into the floor, which opened wide like a chasm filled to its limit with black. I realized then, that the crack was not of the wall or of the doors or the woman, but of me, of my mind. I was witness to the breaking of myself. I tried summoning an aphorism, but then...

I disappeared.

And *I* return. I am on my back, splayed on the linoleum floor of an unfamiliar and cavernous room, staring up at a woman with a flattened head. Her arms swim before me like pale-bellied fish. She drops to the ground and speaks. "They say you look like her."

SPD INTERVIEW RECORD
EXCERPT OF TRANSCRIPTION

WITNESS: Where am I?

GASTRELL: The station infirmary.

WITNESS: Why can't I move?

GASTRELL: I'm sorry about that. You had to be restrained after you regained consciousness.

WITNESS: Who are you?

GASTRELL: Who am I? Who are you?

WITNESS: Morgan Bright.

GASTRELL: Who?

WITNESS: I don't understand. Who are you?

GASTRELL: Detective Abram Gastrell, Scottsbluff PD.

WITNESS: Scottsbluff? What am I doing in Scottsbluff?

GASTRELL: Slow down. Say your name again.

WITNESS: Morgan Bright.

GASTRELL: Christ.

WITNESS: What?

GASTRELL: What happened to Charlotte?

WITNESS: Charlotte? How do you know about Charlotte?

GASTRELL: She's you. We've been talking for almost three days. You told me your name was Charlotte Turner.

WITNESS: Am I in a police station?

GASTRELL: Yes.

WITNESS: How were you talking to Charlotte? She's not real. She's a character, an act.

GASTRELL: Hold on now, I... I'm not sure about that.

WITNESS: And you've had me in restraints this whole time?

GASTRELL: No: you'd been cooperating up until – well, something happened. Charlotte went away. There was an episode ... A struggle.

WITNESS: You're talking about her like she's a real person.

GASTRELL: I'm not sure who is real at the moment–

WITNESS: Let me out of these straps, please.

GASTRELL: I can't.

WITNESS: I'm not going to attack you. How long have we been talking?

GASTRELL: I told you, this is our third day. Do you not remember?

WITNESS: Uh, no. I don't remember. How did I talk to you and not remember?

GASTRELL: All I can say is that it happened. It's all recorded. I'd love for you to explain who you are and why you've been another person up until now.

WITNESS: Can you remove these straps, please?

GASTRELL: We can't do that just yet. I don't even know who you are.

WITNESS: [indistinct]

GASTRELL: Stop that! Stop! What are you trying to do?

WITNESS: Below my clavicle on the left side. Just under the skin. Use your fingers. Tell me if you feel anything.

GASTRELL: I won't touch you – it's not... There's a protocol–

WITNESS: Is there a doctor somewhere?

GASTRELL: Why?

WITNESS: Just get a doctor!

GASTRELL: She's here somewhere. Hold on.

WITNESS: Take these off!

GASTRELL: I said hold on.

[Break taken from 13:21 to 13:26. DOCTOR HEEDA BENTHAM enters]

BENTHAM: Okay. What am I looking for?

WITNESS: An implant. Under my left clavicle. The size of a Haldol.

GASTRELL: An implant for what? Is this something they did to you at Hollyhock?

WITNESS: If I'm not dreaming, it's something I did to myself.

BENTHAM: All right, one moment. [proceeds] The structure on and around the clavicles is unremarkable and identical on both sides. There doesn't appear to be any foreign bodies present. Just a–

WITNESS: No. No. That's impossible.

BENTHAM: Well, hold on. There's a small scar. Freshly healed.

WITNESS: On the left? Where I said it was?

BENTHAM: Yes. Looks like it was repaired with surgical adhesive.

WITNESS: And there's nothing underneath?

BENTHAM: Nothing that shouldn't be there.

WITNESS: My God, she must have found it. She took it out!

GASTRELL: Who took what out?

WITNESS: Doctor Edevane. Can you please remove my straps?

BENTHAM: Not two hours ago you had a complete dissociative episode. Violent. The only reason we haven't taken you for facility observation is Detective Gastrell, here. He says he needs this interview as part of his investigation.

GASTRELL: Is she stable enough to continue, Doctor?

BENTHAM: I'm not endorsing this.

SPD INTERVIEW RECORD
EXCERPT OF TRANSCRIPTION

GASTRELL: What was removed from your chest?

WITNESS: Proof that I am who I think I am.

GASTRELL: Explain.

WITNESS: It was a transmitter.

GASTRELL: Transmitter? For what?

WITNESS: Oh–

GASTRELL: Oh God, what?

WITNESS: About to be [indistinct]. About to be sick.

GASTRELL: Goddammit.

WITNESS: Oh, wow.

GASTRELL: This better not be a ploy to get out of these restraints.

WITNESS: No. Hurry up.

GASTRELL: Fine.

WITNESS: Faster!

GASTRELL: I don't know why they still use buckles instead of Velcro! Here, do it in here. Oh my.

WITNESS: [indistinct] Oh, that was a lot.

GASTRELL: Here. Your face. Use the whole box if you need.

WITNESS: Thanks. Water?

GASTRELL: [complies]

WITNESS: Thanks.

    BREAK taken from 13:59 to 14:13

GASTRELL: We're back from a break. The witness has used the bathroom and I am just dying to know what the hell is going on. While you were cleaning up, I found you – or the person you say you are – in the national criminal database. Morgan Bright, thirty-three years old, of Benezette, PA.

WITNESS: Never said I was hard to find.

GASTRELL: What con are you running right now?

WITNESS: No con. No fucking con.

GASTRELL: No con, huh? That would seem to be a first. You've been booked and charged for everything from shoplifting, to disorderly, to B and E, to felony possession of a controlled substance, to disturbing an official proceeding, and yet somehow I don't see any jail time. I see dismissals, reductions to misdemeanors. How'd you manage that, are you famous?

WITNESS: I had a sister with money who paid for good lawyers. And the B and E was my parents' house.

GASTRELL: They still called the cops on you.

WITNESS: Yeah.

GASTRELL: Add to that at least two – no, four – stints in rehab?

WITNESS: Mm-hmm.

GASTRELL: Nice places. The sister again?

WITNESS: Yep.

GASTRELL: How long have you battled addiction?

WITNESS: A dozen years on and off. But I don't battle it anymore.

GASTRELL: Sure–

WITNESS: I'm sober twenty-one months, and if you knew me before you would have said I wouldn't make it a week, much less two years. Doesn't mean I'm not still haunted by the urge to use. I'll always feel that ... momentum.

GASTRELL: Says here you earned a scholarship to U.
              of Pennsylvania. That's Ivy League, right?
              Good school. You must be smart.

WITNESS: Just smart enough to make it two years
              before being kicked out.

GASTRELL: For what?

WITNESS: Their narcotics policy.

GASTRELL: Hm. What'd you major in?

WITNESS: English Lit and Journalism.

GASTRELL: Not the best job prospects with those two,
              eh?

WITNESS: I'll keep that in mind the next time I go to
              college.

GASTRELL: Sorry. Okay, so why were you posing as a
              housewife called Charlotte Turner in Hay
              Springs, Nebraska?

WITNESS: I don't think you'd believe me.

GASTRELL: After some of the things Charlotte said, I
              have a low bar. Try me.

WITNESS: Okay: Hadleigh Clayden Keene.

GASTRELL: Excuse me?

WITNESS: Hadleigh Keene. You know that name?

GASTRELL: Everyone around here knows that name.
              The Snow Walker. She was found wandering
              the farm-to-markets twelve miles from
              Hollyhock in the dead of winter a couple
              years back.

WITNESS: She's the sister with the money.

GASTRELL: Is this some sort of joke?

WITNESS: I wouldn't joke about her. She was my sister.
              Her maiden name was Bright. Hadleigh
              Bright.

GASTRELL: You're telling me... What are you doing now?

WITNESS: I have to take off my shoe to show you.

GASTRELL: Wait–

WITNESS: See? Right here.

GASTRELL: What is that? A tattoo?

WITNESS: It's a bird.

GASTRELL: Okay?

WITNESS: This was years ago. One of the few times I got her to cut loose. I had a friend with a tattoo gun, so we tattooed each other. One of my many stupid, drunken ideas. Doozies. A dumb game we used to play. Hadleigh gave me this. Anyway, go look at the coroner's photos on the inside of her right ankle. There's a little outline of a wolf. She loved birds and I love wolves. We sort of etched our marks onto each other. It was a way to have a piece of one another forever, or something stupid like that.

GASTRELL: I've seen stupider.

WITNESS: You never did find out why she was out there, did you, what happened to her?

GASTRELL: I expect you're going to tell me you did.

WITNESS: No. I don't know. Not as I sit here. I can't remember.

GASTRELL: Okay, hold on. You can't remember anything from Hollyhock?

WITNESS: Nothing specific. Not... Not right now. My mind is all sort of white.

GASTRELL: Okay. So you're here now and you can't remember anything. Let me play along for a minute. Can you tell me why Charlotte suddenly went away?

WITNESS: I don't know. I remember blackness, and then a gash of light. Then right now.

GASTRELL: Right before ... all of this ... Charlotte talked about seeing a crack in the wall or something – to be honest, it was a little hard to understand. She explained what sounded like some sort of episode in the dining hall with Christmas. And then she immediately had an episode here. It was like they were linked together, the character and the storyteller. And now I'm talking to you.

WITNESS: Hold on, I remember the dining hall. I ... fell? There was a woman on the floor beside me...

GASTRELL: That's Christmas.

WITNESS: Christmas like the holiday?

GASTRELL: According to Charlotte.

WITNESS: And this lady – Christmas – she mentioned Hadleigh, didn't she?

GASTRELL: She did.

WITNESS: Yeah. I remember that. It ... felt like a jolt of electricity. Like, it shocked me awake.

GASTRELL: Were you sleeping?

WITNESS: Was I sleeping when?

GASTRELL: When Charlotte was running the show.

WITNESS: No, no, I wasn't asleep. I was just ... away. I... I don't know where I was. I don't remember anything at Hollyhock to that point. I don't know how long Charlotte was in control.

GASTRELL: You're here now. I need you to explain to me what is going on.

WITNESS: Hadleigh died two and a half years ago. No one knows why or what happened, other than she was found wandering barefoot in the middle of nowhere. Hypothermic, dehydrated, delirious. They got her into the back of a police car, and she died before they made it to the station. I've seen the autopsy pictures. Wrists bent. Fingers frozen into claws. Feet blackened knots of frostbite. That fucking hole in her stomach. No arrests, though. Nothing. Nobody did anything. You did nothing.

GASTRELL: Careful, now. That wasn't my jurisdiction. Hollyhock is in Dawes County. But I know those guys. Solving that case was top of their list. You gotta understand: Hollyhock – it's private. The owners are ... connected. And her husband didn't push it. Do you know how hard it is to get the DA behind something when the family doesn't cooperate? They did everything they could to find out what happened short of having themselves committed.

WITNESS: Yeah, well ...

GASTRELL: You're telling me that's what you did?

WITNESS: [indicating]

GASTRELL: Seriously?

WITNESS: Nellie Bly did it in 1887 at twenty-three years old, and she didn't even have a familial connection.

GASTRELL: I don't know who that is.

WITNESS: Nellie Bly? *Ten Days in a Mad-House*? Jesus.

GASTRELL: Sorry.

WITNESS: Doesn't matter. A little over a year ago, I moved away from Benezette with a man named Darius Stanton. Darius was one of Hadleigh's closest and oldest friends, and we arrived in Hay Springs under false identities: Charlotte and Andrew Turner. I knew the easiest way to be committed was for my "husband" to have me evaluated for "domestic psychosis". Plus, with my shit, there was no way I could be alone for that long. Just no way. I needed someone with me, so I spent the whole year before we left PA trying to convince him.

GASTRELL: And he agreed?

WITNESS: He loved Hadleigh like a sister. As much as I do. And I can be pretty relentless. But the truth? I was doing this no matter what. And I knew he wouldn't let me go alone. So yeah, with his affection for her and a little emotional blackmail from me, he agreed, but only if I was clean. Like, all the way clean. I'd been back using after everything went down. Just enough to keep from going into withdrawal, you know – or that's what I told myself, anyway. I knew I had to be sober if I was going to do this. I went back into rehab. Forty-five days. Using the money Hadleigh left me. I'd done it all before. I knew the steps. I just had to do them. This time ... I really meant it.

GASTRELL: I've heard that before.

WITNESS: I mean, I'd always "meant it," right? You always mean it in the moment. But then you walk out the door and your mind goes right back. You're battling the second you leave. You see the people and the places where you know you can get hooked up and you start toying with the idea, you know? That's how it works when you're just off the kick. You give yourself these little treats, these little daydreams about the pills. But those daydreams burrow in. That's why you've got to push back so fast. You can't do it alone. Darius was there whenever I wanted to slip and he stopped me. It's why I needed him to do this with me.

GASTRELL: And you didn't relapse?

WITNESS: I didn't. I haven't.

GASTRELL: And then?

WITNESS: We created our new personas. Every detail of our fictional lives, going back to birth. Somehow, Darius had no accent, and adopting that clean Nebraska enunciation that sounds like you're doing the weather was no problem for him. I had a touch of west PA yinzer – not extreme, but it took some work to stomp it out. Even now, it doesn't come naturally back. I changed my hair, quit smoking. Probably not the best time for that, but I did it. Darius had some experience doing machinery work during summers in college, but not enough that it was high on his profile. When we got to Hay Springs, he took a job selling for a tooling company. I played housewife. Took up dishes and ironing. Tried knitting. We created a whole new person in Charlotte. We defined her mannerisms, her values, her motives, gave her a complete backstory about our relationship. The struggles over money. Her desire for a child, Andrew's ultimatum that she be admitted to Hollyhock. We lived that fiction for a year. Yeah, I was playing a part, but it didn't take long for me to become it. We never left the stage, you know? Our fake life became our actual, everyday, life. We didn't have much money. We fought about it. I spent my spare time learning about Hollyhock, all the awful things they did to people. The story of Tilda Branch from back in the 1970s. The place closing, then reopening. Their bullshit grand rebranding. Still, though, I got so goddamned bored. Hay Springs was the only place we could afford and it's fucking small. Darius had to travel the counties around Sheridan, over to Dawes, Hooker, Blaine, Loup, and even down to Deuel. I was lonely, isolated. There came a point that I was hardly acting anymore. Charlotte and I shared the same body. The same life.

GASTRELL: I think you still do.

WITNESS: Well, you're wrong. I'm here now.

GASTRELL: Dr Bentham says you've suffered a dissociative episode. She said the same thing about Charlotte, by the way – when we began our interview. Charlotte reported some strange events and said some odd things.

WITNESS: Dissociative episode. What is that supposed to mean?

GASTRELL: I'm just police, but I think it means you're a bit...

WITNESS: Crazy?

GASTRELL: Messed up. Hey, I'm not a doctor, but after all the time I spent with Charlotte, I don't think she's just going away. She was too real when she was here. Call it a gut feeling.

WITNESS: I'm here now. Look at me. I'm real. She's not. I'm in control.

GASTRELL: You were in control before you got to Hollyhock, right? Then you weren't.

WITNESS: [indistinct]

GASTRELL: Right?

WITNESS: I guess.

GASTRELL: Do you even know when she took over in the first place? Or how?

WITNESS:	No.
GASTRELL:	But when she did, what happened to you?
WITNESS:	I... I went away. I only have these ... feelings ... like echoes. I could sense her moving, you know, somewhere in the distance. Something about that place, it ... fed Charlotte, nourished her, made her tangible. It was like I became the idea, and she became the person. That's how it felt is all I'm saying.
GASTRELL:	So, you don't know how she took over and you don't know when?
WITNESS:	It had to be early, I know that. I absolutely remember walking into Hollyhock as Morgan Bright playing Charlotte Turner, I remember Darius leaving ... but something made me forget – made me disappear. Like I'd been ... cut out. That is, until Christmas mentioned Hadleigh in the dining hall.
GASTRELL:	So, you remember getting there, and then, nothing. You have no access to Charlotte's memories?
WITNESS:	I guess not, no.
GASTRELL:	The first thing Charlotte reported remembering was her initial night in the Welcome Room. She took a shower. Ate. They gave her a pregnancy test.
WITNESS:	I remember the pregnancy test.
GASTRELL:	Okay, good...
WITNESS:	Yeah, but I don't remember any Welcome Room. It was called that?
GASTRELL:	Yeah. I don't think Charlotte was lying. She's pretty earnest. Actually, that was one part of talking to her that didn't seem entirely natural. Like it was real, but manufactured. Nobody's that sincere.

WITNESS: I remember a shower too. Just not in the Welcome Room.

GASTRELL: Well, that's what Enid called it.

WITNESS: Enid!

GASTRELL: What?

WITNESS: [indistinct]

GASTRELL: Oh God, are you okay?

WITNESS: I remember. Oh no, oh no, oh no...

GASTRELL: I'll call Dr Bentham.

WITNESS: I am such a coward!

GASTRELL: What are you talking about?

WITNESS: In Charlotte's mind, the Welcome Room was where she went directly after Andrew dropped her off. That was the start of her commitment. But there was a step after being admitted and before the Welcome Room. I'm sure she would have reported it to you if she recalled it.

GASTRELL: She must not have.

WITNESS: That's because I was still me. My shower, my pregnancy test came before Charlotte ever entered the Welcome Room. I was taken into a different room. A yellow room without a name.

TWO

Darius and I check the transmitter in the parking lot and then head inside the building. We wait in the foyer. Hanging from a beam is an ornamental wooden plaque, lacquered to a mirror shine and decorated with pastel flowers and the hand-lettered phrase *You Will Twirl With Us*. Strange, but I knew this place was going to be different.

The foyer opens into a voluminous hallway with dark wooden floors reflecting the chandeliers in their oiled shine. The walls are a deep shade of teal. Despite my nerves, I am disarmed by how warm and inviting it feels. And not fake warmth, either. Lived-in warmth. There's a difference.

We are met by a pair of orderlies. They wear strange dresses that look designed by someone trying to mimic Victorian era clothing without ever having actually seen it. Their feet are shoeless, covered only in strangely textured, ivory white leggings. Footy pajamas for adults. Were it not for the setting, I would probably laugh.

The orderly whose nametag reads SABINA checks my identification and Darius – *my dear Andrew* – is told to return for me in thirty days. We are practiced in the act of a couple suffering marital difficulties, so there is a layer of ice in our short embrace. We exchange our true feelings in a glance. I see his second thoughts, and I'm sure he sees mine. Darius is all I have left that connects me to Hadleigh. He is all I have left, period.

He disappears through the big entry doors. I am taken by the second orderly, *Enid*, down the long hallway. Near the distant end, we go through a door on the right and into a narrower passage.

Everything changes. The walls tighten, funneling us through confusing twists that turn me around. My knowledge of the old asylum's layout is based on an incomplete set of early plans. Those hinted at a section of back and forth, but not this labyrinth, which seems to have no other purpose than to frustrate and confuse. We walk past a narrow window made of wired glass. Little shows through its occluded surface, just the white sky and snowy ground blurring into each other.

More walking and the blue-green paint ends in a flurry of roller strokes revealing a filthy yellow wall beneath. One side of the passage is marked by an oily line of film running the length at shoulder height. Also, it's gotten colder.

Enid squeezes ahead as we come to a door and thrusts a big key into the ancient deadbolt. In recent years, certain sections of the building were renovated while others were sealed and left untouched. The South Wing, for instance, was supposed to become some sort of exhibit as a way of educating the public about the horrors of the past, but it was never opened. I imagine myself inside those blueprints, wandering about one of its unlabeled voids. If I were to call Darius now, would he find me? Five minutes in and I am so far away.

The door opens. Like the hallway outside, the room hasn't received the conspicuous refurbishment that is obvious in the main building. An antique, pull-chain toilet anchors one side of the room. The wall opposite has a set of shelves. There's a pile of folded towels, a basket of fresh herbs, and other apothecary-style knick-knacks. Next to the shelves is an ornate glass pitcher on a stand full of water and fruit. For some reason, seeing these things is a relief. It means other people come through, use the room. It's not like it's a cell.

I'm catastrophizing already.

Enid fills a glass from the pitcher and offers it.

"I'm not thirsty."

"That's okay, drink it anyway."

"Really, I'm fine."

"Drink the water."

"Okay," I say, taking a sip. The taste is blandly citrus, but I can't place the flavor. It's not great.

"Please finish it."

Not wanting a conflict, I drink it down. "There," I say, handing back the glass. She pivots to the pitcher and fills it once more. She holds it out. I wave my hand. "No. Thank you."

Enid doesn't blink, but pushes the offering close, almost touching my chest with it. Her eyes are powerful, resolved. I take the glass, trying to hide my irritation. I'm playing a part, after all. "I'm going to have to pee."

"There's a toilet right there."

I swallow the water. "Will there be a third glass?" I say, petulantly turning it upside down and letting a few droplets hit the floor.

"Not unless you're thirsty," says Enid. "Are you thirsty?"

"I already told you I... *Never mind*. No. I'm not thirsty."

Enid takes something from one of the big pockets on the front of her dress and tears it open. A pregnancy test slides into her palm.

"Okay, now. I'm not–"

"It doesn't matter," she says.

"Why?"

She holds the test out. I take it and pause for her response, but she doesn't answer and makes no motion to leave. I think to say something, but her face says she's staying. I glare at her. *You want to watch? Then watch.*

I drop my long skirt, leggings, panties, and sit on the weathered seat. I try to relax enough to go, listening to my own breath and the faint susurration tucked within the walls. The place is no doubt full of pipes running through every void. It sounds dry, like pouring sand, or maybe the heavy plaster alters the gurgle of rushing water. The floor is mostly raw concrete, scarred and stained with the building's history.

Enid scowls as I steady the test under the stream. Hot droplets splash my thumb and fingers. The walls on either side of the toilet are bare. "Paper?"

"You're about to take a shower," she says, holding open the wrapper for the test. I drop it inside, then pull up my clothes.

"I showered before I left home. I'm clean."

"You're not."

"I'm sorry, what?"

"Here you wash away the historical self," she says, nodding to a door at the end of the room. "There's a basket inside for your clothes. Take your shoes off here."

"What is all this?"

She gestures for me to continue.

I battle with my response as I unlace my boots. I'm here to play a role. Any more combativeness and I risk breaking character, being found out. But wouldn't anyone object to such treatment? Charlotte might not. She'd probably go along with it. She isn't strong.

I peel away the boots and go into the shower room. Cold lights flicker across chipped old subway tiles the color of butter that's sat out too long. There's no sink or anything else one might expect in a bathroom. Just two knobs and a showerhead – and bars bolted along the floor beneath a full-length mirror. The sound in the walls is louder here, closer to where the water comes out.

I remove my clothes, sad for their fading warmth, and drop them into the basket. At the shower, I twist the knob for hot.

The water comes cold and stays that way. I hold my hand under the spray, willing it to change. It starts as a tinge of warmth, almost imagined, but finally steams.

The water is near scalding when I hiss my way under the stream. I should feel like I've accomplished something. After more than a year spent preparing, I've infiltrated a place less transparent than most prisons. I've changed everything to do it. Moved away. Constructed a person who doesn't exist, stepped into her skin, and lived her life. But I don't feel anything like pride. I have a duty to walk the path paved by my own choices. Maybe I will learn the truth. Maybe there will come a toll, and I will be forced to pay it. Maybe none of that will happen. Regardless, I am here, and the shower feels like a final gesture, one last swirl of the soap, where my old existence is scrubbed from the world.

I press a finger into the meat below my left clavicle and note the small nodule there, reliably in its place. A reminder of the truth. But also an escape hatch. *I can do this.*

I shut off the water and step out of the soapy puddle of me running down the drain. Enid arrives with a towel. I wrap myself for warmth and wait for her to leave.

"I need to check you," she says, voice flat.

"What?" The noise in the walls is akin to a curtain of rain that rushes toward you, only heard rather than seen. It gets louder. It surrounds.

"Turn around, Mrs Turner." Her voice hides in the sound.

"Do you hear that?"

"Turn."

I do.

"Lean your head back, Mrs Turner."

I obey.

Her fingers preen my hair, pulling it often enough to make me doubt accidental snags. Her nails catch my scalp. She doesn't see my gritted teeth.

She turns me roughly so that we are face to face. "Open," she says, gripping my jaw and inspecting my teeth and gums until my throat spasms. I inhale her milky breath, sneering when she finally lets go.

The pipes move in the walls. Shifting, coming closer. Carrying their payload of sand. Enid grips my arms. Squeezes them. Over her shoulder in the next room, the pitcher of water crackles. It's a trick of the light, but it seems to be freezing solid before my eyes.

"What are you doing?" I ask.

"Shh!" Her hand passes over my stomach and flows between my legs.

"What is this?"

"This?" She lashes out and grabs my cheek, pinching until I yelp. "*This* is where I dig for the things that you have buried." She spins me around to face the mirror.

A dribble of sweat tickles my ribs, my fear bleeding out in apocrine stink. The pouring sand becomes louder. "Do you hear that noise?"

"Do you hear a noise?" she asks, mimicking.

"Yes," I say, trying to distract myself. "Are you saying you don't?"

Her voice comes distorted to my ears, penetrating the invisible rush that pounds down around me. "Take hold of the bar."

"What?"

She stares at me in the mirror, then angles her eyes to the floor. "I have to search you."

Every sinew draws taut. Complying, I put my mind outside of my body, trying to escape the present, but Enid's insistent fingers keep me there. I wince with every pinch, cry out from penetrating aches in every place that is mine. I am stretched and turned inside out, explored and examined. Violated. I am exposed. *Assessed.* Reduced.

It ends. I release the bar and wipe my eyes. When I try to stand, Enid puts a hand on my lower back and presses me forward until my hands brace against the mirror. Like the flip of a switch, her touch goes soft, suddenly gentle; so light I barely feel it. The backs of her fingers trail over my skin, across my tailbone, thighs, hinting and feinting. She hums a tune in minor keys, whispering uncanny phrases as she goes. *Be lashed by the tongue and insinuate.* Her search is over. Something new begins.

"What is this...? What are you–"

"Paroxysm, Mrs Turner." She pushes into me. "Your first treatment." Her fingers are long.

"No." I want to scream it, but part of me hushes. Like a sudden drop in blood pressure, my protest comes feeble and heartless. Deep within my bowels a shape takes form. A new heart starts beating. Quickening, it swirls and writhes in response to Enid's touch and her whispered incantations. Drawn to her, it responds in contradiction to my fading will. A bright shadow fills my body. It – she – escapes and unfolds. *She* is my paper doll twin, and she moves with the enthusiasm of life.

Enid provokes a swell of heat and a rush of blood into those places where she should not be, and yet the paper doll welcomes it. Enid's touch is her narcotic. Each caress, each punishing thrust, are tastes that she devours and soon she is in thrall.

"I... *No.*" I see myself made an object in the mirror. I shudder with the trespass, the depravity. My cutout is there to receive it.

I hold on to time, praying for it to stop, but the seconds stretch like caramel. Is this a loop with no end? I become light and insubstantial, transparent, as Enid and my scissor-work creation writhe together. Tears that had gathered on the ends of my lashes roll down the cheeks of someone new. In the mirror, I am smiling.

SPD INTERVIEW RECORD
EXCERPT OF TRANSCRIPTION

GASTRELL: Jesus, I need some air. What the hell was that? What was she describing in there?

BENTHAM: That'd be a crime, officer.

GASTRELL: Why would they do that to her?

BENTHAM: Some used to call that therapy.

GASTRELL: Therapy? That's not therapy. That's assault. Torture. That's–

BENTHAM: I'm not saying it was ever accepted, Jesus Christ. But there were always practitioners.

GASTRELL: Your profession has a hell of a legacy, Doc.

BENTHAM: Says the cop.

GASTRELL: Now? Really?

BENTHAM: Obviously, I condemn entire categories of practices done to patients in the name of psychiatric therapy.

GASTRELL: How could what she described in there be called therapy?

BENTHAM: Let's be clear: it's not. But the record of psychiatric treatment of women is rife with monstrous shit like that. Most of the time, it was doctors using them as guinea pigs, just throwing whatever at the wall to see what stuck. Sometimes it was as simple as a doctor using their position to abuse another human being. Other times, there was a specific purpose, especially by places where control of the population was desired. Prisons, armies, institutions like this. It's just another type of identity stripping. Hollyhock House seems to have employed it.

GASTRELL: Identity stripping?

BENTHAM: Dehumanizing ceremonies to weaken the subject and make them more easily manipulated, obedient, pliable. Verbal abuse, physical abuse, sexual, psychological abuse. All, or a combination. Think about how Charlotte regarded Enid after all this. She was completely submissive, possessive even. More than just compliant, she was obsequious. Stockholm syndrome to the point of limerence.

GASTRELL: So, was Hollyhock trying to treat these women at all, or just control them?

BENTHAM: You heard the things Enid said while she was doing it, right? "Be lashed by the tongue and insinuate"? It's the same nonsense that Charlotte has been talking in here for the last three days. Honestly, the idea that they believed that this disgusting act was going to result in some form of … spiritual awakening is more terrifying to me than anything else. Yeah, sure it dehumanized these women and probably made them more easily controlled, but they clearly had larger, unconventional aims.

GASTRELL: Unconventional, huh?

BENTHAM: I'm struggling for the right word. Cultish.

GASTRELL: I can't believe this was all going on out there.

BENTHAM: How could you have known unless someone came forward? The place has been on lockdown ever since it reopened as Hollyhock House. No visitation, NDAs.

GASTRELL: Yeah. I guess.

BENTHAM: It explains the break, though, doesn't it? It explains why Morgan went away and Charlotte stepped into her place. You don't always see this with first time trauma. It often takes chronic abuse for a person to dissociate as extremely as Morgan did, but in this case, not only was the trauma sudden and intense, but Morgan was already playing the role of Charlotte. She had a convenient place to shift the pain of the experience. Morgan let go and Charlotte crawled in. With all Morgan had been through to that point, it's not wholly atypical. She had a history of seeking oblivion. Pushing the trauma on to Charlotte was like finding it again.

GASTRELL: So, like multiple personalities?

BENTHAM: Dissociative identity disorder. I'm not saying that's what it is, exactly ... yet. There's a lot to making a diagnosis, but it has the hallmarks of a DID manifestation. The difference from a more typical case is that here, the patient had created the alternative identity ahead of the inciting trauma – not as a result of it. It really does explain why Charlotte became so dominant so quickly.

GASTRELL: What now?

BENTHAM: I'm going back in there and I'm going to explain this to her. Give her a choice if she wants to continue or be treated over at St Luke's. It's not a psych hospital but they have a good team over there.

GASTRELL: She's already agreed to give a statement.

BENTHAM: Charlotte has, Detective. Morgan hasn't.

SPD INTERVIEW RECORD
EXCERPT OF TRANSCRIPTION

WITNESS: I let myself go. I gave myself away.

BENTHAM: No, don't say that. This wasn't your fault. You are not to blame.

WITNESS: I wasn't completely helpless. In that moment, as Enid was...

BENTHAM: You don't have to explain. We heard it.

WITNESS: As... As Enid was ... you know... I would have given anything to make it all stop. I just wasn't prepared. And then... Charlotte was just ... there. So, I gave it to her.

GASTRELL: It's okay, it's okay.

WITNESS: I thought ... maybe she could be like a suit of armor. If the armor didn't break, then I'd be able to stay and keep my promise to Hadleigh. I surrendered myself instead.

GASTRELL: Any idea what the sound was? Charlotte had described hearing it as well. You both referred to it as pouring sand.

WITNESS: I don't know.

GASTRELL: Did you ever find out?

WITNESS: I don't know.

GASTRELL: You don't remember anything again until when?

BENTHAM: Well, hold on, let's slow down. She needs to give permission to continue–

WITNESS: I give permission.

GASTRELL: That was easy.

BENTHAM: Do you need to rest...?

WITNESS: This is the whole reason I went there in the first place. To find out what happened and tell people. But I can't... I can't remember. What's the matter with me?

GASTRELL: You can remember bits and pieces?

WITNESS: No, like ... my time in Hollyhock feels like a hallway. Like walking with a dim flashlight and finding a clue.

GASTRELL: Like a breadcrumb.

BENTHAM: Very helpful.

WITNESS: My recall goes only as far as the beam. As I walk forward, more is exposed. I don't know why. Right now, all I remember is being in a bed in a room after the thing with Christmas in the dining hall. All I remembered before that was ... Enid.

BENTHAM: Some types of dissociative amnesia work that way. Localized or even selective amnesia could explain it.

WITNESS: I need to know everything that happened before I regained control. You have to tell me everything that Charlotte said because I don't remember it.

GASTRELL: It's hours and hours of interviews.

WITNESS: You can play it back for me, right?

BENTHAM: They're two separate–

GASTRELL: I know, Doc. I know. Morgan: Charlotte was clearly running a different agenda than you were. I don't want to unintentionally influence you or color how you report your experiences by what you learn from Charlotte's interview – she might not have been telling the truth.

WITNESS: Are you serious right now?

GASTRELL: I'm afraid so.

WITNESS: Charlotte is me. I created her! I own her! I own what she told you.

GASTRELL: Listen for a minute! You want to know the truth, right? Anything you learn about the facts of the case will inevitably shape your perception about your own experiences. No matter how well you think you can compartmentalize the two.

BENTHAM: I've told you that from my point of view, as a physician, you and Charlotte are separate people.

WITNESS: From my point of view, you can shut the fuck up. I'm me. [indistinct] bitch [indistinct].

BENTHAM: That won't change anything, but I understand how upsetting all of this is.

GASTRELL: Morgan, can you try to take us forward from that moment you came back into yourself, however far the flashlight beam allows? You said you remembered a bed?

THREE

My mind spins, adrift like a planet thrown from its star. It reaches out to touch the familiar, but nothing is familiar.

There are beds to either side, maybe a dozen, all empty. More across the room beneath towering windows. Some kind of facility. Tidy. Clean. Dark wood trim and a shade of blue-green paint that belongs in a boutique hotel or a spa or... My heart sinks, pulled down by guilt's familiar weight. I've broken another promise. I've relapsed.

Except that my arms and legs are restrained. That's never happened in rehab. I'm not nauseous. There are no shakes or racking muscle aches. No migraine. No imagined handfuls of blues or rimmies or dream-pops or greenlegs. No yearning for the release of pharmaceutical oblivion. This isn't withdrawal. I didn't relapse. I'm clean.

Then it all comes back.

I'm at Hollyhock House.

I don't recognize the room. The infirmary, maybe? A sleeping ward? Why don't I remember? I close my eyes, straining to bring it back. Didn't we just arrive? Didn't I just say goodbye to Darius?

Remember, Morgan.

When you sleep, you still sense the passing of time. Here, though, I don't. It's like being removed from time altogether. Except my body feels older than my mind. It's changed. My skin is different. Dry. I'm heavier. I look down at my hands and see that the fingernails are clipped straight across, squared off. I've never clipped my nails; I bit them. How much time has passed?

Memories populate. I remember everything from before. Our plan. The year spent together in Hay Springs. The day we made the trip across the ocean of snow-laden prairie. Parking outside, walking into the entrance hall. Darius leaving. A room. A shower. And then...

My heart catches. I remember. My body screams. My stomach twists. Pins and needles spill from my groin and swarm across my thighs like cellar spiders. I remember now. My body remembers now.

Enid.

The treatment. The ache. My surrender. Charlotte's rise. My erasure.

A vision bleeds into focus. It has the quality of memory. In it, I am awakened to a laceration of white, a bright chasm forced open in the walls of Charlotte, shining into the place where she had hidden me. I remember crawling through it, returning to the world I'd abandoned, drawn by the mentioning of a name. Hadleigh.

And now I'm in this alien place, a visitor plucked from one place and dropped in another. I have the distinct sensation of a life interrupted, as if my consciousness was a breath hitched in the middle. That hitch is her, coming alive, seizing control, excising me from existence. And I feel it. I feel what it is to have not existed, to be nonexistent. Holding my eyes open as tears wet the pillow, I try to remember, but I can't, and it is like dying again.

I shut them. Shut out the light. Feel for the parts of me that are true. Take clues from the physical world to divine what is real. Run my fingertips on the bedsheets, turn my head on the pillow, breath the cool, dry air.

Based on the orientation, I assume I am inside the infirmary, which is at the distant end of Hollyhock's North Wing. My bed is set against the wall facing the window, though I can't see anything through the blurry glass and gauzy curtains. But that puts me on the western wall. Okay, Morgan, so you're oriented. What now?

I try again to remember, hoping to recall what has happened since I arrived and how long it has been. I breathe, feel the weft of my mind relax, the spaces open up. There's very little that's concrete, but it isn't a total vacuum. Echoes ring of those lost days, and I feel the residue of Charlotte on my skin. I already knew her, and now I sense how she lived as a patient here. She loves the food. She visits something called Home Skills as often as possible. She is given short affirmations that she recites and commits to memory. I can't hear the words, but their unsettling strangeness seeps through. Charlotte made herself an acolyte, taking to her treatment like a religion. Her adulation for Enid is potent, which I don't understand. But undergirding everything Charlotte is a persistent singularity of purpose planted deep into the soil of her. To make a family. I understand that because I gave it to her.

Aside from the rantings of Christmas, there is nothing of Hadleigh in the vibrations of Charlotte. Nothing at all. Did she even know Hadleigh existed? A loathsome fog surrounds me. What did I think I was going to get by coming here? All I want now is to signal Darius and have him pull me home. A new failure in a long chain of them.

I hear my breathing. It sounds louder, somehow. Or perhaps the infirmary is intensely quiet. Where are the nurses?

I find a call button on the side of the bed with my fingers and press it. When nobody responds, I jab at it relentlessly, struggle against the restraints, call out. Scream louder.

Hours pass and my adrenaline bottoms out. I don't want to sleep, but it's unavoidable. Dreams come. It is the first dream that *I* experience within the confines of Hollyhock, and it carries a weight of tangibility that dreaming never did in the outside world.

I am lying asleep on the very same bed, unrestrained. I

luxuriate in the clean, soft sheets, turning on to my shoulder, letting my arm drape to the side and my head sink into the pillow. My dream sleep is light and airy, a prolonged experience of that joyful moment before you must get up to face the day, when the bedding is the most comfortable and you wonder why the sheets don't feel the same way at any other time. This is a good dream. I don't want it to end.

My eyelids flicker open from the dream within a dream, and I take in the room. The windows are clear and the morning light beyond is a vision. Winter is gone. Spring has come. The fields drown in ostentatious splashes of color. I am outside.

I travel a footpath through the meadow, reaching down to touch the carpet of tender new shoots and blooms. I brush the backs of my fingers softly over them, reveling in the fresh beauty of new life. There is a rush in the distance, the unmistakable sound of flowing water. Coming over a small rise, I see a shallow valley and a river at its middle, roiling and violent – the type produced by snow melt in the mountains. But here, there are only gentle hills. I walk along the bank, a safe distance from the rapids, traveling until the landscape changes. The rush grows louder, and in the distance I see the water's destination: a single point where it converges with five other rivers. They all flow inward, and yet don't flood the valley. Where does the water go? The question feels bigger in the dream than it should. It terrifies me. Where does the water from the six rivers go? It is the most important question in the world.

I wake into the wan light of the early winter evening as the echoes of the roaring rivers fade. The dream is so fresh that I can still smell the meadow in my nostrils, feel the lingering sensation of the flowers on my skin. I glance to my hand. My top row of knuckles is dusted. I flutter my fingers and it falls away. It's heavy. Like ash.

There's a shuffling in the darkened entryway to the infirmary, followed by the crisp crinkling of paper. Sand flows through the walls of the building, through pipes and arteries. I remember the noise. The room expands and contracts like a ribcage. Lines of illumination appear dimly upon the ceiling and commence to pulse. Hollyhock is awake.

A voice, disembodied, speaks a word in my ear. My hair pulls tight, and my head hits the bars of the headboard.

SPD INTERVIEW RECORD
EXCERPT OF TRANSCRIPTION

GASTRELL: Charlotte hallucinated her hair being messed with, too.

WITNESS: No, no. What happened to me wasn't a hallucination.

GASTRELL: It's getting hard to tell, Morgan. Wait... What are you doing?

WITNESS: Come here. Feel.

GASTRELL: What now?

WITNESS: Just come here. Feel right here. [Indicates] Right where my finger is.

GASTRELL: Okay. So, you have an old cut on your head. That could be from anything.

WITNESS: A coincidence, then?

GASTRELL: It's possible it filtered through from Charlotte. Just as her aphorisms did. The hair-pulling was already seated within your subconscious. Maybe the line between the two of you isn't as clear as you think.

WITNESS: And the head wound? Is that subconscious too?

GASTRELL: Maybe it was a hallucination, and in the moment you kicked away, hitting the bars of the headboard.

WITNESS: I was flat on the bed. In restraints. I couldn't have kicked.

GASTRELL: What's your theory, then? You seem to be dancing around it like you want me to say it.

WITNESS: That the place is haunted? Not so hard to say at all.

GASTRELL: Like ghosts?

WITNESS: For the record, I don't believe in ghosts. But... that place has a history. Most of it has been scrubbed from the internet, but the scraps I was able to find paint a picture.

GASTRELL: I'm familiar with Hollyhock's past. You think the ghosts of ex-patients were haunting the current ones?

WITNESS: I don't know. It doesn't seem so far-fetched anymore.

GASTRELL: I feel like I've seen this movie before.

WITNESS: Hey, um... Has there been any sign of Darius?

GASTRELL: Not yet. We're looking. We're trying.

WITNESS: Okay.

GASTRELL: Let's move along. You said you heard a voice.

WITNESS: Yes.

GASTRELL: What did it say?

WITNESS: "Irredeemable."

GASTRELL: That's it?

WITNESS: [Indicating]

GASTRELL: What do you think that means?

WITNESS: It feels a lot like the truth.

GASTRELL: No one is irredeemable.

WITNESS: Disagree.

GASTRELL: You can't believe that.

WITNESS: I can believe it for myself. Drug addict, thief, liar, terrible sister.

GASTRELL: Terrible sister? How? You mean, the collateral damage of your addiction?

WITNESS: Can I get a cigarette?

GASTRELL: Wha- Really?

WITNESS: Yes, really.

GASTRELL: You said you'd quit.

WITNESS: That was before. Now I need to smoke.

GASTRELL: Don't know where I'm going to get cigarettes. Maybe one of the beat guys still smokes. We'd have to go outside.

WITNESS: Good.

GASTRELL: Until then, I'd asked about why you say you were a bad sister.

WITNESS: Other than her having to constantly bail me out? I mean, she was a responsible person. I wasn't. She was a good student. I wasn't. She was an athlete. I wasn't. What little attention our parents gave, she got, so I was jealous of that and sometimes took it out on her, even though I just wanted to be her. Regular second child stuff.

GASTRELL: Doesn't sound any different from me and my brother growing up.

WITNESS: Did he ever take money from your purse to buy black market Nuvracet?

GASTRELL: No. He didn't. But I still don't think that makes someone irredeemable.

WITNESS: [indicates]

GASTRELL: So what else is there?

WITNESS: How about my sister is dead. How about that? She was a good person and she suffered and she didn't deserve that. I've never done anything worthwhile in my entire life. I'm a lazy, worthless, shitty person, yet here I am, alive and well. Would you care to hear more specifics?

GASTRELL: That's not necessary.

WITNESS: It's no trouble.

GASTRELL: No. No, I apologize. You feel guilt, all
             survivors do. But you can't blame yourself.
WITNESS: Oh, I can.

TEXT RECORD, PHONE NUMBER
(814) ***-**58

What's up?

Getting ready to go out...

Birds?

Yes, birds, actually. Lol

What are you up to?

Oh, let me check my busy
schedule, um, looks like I will
be working late, then sitting
on the couch with Doctor David
Bowie who may or may not let
me pet her. Should be a super
entertaining evening!

I feel like it wasn't that
long ago you were
harassing me to get out
there and be around
people. Seems like you
have been going out less.

Work's been really busy,
that's all. I'll get back out.
I've got SO MANY friends
as you know. Always
calling me. Life of the
party right here.

You always deflect!
Hey – isn't it six months?

Six months since what?

Since you've been clean.
Do I have the date right?

Yep. You've got it right.

You didn't already forget
our deal, did you? You are
coming out here and we
are going to celebrate.
Responsibly of course.

Oh, come on, that was
just us talking shit.
I'm busy, you're busy.

Are you kidding right now?
I want you to come and visit.
Spend some time with me
and Clayden.

You want me to fly to
Nebraska? Do they even
have airports?

Yes, they have airports.
I'll pick you up. Come
on. I want to see you. I
want you to meet Clayden.

Ugh.

So yes. How is next week?

Oooo, I don't know. The
cat ate the calendar.

I'm calling doozies.

You wouldn't dare.

I would.

Wow. That's the biggest
doozy I think in our history.
When was the last time we
did doozies? High school?

I expect you'd remember.
Timing is everything.

Well played, Hadleigh Bright.
I'll get my flights arranged.

Good. I can't wait.

FOUR

Laying in the darkening infirmary, my mind pivots to the *why* of it all. I think of Hadleigh, of how she'd react if she knew what I'd done in the wake of her death. She'd say I was an idiot, that's for sure, if she'd even speak to me at all. Her dying was my fault, but I know she wouldn't have wanted me to follow her to this place. Still, it wouldn't have come as any surprise to her that I did.

Hadleigh and I had a thing we used to do called "Doozies." As in, "that's a real doozy." It was basically daring someone to do something that risked embarrassment, getting in trouble, or even personal injury. But there were two rules: one, you couldn't refuse to accept a doozy, and two, no one could issue two doozies in a row, so the power swapped hands. There was an element of trust and judiciousness to the game, because if one person upped the stakes for a doozy, then when the power shifted, they could expect to receive a doozy with similar or greater risk to personal jeopardy.

They started small when we were just kids. We might make progressively louder fart noises until we were caught during dinner, or stick our bare butt-cheeks to the front window for thirty seconds. Sometimes it was practical: a doozy to do a chore, take the blame for breaking a glass, or borrow money. The challenges became more elaborate and risky as we aged up. There was theft of our parents' alcohol and sneaking out to run around the block during the middle of the night.

I don't know if Hadleigh ever noticed that I never ratcheted any of my doozies up to a level beyond hers. I don't think it was very conscious at the time, but looking back, I think I wanted to prove myself to her in some way by showing her I was tough and determined, that I could take whatever she threw at me. Surely, I was compensating for the things I couldn't do, whether it was sports or having lots of friends or being popular, that spawned some kind of undiagnosed pathology of mine to volunteer for, and invite, what often amounted to debasing stunts.

When I was fifteen and Hadleigh was eighteen, she took me along to a party with the high school seniors. Hadleigh was hugely popular and here she was, unashamed of bringing her nobody, acne-ridden freshman little sister into the den of the cool. It was a nerve-racking but momentous opportunity for me – a chance to be like her. I remember spending days trying to figure out what to wear, changing my mind a thousand times. It was Hadleigh who pulled a skirt and top from her own closet, tossing them casually – perfectly – onto her bed, saying, "You'd look killer in this. You still have those black high-tops?"

I did. And wearing her clothes, I felt empowered, like I was flying. Pulling up to the party, I remember not feeling nervous at all. I was with Hadleigh and shielded by her armor.

Inside, she kept me close. I met her friends and watched how kind and unassuming she was with everyone she talked to. Yeah, she was popular, but the way she treated people, you wondered if she even knew it.

At one point during the evening, she got around to explaining the concept of Doozies to the group. They all knew and understood Truth or Dare, but Doozies, with its policy of non-refusal and built-in system of stairstep intensity, fascinated them. They wanted to see it in effect. Hadleigh blew them off. "It's just something that Morgan and I do."

They jeered and booed at this, until I volunteered us. I don't know why, really. To get noticed, to show the older kids I was cool, I guess.

"No, Morgan," said Hadleigh. "It's our thing. These numbnuts will just have to find another game to play."

The partiers booed again, throwing thumbs down and talking shit.

"Seriously," I insisted. "Let's just show them."

"Yeah!" they shouted. "Little sister knows what's best!"

"They won't be satisfied unless someone ends up dead or on fire," said Hadleigh. "Bad idea."

I grinned and mugged for the gathering crowd. "Maybe," I said, "but I currently hold the power of Doozies, do I not, sister?"

The crowd *oooed* at the gauntlet I'd thrown. Hadleigh raised her eyebrows and sighed. "You currently do."

"And a doozy can be doozed anytime the one with the power chooses to use it?"

"Do what you want, Morgan," she said, her voice resigned, annoyed.

I looked around the room for something to get us started. I wanted to set the bar low so we could steadily boost the tension. My eyes caught on some candles burning at the end of the kitchen counter. "Put one of those out using a part of your body."

"That's it?" She pushed up from the stairs where everyone was sitting, went over, licked her fingers and pinched a wick. A short sizzle and the flame was out. She went to a nearby couch and sat. The whole room stared at her, waiting for her to return serve. She let them all hang for a long while before saying, "As I explained: in Doozies, the one with the power chooses when to use it."

I booed this along with all the others. "Come on!" I said. "I'm good, let's goooo!" Her friends cheered me as Hadleigh glared. If she didn't want to play, she shouldn't have started telling everyone about it.

"Something good," said a guy wearing an upside-down ballcap. "Make her drink mustard."

"Too easy," I said, feeling the momentum of the situation, the rush of being the center of attention. The others whooped. "Let's hear it, sister."

"No."

"She wants to, come on," said ballcap guy, emphatic.

"Yeah, I want to," I said, going into the kitchen and picking up the recently snuffed candle. "Dooze me."

"No. I don't want to waste it. I want to use it on something good."

I felt anger rising up. I wanted to prove that I belonged and she was killing the moment. "Then pick something good. I'll do anything."

"I didn't bring you here to embarrass yourself."

"That's the whole point!"

"Yeah, that's the whole point," said the others. "Doozies! Doozies!"

We stared at each other forever. Why wasn't she letting me play? Was it really because she was trying to protect me? Was she just being selfish because now I had everyone's attention? Did she really covet a doozy so bad that she didn't want to spend it?

"Whatever," she said, leaning back on the couch, sipping her drink. "But I'm not using a doozy to make you do it."

I reached over to the counter, grabbed the candle and bit off the top. The party roared. I chewed through the wax, pulverizing it between my teeth, masterfully suppressing the urge to gag and vomit. I grabbed a red plastic cup and chased the wad of candle with somebody's warm beer, which I'd never had before.

Slamming down the cup, I was swarmed by Hadleigh's classmates, giving high-fives and fist bumps. It should have been the greatest night of my young life. That moment – the older kids, the excitement of a party in a house without parents, the smells, the idiocy, the beer – it felt like everything. It should have been everything. Hadleigh stayed where she was, a perfect mannequin in a room blurred by movement. Everybody won over but her.

Anyway, nothing seemed to go right after that.

Hadleigh's trip to Hollyhock was an involuntary commitment. So, I went bigger and did it on purpose.

Doozy.

FIVE

Enid comes and my chest fills with gasoline.

"Will you be able to control yourself if I remove these restraints?" she asks. I clench my teeth and smother a snarl. She remains calm. "Are you going to answer me?"

I nod, unsure if it's the truth or not. I have no idea if I can control anything, so overwhelmed I am with rage, my revulsion for her.

"You look like you've sparred with the Devil himself, Mrs Turner," she says, unbuckling my ankle.

Mrs Turner. To everyone else I'm still Charlotte Turner. For the moment, I try to reassume the role, her enthusiasm for healing, her motives. But all I want to do is strangle Enid.

She dabs her hand over the sheets between my legs. "You're soaked."

"What is it?"

"Why didn't you ring if you had to go?"

"I did," I answer, realizing that I've wet the bed. "It doesn't work."

"Of course it does." She depresses the button, then shows me a small device clipped to her dress pocket that lights up orange. "See?"

"It didn't work when I pushed it."

She gives a skeptical shrug and loosens my other ankle.

"I called for help, too."

"It's a big place, Mrs Turner."

"What time is it?"

Working on the thick belts that stretch across my abdomen, she glances to her wristwatch. "A few hours before supper."

"Oh."

"You've been here for over twenty-four hours. Sleeping most of it. I expect you're hungry."

"Yes, of course," I say ruefully, knowing that Charlotte loves the food and wouldn't want to miss a meal. "I'm starving." I'm not. The last thing I want to do is eat. I don't know if I can continue this ridiculous charade. What would happen to me if I stopped? How did I sleep for over twenty-four hours? "Was I drugged?"

"*Absolutely* not. You were beyond exhausted, Charlotte. I don't know how you let yourself get to that point. Had you not been sleeping before all this?" She removes the binding on my right wrist.

I groan to a sit.

"Charlotte, your head!"

My hand flies to the wound. "Oh... Oh, it's noth–"

She sits beside me on the bed. I turn cold in the umbra of her heat. She takes control of my head and spreads apart my hair with her fingers, digs to my scalp. "You've got an enormous gash up here. It's no longer bleeding, but your hair is caked. What happened?"

"Don't know."

She soaks a rag in a bowl on the bedside and begins wiping the top of my head. The dried blood goes wet again. I smell it. I smell her. A nauseating cloud of body odor and essential oils. Sour orange and something else. Her fingers navigate and pick. Fingers I've felt in my hair, in my body, once before, back in that yellow room. My body curls into itself. "That's enough," I say, wrenching away.

Enid gives a questioning look – I know in this moment I've broken character. "Sorry," I say, "it's just very sore."

Enid eyes me as she folds the rag and rises from the bed. I see myself leaping up and wrapping her head in my arms, dragging her to the floor. Roaring, I mount her chest and press my thumbs into her throat. Her windpipe collapses and wet air laps at her billowed lungs.

"Charlotte?"

I snap back to attention.

"Is there anything you need to tell me?"

I shake my head.

"What happened in the cafeteria with Christmas?" asks Enid. "She believes you were plainly hallucinating."

I'm filling in blanks, navigating a past that is at best a blur in the fog. "I don't know what qualifies Christmas to say if another person suffers hallucinations."

"Nothing does. I'm simply asking."

"It was a late lunch and I'm sure my blood sugar was abysmal," I answer. "I passed out. That's it."

She reads me, then smooths her dress in a way that tells me the inquisition is finished. "You'll want to remember that snacks are always available in Hollyhock Hall, as well as enriched water in the Group and work rooms."

"I will," I say, not remembering any of this.

"Your dress is there," she says, pointing to the folded clothing on the foot of the bed.

I take it and sit, waiting for her to leave. When it's clear she's not going anywhere, I lift the dress. It's just like hers, bleached white and no different from those worn by the orderlies who met Darius and me on that first day. Without a body to give it dimension, it looks like a paper doll. I flop it onto the bed, undoing the many buttons that run up the chest, and begin crawling inside it. I should try to break the tension, to ease back into character. What would Charlotte say? "I'd like to request a phone call with Mr Turner."

"You can speak with him at discharge. Not long now." She considers me. "Are you sure you don't want another day to recover?"

I shudder. "I'm ready to get back to the other ladies." Is that the right thing to say? Does Charlotte say *ladies*?

"It's the middle of the hour, so most everyone will be occupied. Why don't you visit Home Skills and read a magazine until it's time for supper?"

I finish squeezing into the awkward costume, then toil with the infinite buttons. Enid offers no help, for which I'm thankful, but she seems to take some satisfaction from watching me struggle.

She leads me from the infirmary. Following behind, I trace my fingers over the panic button beneath my skin, flirting with it like a trigger, fantasizing about shooting off the signal. But I don't do it. It was Hadleigh who'd woken me up – her name, anyway. She keeps me from pressing it. Maybe I won't find out what happened to her, but there is one woman who knows more than I do, and that is Christmas. Dropping my hand from my chest, I walk through hallways I know I have walked, but have never seen.

SIX

Enid strides ahead on some new errand, unconcerned that she has left me alone in the hallway. She doesn't know that every inch of this place is alien to me. I know only the infirmary and the yellow room of old tile and trespass. Unless I'd imagined that, too. But the ache in my gut remembers.

I stand there, looking down at my feet in their heavy white stockings, set starkly upon the dark floor. The wood is so shiny that I lean over and run my finger across the grain to see if it's wet. I imagine them bathing it in New-Age oils and the wood drinking it up because the bones of the place are thirsty. The walls and ceilings are the hue of a lost cavern lake. And me a paper doll floating on the surface.

Having been nonconscious for the first part of my commitment leaves me without knowledge or context. I don't know anyone, or the dynamics of any relationships Charlotte has formed. Any lapses will be read as a deepening of my mental decay.

I know the North Wing layout well enough from the old plans that I can put the infirmary at one end and the dining room on the other. The hallway has doors to twenty or more rooms. Patients' quarters. Okay, great. I'll still have to figure out where I live, but I also can't stand here looking lost while trying to divine it. So, I walk.

At the far end is a museum-style library with books and other artifacts displayed in glass cabinetry. It is a crossroads in two directions, with four entries. In the center are chairs set in a square. Obviously the Group room. I spot one of the glass pitchers of water and note a scratch in my throat. I fill a glass and drink it down, then instantly remember the taste. There had been a pitcher in the yellow room from which I was made to drink. I watched it turn to solid ice as Enid explored me. The aftertaste lingers like the memory, coating my tongue with film.

The short hallway on the right leads to a pair of rooms. One has the word HOUSEWORK hand-painted above it. Ninety degrees to the left is another door with letters in the same style spelling HOME SKILLS. Voices drift from both, fading as I duck back into the library.

Another door leads to a large, windowed alcove. It's the same glass as the infirmary, allowing for a rough impression of ground and sky to show through. It blurs together and I lose the point where the two meet. A wide set of stairs follows the perimeter of the alcove to the second floor. I walk up to a landing where the passage to the second floor has been plastered over. Back in the Group room, the last door leads to the big dining hall. I go through it.

A smattering of patients are gathered inside, sitting in clumps at the long tables, waiting, I presume, for dinner. A numberless clock on the wall says it's a little past four. I walk the length of the room, smiling shyly when the others make eye contact. I'm nervous. I don't know how Charlotte behaved here. I only know how I'd created her. Proper. A rule follower. A pleaser. Obedient. Polite.

I should know all these women's names. I should have a dossier in my head on our interactions, to be able to reference them for conversations. I can't interact with them until I know more, but that is an impossibility. Charlotte would have been content to mind her own business, but she wasn't antisocial.

At the distant end of the room is a second set of double doors, closed. They must connect to the main building and the administrative offices. Not wanting to simply walk in and walk out, I search for a reason to be here and spot another water-filled pitcher against a wall. A striking woman with her hair in side puffs waves at me, and I return the gesture even though I have no idea who she is. Is the wave an invitation to come talk? Something meaningless and innocuous? My act is paper thin. I fill a glass with a plausible amount of water, then swallow it down and stifle another gag. When I turn around, she's there.

"We've been wondering where you went," she says, cradling a black ball of hair just above her ear. She has the deepest dimples I've ever seen. "Glad to see you're okay after all that craziness in here."

"Oh," I say, swiftly calibrating my tone and speech to match Charlotte. "Enid says it's low blood sugar. I hope that's it. Either way, I'm ready for dinner." Charlotte likes food. Maybe I can keep the conversation to that.

She reaches out for the hair at my shoulder and runs it through her fingers. "You're not wearing it up?"

"Ah... I just... I guess I forgot." Shit. Is that a thing?

"So, was Honora in there with you?"

"Honora? Um... No." My mind is a void. I don't know who Honora is or where she went. I forge a plausible lie: "I looked for her as soon as I woke up, but she wasn't in there. Do you have any idea where she could be?" I'm treading water and sinking fast.

The dimpled one points to the two women she'd been sitting with. "Thirza says that she's still in Special Therapies, but who knows? Rhoda was in Specials, too, and she's not back yet either."

"Oh, no." I gasp lightly, trying to walk the line of appropriate reactions. "Just the idea of what they do there..." My voice trails off. I have no idea what they do there, but it doesn't sound good.

She shivers performatively. "Cold packs, and shock therapy and scented candles under your bits."

"What?"

"Well, that's what Beatrice says." She shouts to another patient, "Beatrice! Wasn't it you who said they put incense under our lady pieces in Special Therapies?"

The woman, Beatrice, answers. "It's real. Hysterical suffocation. Fumigation of the vagina with incense to reset an out-of-place uterus and purge toxins. It's real. I read about it." Her tone walks a fine line between actual reporting and sarcasm, as if making light of Hollyhock's strange bygone feel, which I notice more with every passing moment.

"See?" says Dimples, chuckling.

"What is it, Charlotte?" Beatrice hollers. "Is Flory asking if you've got a secret candle connection?" She laughs then, and I follow suit, careful to record their names as I do. Thirza, Beatrice, Flory.

Flory leans in. "As long as the flame doesn't get too close, I could use a little extra heat down there, if you get me."

In keeping with Charlotte, I smile primly, placing my empty glass beside the pitcher. "I'm going to go freshen up before dinner. I haven't been to my room since yesterday. I might forget where it is."

"How could you? You're right next to me!" Flory says, drifting back to the others. Beatrice. Thirza.

If only I could catch a glimpse of Flory visiting her room.

I exit the dining hall and head back through the library, then into the hall lined with patient rooms. The doors to the infirmary hang open at the far end, a mouth waiting for me to venture back and be swallowed.

I grasp a random knob and turn, then think better of it. I can't be seen not knowing where I live. I could begin knocking on doors, talk to whoever I find inside, and try to deduce through oblique conversation which room is mine. Better now than when everyone is turning in for bed.

I raise my hand to knock, when something moves at the edge of my vision. I twitch to it, but the hallway remains empty. Then, a tiny something drifts down from inside one of the chandeliers. I pad through the corridor until I am directly underneath.

It's not a terribly bright fixture; lantern-shaped with four incandescent bulbs inside. It's warm. Comforting, even, just like everything in the North Wing. Paired against the dark teal paint of the walls and ceiling, there's something almost prehistoric about its steady amber light. A campfire in the pre-dawn sky.

On the floor, I see what has fluttered down. A small, mottled gray flake. I kneel to touch it and it disintegrates, leaving a dull smear. Ash.

The chandelier is electric. There is no flame, no source for burned cinders. I glance to the doors on either side of the hallway. One hangs partially open. Standing and straightening the thick fabric of my dress, I slink over. There's a smudge of gray on the knob like the one on my thumb. I nudge the door wide with my hip. It opens into a modest room, full of violet gloam in the dying winter light. Clean, bed made. The only sign that the room is occupied is a framed photo on the desk beneath the window. I recognize it instantly: Darius and I, standing awkwardly beside a horse-drawn carriage during our fake honeymoon.

The moment comes vividly back to me. It had been the start of this whole thing, back when the idea of committing myself was just abstract enough that pulling out was still an easy option. I remember laughing as I tried to stage corny photographic evidence of what I envisioned Charlotte's life to be. I remember the horse taking a massive shit right behind Darius. I'd giggled and laughed as a stranger tried to get one good picture of us together. It was still just an idea then. I don't guess that Charlotte, who had somehow become real, had any idea her honeymoon, her marriage, her whole life, was fake.

Before shutting the door, I stare at the light for another minute, then to the dusky blemish on the polished wood. I stretch my leg into the hallway and buff it out with my stockinged toe before turning into the room.

The drawers are organized with my things, now refolded by Charlotte. In the bathroom, her toiletries – my toiletries – are laid out beside the porcelain sink. My toothbrush, used by another woman. I'm made to feel like a trespasser to my own life. The skin of my back pricks. Something inside me bristles.

My dress is moist and musty with the scent of sweat and panic. And her. She smells different.

A rush comes over me. I tear open the bodice and stomp the dress onto the floor, tear off the bra and panties, then jump into the shower, not caring how cold the water is. The chill summons the familiar ache in my shoulder that tells me who I am. I want this place off me. I want her off me.

The soap and shampoo are pungent. I lather myself, scrub, and rinse quickly, hopping out just as the water begins to warm. I tear both towels from where they're neatly hung, tossing one on the ground for my feet. Burrowing my face into the other, I scream. A rib-shaking, chest-rattling howl, as loud and violent as my body will make. Again and again and again, until my lungs burn.

I scoop up the clothes – they are filthy, diseased – and shove them into the trashcan beside the toilet. Only then do I dry off.

Back in the room, I throw everything from the drawers onto the bed, making sure to unravel every hint of Charlotte, then shove them back into the dresser, holding out a set to wear.

I get it buttoned and stare at the tiny mirror. The dress covers everything but my hands and face. Maybe that's the point. To make us all the same. To erase us. To make us clean slates upon which others can project their desires. Husbands. Nurses. Families. Bosses. Althea Edevane.

SPD INTERVIEW RECORD
EXCERPT OF TRANSCRIPTION

WITNESS: Have you found Darius?

GASTRELL: Sorry, no. Still looking. We're going through papers taken from the house you were renting for receipts for tickets or the like that might tell us where he's gone. We did find this document.

WITNESS: Yeah, that's mine.

GASTRELL: File name: "Hollyhock Research."

WITNESS: Wait. You broke into my computer?

GASTRELL: It's called a search warrant.

WITNESS: I would have given you permission.

GASTRELL: Well, you were Charlotte when we applied for it. I doubt she'd know how to use a computer if we're being honest.

WITNESS: You still would have needed the password.

GASTRELL: DOCTORDAVIDBOWIE. Your cat.

WITNESS: How'd you know I had a cat?

GASTRELL: Her pill bottles. Anyway, you should consider changing your password.

EXCERPT OF
"HOLLYHOCK RESEARCH"

Taken from Personal Computer belonging to Morgan
Bright aka Charlotte Turner (Evidence Tag #N402, Shelf
G4)

Category: Newspapers, *The Antioch Herald*, April 14, 1932

ESCAPED LUNATIC FOUND

State Police say the search for Miss Whitney Keys,
an escaped mental patient, has concluded. Keys
had been under long-term treatment for severe
personality derangement disorder at the Nebraska
State Lunatic Asylum (Hollyhock Asylum) when she
fled the hospital late last week. Hers is the latest in
a rash of escapes, as according to the Dawes County
Sheriff, this is the fourth instance in near as many
months of a patient fleeing the institution.

A source within the department tells the Antioch
Herald that the psychiatric patients uniformly
requested to be detained rather than returned. Miss
Keys was no exception, according to the source,
stating that she preferred death to going back.
On remand to the hospital's custody, she ranted
ceaselessly about "rivers of ash that hide the devil's
finger."

"There is a reason they are institutionalized," stated
Dr. Jeremiah Lord, the Asylum's director. He went on

to add that Miss Key's rantings were relatively mild where delusional proclamations were concerned and extended an invitation to the Herald staff to come see for themselves.

SEVEN

The following morning, I stare into the mirror as Flory's words about wearing my hair up echo in my ears. I throw it into a hasty bun, consider my reflection, and rethink it. Charlotte would probably give a shit about how she presented herself. I release the bun and brush it smooth, then roll each side and join it at the back with a ribbon from a small cache of ribbons in a basket that Charlotte appears to have collected like a crow.

When I emerge from my room, an orderly with a touchpad flags me over to a medical station against the wall. She measures my weight, takes my temperature and blood pressure, then sends me down the hall for breakfast. *Okay.*

The meals are... I don't know. They make no sense. Gourmet feasts served on cafeteria trays. I can understand why Charlotte was seduced by the spread. I am, too. Dinner the night before had been the kind of thing you'd feed a head of state. Impossibly, breakfast is even more opulent. Big, flavorful omelets, toast, eggs any way, pancakes, meats, fruits, berries, oatmeal, lox and more. Still shaken by my lapse of self, haunted by that looming vacuum of time Charlotte took from me, my appetite is nonexistent. I tell myself that I am me again – maybe because there's still doubt – and that now I can do what I came for. I clean my whole tray because that's what I feel Charlotte would do.

An orderly whose nametag says MIRIAM encourages me up from the table as I finish the last of my tea. It's some type of herbal stuff that probably doesn't even have caffeine.

Hollyhock's worst and most hellish feature might be the absence of coffee.

Miriam guides me through a labyrinth of passages and into the central corridor of the main building. Down at the end is a magnesium square of pure white, and it takes me a second to realize that it's the doors to the outside. The real outside. How long has it been since I've seen the world? Miriam knocks on an office door with the director's name hand-lettered on the glass in aquamarine. A voice comes from inside. "Charlotte? Come in, come in."

Miriam gestures me through the door, then shuts it.

Althea Edevane's backside is to me as she bends over, tending to something inside a huge greenhouse-style enclosure set against the far wall. The rest of the room is half office, half parlor. A set of shelves confines books and other memorabilia. Pictures of the director with her son, I guess, dominate an entire shelf. Another series are hung on the wall where the boy is older, maybe nine or ten. My shoulder aches. I imagine a plastic baggie plump with green capsules, then banish the image.

Would Charlotte initiate conversation or wait? I can't stand the silence. "Good morning," I say, almost swallowing the words as they come out.

"It would be better if I could get these powdered oakblues to stop dying halfway through pupation." *Pupation?* She straightens, gently closes the enclosure's elaborately carved wooden door, and turns to me with a smile that smothers her apparent frustration.

"Oh, I'm so sorry," I say. *About what?* I don't know what a powdered oakblue is. A butterfly?

"It's a tiny tragedy every time," she says, holding up a brown, torpedo-shaped pellet for me to see. "You can do everything right and it just doesn't matter. Offer them the perfect diet, keep them in the ideal temperature range, provide ample space to spin their little baskets. But inevitably, some will just

... quit." She suspends her fist over a brass-colored waste bin next to her desk and crushes the husk into pieces.

She carefully wipes the remnants from her palm and gestures to a pair of chairs set opposite each other on a Persian rug in front of the enclosure. "Sit, Charlotte, sit." I do and she follows suit. "The thing with hairstreaks – and most butterflies, in fact – is that they're fast growers. You've got larva, then pupa, adult, then death. The whole thing runs a few weeks. If you make a mistake in guiding them through to adulthood, you can start right over. Try again." She sighs titanically and settles herself further into the chair. "They're so much like us. Did you know that traumas experienced as larva continue through to adulthood? Even though they liquify completely while inside the chrysalis, their spirit carries through, and they remember on the other side. It makes you conscious of the decisions you make while they're young, because you know any damage will be there when they emerge."

Is she serious about all this?

"I'm aware of your little hiccup in Hollyhock Hall. Nothing to be ashamed of. That's why you're here, after all. Would you like to tell me about it?"

What does she know? I decide to stick with the answer I've been giving. "Just low blood sugar, nothing serious."

"That's shocking, the way you eat."

"I... I don't think I'd eaten much for breakfast that day. A hardboiled egg. Some toast."

Edevane grimaces. Does she know what I ate? "I don't want you to think that what happened was solely about you. Christmas has a history of attaching herself to certain patients and then saying ... *things* to them. Disturbing things. Still, I've never seen a reaction quite like yours."

I pivot in a very Charlotte way and politely inquire as to Christmas's health.

"She's had a good response to Special Therapies. She'll be

back in Group today. Slow and steady progress for Christmas, for all of us." She clasps her hands. "What was it she said?"

"I don't know." My answer comes too quick.

"Are you sure? You remember nothing at all?"

I shake my head.

"Well, okay. I'm sure you'll let me know if you do." She points to my head. "I like how you've changed your hair."

A wave of panic. I've got it up, but who knows how Charlotte wore hers – *mine*. I channel her. "Well, I'm here to change, aren't I? Why not try new things? Even if it is just my hair."

"It's very … expedient. I like it." She stands and flattens her dress. I follow suit, relieved to be done. "I'm sure Mr Turner will, too."

Mr Turner. *Darius*. There's a pang in my chest.

Edevane rises and goes to the enclosure, lifts the latch to the door. When I don't react, she tilts her head. "Guided meditation?" she says, and I feel like I'm being reminded of an established routine she and Charlotte have. Inside the enclosure, the corner of a wooden chairback peeks out from an envelope of big green leaves. She spins her own chair to face the enclosure and I find myself stepping inside.

The ground is dirt. I sink into the chair amid the dense vegetation, sending butterflies aflutter. Green, brown, orange. They settle somewhere out of sight. Lights beat down from above in the spectrum of sunlight, and now it doesn't seem like it was built for butterflies at all.

The door closes and Edevane sits opposite, with me still inside.

"Eyes shut, Charlotte."

I comply because I don't know what else to do. The lights filter orange through my eyelids.

"You remember your words of divine sleep?"

Something in my stomach shifts toward her voice. "Yes." Only I'm not the one who says it.

"The words of divine sleep will guide you into the body of

the slumbering Earth, and there you will sleep until I call you home. Do you understand?"

This doesn't feel like a guided meditation. "Yes."

"Okay, Charlotte. 'Fruits of autumn...'"

"'...fields are claimed.'" Charlotte's words in my voice.

"'Then grazing lands...'"

"'...are *winter hained.*'" The stirring inside me goes still. Like it has fallen asleep. Like *she* has fallen asleep.

"Charlotte? Are you awake?"

She's not. I can feel her suspended within my subconscious now, leaving me aware. I don't answer.

Edevane's chair creaks. The door to the enclosure opens, then shuts. She enters and comes close, leans in, breathes loudly through her nostrils. I smell her exhalations, feel the heat of her face on mine. Then she stands and brushes through the foliage at my shoulder and moves off behind me somewhere, twisting through the plants, stopping to rummage, muttering as she goes. *"For those summoned to the halls of the eighth house... I have seen the semaphore, heeded its fire, and carried home the mouth."* Something breaks. A stem or a branch. More words, some hummed, indistinct. *"... resplendent voices perennial."*

She comes around from the opposite side and stands silent in the dirt before me. It feels like eternity. The urge to swallow becomes unbearable. What will happen if she discovers I am awake?

"From this mouth comes the fecund seed." The hem of her dress pushes against mine. Her finger grazes the divot beneath my nose, then traces over my mouth to my chin. *"Be lashed by the tongue and insinuate. Accept this offering. Convey the message in six directions."* There is a quiet snap, like a twig being clipped. "Open your mouth, Charlotte."

I do.

"Eat of the Earth, Charlotte." She lays it upon my tongue.

I guide the object between my molars and bite down, knowing exactly what it is as I do. The tiny package explodes, spurting hot liquid between my teeth and over my tongue. It spreads, thin and runny but with thicker, sinuous parts that might have gone on to form wings or antennae. I push my mind elsewhere, chewing fast, swallowing. The chrysalis sticks in my throat as I struggle it down.

"From this mouth comes the fecund seed."

"Charlotte: wake."

My bowels quake.

EIGHT

Nausea boils over as I crash through the door of my room and collapse across the toilet. Vomit streams from my mouth and nose. My stomach clamps and twists, wringing itself like a dishrag. Lying on the bathroom floor, my mind is awash in theories. Althea Edevane is categorically insane. Or worse, she's coldly rational. Is there a logic to her rantings? Did Hadleigh once sit in that chair, mind pacified by hypnosis, consuming liquid pupae?

I crawl to the sink and wash my mouth out forever.

TEXT RECORD, PHONE NUMBER

(814) ***-**58

Landed.
Pretty sure this airport
only has one terminal.

We are coming around
right now! Yay!

Cool. I'll just wait outside by
arrivals. Did you know you
can't smoke inside airports?

OMG you and Clayden. I
don't even understand it.

Clayden smokes?

Used to. Maybe he can
give you some tips on
quitting, eh?

Godspeed to him.

NINE

Group, held in the chair square in the medical library, is a blur in which time seems to stutter. Maybe it's that I can't keep my attention from Christmas, who sits in the opposite corner in a pocket of air as thick as vapor, arms and hands working the contours of some invisible object. No one else pays any attention.

My participation is limited to answering the prurient curiosity of the other women, which they disguise as inquiries into my welfare. After that, I speak only when repeating the aphorism for the day: *My world is not the biggest world, but it is mine.* I feel strange afterward, acutely aware of my accelerating pulse. It pings like anxiety, but the texture is different. There's no fear at the root of it. Only ... excitement.

I have no memory of lunch, or of Home Skills. I find myself staring at the ornate painted letters above the door for HOUSEWORK. It's like I've been worn and then abandoned, set aside by Charlotte after she's used my body for her own purposes. It is proof that she's regaining her prior strength, the ability to assume control, to put me away. You'd think a realization like that would bring panic. But the truth is, it only takes having your autonomy stolen once to see that freedom is a paper house. When someone stomps it flat again, you just blink.

I go in.

Housework is a mockup of several rooms from a generic home, where the patients go and do … housework. There is a kitchen, a bathroom, a dining room and a children's room, all connected like a diorama reproducing homelife in the 1950s. A few other patients are there when I arrive. Two toil at ironing boards wrapped in black fabric, working the wrinkles out of table linens I'm guessing nobody ever uses. Another is on her hands and knees, scrubbing grout with a toothbrush. The fourth is on dish duty. They all wear large headphones the color of seafoam.

It is a spectacle of absurdity. I marvel at the idea that forcing women to play "House" is supposed to treat a condition allegedly caused by being cooped up in one. I know enough of Hollyhock to guess that it is probably some newfangled repackaging of household duties as empowerment that women can "take back", even though home chores were never – and would never – be taken away. Yet, the other women seem to have found a measure of joy in their labors, their faces the picture of contentment. I can't fathom their mindsets. At the end of the day, they're still cleaning toilets that nobody uses, ironing napkins that will never accompany a meal, and picking up after a child that doesn't exist. I don't want to iron or clean the grout. I never did in my shitty apartment back in Benezette and have no desire to begin now.

I grab a pair of headphones from a basket on the counter beside the pantry. They are smooth all over, with no obvious controls or buttons, not even an on/off switch. Slipping them on, I hear Althea Edevane's voice droning softly over the sound of flowing water in a creek or brook.

"… *but consider that while your body is bound, your mind need not be vassal. For you are perfection, hewn and ground and polished all these millions of years, sharpened and honed into the machines of life, and that without the miracle of creation made flesh from stardust, all life desiccates and the Earth is rendered barren. Let your daily routine serve to honor the painstaking toil of the universe over eons to*

make you, and you in turn make your home, its brick and mortar, a
shell to protect you, and let the places you make within be a sanctuary
in mother-of-pearl for the gem it keeps. For laying beneath and upon
the anonymous fields of wheatgrass and sideoats grama–"

Grimacing, I remove the headphones and toss them into the basket. As I'd suspected, Edevane must be out of her mind.

The kitchen area abuts the children's room, where tiles give way to carpet. A small lamp casts a circle of warmth from a table between twin beds, one of them unmade. There is a dresser, a large dollhouse, a closet, and several open trunks of toys, with many strewn nearby. In the center of the rug is a colossal pile of stuffed animals. Others lay about the room. I can't imagine the banality of the job had by some orderly who is forced to mess the room just so patients can partake in the sacred joy of straightening.

At the unmade bed, I draw the sheet quickly up, not doing my best work. The pillow has a distinct indentation in it, but I ignore that and flip it to the smooth side, quickly pushing away any fantasies that my imagination might spin up.

I indulge a twinge of fearful curiosity, though, scanning the room, thinking of ghostly children playing there, young sisters leaping into the pile of stuffed animals, giggling as they disappear beneath fuzzy faces and furry ears. I think of Hadleigh.

I go across the carpet, picking up stray animals and dolls. Look at me, I'm doing housework, getting better. At the pile, I imagine a child's face embedded among the bears and bunnies and pigs, waiting to pounce.

I kneel and return the strays, then, because I don't know why, start reworking the mound so every member is head-up and facing out. It's how Hadleigh, in her unfailing empathy for the inanimate, had always organized her stuffies; each with its spot and a clear view of the action. I work fast, not allowing my fingers to linger near the mound's many dark crannies for fear of tiny arms shooting out.

I escape the mock children's room for the kitchen. The woman on dishes delivers a tight smile. I return it and take a step in her direction. She points at her headphones and shakes her head helplessly, like someone who signals that they don't speak the language; as if removing the headset is out of the question. I'm sure Charlotte must know her. Do the two of them have conversations when she puts me in the dark?

I wander to the pantry and open the door. A single bulb illuminates shelves stacked with canned food. More cans of food than anyone has ever had in a pantry. There are years' worth of food in here. Something you'd see in a doomsday prepper's basement. The cans have the same generic, faded white labels, as if Hollyhock purchased them from a mock-pantry supply catalog. There are no brand names, just printed words and stock images. "BEANS" in bold letters above a grainy picture of spilled kidney beans, "ALPHABET SOUP" labels displaying large, letter-shaped pastas in a sheen of red. One entire shelf is taken up by cans of "CRANBERRY SAUCE (JELLIED)," and I wonder if that's what's really inside. I pick one up, shake it. It's heavy.

There are no instructions, no orders from anyone telling us what to do, so I start tidying the shelves. The bulb buzzes like a mosquito as I organize cans of vegetables, soup and fruit, as well as glass jars of beige meats suspended within gelatin and those marked "BABY FOOD." I place the cans into perfect columns, facing the labels out in an illusory gesture – something that might make life easier for the nonexistent homemaker into whose pantry I have trespassed.

It takes me the full hour to complete the task, after which I feel a measure of satisfaction in a job well done, even as I know some orderly will be here to undo my work. I've proven to myself that I can set to doing something and finish it. A small victory for my quavering mind. A way, hopefully, to find my ground.

I return the next day and do it all again.

And the next.

ELEVEN

I've come to look forward to Housework despite my best efforts to spurn it. There is a predictable monotony, a routine that I can rely upon, tasks I can do that calm my mind. The idea that the never-ending cycle of housework is the cure for a woman's anxiety, or that it should be her job in the first place, is anathema, and I hate that this place has made it a refuge.

Still, I go. I scrub grout, I vacuum the beige carpet in the children's room, wash the dishes, stack the cans in the pantry. I've taken to the stacking. I like the sounds the cans make, the way they fit together, their uniformity. I'm good at it.

Working my way clockwise from the shelves on the left, I organize the cans by food type: fruits followed by vegetables, soups, then meats.

The meats. They remind me of another thing Hadleigh and I would doozy each other with. We'd be in the kitchen at home and one or the other of us would throw down a food doozy – a "food-dooze", we called it. The point was to create a disgusting concoction and make the other drink it. We'd toss whatever we could find into the blender, producing condiment-bread shakes and mustard-apple smoothies. One time, I did the unthinkable, mixing milk with mayonnaise in even proportion. An unholy brew, so simple, yet sublime in its repulsiveness. I handed her the cup, knowing I'd won, because nothing could ever top my creation. She chugged it, every last drop, and I swear she turned yellow and green in cycles. But she kept it down. I remember the look she gave me, then, a

181

sharp deviousness I'd never seen from her. She went into the refrigerator and came out with a single hot dog, dropped it into the remains of the mayonnaise abomination, and flipped on the blender. When the shake was a bland, gray-pink, she lifted the jar and slid it across the counter. Gagging some, she said, "Doozy. All of it."

My lips curled as I brought the jar to my mouth, the smell something a catfish would turn away. I held my breath and chugged. Lukewarm milk and curds of mayonnaise, firm little grains of hot dog tickled the back of my tongue. My eyes watered and my throat convulsed, but I kept it together … until I was forced to take a breath. The inhalation that came was like squeezing a trigger. I doubled over and unloaded the contents of my stomach all over the floor. The sheer volume was astounding, but even more than that was the sound – my own gag-roaring as the lukewarm liquid blasted my vocal cords, the slap of it hitting the floor.

Our parents came in to find me sitting in a pond of my own sick, honorably bested. I got grounded for that one, as I was the only one in the kitchen when they found me. They could probably have surmised that Hadleigh was involved, but she knew I wasn't going to rat her out. She'd extracted as much misery from my vanquishment as possible while not directly implicating herself. I respected the ruthlessness, to be honest. Chef's kiss.

I'm pushing the final can of alphabet soup into a perfectly straight wall of alphabet soup when the light bulb plinks and goes out. The pantry door is shut. I try the knob, but it doesn't turn, so I kick the door, rattling the attached spice rack. "Excuse me," I say into the gap. "I'm in here."

Something scrapes the shelves toward the back where the light from under the door doesn't reach. It sounds like cans being pushed. I see them in my mind, sliding about like players on a board, then lifted and placed on top of one another. Something presses the air against my face, makes it thick. I wedge my mouth to the door and beg for help.

The clattering and scraping goes quiet, replaced by a noise like knuckles dragging across wood. It moves steadily from the far end, coming closer, then alongside, just off my shoulder. There is a breath, an inhalation through nostrils, but no exhalation. Then the pressure dissipates like a window has been opened. What was here is gone. My neck tingles.

The light flickers back on and it's like noon over crooked towers. My perfect columns of alphabet soup are now a precarious line of battlements pushed to the shelf's edge. They rotate in place like clockwork gears, with the cans turning at different speeds and directions. They grind to a stop. The big, noodle letters on the labels of alphabet soup face out to form a word. Then words become a sentence.

YOU ARE PERFECTION

I try the door again. Call for help. I level my shoulder and burst through, sprawling onto the kitchen tile amid a torrent of spices. Jars fall and shatter, desiccated old leaves and powders pock the floor in yellow, brown and rust. Cans roll from the shelves, smacking the ground again and again like a metronome.

"Mrs Turner!"

Anise is there with her hands on her head. "What is going on? Are you all right?"

The other women close in like cats to fresh milk.

Anise bends over and gathers spice shakers.

I lean to the side and gaze into the pantry. The words are still there. "Look!"

Anise walks inside and consults the wall of soup, then, seeing the sentence, points and turns. "Ah, I see," she says, putting her hand on a hip. "Very nice, very nice, Mrs Turner."

The others collect beside the door and peek inside. They instantly begin clapping, then twirl in place. Anise joins them. "Rejoice, Mrs Turner!" She claps, she twirls.

"But I didn't do it!" I stand from the floor.

Anise stops, the joy drained from her face. "Who did then, Charlotte?"

The others spin out their momentum, then stand with hands clasped, heads pushed forward on long necks, waiting.

Seconds bleed away as I try to answer her question. The ghosts of all the people who died in this place, is what I want to say. Rageful spirits bent on retribution, taunting and torturing the living, just as they had been while housed here. It is the only thing that explains the hallucinations, the pulling of hair, the delivery of unsettling messages via cans of soup. That, or an inconceivably elaborate prank. Or my mind is crumbling. But I don't believe that. Not entirely.

Anise tilts her head, prompting me to answer. When I don't, she touches my shoulder lightly, as if she fears I might collapse under the pressure. "Charlotte?" Her voice is soothing now, quiet. "Why don't you come with me?"

I flinch away. "I have been so exhausted. I probably didn't eat enough at lunch. I'm sure that's it." I don't remember lunch. "I was in there daydreaming and forgot I'd stacked the cans like that. But now I remember." My fingers are shaking. I shove them behind my back, lace them together and squeeze.

Anise says, "That's fine, but in light of … things … I think we should have you checked out, just to be safe."

"But it's not the end of the hour yet!" I say, my voice cracking. "I really should move to another station."

Anise steps forward, hand outstretched. "I have some clary sage oils in the infirmary. I could do a tincture."

I retreat into the kitchen. I'm not going back to the infirmary.

"Charlotte," says Anise, exasperated. "Come, now. Come with me."

Turning on the water at the sink, I squeeze some soap onto a scrub brush and pick up a plate. "I'll be fine," I say, working the brush around the plate, proud of the calm I've forced into my voice. I glance over my shoulder at her and grin.

Her eyes go wide.

I look back. The plate is coated in blood. In my other hand is a knife, its blade embedded and parting the flesh of my thumb.

I watch in awe as it glides effortlessly through the skin and muscle, so cleanly, so perfectly, that at first there is no pain. There's another hand on the knife, and then it's gone.

The blade hits bone and the plate clatters off the counter onto the floor. I jam the despoiled thumb into my blouse and collapse.

Anise is there, wrapping my hand in a dishtowel. She gets her head and shoulders under my arm and ushers me out of Housework.

"Nonononono," I cry. "I can't. No!" Anise is stronger than I am. "Don't make me go to the infirmary!" I stiffen like a board, pinning my legs straight in front. Anise struggles me forward through the medical library, past a woman in a spring dress pouring herself a glass from a pitcher. Her hair floats languidly about her head like she is underwater. She speaks as we go by.

My world is not the biggest world, but it is mine.

EXCERPT OF
"HOLLYHOCK RESEARCH"

Taken from Personal Computer belonging to Morgan Bright aka Charlotte Turner (Evidence Tag #N402, Shelf G4)

Category: Historical research, treatment devices/techniques.

Elizabeth Collar

TEXT RECORD, PHONE NUMBER
(814) ***-**58

I'm not mad at you.

Hey. I'm NOT mad at you.
I'm sad. I want to help!
However many times it
takes. I know what you're
dealing with seems
insurmountable. You didn't
have to leave early. We
could have worked through it.
We WILL work through it.
I can come out and be with
you while you get clean
again.

Can you at least call me? Please?
Morgan?

TWELVE

I worry my teeth will shatter. When I try to bring my arms around my shoulders, I find them bound. Frozen wet sheets swaddle me from head to foot, as I lay upon a flat metal table. My shoulder screams, the ancient wound within stressed to its limit. I squeeze the muscles of my arms and legs and stomach, but the sopping sheets contract in response.

The room is expansive, lit by dull sconces glowing cold light along the walls. Rows of extra-wide tables fill the room, all empty but for the one I occupy. The echo of dripping water bounces between tiled walls.

Housework seems like a bad nightmare, coming to me in flashes. The pantry; *the presence*. Cans of soup sending a message. Charlotte swimming up from the depths to take hold of the knife. My flesh blooming open. I wiggle my thumb beneath the mummy wrap to test if it was real. I feel the bandages, the ache of the wound. The time between then and now is a dimensionless bridge. Have I been here for hours, days? Has Charlotte used my body to go about her routine while I am interrupted?

I push my head back, angling my chin high, and strain my eyes toward a cast of light. Behind me is a wheelchair with someone in it, silhouetted against the light from an open door. She is restrained, head tossed back and mouth agape. I engage in another fit of struggling against my bindings. Wriggling my head until it hangs backward over the table's edge, I get the full, upside-down picture. She's big. Muscular. Built like someone who moved things her entire life. The old wheelchair struggles to contain her.

Around her neck is an Elizabeth collar, a device I recognize from my research. A leather collar wraps her neck from chin to clavicles, where it expands to form a wide dish of leatherbound metal over her shoulders and chest. If her arms weren't already crosswise bound, the contraption would prevent her from touching her face.

"Hello?" My voice is a rasp. "Hey. Are you awake?" She doesn't move. Staring at her slack face, I follow my imagination into dark corners, where familiarity with obsolete practices lingers. Lobotomization, trepanation, cerebral diathermia, insulin comas. Orbitoclasts jammed to the hilt into the corners of fearful eyes. "Hey!"

The women starts, then groans, easing her head up and as far forward as the collar will allow. Bringing her head upright, she's silhouetted against the door, her eyes mere pinpricks of light. She looks around and tries her arms. Her eyes shift to me. "Fucking what day is it?"

"I don't know."

"That you, Charlotte?"

Flory and the others had mentioned two women who'd been taken to Special Therapies, Rhoda and Honora. I don't know which one this is. There is a note in her voice I recognize, and it's a sound I have immediate affinity for. I know that she and Charlotte have spent time together as friends, and I wonder if my affection is really Charlotte's own passing through to me. Her bindings creak. My gut says it's Honora. "*Honora?*"

"Who else?"

"What have they done to you?"

"It was the electroshock today."

"Oh, no."

She clears her throat loudly and launches a ball of phlegm into the tiled wall. "Why 'oh no'?" she says. Her voice is calm and centered, like she's having a chat over coffee. "Shocks are like little chisels, just chipping away at your memories. It makes you forget. Convenient if you don't want to remember."

My mind is a junkyard of bits and scraps of information I gathered in the year running up to now. Electroshock has a long, controversial history. And I don't know if that is what Honora received exactly. If anything, she probably received electroshock's more refined cousin, electroconvulsive therapy – still controversial, but with far wider acceptance than the earlier, more brutal iteration. Her comments about memory, though …that sounds like the original. I remember reports of how patients came to look forward to the shock treatments, exactly for the reason Honora said. Because it dulled everything, especially the past. Of course, I don't know what past Honora wants to forget; *I've* never met her, and Charlotte holds the missing pages. My train of thought disappears as the penetrating cold screws down.

"Honora," I say with a shiver, "what's happening to me? I think I'm dying."

"The cold packs? Nah, they're supposed to make you feel like that."

"I think my heart is slowing down."

"A trick of the mind. But you might wish you were dying soon enough."

"What?"

"You and me are going to the South Wing."

"The South Wing is closed, Honora. Anyhow, my commitment is for thirty days. I asked to call Andrew, but Enid said my time here is nearly at an end."

"Just wait. You wouldn't be the first to be so sure, and then find out."

"You don't know that. Why do you say that?"

"Because of Christmas."

I adjust my head so that my neck doesn't ache as badly. My view of Honora remains upside-down. "What about Christmas?"

"Christmas shows them who to send south. Haven't you noticed?"

"None of that makes sense, Honora. Listen to yourself."

Honora harrumphs. "If Christmas homes in on you, you're *It*. I've been It since before you got here. Rhoda's been It." She shifts uncomfortably in her collar. "Now you're It, too. And Doc Edevane knows."

"Christmas is a patient here, just like you and me," I say.

"Hmm, I don't know. They say she's chronic – in and out all the time – but I don't think she ever leaves." The wheelchair creaks. Honora swallows loudly against the collar. "Hollyhock pays attention to whoever she singles out. That's who goes. You've been picked. I've been picked. I haven't seen Rhoda for days now. Pretty sure she got picked, too. And more before you ever showed up. Jennie, Decima."

"That's ludicrous. Christmas hasn't *picked* me." Doubt creeps in as I say it. I don't have access to all the days that it was Charlotte and not me.

"Oh, she has. She's come at you twice now. Group, then your little thing in Hollyhock Hall. Everyone heard about that. If that's not being homed in on, I don't know what is. But now she's got her mark on you and that means they'll carry you south."

I don't remember anything about the group session Honora is referencing because it didn't happen to me. But I do have the tiny glimpse of what happened in Hollyhock Hall. I have the words spoken by Christmas that awakened me from wherever I was and ripped Charlotte from the helm of my body. *They say you look like her.* "Why does Doctor Edevane care what Christmas says?"

"I don't know. She shows the doctor who's guilty."

"Guilty?"

"All the women I've seen go south. They've made mistakes. Real mistakes. Not this husband-wife-set-your-car-on-fire-tiddlywinks. They carry bigger regrets. Christmas knows and she homes in."

"You're telling me she senses guilt?"

Honora lets out a resigned sigh like a punctured tire. "She's got... It's like a sixth sense."

"A sixth sense ... for other people's guilt?"

Honora grunts, shrugs beneath the collar.

I force my head backward, trying to lock eyes, but she's staring off. "And what guilt do *you* carry?"

Honora is quiet at first, but I can hear the noises in her throat as she assembles the words. The points of light in her pupils return to me. "I carry my child's casket." Her throat clicks once more against the collar. "She was two months. All I remember was that I walked into the nursery and then I walked out. They told me afterward what I'd done."

I hear what Honora has confessed to, but my mind pushes back. Infanticide and its ties to postpartum psychosis is something you read about, not a thing that happens to someone you know. There is a lump in my throat like I've swallowed peanut butter. How is binding this woman to a chair and strapping on an Elizabeth collar supposed to make her better? "Why did they put you here, Honora?"

"And what did you do?" she says, apparently uninterested in talking any more about herself. "What does Christmas see?"

My guilt is my own. I push it deeper.

"You don't have to tell me," Honora says a second later. "Christmas knows. Means Doc Edevane knows as well."

I struggle against the icy cocoon.

"Hey, calm yourself," says Honora. "That won't help."

I flail harder, fighting the suck of the wet sheets. I fill my chest and press my shoulders, determined to snap the belts that hold it all together. The wound on my hand opens. The blankets go red. My warmth spills out.

"Oh, you got a gusher there." The wheelchair creaks. "*Oh.*"

I glance back. Honora's hair floats about her head like she's underwater. My mouth falls open.

Honora pushes her toes along the ground and begins rolling backward toward the open door, hair swimming.

"Honora! Where are you going? Honora!"

She disappears into the adjacent room.

Minutes pass. Could be longer. It gets colder. Jets of steam vent from my nostrils. I know there comes a point that the cold goes away, replaced by the illusion of warmth that comes with hypothermia. I wonder if I am dying. Is it always this ... quiet?

An uneven line of illumination appears on the ceiling. The air turns thick, filled with the heavy smells of wet salt and iron. The sheets grow warm – actually, truly, warm – and tight at my feet, binding my heels and ankle bones against one another, then constricting my stomach, chest, shoulders. It courses in peristaltic waves, squeezing harder and harder. My ribs bend. I sip inhalations between contractions. The sheets, soaked and bloody, turn translucent, then pliable. They spread open at my shoulders. Angling backward over the table's edge, my arms come free. Naked belly and hips escape from the sac, and I slip to the floor beneath a hot fluid cascade.

Streaks of color swirl through the water and down a drain in the floor. The smell has changed; the salt replaced by sour sweet. I taste the air, smacking it in my mouth as a familiar vision resolves to focus.

It's Thanksgiving dinner. Hadleigh sits across the table, engrossed in conversation with our parents and relatives. I vie for their attention, offering riddles and stories sure to entertain. When they continue to ignore me, I try for Hadleigh, prompting her with private jokes and shared language. But her focus is steadily elsewhere, her face inscrutable. Finally, she finds my eyes with hers and smirks, then angles them to my meal.

A can of cranberry sauce lays sideways on my plate. I look at Hadleigh and shrug, but then I know what this is. She whispers, *"Doozies."*

Grinning, excited to impress her with my bravery, I spear the can with my fork and cut through the metal with a serrated knife. Gelatinous preserves escape in flesh-colored clumps along with an odor like meat soaked in formaldehyde. I scoop it with my fingers and shovel it into my mouth. Even as it congeals into vaguely organic shapes and takes to squirming on the plate, I eat and I eat. Every bleb-covered chunk, every grit-filled node, each unidentifiable, shuddering thing, I devour as my throat revolts and my stomach clenches. To prove I am worthy of her attention. To show I can take any challenge she sets before me. To make her proud.

SPD INTERVIEW RECORD
EXCERPT OF TRANSCRIPTION

[Detective Gastrell enters room at 8:43 pm]

GASTRELL: Food's on the way. It's not really my business, but do you want to take a break from the double burgers? Maybe some chicken or Chinese? Change of pace?

WITNESS: I've been eating oysters and yogurt and fucking chia seeds for two months. I want regular fast food. Oh, and a shake.

GASTRELL: I anticipated that.

WITNESS: Thank you. What's in the folder?

GASTRELL: Some more items from your home.

WITNESS: Okay.

GASTRELL: Gotta say, you were really playing the Charlotte role.

WITNESS: What do you mean? Other than, obviously, everything.

GASTRELL: Well, this, for one. What's that?

WITNESS: A picture of the nursery.

GASTRELL: A nursery for a child you were never going to have?

WITNESS: We had neighbors. Hay Springs is a small, small town. If even one person found out the truth about us, our whole cover would be blown.

GASTRELL: Maybe you should have moved to Lincoln.

WITNESS: I'll remember that the next time I assume a false identity. But also, we didn't know how thorough Hollyhock was going to

195

be on the intake. And it's good we had a nursery done up because Doctor Barker did his evaluation on a home visit. He saw it all. We figured if he was convinced of my desperation–

GASTRELL: Charlotte's desperation.

WITNESS: Right – Charlotte's desperation to have a child, then he would be more likely to give a diagnosis and recommend commitment. It was insurance in case he had any doubts, which he didn't.

GASTRELL: I think you convinced Charlotte.

WITNESS: Charlotte isn't real. She's whatever it was your doctor said – an identity created by trauma.

GASTRELL: And what's this?

WITNESS: Oh. Heh. The Sparrow and the Nuthatch. Why do you have this?

GASTRELL: It was sitting in the crib. Hay Springs PD thought that was odd. I do, too.

WITNESS: Why? It's a children's book. So what?

GASTRELL: All the pages are torn out of it.

WITNESS: Yeah, that was me.

GASTRELL: Kinda odd. Care to explain that?

WITNESS: This book is old. I was a kid. Five or six. It had been Hadleigh's favorite story when she was my age. Look [indicating] she wrote her name inside the cover. I don't remember what happened, other than I must have been mad at her for something, or jealous, and I was a child, and so I did the meanest thing I could think to do at the time. I actually loved that book, by the way. By then it was more mine than hers anyway. She'd outgrown it. But that's how kids' brains work, I guess. I destroyed one of my favorite things to spite Hadleigh.

GASTRELL: Kids do stuff like that all the time. Why do you still have it?

WITNESS: I felt bad. Kids do that too, you know? I dug it out of the garbage after our mother threw it away.

GASTRELL: Why were you mad – or jealous – of Hadleigh?

WITNESS: I worshiped Hadleigh. But she was out there doing things. Living her life. I was a weak kid already, and my arm made it worse, I was always getting hurt. I sort of folded in on myself. Sometimes, I lashed out in my own little ways.

GASTRELL: What happened to your arm?

WITNESS: Well, that's the whole thing, isn't it?

GASTRELL: Whole what thing?

WITNESS: How I ended up addicted to pills.

GASTRELL: Like a sports injury? Something like that?

WITNESS: Nah, it was an old bone break. Right up here.

GASTRELL: Shoulder?

WITNESS: Humerus. Top snapped right off. By my twenties, I had the worst case of osteoarthritis you ever heard of.

GASTRELL: Like what old people get?

WITNESS: It can happen at any age. Usually from badly healed bones. When I was little, I fell off the swings. Went too high, lost my grip, and dropped. Landed on my shoulder. They said it was a clean break, but it never healed right or worked as well as it should have. It always felt different, but didn't become really unbearable until the end of high school, when I had my last growth spurt. It was agonizing then. Anytime I moved it was like being punched in the shoulder or having my nerves set on fire. Debilitating. I went on to college, which... You know that story. I don't even remember when I first tried pills. I was probably complaining about it. Someone had blues or rims and I swallowed some. It was like a miracle. Not only was the fire doused, but all of a sudden I was soaring through the clouds. No more pain. You know how it goes from there.

GASTRELL: Yeah. I do. Did you ever get it fixed?

WITNESS: We didn't have the money when I was a kid, and my parents never believed it hurt as bad as I said. Told me to toughen up. Hadleigh paid for an operation when I was twenty-seven. That helped some. But by then I was already parachuting rimmies and stealing money to buy dream hammers or anything else I could get cheap. Didn't matter by that point.

GASTRELL: I'm sorry.

WITNESS: Wasn't your fault.

GASTRELL: A person can express empathy without needing to be responsible. That's all I'm doing.

WITNESS: [indicating]

GASTRELL: You mentioned that you still feel the pull of addiction. Momentum, you called it. Wouldn't Charlotte have felt that?

WITNESS: I'm sure she did, but maybe it came through as something else for her.

GASTRELL: I think Hollyhock was her addiction.

WITNESS: Yeah... Yeah, maybe.

TEXT RECORD, PHONE NUMBER
(814) ***-**58

I lied to you.

I know.

I hate myself.

I'll never ever hate you for
what you do on a relapse.
It's not you. It's the pills.
It's a disease. You should
know that I can separate
the two.

I checked Stone Crescent.
They can take you right
away. I can be out there by
tomorrow night to help
you get situated.

You're wasting your
money.

They should tell you when you
first show up for rehab that
relapse is part of the process
Hello, welcome to rehab.

You are going to relapse
within a week of walking out
of here. Then people wouldn't
think of it as a failure – then
YOU wouldn't think of yourself
as a failure when it happens.
It's expected. Rehab isn't one
place but a series of places. Until
one time, hopefully, you stay
sober. I'm going to be there for
however many times it takes.

                              I don't deserve that.

You've lied to me before. You
relapsed. You left early. I still
wish you'd stayed so I could
get you in somewhere closer
to me, but hey, we'll do the
trip again when you're out.
I'll be there next week to help
you get moved.

                        No. No. Don't come.
                      I can check myself in.
                        Darius will take me.

If you say so. I'm glad you
have him. He's an angel.

THIRTEEN

Hunched on the bedspread, I examine my fingertips in the moonlight. Lacerations crisscross the pads in every direction, sticky with clotted blood that will harden into scabs. Someone has cleaned me up. I don't know how I got here or when.

My perception has been distorted by this place. What is real and what isn't, the line between dreaming and reality, even time itself. Every passing day is marked by leaps of hours – if I see the day at all. It's like sleeping, except that I know I've been awake, going through my day. But I don't even feel the gap of time. It's been plucked out of my experience. And if I'm not there, I know she is.

I roll on to my back.

She stands at the foot of the bed, her back to me, wearing the same dress she'd been wearing inside the medical library when Anise had dragged me out.

"Charlotte."

She turns her head to the side, as someone who hears a faraway call, and I know it is her because she is me. Except that she is radiant. Her skin is clear and glowing. Her eyes twinkle. She has long, rich hair done up in an elaborate lattice running loosely over the top of her ears and to the back, where loops of it hang like vines in a garden.

"I'm here now," I growl. "Go away."

Serpent-like, she draws her hands up one side of her head, setting her fingers to the delicate task of undoing the braids. Hanks tumble thick and heavy about her shoulders. Hair unbound, she sets her arms peacefully to the sides and rotates in place. A slow twirl.

"What do you want?"

Her hair rises from her head like a crown of sunlight. She angles her head back. Her chin gleams.

I must try to outlast the hallucination. I count my breaths.

One.

Two.

Three.

Four.

Five.

Six.

Seven.

Eight.

She opens her mouth toward the ceiling and a creature made of light emerges. A slender body with a hundred legs crawls onto her face. Wings unravel, blanching the room, turning shadows black. It flutters, then launches upward, disappearing through the ceiling.

She lowers her head. Her mouth is a tunnel of flesh. I hear words like a radio transmission.

Build for them the nacreous home.

FOURTEEN

The voice was mine, the words were not. They play on a loop from the moment I wake, all the way through breakfast, an uncanny refrain that I don't understand, aside from the tone, which is imperative. Not a platitude, but an order. *Build for them the nacreous home.*

Although I am more confused than I've ever been, Charlotte's latest appearance has me feeling newly determined to pierce through the nonsense of this place. I can answer her taunts, her vague admonitions. It's like Doozies.

There's something about the recordings. I put on a pair of headphones in Housework, but they aren't working. After trying five more pairs, I conclude that they must be turned off.

Though I try to keep my bearings, I move through the day in the strangest way; a vehicle straddling the centerline over lanes going opposite directions. There are moments when I catch myself embracing the course of therapy, find myself looking forward to Getting Better. I daydream about Andrew, a person who doesn't exist. I volunteer in group session before I can stop myself, then end up speaking long and sincere about the work of marriage and the struggle to keep one's identity separate from one's husband, and only afterward realize that at some point I'd forgotten I was acting. Charlotte lurks at the edge of my thoughts, pulling strings in the shadows of my psyche. She is my creation, not the other way around. I say it aloud when I'm alone. But I'm not alone, am I?

Time skips.

How can I pursue her if she can erase the ground?

I wake up in Home Skills, standing before the big table in the middle, holding paper envelopes in my hands. Laid out are sewing patterns for clothing. A man's pants and shirt next to a casual dress. Beside the slacks is a pattern for a girl's Easter outfit. Nestled against the chest of the woman's paper bodice is a little boy's church suit. She's got him in her invisible arms. They rustle in a draft.

I gather the big leaves of paper, folding them along their well-worn creases, and return them to their envelopes. There is a large console with tiny drawers. I open the first one and shove the patterns inside, slam it shut.

I understand – I *know* – that Charlotte often visits this place, that she steals minutes and hours away from me to do so. I feel like she's placed me here purposefully, to show me what she's been doing. What is she doing?

She leaves a hole where my memory should be every time she comes. *Holes.* Holes burrowed by the worm that is her through the gray mud of my brain. Does my brain look how it feels? At autopsy, will the medical examiner find it eaten through with channels and voids, like a bucket that crawls with fish bait? Tears threaten. I push them away. There is no point to what I am doing here. There has long been no point.

In a basket by the cabinet are knitting projects. One is rolled up and bound neatly in ribbon with a small tag that says "Charlotte" – a scarf for her false husband. It's a two-tone blue rectangle with a basic Celtic knot pattern running through the center in purple and green. I unroll it slowly, fearful that the knots will unravel into words – more aphorisms or a message of my coming doom. But the scarf is plain, innocuous. Charlotte doesn't torture me without purpose. There is a structure to her behavior that I can't divine.

I hold up the scarf and stretch it long. When I bring it down into my lap, Christmas is there. She makes a noise – a hiss – as if I were the one who had snuck up on her.

"Oh my God, you scared me," I say. The woman weaves through my life like a wandering stitch.

"You scared *me*," says Christmas. She leans over and runs a finger along the edge of the scarf. "Your knots are all bunched."

The conversation I'd had with Honora is still fresh in my mind. Christmas and her "homing in." I crumple the knitting and lean over it.

She sits in the opposite armchair with a grunt.

"How are you feeling?" I ask.

"About what?"

"Didn't you have an episode in the dining hall? I was there."

"No episode."

"But you had to go to Special Treatments."

"I go to Specials all the time."

I try to figure how to best ask about an event I don't understand. "Christmas, what happened to me in there?"

She pulls a strand of yarn from a ball and wraps it around a finger on her opposite hand. "Something happened to you in the dining hall?"

"In Hollyhock Hall. You… You said a name to me. You told me–"

"Did I tell you something?"

"Yes. Don't you remember?" I push to the edge of my chair. "Tell me the name you said. I'm begging you." I need to hear it.

The ball of yarn shrinks as the spool on her finger grows. She glances up. "I don't even know you."

"What?" My teeth snap the air.

She draws her legs up and looks away. The air at her shoulders becomes dense and hums. "The other lady in your head," she says, pointing her yarned finger into my face. "*Her* I know. We have conversations."

Instead of worms, I see a chrysalis-shaped aneurysm in my brain. It explodes liquid butterfly.

"I told her what would come. I warned her," says Christmas, angling her face and eyeing me with suspicion through a shroud of quivering atmosphere. "But she stopped being afraid once she knew her future."

"What future, Christmas?"

"See?" She slips the yarn from her finger into the basket and rises from the chair. "I knew you weren't her."

I almost fall forward, taking hold of her lantern sleeves. "Tell me, please!" The vapor goes tense, shimmering like a warning. I release the fabric and Christmas dissolves out of the room.

TEXT RECORD, PHONE NUMBER

(814) ***-**58

Congrats on finishing, Morgan!
Let me know when you're back
home okay? Say hi to Darius for
me.

Hey, call me when you can. I
have some news too.

SIXTEEN

The gurney rumbles beneath golden chandeliers and past indistinct doorways. Anise glances down, smiling pleasantly. I ask where I am being taken. She laughs lightly. "That's very funny, Charlotte."

We roll into a windowless room. The brightly lit walls are clad in subway tiles of butter, identical to those in the room I'd once entered as me and exited as Charlotte. A pit expands in my stomach as feelings of the experience return. The violation is tactile again, the memory of it echoing through my bones and spreading like a disease across my skin. A ridiculous thought occurs to me, that I will need years of therapy when I leave here, and then I wonder what makes me think I'm ever getting out.

The IV in the back of my hand aches. I can feel the needle pressed up against the inside of the vein. There's a Boyle's apparatus spiking with medical equipment on one side of the room and on the other, a large metal box with dials and wires. There is only one place this can be. I don't know why I am here. Honora's voice is clear in my mind as Anise kicks down the brake on the bed. *It makes you forget.*

Maybe I'll forget. Is that what I want? To forget everything that put me here, put Hadleigh here?

I don't deserve to forget.

Miriam assists Anise. She checks my restraints, tightens them.

What was I doing, coming here? Did I think I was brave? Are you still brave if you can't run away?

209

Edevane appears above me, her smooth face upside-down, holding a large tool that looks like forceps with sponges shoved onto the tines. She smells like herbal tea and peppermint. "Good evening, Charlotte. You finally got your wish."

My wish?

"Not everyone is a candidate for electroshock – but considering your most recent episode and persistent requests, I've come around. It's best we exhaust every option that we have. So," she says, smiling cheerfully, "let's proceed."

Anise shoves a rubber mouthpiece between my jaws. "Bite down so we know it's in place." I do. I don't even fight it. I can't.

"The usual starting point, Miriam," says Edevane.

I don't want electroshock. I never asked for this. I don't want it! There's a mistake! Something happened to me! There's two of us! I'm not her! Please please please please. I don't make a sound in the external world. Charlotte has my tongue.

A switch is thrown. The room vibrates.

Edevane gazes down. "Now, before we start, the typical pulse duration runs about one-half to three-quarters of a second. Depending on how you respond to the minimums, we could go up to a second and half. If it's all positive and your symptoms allay, then we can talk about continuing the course. Are you ready?"

Charlotte produces an agreeable noise through the mouthguard. My head nods.

Anise comes alongside with a small, hand-held valve connected to the intravenous line. "Goodnight."

Her thumb depresses a plunger, sending the medicine into my veins. In the space of a second, my eyes close and my body undergoes paralysis. I sense Charlotte dropping away like a rock thrown down a well, while I remain entirely conscious. I have no way to communicate. No way to tell them that I am still wide awake.

"Eight hundred milliamps, Miriam, please," says Edevane. "One half-second."

The shock comes. It is like walking through the woods and catching a spider's web across my face, only the web is made of the sun, burning through the skin of my nose and into my sinuses, my bones. I can't scream. The pain stays inside.

I hear Edevane's voice. "Did the pulse deliver?"

"Yes. One half-second."

"Why is there no seizure?"

"No change in BP or heart rate either," says Anise.

"Let's go again," says Edevane. "One second."

No! Nooooooo–

The darkness is awash with light. The spiderweb becomes a bale of razor wire, searing its brand on the bones of my skull. I shrink and collapse into a ball, trying to make the essence of me insignificant. To hide from the pain. When it finally subsides, I know. I understand. Charlotte carried me to the roof and called for a storm, then abandoned me when it arrived, a lightning rod to be struck. To be annihilated.

"No change," says Anise.

"No seizure either," says Edevane, perplexed. "I've never seen this. It could be voltage. We'll go once at three hundred. One second duration. Go ahead."

I lie upon the open plains of myself, curled beneath roiling clouds. There are no trees, no places to shelter. The full expanse of night sky bleaches white. I cover my head just as the light finds me.

"Small jump in BP and heart rate that time," says Miriam. "A blip."

"There is something..." says Edevane, her voice trailing off. "She's resisting the electroconductivity ... absorbing it."

My body isn't. I am.

"What do you want to do," asks Anise.

"What was the heartrate spike?"

"Seventy-one to seventy-four," answers Miriam.

"It should go to twice that. Let's see what happens at five hundred volts, six seconds."

"Okay."

I shriek voicelessly as the web of silken fire fills the sky and descends through the clouds. The person I am begins to fracture, exposing my core. I am reduced to the animal desire to flee from the suffering. I call to Charlotte in the darkness and offer myself. Anything to make it stop.

"Still no seizure."

"Eighty-five bpm," says Miriam.

"Did we miscalculate the sedative?"

"I don't think so."

"Perhaps she's oversensitive. Reduce the anesthesia."

"Reduce?" asks Miriam.

"I need to be able to gauge her reaction."

"Sedative shouldn't affect seizure response."

"I understand the physiology. Reduce it."

"Backing off."

Light in the shape of bars appears overhead. I am partially back in the room, even though my eyelids won't open. The shadows of Edevane, Anise and Miriam pass above. Nothing works. I try to speak. My tongue shifts against the rubber.

"Alright," says Edevane. "We get one, maybe two more before she comes out. We need the seizure response. Seven hundred-fifty volts, please."

"Seven-fifty?" asks Anise.

"I know what I'm doing. Seven-fifty, six seconds. Now, Anise."

No. No. No. No. N–

My first thought is that I am dead. Except that I'd always expected nothingness with death. If I've arrived in the afterlife, it seems the same as normal life. It can't be a delusion because I'm not awake, and it can't be a dream because I'm not asleep. So it must be the afterlife – how else could I be delivered to this new place from atop an electroshock table at Hollyhock, if not by the journey from one life to the next?

Or have I skipped the afterlife altogether and been reincarnated?

Because now I am a child in a bed. A little boy. *No*, I am not him, I am inside of him, a passive observer of what he does, sees, what he feels.

Right now, he's anxious, flinching as someone comes into his room. He looks away, trying to avoid them, wishing that they would go. The person, a woman, places a tray on his bedside table and sits on the edge of the mattress. "Sweet boy." There's no mistaking a mother's whisper. She rests a moist rag on his forehead (I can feel it), making an empathetic *tut-tut* sound between her tongue and teeth. She administers a spoonful of medicine, adjusts his sheets, and leaves.

The light changes. It's a different day. The boy in his bed. His mother coming in with her tray. Gone is the warmth from the previous day. She fills a syringe from a vial. His body goes rigid. Her fingers clamp upon his arm. The needle goes in. The bed goes wet.

The scene through his eyes loses color, bleaches gray, then the bars of light reappear above me.

Edevane's voice fades in from a distance. "... total tonic clonic seizure. Anise, how long did it last."

"Seventy-five seconds."

"Jesus," says Miriam.

My eyes crack to a blurry scene. "Oh, there you are," says Edevane.

My mouth is moving. Sounds come out. Miriam removes the mouthpiece and wipes my eyes as I struggle to report that I'd been conscious, that the pain had found the center of me and stricken it, that I'd played the role of a child suffering some kind of abuse.

"Calm yourself, calm, calm," says Edevane. "You'll regain your faculties in short order."

I mumble something that sounds like language, my mouth trying to form the word *dream* but failing.

"Soon, soon. I predict a long and relaxing evening of sleep for you, Charlotte. We had to take the intensity far higher than I'd wanted in order to get any type of physiological response from you." She undoes the top buckle across my chest and leaves the rest to Anise and Miriam. "Eat up and sleep well. I'll be back to check on you in the morning." Her footsteps recede, then stop. She says, "Her jaw was creaking. Let's do acetaminophen and mandibular massage before bed, alright?" The two orderlies answer that they will.

I let out a squelch of sound, then again. I shout the words I want to say. Poorly, but they regain their form second over second. Anise places a hand on my chest, tells me to relax. My eyes strain to Edevane, who has halted in the doorway.

"Did you say you had a dream?" she asks.

I struggle to get my mouth to move at the speed of my thoughts.

"No," she says before I can speak. "I wouldn't expect you had any dreams. Not with this sedative."

"Not dream," I say, the words blunted on both ends. "A vision. Awake. I was awake."

Anise jumps in. "We stopped the flow–"

"Shhh," hisses Edevane, cutting her off and stepping back into the room. "No, I don't think so, Charlotte. With this cocktail, you're either here or nowhere. There's no in between."

"Where I was. That's… That's where I was. In between."

"Okay, well, you're all right now. Recovering. Your vitals are as they should be. I'll look back over the data for when you were under. Sort out this *in-betweening*." Her heels squeak as she pivots, but she turns back. "This vision. Can you describe it?"

I close my eyes, and it is as vivid as it had been the first time. The dream quality slips away. The edges are crisp, the colors saturated. "I was in bed. I mean, I was literally just lying in a child's bed."

Edevane comes closer, her face performatively empathetic, almost bored.

"He was sick, I think. His mother was there, she was tending to him."

"Do you know who she was? Or the child?"

"I don't think so."

"Maybe an old friend?"

"No. I didn't know them."

She blinks. "And ... what happened?"

"The mom, she gave him some medicine, put a rag on his head. Gave him a shot. He seemed afraid."

She nods. "Thank you for sharing. We may have overcompensated when your body wasn't responding to the therapy. How the mind reacts is always a lesson in unpredictability. Sometimes it shows you things you thought you'd never see."

EXCERPT OF
"HOLLYHOCK RESEARCH"

Taken from Personal Computer belonging to Morgan
Bright aka Charlotte Turner
(Evidence Tag #N402, Shelf G4)

Category: Newspapers, *The Omaha Picker*, November 6, 1979.

LEGISLATURE CLOSES LONGEST OPERATING STATE PSYCHIATRIC HOSPITAL IN THE MIDWEST

Piper Gilstrap, Staff Writer

–In what has been described as an "inevitable" move, the Nebraska State Legislature has voted overwhelmingly to cancel funding for Hollyhock State Hospital, which has operated in near obscurity since 1896 in a remote section of Dawes County.

The closing comes on the heels of decades of controversy, often blamed on a combination of mismanagement, poor oversight, and woeful funding. The decision was celebrated by patient advocacy groups who have actively pushed for the hospital's closure after decades of reported abuses.

"I don't know why they ever put it out there, to be honest," said William Riggs, a lawyer for the patients' representatives. "It's remote even by today's standards. Can you imagine what it was like fifty, a hundred years ago? The roots of that place are rotten, and the people in charge were given carte blanche to do whatever they wanted to their patients. You see it with what happened to Tilda Branch and her girls. It's sickening to me that things had to get so bad before these lawmakers started paying attention. But I'm glad it's over. Good riddance."

SEVENTEEN

I sit in my room at the tiny desk, watching the woman in the field doing the flips. The experience of her, the dream – if that's what it is – is so clear. I can only guess to what end she works, but the effort imbued in her movements tells me that she knows. Her persistence in executing the choreography is inspiring, because from my vantage point she is trapped in an endless – and purposeless – chore. An inescapable loop. I want her to find what she is seeking or to win at whatever game she is playing. I want to see her again. I want to watch her crack the system which has her trapped. I don't know what victory looks like for her, but I want to be there when she claims it.

EIGHTEEN

Honora eats her food like someone who's forgotten they're institutionalized. She is completely engrossed, sampling from here and there on her tray like it's a miniature buffet and making satisfied little noises as each flavor strikes the palate. She surprises me when she finally looks up from her tray and speaks. "So?"

"Yes?"

"You did shock?"

I nod. I leave out that I'd apparently requested it.

"Did it make you forget?" she asks, reaching across and spearing a piece of my cantaloupe, which by this point has become part of our routine. I would miss it if she got through a meal without stealing some of mine.

"No," I say, thinking how to explain what happened, or whether to try at all.

"I'm not forgetting either," she says, crushing the fruit between her teeth.

"I'm sorry." I reach across and she allows my hand to linger on hers.

"It's Isobel. She won't let me forget."

"Was that her name? Isobel? It's beautiful, Honora."

"*She* was beautiful." Honora gazes off and then back. "When I tell you that I want to forget, I don't mean that I want to walk away from the memory of my daughter. I wish I could carry her forever. What I want to forget is that I was her mother."

My heart clatters apart. "Oh, Honora."

"I had a photograph. I want to look down at her face and know that whoever she is, she's someone special. Someone who will brighten the world wherever she goes. Maybe she's a niece or a sister. I'm sure I'll suspect that she's my daughter, but I want no memory of having a child. I don't want to forget her, just who I was to her."

I've always thought that sorrow was a kind of dense fog or deep mud that you push through, knowing that one day you'll end up on the other side. Not that you won't feel it always, but that at least you'll be able to move, to function again in the world. My sorrow for Hadleigh is that way, and I've been able to redirect it into investigating the question of her death. Maybe it will surge again when all of this is over, maybe the mud will deepen and I'll have to fight through it again. Honora's sorrow is different, though. I can see the shell of it hardened around her. "I'd love to see that photograph."

"I had it," she says, gesturing to an orderly standing nearby. "They took it away. I had a locket."

"I've seen a locket."

"Yeah, Doctor Edevane keeps all the contraband jewelry there in her office. I know."

"It's in the raven's beak."

"Pretty sure it's a crow, but yes. That's the one."

"They should at least let you have the picture inside."

"Hollyhock is all about new beginnings. Resets. The future. I'm sure you've heard. They won't have me lingering on the past."

"The past is part of you, Honora. They can't take that away."

"It won't be *my* past anymore. Not if I finally forget who I am."

SPD INTERVIEW RECORD
EXCERPT OF TRANSCRIPTION

GASTRELL: We pulled the texts from your phone number for the months leading up to Hadleigh's commitment. They're interesting. Can't say I was expecting all that. Here.

WITNESS: I don't need to see them. I know what they say.

GASTRELL: They helped me understand things. Your rationale for doing what you did.

WITNESS: My rationale? That's a nice way of putting it.

GASTRELL: What would you call it?

WITNESS: Paying a debt. Accepting responsibility for a terrible mistake.

GASTRELL: We all make mistakes.

WITNESS: You'd put what I did in the "we all make mistakes" category?

GASTRELL: I wasn't there. Things happen. Considering your past ... the drugs and all.

WITNESS: Did you ever make a mistake that got someone killed?

GASTRELL: Fortunately, no. And neither did you.

TEXT RECORD, PHONE NUMBER
(814) ***-**58

Seriously, you gotta answer
the phone. I finally had to call
Darius. He said you're around
and clean and all that. I'm so
happy for you, but please
call me back!

NINETEEN

More than once I have found myself sitting at the desk beneath my window late at night. Sometimes I remember sitting down, other times I don't. Charlotte comes and goes, using me when she likes and leaving me when disinterested. The irony of being housed in a place that is supposed to treat conditions like mine is rich, as the last thing I would ever do is confess my reality. I can only hold on to myself for as long as possible and hope something comes of it.

The window mixes the night just as it does the day, with a spill of periwinkle at the bottom where snow covers the land, bleeding into the black-purple middle and rumors of lilac up high that might be clouds or ripples in the glass or make-believe anomalies of my own creation. Tonight, I see no difference between myself and the world through the window. Neither of us knows what we are anymore. Though we are both more than one thing.

I ask myself just what it is I am supposed to do now. What was I ever supposed to do? Even when I was a whole person, there was no plan, just a wish. A hope that some clue would jump out at me, or that I might... What? Break into a file cabinet and peruse Hadleigh's records?

I was a person running into the burning house with full knowledge that the people inside were already dead. Was I trying to prove something by returning to the scene of the crime? Was I so foolish to think they wouldn't have cleaned it up by now? Or were my reasons less conscious? A brazen act of contrition offered to a ghost?

I flirt with the idea that I always knew I'd never find out what happened to Hadleigh, and that the whole charade had always been pretext for the real purpose: that I wanted to be punished.

When the cold becomes unbearable, I leave the desk and crawl into bed. At least the blankets keep me warm. I lay down on my side as I do every night, facing the door.

The draft at the back of my neck is imagined. Such things happen to me in the twilight of wakefulness. Ever since childhood, I have experienced the strange tricks of perception that strike during that transitory phase between consciousness and the atmosphere of dreams, where hallucinations overlay the real world, allowing the joys and horrors of sleep to cross from one realm into the next. Mixed, just like the world through Hollyhock's windows.

The onset of sleep is a time for strange noises, bumps and knocks, shadows that move, flashes of light through eyelids, shifts of fabric and hair; all suggesting the presence of something, when there is nothing. Fingers of cold caress a line from my shoulder and over my ribs, but they are no more real than any other hypnogogic mirage.

The chill comes again, and this time my eyes snap open. I feel it at my back. The sheets lift and go taut, pulling out from where I'd trapped them. They billow behind me, rising from the bed, exposing my back. I anticipate a touch. Electricity sparkles down my spine.

Someone slides in with me. I lay paralyzed, eyes wide and dry, anticipating their touch. I hear Christmas's breath, her voice of drifting atmosphere. *They say you look like her.* The sheets settle. Do I share a bed with her now? There is no more movement, and as warmth returns I begin to doubt that it has happened. Courage harnessed, I roll on to my back.

They are right next to me. The sheets reflect the shape of an arm. It slithers across my stomach without touching the skin. The impression of a hand forms, small and childlike. A finger points to the door, and I turn to look. The space beside me is suddenly vacant.

I slide from the blankets and move to the door and crack it.

The chandelier outside my room blinks on as flakes of snow fall from within its vitrine housing. Down the hall, flurries sparkle in shafts of light, leading to the old library.

Stepping into the hallway, I draw the door quietly shut and reach into the silent shaft of snow. It's light and gritty, and I realize it's not snow at all, but ash. For all the fear that lives in my bones, I am cognizant that this is a crossroads. Something has come and presented a choice. Wiping my hands, I follow the lights all the way to the Group room. The precipitation stops inside each chandelier as I go by.

The old library's glass cabinets glow to life like life-sized snow globes. The water inside the pitcher is frozen solid. The ash fall guides me to Housework. It's dark, but a light comes on.

Towering figures stand in silhouette. I falter backward, realizing as I do what I'm looking at. Someone has sprung the legs on the ironing boards and stood them on end, aiming their tapered noses ceilingward. I blame Thirza or Beatrice – they seem the type who would play such a prank. I recover my composure as the lamp in the children's room glows bright, illuminating the dollhouse. "Hello? What...? What is happening? Did Christmas send you?"

I can't be sure if it is my own memory or something told to me, but there was once a children's program, a cartoon show maybe, long ago, about the ghost of a child who lived in harmony with the humans in his world. A nice ghost. Maybe I'm remembering something else, as I can hardly touch the threads of the story. Gasper? Gasper the Kindly Ghost?

The idea by itself brings comfort. I would rather have visions produced by a phantom than confront the prospect of my own lunacy.

The dollhouse is large, comprised of four floors. Little wooden figures lay about inside; a man in the easy chair, a little girl in her room, which also happens to contain its own miniature dollhouse. I wonder if there is an even smaller dollhouse inside the miniature, and another inside that. A little boy is in the bed in his room. On the second floor is a nursery, with animal print wallpaper, a diaper-changing station atop a dresser, and a toy box. The crib is missing. Down in the kitchen, a woman lays on the floor next to the stove. There's a pie in it. Behind the oven is a hole that goes through to the outside, chewed by a rodent. I poke my finger through the oven door and out the back of the dollhouse.

In the attic are tiny replicas of children's toys, and among the mess, the crib from the nursery. The baby is wedged inside. When I tap the crib on the ground, it pops out. It looks all wrong. Legs sprout from the shoulders. Its arms are shoved into the gaps for the legs. Rather than leave it as is, I tear it apart and rearrange the limbs to erase how it makes me feel.

I set the dining room table upright and place the family members into the chairs. Father, mother, little girl, little boy from his bed, baby from the attic. I stare at the scene, question why I bothered, then smash it to pieces.

The lamplight drops away, so I move to the kitchen, where the ironing boards have shifted. They form a corral that leads me to the pantry.

"Thirza? Beatrice? Honora?" There's a line of light below the door. A can clatters to the ground. This is it. This is their big reveal. I knock, say their names again. Another can strikes.

I rip the door open. The pantry is empty. I step into the threshold, but not so far that the door can trap me inside again.

A can of cranberry sauce falls from the shelf and rolls to my toes.

I hear a utensil drawer flying open in the kitchen. The ironing boards have reset again, funneling me to the open drawer. I dig around and grab a can opener, then rush back to the pantry and pick up the can. It rumbles in my hand. I yelp and let go. It rolls to the wall, stops, then comes slowly back to me.

The opener cuts the steel with a hiss. A fever builds behind my eyes as I crank the handle, the blade chewing into the lid until it hangs by a fragile strand of tin. I bend it back.

My face reflects from the mirror surface of wet red-purple. "I don't–" The can flutters. This time, I don't drop it. I break the lid away and invert the can above my palm. A plug of jelly emerges with a sucking noise. A quarter inch, an inch, then it slides quickly out, *thwauk*, into my hand, a perfect cylinder.

I lift it to the bulb overhead, illuminating the jelly everywhere except in the dead center, where a shadow is suspended.

I press my fingers through the congealed sauce, taking hold of something fleshy. Soft and pliable. The jelly drops away and the thing inside falls open like a rope. It looks like a gigantic worm – waterlogged, skin partially sloughed. I can tell it's not a living thing, more a part of one. Blue veins run shallow beneath the outer membrane and the ends are cut jagged. An umbilical cord. I hurl it down. "If you are sleeping," I growl, "wake the fuck up, right now."

The cans of alphabet soup do their clockwork dance. Amid a wall of letters, a new word appears: HADLEE.

I behold it in oracular wonder. "What about her?" I rush to the shelves. "Is she here? What do you mean?"

Another can pushes from the shelf, slaps the floor.

My breathing is desperate and ragged, as I obey what feels like a command, leaning down and lifting the can.

It vibrates. I set it on the floor and stand away. "No." The wall of cans moves again, the towers twisting faster, frenetically. A new sentence appears. U HAV THE TOKN. The cans spin and fall. I scrub my hands over my face, beg for it all to be over. Beg to wake up. Turning to the door, the ironing boards stand shoulder to shoulder like faceless nuns, blocking my escape.

Only when I drag the opener into my hand do the cans cease their mania. I snap it down on a lid and feverishly turn the handle. The movement within responds, becomes stronger, manic. Whatever is inside, needs out. I remove the lid, carefully extract the contents and hold it to the light.

"Oh my God." Cradling it against my chest, I obliterate the gelatinous mold into which the tiny body is folded. "Oh no, oh no, oh no, oh no, oh no."

Having been packed so tightly, its misshapen limbs are almost melded together, folded and creased like a canned chicken, packed so tightly as to become a single, cylinder-shaped thing.

It is a baby too small to have ever been born. Using my pinky, I wipe the sticky crumbles from its face, its nose. Had I imagined the vibration? Had I been too late? Did I not read the signs? I take the tiny hands, smaller than my own fingertips, and hold the body out, stretching the arms wide like a baby bird. It is beyond comprehension. The limbs are wrong, out of proportion. Holding in a scream I will someday release, I press it to my chest, praying that its movements had been imagined. That I had not been too late. That surely it had not been alive. Not ever.

Ash is falling again. Flakes stick to the wet lines on my face.

I look at my hands, now full of ash which I have smeared across my chest. I am captured in a moment of relief, as now I can tell myself that none of it was real, a hallucination played out on the stage of my corrupting mind. I welcome the delusion – I want the delusion – if it means that what it shows me is not the truth. What would be the truth anyhow?

Gasper doesn't talk, but he sends another can from a shelf. It rolls to my knee. Then another and another. They line up, vibrations forming a chorus that shakes the ashen landscape.

Is it a delusion?

Is there a ghost?

Am I him?

TEXT RECORD, PHONE NUMBER

(814) ***-**58

I really thought you'd be
happier for me. For us.

> I would be. I mean, I am.
> I just want you to be sure
> that you're sure, that's all.
> Sorry. Bad timing.

Why are you saying this?
He's the best thing that's
ever happened to me.

> I'm not saying anything
> about *him* I'm just
> saying you want to be sure,
> right? I'm just thinking about
> mom and dad. I'm sure they
> seemed perfect for each
> other too at one point. We
> saw how that went.

Me and Clayden aren't
mom and dad. And also
how dare you! Could
you not share a little bit
of joy with your own

sister? I've found the
person I want to spend
my life with.

It's like we're kids again
and you're tearing up my
birthday cards.

        You look out for me. I'm
        only looking out for you.

Doesn't feel that way.

            Sorry.

You're the one that pushed
me to get out and date. You.
Now I'm engaged and you're
acting like it's YOUR funeral.
I don't know why you ever
gave me advice when you
were just going to act like this
if I found someone. You're
seriously acting jealous just
like when we were kids.

        I'm not jealous that you
         found someone.

Then what? Tell me what
I'm missing. Are you back
using? What is it?

       That's where we're at? Anytime
       I say something you don't like

it must because I'm dosing
again, right? Fuck you.

I didn't mean it like
that. I'm sorry.

I'm not jealous. That's the
truth. Maybe I'm possessive
of you. Maybe I'm afraid
you'll abandon me. I know
you won't. It's just deep down
I guess. I want you to myself.

I would never abandon
you. You know that.

TWENTY

I'm at the window again, entranced by the woman and her flips. I am shocked when she stops and stands. I fear she will look over and see me, but I am wrong. She does nothing to suggest she knows – or cares – that she is being watched.

She leans forward. Farther and farther until I am sure she will fall straight into the mud and snow. Yet, she remains suspended, going past where any normal person would collapse. Her forehead begins to pull up from the rest of her, distorting her face. Her neck and body follow. She grows tall and thin – many, many feet beyond her original height. No wind reflects upon the prairie, yet she stretches long like a streamer, and undulates.

SPD INTERVIEW RECORD
EXCERPT OF TRANSCRIPTION

GASTRELL: Who is she? The woman outside doing flips.

WITNESS: She's "women."

GASTRELL: What does that mean?

WITNESS: I don't know. She's just... doing what all women do.

GASTRELL: Flips in a field?

WITNESS: You wouldn't understand.

GASTRELL: Is it a dream?

WITNESS: Feels different than that. Feels like I'm being shown something. But, yeah, it must have been a dream.

GASTRELL: Anyway, here. Rustled these up for you.

WITNESS: Oh my God, you're a wizard. I need one of these. You have no idea. Jesus, they smell so good.

GASTRELL: We have to go outside, though.

WITNESS: I know.

GASTRELL: Not exactly protocol, but I think we're way past normal, eh?

[Break taken from 9:25 am until 9:28 am]

WITNESS: Got a light? Thanks. Oh shit, that's amazing.

GASTRELL: I'm glad.

WITNESS: I don't know why I ever quit.

GASTRELL: Make it quick, it's cold as hell out here.

WITNESS: You should have one.

GASTRELL: No thanks.

WITNESS: Suit yourself.

GASTRELL: It's Casper, by the way. Casper the Friendly Ghost.

WITNESS: How do you know that?

GASTRELL: I've got a few years on you, Ms Bright.

WITNESS: Isn't that story over a hundred years old?

GASTRELL: About that, I think. But anyway: it's Casper.

WITNESS: Right, okay. So, I was close. I still like Gasper.

GASTRELL: And you think this "ghost" was communicating with you? It wasn't a delusion?

WITNESS: I can accept that I had delusions. And I'm convinced that some, maybe all of them, were Charlotte. Who knows? She was there for them, and when I didn't see her, I felt her. Like she was trying to push me. But then there was Hollyhock. It had its own thing going. We both knew it. She knew it. And Gasper only appeared when Charlotte wasn't there. If Gasper was external, not a product of my mind, then I'm not all crazy, am I?

GASTRELL: Stomp that out. Let's get inside.

WITNESS: One more? Please?

GASTRELL: Let's go.

TWENTY-ONE

Hollyhock has set my mind askew, like trying to cut a length of string to match another, finding it too short and then cutting the original to match the second, overcompensating, and continuing the pattern until the pair become shorter and shorter. So goes my sanity. Much of the time I don't know what is real or the truth; guessing fact from delusion feels like spinning the roulette wheel.

I'm almost never there – aware – for meals now. Usually I come back to myself just after eating. Charlotte loves the food, and so I guess she pushes me aside so that she can eat. I get to bus the empty tray. I never taste food because she doesn't let me eat. And I'm never hungry because I'm always full.

Dilute light sifts through the window above the desk in my room. I lean down to inspect a painful blister on my right index finger that I don't remember getting.

It's the middle of the day. I should be out with everyone else. I get up and check the door. It's locked. I pound and shout. Press the call button. There's the slightest taint of smoke on the air. I press my nose to the door jamb. There's a single knock. It opens. Enid breezes in with lunch.

"Why am I being kept in my room?"

She leaves the tray on the desk and turns to leave.

"Do you not smell that smoke?"

She gives me a searing look, then quickly exits. She doesn't even stay to watch. I guess because I'm such a good eater.

This time Charlotte doesn't tap me out for the meal, or dinner when it's delivered. I barely eat, pressing the occasional pomegranate seed between my lips or sipping tea. I don't rejoice at Charlotte's inactivity – she always comes back. I read her quietude as confidence, that she need not interfere with the course I am on because it is the course she's set. And I don't know where that goes.

Enid escorts me from my room before breakfast the next morning. She refuses to answer when I ask about my confinement the prior day. We walk through Hollyhock Hall and into the network of passages that lead to the main building. It's too early for my session with Doctor Edevane. Am I going to the yellow room? I lag behind.

We arrive in the corridor of the main building. Darius stands outside the door to Edevane's office. Has it been thirty days? I freeze, hoping that he is truly there and not a cruel construct of my addled brain or the worm that lives inside it.

"Charlotte." He runs over. Enid doesn't fight me when I break away to meet him.

His arms swallow me. He feels real enough. I reach up to a curl of hair at the back of his neck and pull it. He says *ow* and I know it's the real world. His shirt is wet before I notice I'm crying. Mouth to my ear, he whispers, "Are you okay?"

Still beyond Enid's hearing, I speak the answer into his shoulder. "Get me the fuck out of here."

We break and his eyes seem to say, *Hasn't that always been the plan?*

I answer as Edevane's door swings open. "There's something wrong here."

The director rounds into the hallway and takes Darius's hand. "Mr Turner, so good to see you."

"Doctor."

"Come in," she says.

Enid follows the three of us inside. Edevane goes to a small table beside a run of windows opposite the hairstreak enclosure, which has already captured Darius's attention. I know his *what the fuck is that* look.

We sit. Enid positions herself inside the door next to the bookshelf. My eye runs to a glint of silver on one of the lower shelves. Honora's locket hanging from the raven bookend, the one with her daughter's photo inside. The raven seems to expand and contract like it's breathing. Do ravens share an affinity for shiny objects like their crow relatives? Is it a crow, after all? Does it blink? Is Gasper here?

"Mr Turner," says Edevane, presenting an embossed folder with the Hollyhock logo on the front. "That is your copy of Mrs Turner's thirty-day record and assessment. She and I have gone over the bulk of it already."

We have?

"Okay," he says, hesitantly.

"Charlotte is a model patient. She has been a willing and active participant in her treatments. She is eating very well, as you can see." Edevane reaches over and gives my arm a pinch. "I want you to know, first of all, that she has devoutly and enthusiastically fulfilled her end."

"There's a 'but' coming."

"I can see sugar coatings are wasted on you." She smiles warmly and clasps her hands. "It is we who haven't met our benchmarks. Our failure, not hers. Not all programs work for all people. But now we have enough data to better tailor your wife's treatment."

"You want to recommit her?"

"I want to recommit *to* her, Mr Turner." She points to me without looking. The tip of her finger is an eyeless worm. "I know we can bring her to full health. The problem is… Well. It is possible that Charlotte was underdiagnosed prior to her admission."

"You said thirty days for domestic psychosis. That's Hollyhock's specialization, isn't it?"

"Unfortunately, Mrs Turner's behavior has bled over the boundaries of that diagnosis. She's become erratic and unpredictable, driven by heightened paranoia and increasingly vivid hallucinatory episodes. There is only so deep we can go on a thirty-day commitment. Most of the time, yes, a run-of-the-mill case of domestic psychosis can be – I won't say 'cured' because the psychogenic ailments are more strongly rooted than the physical in most cases – but they can be managed. Sometimes, though, we dig down and find the roots have burrowed deeper than what one month's treatment can uncover. We just need more time, and I'm quite happy to tell you that Charlotte has not only agreed with my recommendation of a second commitment, she requested it."

I hide my reaction. This is why Charlotte had been leaving me alone. She doesn't want to leave.

Darius sits straight and makes himself big. "Charlotte is welcome to her opinion, but none of this is up to her, is it?" he says, playing his part. "I don't like the idea of paying you for another thirty days when all she's done is get worse."

"Well, as an administrative matter, a second commitment would be sixty days."

My throat snaps closed. My eyes flick to the door. Can I run? Would I make it? Charlotte, as she is currently manifested, has never existed outside the confines of Hollyhock. Can she live beyond its walls? Maybe it's as simple as going outside.

"No. I appreciate your efforts, Doctor, but I don't think so." He stands and extends his hand. "Come, Charlotte."

I push my chair back from the table.

"Her mind is healing every day," says Edevane, gripping my wrist. "She just needs more time."

"Let go of her."

She releases and holds her hands up in surrender. But I can see she's only reassessing.

"I'm not paying you more after she's gotten worse."

"There will be no additional fee. I want to see her treated."

"We're still leaving."

"Mr Turner," says Edevane, her voice clear and level. "Your wife's delusions are all her own. I assure you." She flips up a touchscreen from the center of the table. "I won't attempt to physically prevent you from leaving with her. But please, let me call up some footage before you go. You'll want to see this. Indulge me."

We share a glance. He sits.

The screen angles back and she taps it. I try not to show any curiosity. She pivots the screen to Darius, but makes sure I can see it, too.

The camera view is of the old library. Miriam has just ended the session. Edevane advances the clip until all the women have left the room, with me standing to get a drink from the pitcher. But it's not me. It's Charlotte. I hate the water. The clip is from before I regained control. Charlotte takes a sip, then flips her head toward one of the four doors and starts talking. No one is there. She walks into the doorway and says something else. Returning to the water, she twists to address a different doorway. She is animated, yelling. This repeats until it becomes a five-way conversation involving one person. The clip ends.

"What the hell is this?" asks Darius, real fury sparking in his voice. His efforts to remain Andrew are fading. He shoots me a glance. I can only give him confusion.

"This next bit happened a few days later."

The video skips. Darius watches me fly from the pantry in Housework, converse with Anise, and then rush to the sink and open my hand with a knife.

He grabs my hand and flips it over. My thumb is out of bandages but still bears a line of stitches. His rage takes hold. "This is negligence!" he says, raising his voice. "She can't be allowed to harm herself like this. You let them have knives?"

"So you agree she can't be trusted not to harm herself?"

"No. No. Stop that. That's not what I'm saying. You made her this way–"

Edevane holds her hands out. "There is a delicate balance between treatment and the need to keep our patients socialized and independent. We can't heal your wife by giving her foam cutlery and placing her in a padded cell. And I assure you, this is the first time this has ever happened."

"Charlotte," he says. "What did you do that for?" His face is broken. It's not an act. He's doubting my sanity. Rightly so.

"I don't know." Because if I tell the truth – that I have been subsumed by the woman that he and I created – then I truly belong here. I need him to drag me away without confessing it.

There is a frenetic energy to him now as he looks between me and Edevane. He presses his hands on the table, then places them in his lap.

"Mr Turner?" says Edevane, making her tone soft. "I want to see you reunited. But Charlotte is in no state. She knows this." Darius doesn't answer. The video skips. "This is our Special Therapies room. The swaddling you see is a widely accepted psychiatric pacification technique. We use it after someone has suffered an episode."

"Pacification? She had to be pacified?"

"Patients are bound in a cold pack which slows the circulation. Most find it soothing."

She speaks as the video, which is silent, shows me pushing out from the cold wrap and flopping onto the floor. I register the faint odor of rot as it plays. Darius is intent on the screen. Watching now, I do look deranged. The video doesn't portray what I so vividly remember – being evacuated through a spiraled organ of flesh. What Darius sees is a woman escaping from the cold pack, then digging at the drain in the floor, yelling at it, her naked body flexed and bristling with maniacal energy.

Darius's face drops. I can see his spirit melting. He squeezes my hand. "Charlotte?"

In every corner of his voice is a plea to have me confess that it was all an act. The video has convinced him that I am genuinely out of my mind. And I guess I am.

Darius clears his throat loudly and stands. "Let's go, Charlotte. We'll get you help somewhere else." I stand from the chair, only to have Edevane press me back into it.

"I'm sorry, Mr Turner, but she's not going anywhere."

"You don't seem to understand," he growls. "I will kick over that table and carry her home."

Edevane doesn't move. She's phlegmatic and cool-headed. "I don't want to add to your distress, but I insist that we retain custody. Due to some … recent events."

"Recent events?"

I look to Edevane. She *winks* at me and addresses Darius. "Yesterday, your wife committed an act of arson. Our Home Skills room is closed until we can remediate."

"Arson?" He flashes to me.

I don't remember any of it. "I…"

But then, *of course*. Charlotte moves inside me. She's been there, watching, listening. She pushes a memory up from the depths. I can tell by the feel of it, the taste, that it is hers, not mine.

Charlotte stands before the big worktable in Home Skills. Fabric patterns for a man, a woman, and two children are spread out, arranged so that the woman is featured at the center of the family.

The air is blue with smoke. A bite of searing pain shoots through her hand – my hand – and up her arm. Flinching, she drops a match, still burning, to the floor.

There is a blur of activity. Someone tackles her out of the room and, though she offers no resistance, pins her down hard upon a bench in the hallway. She has the patterns from the table. The orderly tries to pull them away, but Charlotte's grip is a vise. She rages when the papers tear.

Anise shoots down the hall, dragging a hose from a port on the wall, and douses the room.

It ends. They're all staring. My mind spins. I whisper, "Where did you get a match?"

"What's that?" asks Edevane.

"Nothing," I mumble. *I'm talking to Charlotte*, I think. But Charlotte stays quiet.

"What kind of hospital is this?" roars Darius. "First a knife, and... How did she get access to fire?"

"That, I'm still trying to figure out. Your wife is resourceful." She places her hands on the table, a gesture of nothing to hide, and sighs wearily. "As you can see, we have a situation. I would like to try and work with her here, rather than asking the police to intervene. They only set you back."

"Call the cops," answers Darius. "We'll take our chances. Let's go, Charlotte."

"The thing is," Edevane continues, "Mrs Turner can be held with or without your consent. Contingencies for criminal behavior and your acknowledgments of understanding are all in your folder." She slides it toward him. "Besides," she says, tapping the screen and rotating it, "I've already contacted the police." A feed shows a police cruiser sitting out front. "They've been briefed on the felony, but please go and reason with them. It's your right."

Darius's gaze is a blanket. "Charlotte." His eyes say that he is finished with the charade, but he's asking my permission to openly renounce it.

"I expect it would take a day or two for the paperwork to push its way through the courts, but we will get an order for Mrs Turner to be held indefinitely ... or until her psychosis abates. Then, of course, she'd face the arson charges." She pauses, letting it all sink in. "Or: you agree to sixty more days, and I tell the officers outside that we've resolved our differences."

Darius looks to me. His face is resolute. Every molecule in my body pulls to him. I wish to stand and leave. Disassemble the lie of our manufactured life and return to Pennsylvania, a thousand miles beyond the reach of this place.

But Charlotte has played a hand that forces mine. There is no fleeing. I'm left with only one option. To tell the truth.

The truth? I'd stop you.

You aren't real.

Don't say things you don't believe. You're just getting cold feet. You made all those promises to yourself and now you want to run away? We both belong here. The truth is you want to be here. I'm going to get better and Andrew is going to be so proud. And you're going to see what happens when the Earth speaks a name through the instrument of mortal flesh. Hadleigh did.

What do you mean?

There's no answer.

Hadleigh. Dead now two years. A funeral. Cremation. A dusting of ash scattered where blue herons parade through the reeds. She is an anchor in the pit of my stomach. She is the iron ache of guilt. A deficit of conscience that can never be fully paid. Something of Hadleigh remains in this place. Christmas, Gasper, Charlotte – they all say so. I can't leave without understanding. She is owed. By me.

The trip to Housework had been of a different character from my other hallucinations, possessed of a divulging, conspiratorial spirit. Something done for the purposes not of torment – though the images will be forever etched in my mind – but of revelation. I hadn't been harmed; I had been shown. It was an invitation to see, to stay and learn the truth.

Turning to Darius, I realize I've made a decision. "Andrew," I say, infusing my words with the person I am, hoping he will register the subtext. "As you can see from these videos, I have to stay. I have to know *the truth* … of my condition. In order to fix things. So that we can have what *we've always wanted.*"

Knowing him like I do, I read the contours of his face, the subtle tilt and tone. He holds my gaze, and in an exchange of looks an entire conversation unfolds: He shows me his fear; I project strength to reassure; He begs me to end the game, to sprint away; I explain that I may yet uncover the truth; He tells me that I am not safe here; I say that I will trigger the panic button in my clavicle if I feel in grave danger; He says he loves me; I love him back. There's no revelation in it – we both knew – but now it is voicelessly confessed.

Edevane wears a satisfied grin.

Darius clears his throat and swallows hard. "I don't care anymore about your condition, your psychosis or whatever they want to call it." Andrew is gone, but the tone of his voice is acceptance. "I want my wife back."

"And you will have her, Mr Turner," says the director, standing opposite. "In sixty days. When our work is finished, and without any pending criminal charges." She moves across the room, the weight of her presence so much larger than herself, like an invisible wave that pushes Darius and Enid into the hallway. She turns back. "Enid, why don't you go ahead and tell the officers that we have resolved our issue. Come, Charlotte. A round of goodbyes and then back to work."

Darius stands in the doorway, his eyes red and glassy. It takes everything I have not to crumble. But I have made my choice. I steel myself, stand and follow. Edevane moves into the hallway, and in the moment that we are separated, I reach down and steal Honora's locket from the raven.

TWENTY-TWO

In the minute of our final embrace, I know Darius's sorrow. He is an ocean. I know his anger. He is a pyre. He knows I am in danger. Not the vague hazards we'd talked about when hatching our plan – those that felt real enough to cause the type of fear born of not knowing. This is like being suspended above a dimensionless chasm.

I am part of Hollyhock because my past pointed me here. Even if I allowed Darius to drag me away, I would be pulled right back. Fate, well earned. I give him a last squeeze and watch as he recedes down the long hallway. I will him to set his eyes east and go there. To never come back, for the chasm would claim us both. I don't deserve him, anyway. That's a fact of nature.

And even if I did, it doesn't matter now. I am no longer me. I am a shell in which two forces vie to expel each other. Only, I don't know how to push Charlotte out. My eyes don't penetrate the places she swims. I suspect the opposite is true for her. When she finally comes for me, she knows where I am.

Enid pulls gently at the fabric on my shoulder as Darius reaches the double doors. She smiles when I jerk out of her grasp.

"I'll be down to see you soon, Charlotte," says Edevane. "I'm drawing up your treatment plan now."

Enid goes, I follow. A refrain of my first day. Some distance yet from our route into the north wing, she turns into a hallway on the left. It ends abruptly, a once-open passage now plastered over.

TWENTY-THREE

Growing longer and thinner, the woman is a wave of fabric, a ribbon beating on the wind. I have seen her face and do not recognize her. And yet, I know her. I have seen her in the face of every woman. Feet still planted in the hoarfrost, she is pulled and drawn long by her station. Slow at first, but then more rapidly the farther out she goes. Soon, her head and shoulders are distant, too high in the sky for me to discern. Even in the midst of – what is this, a fever dream, a hallucination? – I worry for her as she climbs toward the clouds, and I know this is no ascension, no rising to a better place, no actualization of self.

I see along the length of her, a life. Birth, a childhood, a time of learning and wonder, of limitless horizons. But the passage of time is a thief. The obligations set upon her by the circumstance of her birth foreclose opportunity as others graft their horizons upon her, buttressing themselves in her strength and steadfastness, stressing her ligaments, the sinews which hold her body together and her mind connected.

She is the strength of womanhood under duress, pulled by the world to its purposes. She is an unbroken circle; comforting, giving warmth, protecting, securing futures that aren't hers. But she forgets those dreams of childhood, aspirations both fanciful and practical, as the space in her mind is crowded out by the dreams of others, and at long last she forgets herself. It seems that she might stretch forever, but the limit is reached. Her feet leave the ground and, like the tail of a kite broken free, she flies away.

EXCERPT OF
"HOLLYHOCK RESEARCH"

Taken from Personal Computer belonging to Morgan
Bright aka Charlotte Turner
(Evidence Tag #N402, Shelf G4)

Category: Marketing/Public Statements, Press Release.

HOLLYHOCK HOUSE VOWS TO SET THE BAR ON ENLIGHTENED PSYCHIATRIC CARE

–Dawes County, Nebraska
"To move beyond the past, you must first occupy it," says Althea Edevane, the inaugural medical director of the newly refurbished *Hollyhock House*, a psychiatric hospital catering exclusively to women. "With the increasing diagnosis rate of domestic psychosis, offering places for women to be treated in a nurturing and respectful environment is vital. Thankfully, the recent passage of the Nebraska Family Protection Act provides a means for bureaucracy-free mental health care."

The building, formerly operated as the Nebraska State Lunatic Asylum before being renamed Hollyhock Psychiatric Hospital, will soon reopen under private management. The property, which has sat vacant for decades, was recently purchased from the state.

"As we launch into this new era of women's mental health treatment, our first commitment is not to repeat the awful

247

mistakes of the past," says Dr. Edevane. "Hollyhock House occupies considerable square footage across two wings. The hospital will operate out of the North Wing only and has been renovated into a first-rate, luxury treatment facility. The South Wing shall remain untouched, and we hope to reopen it to the public as a permanent exhibit. We have a unique opportunity to put the past on trial, to contrast the antiquated and cruel techniques of the old state asylums and Magdalene hospitals with genuine medical progress. There is a way to provide psychiatric care in a loving and respectful environment."

The doors to the future open on December 31st. New patient evaluations are underway and may be submitted through the web portal.

For all other inquiries, please contact hospital administration or visit our website at www. welcometohollyhock.com.

NEBRASKA STATE LUNATIC ASYLUM

"HOLLYHOCK"

SOUTH WING

PLAN OF THE HOSPITAL.

GROUND LEVEL

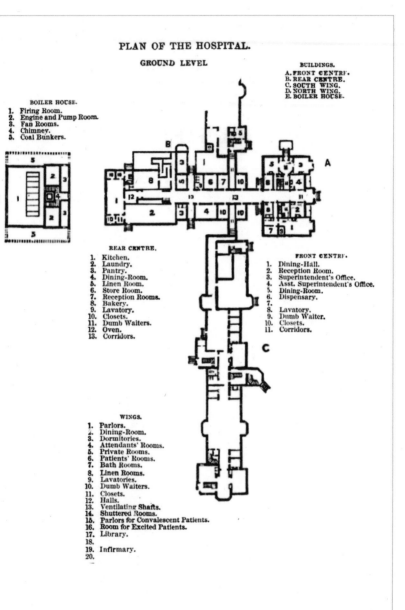

BUILDINGS.
A. FRONT CENTRE.
B. REAR CENTRE.
C. SOUTH WING.
D. NORTH WING.
E. BOILER HOUSE.

BOILER HOUSE.
1. Firing Room.
2. Engine and Pump Room.
3. Fan Rooms.
4. Chimney.
5. Coal Bunkers.

REAR CENTRE.
1. Kitchen.
2. Laundry.
3. Pantry.
4. Dining-Room.
5. Linen Room.
6. Store Room.
7. Reception Rooms.
8. Bakery.
9. Lavatory.
10. Closets.
11. Dumb Waiters.
12. Oven.
13. Corridors.

FRONT CENTRE.
1. Dining-Hall.
2. Reception Room.
3. Superintendent's Office.
4. Asst. Superintendent's Office.
5. Dining-Room.
6. Dispensary.
7.
8. Lavatory.
9. Dumb Waiter.
10. Closets.
11. Corridors.

WINGS.
1. Parlors.
2. Dining-Room.
3. Dormitories.
4. Attendants' Rooms.
5. Private Rooms.
6. Patients' Rooms.
7. Bath Rooms.
8. Linen Rooms.
9. Lavatories.
10. Dumb Waiters.
11. Closets.
12. Halls.
13. Ventilating Shafts.
14. Shuttered Rooms.
15. Parlors for Convalescent Patients.
16. Room for Excited Patients.
17. Library.
18.
19. Infirmary.
20.

TWENTY-FOUR

The faint outline of a door is the only blemish on the wall inside the short, dead-ended corridor. Enid removes her nametag and rubs it beside the gap. There's a click and the door eases open. She pulls it the rest of the way with her fingers and goes through. A set of steps descend below the plastered-over hallway and into a dimly lit old passage that crosses beneath the main building.

I reach the bottom and stop. "You're taking me to the South Wing. I thought the South Wing was closed."

She turns and shrugs, smiles puckishly.

The look says it all. They never closed it. Honora was right.

"I want to stay in the North Wing."

Enid barely acknowledges I've said anything, mutters "Come," and starts through the passage.

It is like walking through the buried skeleton of an ancient beast. The marrow is gone, but the hollow bones of this place *sing*, amplifying a frequency somewhere down in the soil. It is everywhere, tickling the hairs in my ears. My blood vibrates in response. Charlotte, though, is pacified. I can feel her nestled within the bedding of my consciousness, napping, dreaming a joyful dream. To be here is all she wanted. I know that now.

I smell the ancient soil where Hollyhock's foundations are rooted. It has the musk of something that once lived.

I imagine Hadleigh walking this same path two years prior,

not crazy, but driven to madness. Had harassment by apparitions led to cold packs and electroshock? Had she suffered the slow withering of her memories? Did she know who she was when the end came?

Will I?

I just want to know who I am when I die.

The floor of the passage is unfinished hardwood, with a centerline that shines from decades upon decades of feet. Outside of that well-traveled path, the floor is hazy with dust. Footprints meander to the sides in places. I wonder if any are hers.

Staring at the back of Enid's head, with its elaborately plaited braids and lively sprigs of clove, I think about what a good handle all that hair would make. I fantasize taking hold of it and using every ounce of my weight to crack her skull on the ground, then watching her face go confused and effortful as she died.

We go up a second set of steps and emerge into a new corridor streaming with winter sunshine. It offers a shocking contrast to the North Wing, which was defined by an aesthetic of holistic warmth you see in wellness advertisements: teal-blue walls, dark hardwoods, and incandescent lanterns presenting a welcoming, cozy environment. It could easily have been the health retreat that its new skin was made to suggest.

The South Wing makes no pretense. Its old bones ring with a clarity of purpose.

The construction is original, of this I have no doubt. Whether it is the walls undulating over plaster and lath beneath butter-yellow paint, the dark crown molding, or the brass hardware of knobs and hinges, it all wears a century and a half of patina. Simple. Strong. Reliable. A loyal servant to cold utility, meant to last forever.

Old hardwoods run down the hallway. Any varnish or lacquer has long rubbed away, with only tiny tracings of brittle amber pinched between the planks: narrow, historical crevices accumulated with dust and dirt, strands of hair, flecks of skin. Tears. Blood.

To our right are the same tall, wired-glass windows as in the North Wing. On the opposite wall are a series of heavy wooden doors in heavy wooden frames. Screwed into the center of each are corroded metal frames meant for placards. Most are empty. Some are not, with yellowed card stock identifying the room's purpose. Our route carries us past CALMING and HYDRO as well as others faded beyond legibility.

Enid nudges a gurney flush to the wall. "The South Wing houses fewer women," she says, as if answering a question. She glances back. I wear a placid expression. Maybe if I play the role better it will keep Charlotte at bay. Or maybe she'll disappear forever now that she's gotten what she wanted. I'm still spinning from the arson, the blunt cunning of it to ensure I couldn't leave. How did she get a match?

I found it.

Where?

On my desk.

One match? On the desk in my room?

My room, Morgan. Strike anywhere.

We arrive at a door. Enid unlocks it and we are met by a second, short hallway. The echo of women's voices bounces to us. "The community room is here," she says, leading me in as it opens from the hall. The talking stops.

The room is the size of a funeral parlor. Everything is packed together, dark and old. Ten or so women sit closely together at a round table, looking like a sedge of cranes. They stare expressionless, except for one that grins crocodile wide. I must know her because she clearly knows me.

The low ceiling presses down, hanging there almost, threatening to come loose and crush everyone inside. In the far wall is a cutaway to a small kitchen with a counter and tray return. Above the cutaway is a small clock with no hands. There's a rocking chair next to a standup mirror in the corner.

An orderly emerges from a door to a second hallway next to
the tiny kitchen. She is cube-shaped, neckless, and nearly fills
the doorway as she exits it. A human bear.

"Charlotte Turner," says Enid, "this is Mamie."

"Mrs Turner," says Mamie the bear, taking hold of my hands.
"Most of these ladies call me Aunt Mom – they seem to like
that one, so I figure just go with it, right? I'll be seeing to your
treatment here in the South Wing, along with Hettie." She
circles her thumbs over the backs of my hands. "Hettie's busy
right now." She releases my hands and swirls hers together.
"Anyway, lunch comes soon, so make yourself at home. I hear
you've gotten quite good with your needlework. Oh: and no
more fires, okay?" She scrapes her pointer fingers against each
other. *Tsk tsk.*

I must nod a vague agreement because Mamie continues on
as if I did.

"Good, good. There's a basket of yarn and all the fixings
over by Iva." She points with her forehead to a corner of the
room where a woman sits in an armchair, staring out a row
of thin windows just under the ceiling. They aren't wired, but
being so high up, they're no more than a triptych of frames for
the white sky.

Enid nods at Mamie and leaves.

"Lunch in ten, give or take," says Mamie, turning to follow
Enid.

I cross over to the staring woman. The floor is the same
trampled wood as in the hallway, covered in a patchwork of
area rugs that look donated. "Hello, Iva," I say, doing my best
to channel Charlotte's sanguinity. I hardly know why I keep
up the act, but I do. I guess because I'm here, and drawing less
attention to myself is my current strategy. "I'm Charlotte."

"Come sit."

There's a plastic chair nearby. I slide it over and sit it beside
the yarn basket next to Iva in her armchair. Iva looks strung
out. She's wide-eyed and jittery, a squirrel that ate uppers. Her

eyelashes are sparse and mangled, hanging like spider legs. Her hair, frizzy and unbrushed, is pulled up on top and secured by a simple band. It's bleached to the point of cooked, but also grown out, showing dark roots. She taps a fingernail on the fist of wood at the end of the chair's arm. I trace my eyes to where she's staring. "What are you looking at?"

"The outside. You should, too. Because when things are dark, you can remember it. I don't know why these other ladies use their community time gossiping."

"Gossiping can be a good way to make friends."

Iva doesn't react.

"When is Group?" I ask. "Housework?" I regret mentioning it as my mind flashes to the pantry.

Iva breaks from the window to look at me, brow furrowed, then back to the rectangles of white. "No Group. No Housework."

"Home Skills? Individual sessions?"

"We don't have those here. Just Calming."

"Calming?" There was the door in the hall with the same word written on a placard.

"You should look outside and remember it," says Iva, rubbing her red nose. "Take pictures and save them to look at later. Take as many as you can. Calming lasts forever."

Like Christmas, Iva seems possessed of some knowledge or understanding that eludes me. I'm weary of the vague affect that Hollyhock bastes upon its wards, making it impossible for them either to understand or articulate the goings-on.

I stand from the chair, fed up with this world comprised of shadowed corners. "Iva," I say. "What do you mean?"

The attention of the other women flutters toward us, then away.

Iva only stares. I place myself between her and the window. Her countenance remains stolid, as if she sees through me.

"Why?" I try again. "Why should I look outside the window and remember it? What is Calming?" I loosen a length of yarn from the ball, looping it over my thumb. "What happens here if there is no Group, no Housework, no Home Skills? What are we expected to do?"

"Just … enjoy the view."

An urge pours through me, and I lunge, pressing the lengths of yarn across Iva's neck. I lean forward, my hands sinking into the cushion of the armchair and canting it back on two legs. Her thin wrists shoot up against the red string, which makes it appear like her neck has already been slit.

"It's lunch," she says, finally looking away from the window and into my eyes. "Protein."

I check my hands, still clutching the yarn garrote.

Iva leaves her chair and walks to the far end of the room, where the others gather around a new orderly holding a tray of large plastic tumblers. I follow.

I'm last to take one. "What is it?" I ask of the curly-haired attendant whose nametag says HETTIE.

"Vitamin lunch," she answers, turning away with the empty tray.

It's a smoothie, thick and purple-red. I tug out the metal straw and touch the bottom of it to my tongue. It's creamy with a tart hint of fruit, nuts, banana, and some earthy flavors I can't place.

Standing at the center of the room, surrounded by women who sit and chat while enjoying their liquid lunches, I question existence. I marvel that life brought me here. Is it real?

I can't place.

SPD INTERVIEW RECORD
EXCERPT OF TRANSCRIPTION

WITNESS: How are things going, Detective, in your estimation?

GASTRELL: Sorry? What things do you mean, exactly?

WITNESS: This whole business with Hollyhock.

GASTRELL: Well, that's why I'm sitting here talking to you. To figure that out.

WITNESS: Ah.

GASTRELL: Are you all right? Wait: Charlotte?

WITNESS: That's right.

GASTRELL: Where's Morgan?

WITNESS: She'll be back.

GASTRELL: Are you playing with me right now? Sit down.

WITNESS: I apologize. What were you saying?

GASTRELL: Is Morgan okay?

WITNESS: Now that's a loaded question, isn't it?

GASTRELL: Tell me.

WITNESS: Yes, yes. She's fine. So? The investigation?

GASTRELL: We're trying to make sense of things. The more we learn, the more shocked I am you're here at all.

WITNESS: Why?

GASTRELL: Because I can't figure out how you escaped. The whole place was transformed.

WITNESS: Transformed?

GASTRELL: Yes. You know this. Here, these were just taken. We can't get any closer or the cameras malfunction.

257

WITNESS: What...? What am I looking at?

GASTRELL: Whatever became of Hollyhock.

WITNESS: Well, I don't even know how to look at this,
              Detective. Where is the sky? The ground?
              Am I holding it–

GASTRELL: Turn it like this.

WITNESS: What is that?

GASTRELL: We don't know. Nothing makes any sense.
              My eyes can't translate it. Those crystals.
              It reminds me of a picture I once saw of the
              inside of a glacier, except glaciers aren't
              that color, are they? It seems to change the
              longer I stare. More than anything, it... It
              makes me think of my father.

WITNESS: Was he an Arctic explorer?

GASTRELL: No. Nothing like that. It's the sadness of his
              death. I look at this and that's what it makes
              me feel. Don't you feel the sadness? Like it's
              coming through the paper ... a sense of loss,
              when you look at it?

WITNESS: To me it feels like a celebration.

GASTRELL: I don't know. Anyway, let me get that back.
              Yep. Thanks.

WITNESS: The Earth with her many teeth.

GASTRELL: What is going on with you?

WITNESS: Me? I'm feeling fine.

GASTRELL: Sure? You want to take a break? I need to
              get Dr. Bentham. I can grab some more food.
              Another burger?

WITNESS: I'm not feeling my appetite. You should tell
              whoever you ordered those burgers from
              that something must have gotten into the
              beef. It tasted like pennies.

GASTRELL: Now, hold on. I ordered three burgers and
              you ate two of them. I've never seen anyone

eat a cheeseburger as fast as you did. Now you say it tasted bad?

WITNESS: I can't say. Sometimes hunger trumps the palate. I wonder if we might find some raw oysters the next time around. Yes. Oysters, salmon and roast tomatoes would sit well with me. Something citrusy. Grapefruit? Are those in bloom this time of year?

GASTRELL: In bloom? I think we're probably limited to fast food here in the police department, but I'll try to change it up for the next meal.

WITNESS: When will that be? I'm pretty hungry.

GASTRELL: You just said you had no appetite.

WITNESS: No.

GASTRELL: Yes. You did.

WITNESS: Why would I say that? I'm starving.

GASTRELL: Morgan?

WITNESS: Yeah.

GASTRELL: Do you realize what just happened?

WITNESS: Hmm?

GASTRELL: What's the last thing we were talking about before food?

WITNESS: I don't... I don't remember.

GASTRELL: We were discussing these photos, Charlotte and I.

WITNESS: Maybe I zoned out.

GASTRELL: No, she'd put you away. Are you in danger? Can she hurt you?

WITNESS: I'm not going to hurt myself.

GASTRELL: But what about her? What can she do to you? I'm messaging Dr. Bentham. If she gives approval to continue the interview under her supervision, then fine. If she wants to take you for observation, which I'm sure she will, that will be her call.

WITNESS: And what if I walk out of here?

GASTRELL: Will you?

WITNESS: You'd be fucking nuts to think I'd consent to any psychiatric treatment after what I've been through. Maybe you need a doctor.

GASTRELL: I think I will when this is all over. I think we all will. I'm bringing in Dr. Bentham. She'll be present for the rest of our interview, however long that lasts.

TEXT RECORD, PHONE NUMBER
(814) ***-**58

Are you really doing this?
Are you really not coming?

> I told you, I can't get
> off work. I tried.

Can't get off work for your
sister's wedding? I still can't
believe it. It doesn't feel real.
Are you going to make me
ask the question?

> I'm clean.

This makes no sense.

> It is what it is.

It is what it is? Who talks
like that? I'd quit my job
to be at your wedding if
that was the only way I
could be there!

> I'd never ask you to
> quit your job.

You wouldn't have to!

Why do you act so surprised?
You're a better person than
I am. You always have been.

That's not true! Why do
you insist on acting like
this? What is going on?
You're making me feel
crazy. Who are you?

The same person I've
always been, Had. You
just haven't been
paying attention.

You are breaking my heart.

I'm sorry. I really am.
But this is me.

TWENTY-FIVE

There are eleven women in the South Wing. After the shake lunch, Hettie leads us into the kitchen and to a door in the corner. She throws it open, allowing in a rush of brittle air. The other women squeal and ruffle themselves like ducks shaking their feathers, but I don't move at all. It's the first fresh air I've tasted in a month, and I couldn't care less if my organs freeze and shatter.

We slide our stockinged feet into thick plastic galoshes and start off on a walk behind Hettie. She's big like Mamie, jocular, too. They could be twins if they didn't otherwise look so different. Mamie's hair, thick and dark brown, is long enough to be wrapped around her head at least twice. I imagine that taking it down, she looks like one of those women they find in anti-government communes, wearing pioneer dresses with hair past their waists, whereas Hettie has pounds of white-yellow curls that make the top of her head look like a colander of boiled cavatappi. Mamie's hands are huge and scarred. Hettie's round nose has been broken at least once.

A narrow sidewalk, shoveled of snow, traces the outline of the building. Some distance behind is the powerhouse. To this point, I've only seen it illustrated on the architectural plans. It's not much more interesting in person: a peeling white cube full of boilers and smokestacks, and that's about it. I consider the idea of trying to run, but I wouldn't get far in the inflexible boots, and even if I escaped, then what? End up like Hadleigh?

We round the corner at the back. Between it and the powerhouse is a small yard trimmed in chain-link fence. There's an old aluminum swing set in the middle. *A swing set.* The past plays in my mind, a scene as old as I can remember. The blue summer sky dotted with puffy clouds so perfect they look fake. The *tik-tik* of a sprinkler, the smell of cut grass. The terror of swinging too high. Fear, panic. The realization that I have lost my grip, the lift in my stomach, and the sensation of falling backward from the seat. The short delay between the sound of my arm snapping like a gunshot, and the flood of agony that fills my little body so fast I almost self-destruct. Then the guilt of having done something stupid, of making everybody worry. That was the beginning of everything.

Hettie tells the first two women in line to use the swings. They pace to where the path forks into the yard, flip the swings to rid them of snow, and sit. The next two women follow, assuming positions behind the first group, and begin to push. The scene is utterly surreal: mental patients lining up to push each other on a pair of swings like they're in nursery school.

Panning the surrounding fields, I try to make the topography match what I know of it from satellite images and maps I've studied. There's a swell of land out past the powerhouse toward the distant end of the South Wing, a gentle rise of the prairie that disappears into the horizon. You couldn't call it a hill. Clouds move behind it with all the contours of winter, from marbled white to imminent slate. Their patterns conjure a sense of déjà vu, and I am certain I have seen this spot of anonymous earth before. There is a patch of mud on the rise where the grass and snow have been worn away.

Hettie tells me it's my turn. I mumble that I'd rather not. She says that I have to get my exercise, and I want to ask what possible exercise is to be gained by being pushed on a swing by another grown woman. But fighting with her, I already sense, is pointless. I shuffle around to the front and sit stiffly in the chair. My hands and fingers squeeze the chains so hard that they might grow together. Iva sits beside me.

Hettie pushes us both. Sitting rigid as a block of wood, I hold my breath and shut my eyes and wait for it to be over. My shoulder aches in a way it hasn't in years. I haven't been on a swing since it all happened. By the end, my armpits are drenched with icy perspiration and my vision tunnels.

Afterward, we follow the sidewalk back into the kitchen, down a hallway past more closed doors, and into a large ward that mirrors the infirmary in the North Wing. Hettie stands in the center aisle between the two rows of beds as the women come to stand at the foot of each. Hettie directs me to an unoccupied bed.

She bends over and reaches down to touch her toes, grunting, and from here we are led through a series of awkward stretches and dances. It reminds me of old black and white footage from long extinct health retreats showing people on a lawn in grid formation, arms outstretched and swiveling robotically from side to side. I imagine giant rubber band machines are next, with Hettie seeing to it that we are shaken into shape.

The whole strange thing concludes with us twirling in place like paper doll dreidels. We are given a few minutes of rest. Most of the women lie on their beds and chat quietly enough that I can't hear them. I lay back on the thin mattress.

There are some twenty more beds, all empty, but dressed for occupation. At the end of the room is the bathroom, tiled in old yellow and lined with doorless toilet stalls. One of them sits in full view of the ward. Outside the bathroom is a stairwell. The door is closed and secured with a padlock. Next to that is the wooden frame of an ancient dumbwaiter boarded over with plywood.

Something slips from the large pocket on my right hip and settles into a divot on the bed. The locket. I'd forgotten I had it. I bring it to my chest and press a fingernail against the tiny clasp. The child inside is days or weeks old, with a swirl of black hair and blue eyes. Even at such a young age, she is her mother's daughter. Honora's daughter, *Isobel*. There is a simple nightstand beside the bed. I slide open the lone drawer and place the necklace beneath a stack of folded linens.

Hettie leads us back down the hall to the community room. I drift from the group and head toward the knitting, but the women continue through and out the door on the other side. Puzzled, I jump into the back of the line.

"Pardon me," I say, tapping the shoulder of a tall young woman in front of me. "Where are we going?"

She smiles. "You're the new girl, Charlotte."

"Yes, I–"

"I'm Decima. Nice to meet you. We're on our way to Calming."

"And what happens there?"

"Just remember that no matter what you see, you always return to the cabinet," she whispers back. "It's not real, but you won't know it at the time. You always return to the cabinet."

I must make a terrible face, because hers changes as well. Brow furrowed, she says, "Look outside, imagine a world. Use that to help you through. Until harmonization."

"I don't understand," I say.

"Well, you should."

Hettie reaches the door marked CALMING and unlocks it. The line funnels in. Her palm hits my chest. "Wait. Not you."

"Why not?"

"You haven't produced yet."

"Produced what?"

"Not until you've produced, Mrs Turner," cutting me off before I can protest. She points down the hall. "Back to the community room."

I go.

The community room is just me in the big armchair next to the basket of yarn. Mamie moves around in the kitchen. I sift through the yarn selection, balls and hanks and cakes in every color, eventually lifting a wad of deep teal and running it through my fingers. I can't fucking knit right now.

I get up and wander the room, searching the bookshelves and cabinets for something to keep me from dying of boredom. I burrow through stacks of crinkly old magazines, looking for crosswords that haven't already been completed, wondering all the while what "producing" means. Mamie floats in and out as she attends to her duties.

Eventually, I settle on a puzzle, pouring the worn-out pieces across the table. The box shows a forest with a blue light floating deep within. A will-o'-the-wisp. I organize the pieces, flipping them all the same way, setting the edge pieces to the side, as is standard, and then separating the rest by color. I lose myself in the process.

Hours later, I surface for air. The light through the windows is dusky purple. I push up in the chair, straightening my back to a crack of bones. Mamie's reflection appears in the stand-up mirror in the far corner by the rocking chair. I turn to the kitchen, where her top half is visible through the serving window. She lifts tumblers from a large stack, arranging them somewhere in front of her, then readies a row of blenders, whose open mouths peek over the bar top. She dumps a large scoop of ice into each one, then adds frozen berries and some type of milk, probably oat or cashew, then squeezes in dollops of thick syrup from a clear bottle, and methodically spoons in different colored powders with a metal ice cream scooper. She disappears to the back and returns with an armful of cans. She uses a machine to open them, then lifts the first can over the blender.

A glistening, bloody cylinder slides out. I see the pantry in Housework, the wrinkled skin of a strangely proportioned infant. She slices the gelatinized fruit with a butter knife and plops the sections into the blenders. The lids go down. I flinch when they roar to life.

Lining the tumblers on the bar top, she fills them from the blenders, caps each one and adds a straw. All but one go into the refrigerator. Mamie floats out from the kitchen and sets it on the table for me. "You've had a busy afternoon," she says, tilting her head to look at my progress. "I've got a little more shake back there if you finish. The advantage of being the only one in here."

"When are the others back?"

Her eyes flick to the hallway. "Not until late. You can turn in whenever you want, you know." She looks at the table. "That puzzle is missing a piece."

I slump in my chair and eye the smoothie. "What goes on in there?"

"In where?"

"In Calming."

"Name's right on the door." She turns for the kitchen. "Calming."

It is black outside when I finish the puzzle, all but the centermost piece – the glowing blue orb representing the will-o'-the-wisp itself. Not long after, Hettie comes in, followed by the other ten women. They process through the community room in single file, stopping only to take a smoothie from the tray.

I watch them for eye contact, but none give it.

TWENTY-SIX

Whatever goes on in Calming is a mystery, and so my mind mercilessly fills the void. It populates it with the vast parade of gruesome horrors that is the history of the asylum system in America, trying each one on to see if it might fit what is happening here. It could be anything going on behind those doors, so creative were the architects of experimental treatments foisted upon the institutionalized. In my time spent researching, one truth came to stand above all others, axiomatic in understanding these places: don't bother looking for smoke, because there's always fire. On the rare occasions when smoke escapes a place as buttoned down as Hollyhock, it means the fire is raging.

Prior to deciding to institutionalize myself, I devoured everything there was to know about Hollyhock's past. Most came from newspaper reports and some legislative records, or the occasional interview. There was a steady stream of rumor and myth about the abuses taking place within its walls, but little was ever investigated and even less was ever confirmed. Budgets were light and the public wasn't pushing the issue – there was nothing concrete for them to rally around. Nebraska State Lunatic Asylum operated in obscurity in a remote section of the state that no one would purposefully visit. It seemed intentional. The ideal way to keep any smoke from being seen.

It all came crashing down in the middle 1970s, when a woman named Tilda Branch showed up at the asylum's front door. Tilda had spent most of her adult life searching for her twin daughters, having gotten pregnant as a teenager and given them up for adoption since termination wasn't an option. With no means of support, it had been the right decision at the time, especially as the girls' father had quickly fled. But it had always haunted her. She loved them from afar, and swore to herself that she'd find them when she was able to get on her feet. They might never forgive her, they might hate her, but at least they wouldn't be in the dark any longer. They'd know who their mother was and why she'd done what she did. If they didn't want anything to do with her after that, well, she was ready to accept it.

As Tilda got older, got a job, went to school, she set forth on a tedious journey through a labyrinth of bureaucracy and red tape that led her from one adoption agency to the next. She learned that the girls had been given up, not just once by her, not twice by their adoptive parents, but at least twice more. In and out of foster care. She followed a trail across the country from where they'd been born in Virginia, to a small, broken-down settlement in north-eastern Colorado called Crook.

There, in a tiny ramshackle house, she'd met Jinnie and Russell Lawson, a couple in their sixties living on government support. Yes, they said, they had adopted Stacy and Gail, which were not the names Tilda had given them: Eleanor and Olive.

The Lawsons openly admitted to going after the girls for the state support checks and tax credits, but even those windfalls hadn't been enough for them to continue as their parents. The girls had "mental problems", said the Lawsons, and handed Tilda a file from a place one state over called Hollyhock Psychiatric Hospital.

Within days Tilda was there. They refused her entry. Undeterred, she returned with a police officer, a young lieutenant who'd been drawn in by her story. When they dodged his questions and then tried to keep him from going in, he commandeered a nurse and demanded to be taken to wherever they were keeping Stacy and Gail Lawson.

Tilda later described following the officer and the nurse through a "yellow maze" that led to a dim, yellow room with a large piece of furniture sitting in the middle.

The Utica Crib was invented in the 1800s by the first director of Utica State Hospital in New York, Amariah Brigham. This "immobility device" was an adult-sized crib with a heavy, slatted lid designed to sandwich the patient inside, preventing them from sitting or rolling to their side. Patients were commonly kept inside for days or weeks. After a series of deaths, a vocal group of doctors at Utica protested the crib's use, resulting in its removal after only three years. The extent of its implementation at other mental institutions was never reliably catalogued.

But Hollyhock had one.

Eleanor and Olive, aged twenty-two and a half, were shut inside it together, where they had been for three years. Tilda never spoke again, all the way until she committed suicide two months after seeing them. The photographs explain why.

The sisters' bodies had melded to the slats inside the crib, as well as to each other. Infection and necrosis had set in where wood and flesh grew together. In some places the skin had blackened and died; elsewhere it had grown around, subsuming the architecture. They were still living, but incoherent, unable to communicate through chapped lips caked in the infant formula that had kept them alive. Medical specialists tried to extract them. Both died in the process, their bodies collapsing like tents over brittle bones, their organs having the consistency of meat pulled from a slow cooker.

I thought that the photo of the women in the crib was the worst thing I'd ever seen until I found the closeups of the wooden slats taken from inside it, where Eleanor and Olive had clawed deep gouges with their fingernails. That, more than anything else, brought their suffering alive. I felt their panic, their struggle, their desolation, and finally, the death of their hope.

Though the discovery of Tilda Branch's daughters led to the asylum's closing, the account felt to me like the tip of the iceberg, with the full extent of human depravation hidden beneath the surface, behind the walls. Walls that now stood open again for business, walls that had so recently claimed my own sister. Is there a room full of Utica Cribs behind the door marked "Calming?" Did Hadleigh go there? Will I?

EXCERPT OF
"HOLLYHOCK RESEARCH"

Taken from Personal Computer belonging to Morgan
Bright aka Charlotte Turner
(Evidence Tag #N402, Shelf G4)

Category: Historical research, treatment devices/techniques.

The Utica Crib

TWENTY-SEVEN

It has always bewitched me how snow produces its own light. I'm sure there's an explanation that makes scientific sense. Something about city lights bouncing between ground and cloud to reach the rural places where the lights of civilization don't normally venture. Diffusion of photons through crystals. Whatever. It's one of those things that I'd rather not fully understand.

A cool glow illuminates the windows, even though I can't see the moon. The other ten women are silent, having made their way into the ward from Calming and gone straight to sleep, as they do every night. Peace eludes me even though I am plenty tired, worn from the stress of not knowing – or, more accurately, not learning. Nothing happens in the South Wing. There is no therapy. No "getting to work" that Edevane had played so keen on doing. There's exercise, eating, the Calming Room for everyone but me, and time spent lingering. I have more questions now than when I first arrived.

My shoulder aches. Which always makes me think of Hadleigh. I can't help but see her when the pain comes. Falling from the swing was the moment our trajectories diverged; when mine lost its momentum and Hadleigh's continued skyward.

I went from being an active, rambunctious kid, to a fearful, shy one. It hurt too much to go out and play with the other kids. Even running made my arm and shoulder flare up. I folded inward, lost my confidence. No one believed the pain was as bad as I said, because I kept complaining about it long after the break was technically healed. I mean, now we know it was "chronic fracture pain" and then the osteoarthritis. Hadleigh never said so, but I think she thought I just needed to get over it. And she seemed to believe that if she could coax me out of my shell, I'd realize I wasn't suffering as badly as I thought I was.

It must have been summer, maybe three or four years after the accident. We were in our front yard. The grass had just been cut. There was that smell. Hadleigh decided she was going to teach me to do a cartwheel. She knew I loved watching her do them but was too afraid to attempt anything that put weight on the bad arm if even for just a moment. I refused, but Hadleigh was relentless, like if she could get me to do this one thing, everything would be okay from then on out.

Eventually I agreed to try – I wanted to make her proud. She showed me every step of the move, even taking hold of my legs to support me as I repped it in slow motion. I gained confidence with each roll, even as my arm and shoulder flashed warnings.

Hadleigh built me up bit by bit, and soon my child's mind was convinced that this cartwheel was the most important thing in the world – the solution to everything. If I was successful, I would be reset, the pain would be defeated. I would be myself again.

I gathered all my belief, my faith, summoned that ebullient and unsoiled childhood passion that you harness with your entire being to make it snow or to be able to fly, and when Hadleigh gave the signal, I ran. I ran across that grass like I was possessed, ignoring the clatter of my bones, the radiating cry of electric nerves. Springing forward from my toes, I rolled and planted my good arm. Coming around, I was light and limber, a whip of greenwood snapping into position.

My left arm stuck the ground and collapsed like a tower of popsicle sticks. I crumbled, head pinned to the side, spine twisted. Joints aflame.

Hadleigh huddled over me as I sobbed, defeated, convinced there was nothing that would ever fix me. I think Hadleigh realized it then, too. After that, she stopped trying.

The next morning, we follow Hettie and Mamie out to the swing set. I gaze into the distance, at the rise with the spot of mud there in the snow. Hettie asks me if I want a turn on the swing but I don't respond. She doesn't force it. We go back inside.

At lunchtime, Enid appears in the doorway to the community room with Honora. My heart inflates at the sight of her; a friendly face, even though I suppose I should mourn her presence. After meeting Mamie, she comes straight to where I sit at one of the round tables by myself. I leap up and squeeze her big shoulders. Her embrace is a little placating, which is good enough for me. Coming from Honora, it seems a considerable show of emotion. She's warm and real. Nothing has changed about our circumstances, but just seeing her is enough to give oxygen to my flickering hope.

"Didn't guess on you beating me here, but you did," she says, breaking free. She eyes my tumbler. "What's in there?"

I pick it up and give it a wiggle. "North Wingers."

"Oh goodie."

"Liquified."

"Hm-mm, for the digestion," she answers.

"What happened to you?" I ask.

"Told you when we first met I was a lost cause."

I wasn't there when we'd first met. "For how long did they send you here? I got sixty more days."

Honora slides my tumbler to her chest. Pinching the metal straw between her teeth, she takes a pull. "Those ladies taste good. Maybe there's a little bit of Rhoda in there."

"No, Rhoda's in here." I point.

Honora leans to the side and locates her at another table, then makes a noise that sounds like she's spotted a target.

We sit quietly. I am bolstered by the presence of this woman I barely know. It's not even companionship, really, though every time our paths cross, I feel more tied to her. It's strange. Different from the way friendships usually grow. It's an intersection of paths, or better: a pair of strings that come from distant corners and meet, then twist together, bound by chance or opportunity or fate. I feel like I need her more than she needs me.

Mamie assembles everyone for Calming. I stop Honora when she begins to stand, explaining quietly that this activity – whatever it is – isn't meant for us. We have to "produce", and that no one will explain to me what it means. Honora settles back into her chair, expressing no further curiosity. I suppose you reach a point where you accept that trying to figure it all out is wasted energy.

We spend the afternoon working puzzles. Most of them are old and missing pieces. It frustrates me, but Honora doesn't care. She's found a pair of the ubiquitous headphones and smiles blithely while sorting pieces. I try listening, but the pairs I select are all off or don't work. After dark, the women come through in single file and receive their smoothies from Mamie. All but Iva. Mamie motions to Honora and me, who follow. I ask Mamie about Iva. She says that Iva is speaking the words of the Earth. Honora nods at this like it was exactly what she'd expected to hear. I say nothing.

The women crawl into their beds, with Honora taking the vacant one across the aisle from me. The lights go out.

TWENTY-EIGHT

I sit up in bed sometime before dawn, having stitched together small patches of sleep. Honora's breaths are steady. I pivot to the bathroom and the lone toilet.

I go inside and sip from the sink, then wander quietly out of the ward and into the community room. The lamp beside the standing mirror is on. I haven't seen any sign of Gasper since the North Wing. I stand between the tables, waiting. I want to be as inviting as I can, a willing listener, should he wish to reveal himself. The scene is static, the lamp's light steady, unmarred by drifting ash. Maybe ghosts are limited by geography.

I sit in the rocking chair beside the mirror and wait. It's then I realize that's exactly what I'm doing. Waiting for something. Maybe he will come. What a strange feeling to anticipate an arrival without being party to arranging it. The rest of the room is dark, the corners veiled in shadow, the kitchen behind the serving counter a black rectangle. I'm restless. I trace imaginary lines between the lights in the ceiling, waiting for one to flicker on and signal the start of a new happening. But the shadows stay home, and the lights remain off. No cascade of sand streams through the walls, nor does an ethereal glow draw lines across the ceiling. I feel attuned to this place, in a way, no longer fearful of its parlor tricks. The next time it tries, I will laugh.

Paper crinkles behind me.

I twist around. The books, puzzles, magazines and games are neatly stowed. The basket of headphones is heavy and still.

I turn to the mirror and rock forward in the chair, leaning inch by inch until the side of my head appears. My hair, an ear. Charlotte's smiling face.

I spring away, jabbing my back into the edge of a table. Charlotte stares out from the mirror, her grin dimming to a flat line.

"What do you want?" I croak.

She straightens her dress, which crackles. It is covered in a patchwork of sewing patterns bound to her clothing by yellow-topped straight pins. Tiny arrows shot into spots of red, targets made of blood. Her hair is down, and she wears a pair of big, aqua green headphones over her ears. I realize they're the same color as Edevane's eyes, and if I let mine blur, Charlotte resembles the Director if she was an insect.

Easing against the back of the chair, she rocks and begins looping yarn. "Join me."

I'd rather smash the mirror.

"No more destruction of property, Morgan. You've done enough damage."

My legs walk me back to the rocking chair and I fall into it. Thrown, almost.

I stare at this person who is me-yet-not-me, moving my face closer to the glass until I feel the heat of her. "Why are you torturing me?"

"Because I'm not strong enough yet to erase you."

I scoff.

"I will be soon, though," she says, pulling a knot. "Things would be so much easier for me and Andrew if you saw eye to eye with us."

"There is no Andrew. There is no you."

"So, get up then, Morgan. Walk away."

I can't.

"It's what you wanted, isn't it?" she says. "Hadleigh is just a story you tell yourself to justify whatever this is … your clumsy suicide."

"I–"

"*I'm* talking." She shoots a glance, then goes back to knitting. "You never thought you'd find out what happened to Hadleigh by coming here. You saw it as an act of repentance, something that a nobler person than yourself would do. And if death came as well, then fine. You'd set the ledger straight – but only if a force outside yourself made it so. Because you're a coward. Couldn't be bothered to do the honorable thing: stick a gun in your mouth or open your arteries." She pauses as my mind boils to respond, to say something to push back on allegations that if left to hang will become true.

"There's nothing I'm telling you that needs to *become true*. It already is true," she says, "so stop your denial. I've spent more time swimming the currents of your subconscious than you have. You're not a great person, Morgan."

She flips another loop and tightens the cast. "What are they always preaching to us here? Hollyhock is a place of renewal. Rebirth. It was because of your weaknesses, your destructive nature, that Hadleigh was set on the path which killed her. But light was born of it – life, Morgan: *me*. See, you're the larva, Hollyhock is the chrysalis, and I am the hairstreak who will hatch. How clean. How simple. Poetic. Natural. There could never have been me without you. You've played your part. And so, in a way, you've made it all okay."

She starts humming, and soon it becomes a song.

"*I left my baby lying there, lying there, lying there,*
I left my baby lying there, to go and gather blaeberries.
Ho-van, ho-van gorry o go, gorry o go, gorry o go;
Ho-van, ho-van gorry o go, I've lost my dearest baby-o
I saw the little yellow fawn but never saw my baby.
I traced the otter on the lake but could not trace my baby.
Ho-van, ho-van gorry o go, gorry o go, gorry o go;
Ho-van, ho-van gorry o go, I never found my baby-o."

I know the song. I've always hated it. Our aunt – our

mother's sister – sang it to us whenever she came to visit. Who would sing such a thing to children?

"Well," says Charlotte, breaking off mid-verse, "you just don't understand it."

I stare at the mirror, bewildered over the unimaginable circumstance of conversing with an exact copy of myself. "The song is about a child's death."

"No!" she snaps. "It is about a *mother's love*." Her lips shake as she lingers on the last word, teeth subtly bared. "But you wouldn't know anything about that."

"Neither would you," I say. "You're not real. I made you up. Go away. You served your purpose. Leave me alone to do what I came to do."

Charlotte pouts her mouth mockingly, but it turns real. "My mind is healing every day, *Morgan*. I'm taking the steps." She resets her face to relieve the knot of frustration I seem to have caused. "You put the patterns in the wrong drawers. Tried to hide them from me, tried to take my family away. But I found them."

"Why are you even here?"

"Why am *I* here?" she asks. "You brought me!"

"No, I didn't."

"You would spurn the gifts of the Earth."

"You're insane."

"Insanity is the inability to distinguish fantasy from reality, Morgan. Only one of us suffers from that. I see the world."

"You're an idea living in a mirror. *This* is the real world." I slap the arms of the rocking chair. "Why am I arguing with you? You don't exist. If you were in control, you'd be on this side of the glass."

Charlotte raises her eyebrows. "Soon."

"I'm leaving."

"You don't even know what you came in here for, do you?"

"Couldn't sleep."

"Lie. You came here to wait for me, Morgan." She smiles, but it warps. Her face twists and gurns, stretches like a funhouse mirror. "You came to me because I sssssssummoned you." She removes a fabric pin from the dress pattern at her shoulder and adjusts the paper. "See, I've been doing the steps into the sky. I'll be reunited with Mr Turner," she says, stabbing the pin through the pattern and into her flesh, "and we will have a family."

"There is no Mr Turner! He's made up, just like you!"

"Your lies can't infect me." She dabs a droplet of blood from her arm and scrubs it across her teeth.

"You should find a mirror that works and look at yourself." I push up to leave. Only I can't. My hands won't move from the arms of the chair. It continues rocking even as I lift my feet from the ground. "Stop it. Stop it now, Charlotte."

She stares out of the mirror with a red sneer. *"The sickening mind is a master of deception."*

I wrench my arm free and fight to stand. Charlotte chuckles, the tone of it just contemptuous enough so that it's clear she's allowed it.

"Don't you want to know why I wanted to chat?" she says.

I don't answer.

"Despite our difficulties, I feel a connection between us. Together we're touching the sublime. We are almost ready, Morgan. We have made our spirit bed, and it is lush. It nourishes."

"What the hell is wrong with you?"

She shakes her head somberly. "It's all there in the recordings, Morgan." She gathers her knitting and holds it up. "What do you think?" she says, pulling the garment taut: an infant's onesie.

A rush of energy pours through my body and I break free of her. I lift the rocking chair and smash it through the mirror. Glass sprays the wall and floor. Mamie bursts in, wearing her billowing nightshirt. I swivel to face her.

"Drop it, Charlotte," she says, flipping on the lights. "Drop it!"

"This isn't for you, Aunt Mom," I say – only it's Charlotte speaking. In my hand is a shard from the mirror. I try letting go, but Charlotte's grip is stronger. She draws it toward my chest.

Mamie edges closer. "You stop that right now, Charlotte! You hear me?"

I use everything I have to push back on Charlotte. Would she really kill me?

Mamie makes a move to come closer, but my other hand wields a second icicle of glass. "Stay there, Aunt Mom. I'm just doing some self-reflection," says Charlotte. "Wait and see."

The first shard reaches my chest. The delicate tip disappears into the skin. Deliberate, slow. And I realize this is not a mortal assault, but a procedure. Charlotte draws the edge just below my clavicle, then drops it, and using a finger, applies pressure to the opening. Paralyzed, I watch as my last line of defense squeezes out and falls to the floor. Charlotte dissolves away.

I lunge to the blood-spotted ground and scramble for the implant.

Mamie gets there first.

TEXT RECORD, PHONE NUMBER

(814) ***-**58

Called you. No answer.
Are you using again?
Don't lie to me.

TWENTY-NINE

Doctor Edevane rolls the transmitter between her fingers. "You were communicating with someone."

Sitting on the bed, I say nothing. There is no safe explanation. I suddenly feel sick.

"What happens if I press this little node, here? Who comes to Hollyhock, Charlotte? Is it your husband? I thought he was a tool salesman, not a spy. Are you a spy, Charlotte?"

A splash of bile licks the back of my throat. She knows. Maybe not everything, but enough. At the same time, there's a trickle of relief. She'll call the authorities. Have me turned in. I won't be here anymore.

"What possessed you to smash the mirror in the community room? Aunt Mom had to clean that up and now I've got to order a new one." She pauses for me to answer. I don't. "Your antics are going to make it difficult to keep your second commitment to a mere sixty days, Charlotte. You've regressed. Are you no longer taking the steps?"

My stomach gurgles loudly.

At this, her eyes fill with puckish light. She tilts her head. "Do you not feel well?"

"Strange question to ask of someone in this place."

"You don't sound like yourself, Charlotte." She points vaguely to my middle. "An upset stomach?"

"It's always upset."

She stands from the mattress. "You should pay attention to your body. It speaks to the Earth."

"That's stupid." Fuck her.

"Is it?" she asks.

I stare off. She keeps talking.

"I don't know… Body and Earth commune with each other because they are each other. The experience of your life is a tiny interlude across billions of years where the Earth divides herself into physical bodies which are separate. When you die, you will be part of her again, and your spirit will become her breath. Ask yourself why she would allow you to break free to wander for mere decades upon her skin? She speaks the answers through your body every second of every day. I'd suggest you give her a listen. Sometimes she's not saying what you think she's saying. The other women understand this, why don't you?"

"Because I don't want to be part of your cult."

"Oh, Charlotte." She makes a tutting noise. "Cults don't keep their promises."

I roll my eyes.

She breathes an exhalation and wraps her shawl in toward her neck. "It doesn't matter to me that you are a spy, Charlotte, or whoever you are. I made a commitment to you, and Hollyhock will follow through. You will become yourself and you will rejoice in it, believe me." She examines the panic button between her fingers. "You risked a lot bringing this device into my hospital. I shouldn't admit this, but I admire you for it. I'm a risk-taker, too." She pinches the transmitter until it clicks, then tosses it onto my bed as I behold it in complete shock. "Let's roll the dice."

She leaves me then, alone with the panic button engaged. I sit there forever, my mind thumping in a fog. Why was she unaffected by the fact that I am not who I said I was? I should be dragged out of here, hustled to the front entrance and handed over to the authorities. Why doesn't she care that I've deceived her?

I touch the tiny bandage over the wound Charlotte carved in my chest.

Wherever Darius is, I pray the signal doesn't reach him.

TEXT RECORD, PHONE NUMBER
(814) ***-**58

Hey.

What's going on with you?

What do you mean?

I feel like I'm in an alternate
reality or something. Are you
clean?

Yes. Stop asking me.

Everyone is acting strange.

Everyone?

Well, Clayden is being weird.
Distant.

He's probably just
adjusting to married life.

By being quiet and acting
depressed all the time?

I don't really know him
well enough to say, Hads.

Then what about you?

What about me?

Honestly, you tell me, Morgan.
You don't call me. You hardly
text. It's like everything
changed with the wedding.

I'm just letting you live
your life. Giving you your
space. Is that a problem?

See, my real sister would never
care about giving me my space.
You've always been in my
business. Me being married
wouldn't change that. I miss
it. Where did you go?

I'm right here. Sitting
on the couch with DDB.
I'll try to be in your
business more.

This is all bullshit. It's like
you're gaslighting me.
Something is up. Don't tell
me I'm imagining it.

I think you need to get
a grip.

Why are you being like this!?!

THIRTY

The door to the ward creaks open, waking me. I twist my head slowly around, cracking an eye. A shadow looms in the entry enclave. I stare, waiting for it to move or disappear, another apparition in a place where I have come to expect them.

It moves in from the entry and the snow light betrays no apparition at all, but Mamie. She seems to float, steady and full of inertia, a refrigerator on wheels. She settles at Rhoda's bedside and rouses her. Rhoda gets upright and follows Mamie out.

THIRTY-ONE

Honora and I sit with a pile of puzzles at one table while the other women huddle at another in their white scrum. In the wake of the mirror incident, they whisper and glare.

"Just tell them you got a good look at yourself," says Honora. "And that you no longer wanted the torture of it. They'll understand."

I force a chuckle, but my stomach cramps. It's been cramping since my confrontation with Charlotte. I want to confide in Honora, otherwise I am entirely alone. I know she can't help me, but the solitude is a bottomless well. Acid gurgles audibly at the base of my esophagus; the well of me.

"They took Rhoda last night," I say.

"Oh?"

"*Yeah*." I glare at her, annoyed by her lackadaisical response. "They took her somewhere. Just like they did Iva."

"Hm-mm."

"*Hm-mm?* What's the matter with you? Doesn't that worry you? We're here, too. When are they going to take us? Where?"

Honora pulls the headphones up from around her neck and holds one open over her ear. "You really should listen to the recordings. They're stranger than a box of weasels, but also kind of soothing. There's a message wedged in amid the gibberish."

I don't tell her that ever since I experimented with the headphones the first time in Housework, I can't hear anything when I put them on. The voice inside always fades away like the volume is being turned down. "Does it say where they took Rhoda and Iva?"

The last words garble as my mouth fills. I try to swallow it back down, but my stomach heaves. Vomit spurts through my fingers across the table.

"Charlotte!" Honora hunches over me, rubbing my back.

The other women twist their heads like a clutch of barn owls.

"I'm fine," I grunt, waving my hand to dissipate their attention. Mamie rushes over.

A thick layer of phlegm coats my throat. I try clearing it, forcing air up my windpipe until it sounds like a jet engine. It only fills more. My airway spasms. "Something caught..." I gasp. I'm going to suffocate. I try to force a cough, only now there's nowhere for the air to go, blocked by the thing lodged in the base of my throat. I've been on a liquid diet. There hasn't been anything solid inside my stomach for days and days. Did I swallow something in my fugue wanderings? A wad of paper towels? A tampon?

Did you do this?

You did, answers Charlotte.

Honora pounds on my back. Mamie pulls her away. "She's fine. She's fine! It means it's finally begun."

"*Begun*," says Honora in a hushed tone. Her expression goes flat.

"Begun!" cries Decima. The others echo her.

I plead silently for help as they watch, greedy with anticipation. No air goes in or out. All I can think is how choking to death is the worst way to die, because you know it's coming and you're forced to watch yourself leave the world. My abdomen clenches. I lurch over the table.

My diaphragm convulses to expel the blockage. Mucus rappels from my mouth. I am a cat bringing up a hairball. A bird vomiting the contents of its stomach into the mouths of her young. A serpent regurgitating a pellet of undigested fur and claws. The others begin speaking in sync. A whispered chant. I gape as Honora joins in. The object climbs my esophagus. I stiffen. It crawls over my vocal cords, mashing my tonsils with its girth, and edges onto my tongue.

What emerges from my mouth is accompanied by the putrid smell of old infection. The weight of it passes over my teeth and lips, but remains anchored to the back of my throat by tensioned ribbons of yellow-green phlegm. I cough and gag. It hangs there, stubborn, until I take hold and rip it away, snapping the strands.

I recoil from the table with a rasping shriek. The others step onto the chairs around it, cooing almost, reciting their invocations. I don't hear what they say, don't care, too distracted by the thing that has come out of me.

Mamie steps cautiously from among the other women and regards the fleshy node. She smiles wide, lips quivering with reverent energy, as she peels away the custard-soft yellow coating. Its acrid stink abrades my sinuses and I dry heave.

Revealed inside is a half-moon dumpling of folds in pink and gray. Part oyster, part genitalia, entirely neither. I cry out, begging to know what it is and why it has come out of me. My voice is husky and raw, full of accusation, as if Mamie herself had placed the thing inside me. Had she?

"Charlotte." Her eyes gleam. "You've produced." She squeezes my arm as I am paralyzed by disgust. "And..." She slides a finger into the organelle's slick folds and presses it open. Looking first to me and then to the others, she cries out, "The spirit bed is fecund!"

The women's teeth shine. They clap and twirl. Honora levitates to her tiptoes and joins them.

Mamie holds it open like petals on a tulip. Nestled in the peach-pink center is a sky-blue pearl.

All I know is that this is a thing that should not be. It is a repulsive amalgam of flesh; an aberration, an abomination. It is not of me, it is not of nature. My face goes hot. I leap onto the table and swat it to the floor. I dive after it, to seek and destroy, to smash it like a slug.

Hands seize my ankles and pull me away. Mamie pounces onto the ground, her ursine bulk thundering through the underbrush of tables and chairs, until she finds the gem and gathers it into her paws.

Lightheaded, I pull myself up and stagger out, shouldering the wall for support, then make my way through the ward and to the bathroom, where I ply my hands with soap and drive my fingers into my throat.

SPD INTERVIEW RECORD
EXCERPT OF TRANSCRIPTION

GASTRELL: She's gagging.
BENTHAM: Turn her over, turn her over.

THIRTY-TWO

Sitting in the corner of the ward, from where I have not moved in a day, my body disappears. I see the hands and the fingers, the calves and ankles lurking beneath the painted white stockings, but they are someone else's. So long as I don't move, I won't have to acknowledge this living corpse or the thing it delivered up.

Though I give out no warmth, I am no longer shunned. My fellow patients smile and blush. They emanate the giddy energy of those who know what's coming but don't want to spoil the surprise. One of them, a skeleton called Beryl, leans down to congratulate me. "Today," she says, "you will go to Calming." I give her nothing. She reminds me to think of something other than darkness. Though I spurn her, the intrusion vaporizes my meditation, calling my mind back into my body. I roll my lips to show her my teeth. Unfazed, she holds up a finger and notes that everyone's experience in Calming is different, and that nothing she could tell me would help me understand.

Charlotte remains silent.

In the community room, I try speaking with Honora, but I cannot reach her. She acknowledges me, wishes me a good morning punctuated by an unwelcome quotation from the bizarre teachings of Edevane. I sidestep it all, try to engage, but she wears a skin of blithe satisfaction that deflects my attempts. After lunch, which I don't drink, Mamie leads everyone but Honora down the corridor to the door marked CALMING. She turns the lock and pulls it open, painting a stripe of daylight across the darkened interior. I'm ready to see a line of Utica Cribs, their lids open wide to swallow us.

There are no cribs, but the room is full of fossils, pieces of Hollyhock that time doesn't touch. Rows of hulking wooden chairs stand like druids called to ritual. The thick wood is worn smooth from use and blackened by the oils of the many bodies they've cradled. Iron-clad boxes hang upon hinges from the chairbacks like hooded cloaks. Not Utica Cribs, but I know what they are: serenity cabinets. Relics of the cruelest heyday of the old state asylums, designed to deprive their captives of their mobility and their senses, to smother their protestations until docility returned.

The walls and ceilings are torn open, exposing ancient framing and crooked piping. Lath and plaster lay in piles along the baseboards, evidence of more recent demolition.

Everyone sets eagerly across the floor, climbing into the chairs and strapping themselves in. Mamie props open the door – there is no other light – and comes inside to assist. I don't move. She kneels to tighten the restraint of a woman seated nearby, glancing up to me as she works. "Find a cabinet, Charlotte. When I'm done with Gretchen, I'll help you in."

"No."

"Remember the words of the recordings, Charlotte."

"I don't listen to them."

She tilts her head and smiles incredulously. "You listen more than anyone here, darling. Most nights I have to pull them off of you." I turn to leave. Her hand is a vise on my arm. Foul breath seethes through her teeth, mixing with whatever oils she's bathed herself in. She pushes me to the back of the room and thrusts me into an empty cabinet. She quashes my squirming and easily secures my limbs. "We are the machines of life, Mrs Turner. Your spirit bed is fecund, and you have produced. Stop being so spoiled! I wish I was in your place."

The hinge squeaks as she brings the box up and over the back of the chair. I begin to hyperventilate. The hood covers my head and chest, then comes to rest on the arms of the chair. Small, half-moon cutouts allow for my wrists. I watch her feet as she walks away. The other women whisper cheery "Thank you, Aunt Moms" as they don their cowls. The door closes and it is the blackest place there is.

The others don't respond when I call out to them. I screech and grunt, struggle to free myself. Time stretches. I wait for Charlotte, but she doesn't show. This is what she wants. This was the step she'd been looking forward to when she torched Home Skills and secured my second commitment. I go quiet. The silence in the room is as perfect as the dark. Beyond the sensation of the chair beneath me, there is nothing to tell me that I exist. And now I wonder if this is the point.

The pouring of sand begins. It climbs and roars like it's being emptied from a truck. And I feel it, some torrent of emotion washing over me. Loss, despair, sorrow, solitude, confusion, rage. I am recipient to the feelings of others without seeing or hearing them, and that is unequivocally what this is: a transmission, with no loss of fidelity, a communication without language. Undergirding it is the desolation of emptiness, an endless nothing. And I know that this is the language of the dead.

A draft turns the skin of my ankles to gooseflesh and a scuffing on the floor follows – to my left, then somewhere in front. On both sides at once. Behind me. I try to keep track, to echolocate until I realize it's not one or two. The ghosts have left the walls, and the room is full of them. They walk, they breathe.

"Hello?" I whisper.

A scream splits the air. One of the other women. It's a sudden bark of questioning fear, allayed by a gasp, and then a long, witnessing howl, filled to its volume with distilled agony.

"Somebody help her!" I cry. "Mamie!"

"Shhhh," someone says as silence returns.

"Quiet!"

"Didn't you hear her?" I yell.

"Shut up, Charlotte!"

I rattle the restraints. "Are you okay?"

"You're ruining it! Why are you ruining it?"

"Mamie!"

No one comes. The sound drains from the room. Sucked out like a vacuum. No more screams. No scuffling, no sand. No emotional vapor.

Time means nothing in the infinite black.

Sometime later, the quiet ends with Mamie's voice. The others overwhelm her with complaints about my disturbing their "harmonization". We are pulled from the cabinets and she holds me back as the others process by, crisping my skin with their glares.

"I don't know why you insist on questioning things and behaving the way you do, Charlotte," she says. "Harmonization is sacred. Not to be interrupted for any reason. No matter what you see or hear."

I stare at the ceiling in my bed, haunted by the sound of Decima's screams – it had been Decima in Calming – echoing in my ears. I hear it fresh in my memory, the shrill, unlevel sound of fear turning to bodily suffering. I don't know what she experienced, but I heard in those screams her humanity peeled away, exposing the raw animal inside. And then I heard that animal whimper for death. I gaze down the beds. They all sleep soundly, as if nothing had happened, Decima included.

The sound of splashing comes from the bathroom.

I roll over. They've left the lights off. The splashing continues, coming from a darkened stall with the single toilet that sits visible to the room. She's on the seat, nightgown pulled to her waist, leaned over with one arm buried in the bowl. Her wet black hair bounces as she lurches up and down, her fist a plunger, sending water across the tiles and herself. She stops abruptly, conscious that she's being watched. Her eyes angle up, points of light in the shadow.

"Go back to sleep, Morgan," says Charlotte.

And I obey.

THIRTY-THREE

The phone vibrates on the coffee table. I roll to the edge of the couch and strain my fingers to reach it, but only push it farther away. I'm hungover. My head rings high and bright. The sun threatens to split my skull in half. I groan up to a sit and look for a drink. Everything has an aura. My mouth is cotton and wasp's wings.

The apartment is wrecked. I don't know how many people were in here last night. There's dried-out boxes of shrimp fried rice, a spilled ashtray (my apartment is non-smoking but my landlord hasn't said anything yet), a couple of roaches, and even a baggie with some greenlegs still inside – which is shocking, because if I was at a party and no one was looking, they'd be in my pocket or down my throat. It speaks to how gorked everyone was. There's a glass half full of water, but it turns out to be warm gin when I smell it. I take a swig anyway, swish it around, and swallow. Because fuck it.

I stand up and stumble. My legs move like chopsticks. I lean over the glass top of the table and glance at my phone. One forty-five in the afternoon. A missed call from Hadleigh.

Needing to pee, I zombie shuffle toward the bathroom. The door to the apartment is partially open. "Oh fuck," I say, dashing over, fully aware that Doctor David Bowie is a runner.

The hallway is clear to both sides. "DDB? DDB!" I leave it cracked in case she's out there and wants to come back, then begin darting around to check her favorite hiding places: top of the fridge, in the big mixing bowl on the low shelf, behind the toilet. I toss the couch of its lumpy pillows and frayed blankets, maniacally flip the cushions out over the floor. Leaning over the back, I check the window. It's locked.

I'm instantly sober, my attention sparking with the urgent need to find my cat. But first, those greenlegs.

I take out the baggie, set it on the table and smash the pills with an empty bottle. I dump the powder into a little mountain and shove my nose into it, sucking in as much as I can. I shoot upright in a cloud of dust. It stays suspended in the air, rather than drifting down as normal. It shifts around, forming the shape of a cat. I reach out with a finger and write in it. When I'm done, the word says S H O W E R.

I leap from the couch and run to the tiny bathroom connected to the studio, ripping the shower curtain to the side. The air goes still in my throat. Toothbrushes tumble from the sink.

DDB is nailed to the tile inside the shower, her belly split open down the middle. The skin of her stomach, neck and face are pulled out to the sides, stretched taut like the inside of a red balloon, and then pinned to the wall. Her balled-up organs are a pendulum of offal, hanging loose by a sinew below her cracked ribs. Veins and arteries have been excised into branches that stretch from her heart in six precise directions. Like a clock, or a compass.

Entire sections of her insides are studded with colorful pills shoved into the flesh in a spiraling mosaic of exquisite design. Her paws are covered in glitter. The claws have been pulled but remain attached by nerves. Blue painkillers are stuffed into the holes.

I step into the tub, wailing, trying to figure how to get her down.

Her lungs inflate. She opens her mouth and mews.

Then it's dark. Entirely dark. I move to brace myself on the wall, to feel my way to the living room, but my hands are tied down. So are my legs. It's pitch black when it shouldn't be. The light from the front should provide plenty of sunlight to the bathroom. Why am I suddenly sitting down?

Then I know. I remember. I'm in the cabinet. How is it possible that I was somewhere else, acting out a past that never happened without knowing my reality? Thinking of DDB, I begin to sob. I know she's all right. I hope she's all right. She's with Darius. But why is someone doing this to me? I think of Charlotte and feel my soul turn black.

Is it you?

Not me. Them.

Explain. Who's them?

You should have listened to the recordings.

You won't let me!

It's the harmonization stage. Sometimes the angry ones get in first.

TEXT RECORD, PHONE NUMBER

(814) ***-**58

That's where we are now?
You hanging up on me?

You are outrageous.

I just want to know the truth.
I feel like I'm going crazy. It
happened on the trip out here
didn't it? You cut it short. But not
because you were using.
I should have seen it.

Honestly, you shutting me
out hurts more than
anything else. Please stop

Answer me!

Nothing happened.
How many times do I
have to tell you?
I can say it until I'm
blue in the face, but
you won't listen.

Then why is Clayden acting
the same way you are?

I don't know. I'm not him.
Can't you just take my
word for it? Don't I
deserve that from you?

Don't I deserve the truth
from you?

Yes and I've told you the
truth and you've chosen
not to believe me.

Do you have any idea
what it's like to see the
world for what it is and
to have the most important
people in your life tell
you that you can't trust
your own mind?

Yeah I'm sort of getting that
from you right now.

I just want to hear it from
you. The truth. Please.

Please?

Morgan?

Morgan?

THIRTY-FOUR

We had a long driveway back home. It sort of curved around and down to the road. It wasn't a busy road. On the other side was a field. There were cows in it sometimes, but strangely, it had no fence. The cows didn't leave for one reason or another.

Some evenings Hadleigh and I would set up lawn chairs and read books beneath the floodlight on the garage. There came a time when she stopped. Busy with school or friends, I guess. But I kept doing it in the hope that she'd come back.

Today is one of those days. It's late summer, but already the nights are breaking the heat as soon as the sun hits the treeline. I drag my lawn chair out from the garage and sit with a novel plucked from my parents' bookshelf. It's scary and gripping: a coastal tale about a missing child. I read for a bit, then pause and drop the book to my chest to consider how the fading sun has lit the clouds over the cow field.

And there's Hadleigh, standing in it. Her white shorts and shirt and hair flutter in the breeze as she stares into the distance. I don't remember if she was on her way back from somewhere and maybe had decided to stop and catch the sunset.

I lift the book to start reading again as she turns her head to me. I pause and she says something. It's weird. She's too far away for me to hear her. She must know this. I shrug and holler that I can't understand what she's saying, then go back to the book and quickly forget the exchange. The quality of it was surreal enough that it feels almost imagined.

"I'll know," she says from above.

I look up to the sky. Hadleigh is twenty feet high, standing in the open air above the drive. Floating.

My skin is stricken cold. I can feel my face going tight. *I am imagining this*, I tell myself. I make her not real by focusing on the words on the page before me.

But she remains in the air, a wind-whipped blur in my periphery. She's waiting. To judge or confront me for a thing I haven't yet done. She is the personification of future consequence. Inescapable, imminent. I don't look up.

A flashlight beam clicks on to my left, illuminating the pages. My father, worried about my eyes going bad. Thinking the vision broken, I turn. It is her face instead of his, a pair of blinding floodlights where her eyes should be.

She smiles and says, "I'll know."

THIRTY-FIVE

Calming is a visitation or a hallucination, or maybe both. Hallucination brought by visitation. When Mamie closes the door there is silence, then the rush of sand, followed by a gathering that fills the spaces between the cabinets. I know now that we are supposed to be waiting for something, the *right* thing, and in the meantime must bear the dreamlike assaults brought on by the rageful things that Hollyhock confines. They come from the walls.

Some days I sit in the dark and listen as others murmur and beg. They don't remember that their bodies are still here while their minds are dragged to Hell. You don't know it when they come for you, only when it's over. The return of darkness tells you it wasn't real. In that respect, it is like dreaming. Except we aren't asleep when they come. It makes you wish you were dead.

When they come for me, it's bad. The scene with Doctor David Bowie has played fresh over and over, with subtle and excruciating adjustments designed to heighten my torment – or the titillation of whoever summons it. Not once have I had déjà vu as it happened, or suspected it was anything but real until it ended. It is the same every time I watch my family, old friends or classmates I hardly knew, have their bodies broken, their flesh rent, their skin and organs repurposed into glorious monuments to pain at its most exquisite. The cat is always the worst. Something about innocence.

Some of what they show me seems random, but it always

feels deeply personal as it's happening. Piglets taken from their mothers and vacuum sealed into cans while still alive, a tree cut down branch by branch over a thousand days, even as new growth struggles to make up for the loss, but never can, until it finally dies. I feel the death and I die, too.

I see the six-way river, and myself dangled over its confluence.

More visits from Hadleigh, telling me she'll know.

Calming has made me shun the light and embrace the dark. Sitting in the chair beneath the wooden box is the only time I know I can trust where I am. Outside of the serenity cabinet, I can never be sure that it isn't another time- and perception-altering vision done by whatever visits me inside of that room. What if I've been going to Calming for longer than I think? Were my earlier episodes of confusion and hallucination just nightmares from the cabinet, cut and pasted into my seedy recollection? Are any of my senses reliable? My mind sloughs away.

Activities like eating in the community room or doing puzzles with Honora or walking to the swing set carry a hollow feeling of unreality. Knowing that the cabinet is there, and that I might be inside it, makes every moment tenuous – the ever-present shoe, always about to drop.

But not all the visits are malignant. Some are like art; in the way that art can be a medium for communication across cultures and language. Like the woman who does flips and then flies away. I don't know for sure, but she feels like a visit, even though I think I remember her from the North Wing. Gasper, too. I don't know now if he came before all of this, or if I've cut and pasted him from the Now into my recollection of the past. But even those visits are not what we are waiting for. If they were, I feel like Charlotte would intervene. She remains silent.

One morning, I watch Mamie in the kitchen, buzzing about, dumping ingredients into the smoothies, and it occurs to me that these uniform meals are the common denominator for a cadre of women experiencing thematically similar hallucinations. Which of the powders that she dumps into the blenders is the LSD or psilocybin or some other psychedelic? I almost kick myself that I didn't realize earlier that our liquid meals must be laced with whatever is causing us to go crazy in the black boxes, to make me think I've coughed up a phlegm-coated meat ingot. It's an elaborate setup of some kind. They drug us, put us into strange scenarios, poison our minds with hypnosis and suggestion. It's so obvious and I'm so stupid.

I offer my theory to Honora, who looks at me as if *I* am the weirdest thing in this place. Without any irony whatsoever, she says that I am delusional and offers to prove me wrong by drinking both my breakfast and lunch smoothies. I accept. Assuming she's on twice the dose of whatever they're giving us, I watch her all day for changes in behavior, but she acts no differently and reports no ill effects beyond a slight stomachache from eating too much.

On my way to Calming I tell myself that Honora has a stronger constitution making her able to absorb more of the drugs without ill effect. I go to my cabinet clinging to the illusion of autonomy.

Ten hours later I emerge, crying like a child, having watched Hadleigh pull her own teeth one by one, then swallow them in front of me.

TEXT RECORD, PHONE NUMBER

(814) ***-**58

I know the truth.

> Oh do you?

It doesn't matter that
neither of you will
admit it. I know.

> Well you've worked it
> all out apparently.
> What do you want me
> to do?

I want you to be a
FUCKING HUMAN
BEING. I just want you
to treat me with dignity.
I want to hear the truth
from your mouth.

> I can't give you the truth
> you want because it just
> didn't happen, okay?
> That's that.

You're actually an awful
person. How did I not see it?

Goodbye.

You and Clayden were
my world and you destroyed
it together.

You clearly live in your
own world now. Enjoy it.

THIRTY-SIX

Storms outside make it dark. Honora works on the *Oliver Twist* puzzle missing the piece that completes the Artful Dodger's face. I grab her hand across the table. "Honora." My voice is a croaking whisper. "Something terrible is happening here."

She looks up, face mildly amused, like there's a kite flying in the distance. She pulls the headphones to one side. "Hmm?"

"You need to stop listening to that shit," I say. She dodges when I grab for the headset. "The Calming Room is not a good place. You can't let them see you produce. If you start to feel bad ... uh ... nauseous, get to the bathroom and cough it up there. Flush it. Don't let anyone see. Anyone."

"I don't think I can do that."

"Of course you can!" I snap, squeezing her wrist. "They took Rhoda, and Iva before that. Where do you think they've gone to?"

"Same place we'll go."

"And where is that? Since you seem to know."

"To meet the body of the Earth and to sing upon its breath." She ticks her finger back and forth as if she's reciting a central tenet.

"Honora, no. No. Please. Stop this. Please take the headphones off."

She looks at me and I can see the gears turning, some small fragment of what I've said trying to grab hold of whatever is left of her rational mind. Finally, she says, "This puzzle is missing a piece."

"Honora..."

She lets the headphones snap down over her ear and goes back to work. It's like the clap of thunder that releases the first gouts of rain. I hear it. The thunder, the rain.

Watching Honora's face, I feel the emptiness of loss. Until now, I have clung to the idea of her as a fellow conspirator, the one person who saw through the cracks in this place. But now she is distant, swallowed by the siren's song of her recordings. And having watched the nascent threads of our bond dissolve, I am more alone now than had we never met.

The cabinet comes down.

Darkness, silence, pouring sand, a gathering. I wait, hoping that this will be one of those days that no one comes, but I am not so lucky.

A breath of frost chills my face, and I smell the Earth. Decay, humification. The temperature plummets to bitter cold, flash-drying the insides of my nostrils. I feel lifted, then passed through a boundary; something – the world – is peeled away in the process. The temperature rebounds, crawling back to a place where I am merely shivering. Soon, relative warmth returns. I am aware of myself, of my body still in the cabinet. The character of this visit is different.

A scene presents itself, with me at its center. It is autumn. The prairie is waves of bronze, copper and gold, with tassels of bluestem blazing streaks of red from horizon to horizon. There's a creaking of chains. I'm on the swing set.

"Hello there." A man sits on the swing beside me. Late thirties or early forties. He waves nervously, pressing his lips into an anxious smile–frown. He's wearing a smock – the type of old baptisms in the muddy waters of local rivers. He's soaked, dripping. Like he's been sitting beneath a faucet. "Can you hear me?" His words ebb, slightly out of sync with his mouth. I can't get my eyes to focus right. His image goes in and out like a transmission, and when he comes through clear, it looks like he's melting.

"You're dripping," I say.

"They tell us this is the only way to hold the connection." He smiles at me, shy. "You're wherever you are, and we have to sit in this tepid water."

I twist in the swing and look around. Aside from the change in season, I am still very much at Hollyhock. The building. The snaking sidewalk. The chain-link fence, the small rise in the prairie beyond. "Are you at Hollyhock right now?" I ask.

"Yes. In the room with all the tubs."

HYDRO. I haven't been in that room. None of the patients have. "You're real," I say, trying to make it so. "Not a hallucination."

"Um," he says, his tone clearly suggesting he'd not expected me to be confused. "We're real, you and me. Meeting inside a kind of hallucination, I guess. That's how it was explained to me, anyhow. This is where we come for harmonization."

There's a twinge of something along my spine. A reflex I know as the one you're supposed to obey when it comes. Flight. Except here, there's nowhere for me to go.

"Harmonization?"

"Right," he says. "So before … everything happens, the three of us can meet."

"The three of us?"

"This must be as strange for you as it is for us," he says, lips moving for another second after he's spoken. Even with the strange drips, like the atmosphere turning liquid and gathering into droplets that fall down his face, his eyes are clear. He's got dark blue eyes, like marbles. "It's been the weirdest journey. But I'm thankful. Sometimes I can't believe it's real."

"What's real?"

His eyes narrow as his brow draws together. "You don't…? You don't know?"

"What? What don't I know?"

He pulls his hand away from his chest where he has been clutching a wooden picture frame. Inside is a photograph of a family. He's there with a woman I assume is his wife, and between them, a little girl, maybe four or five years old. Freckles. Straw hair falling over a flannel shirt buttoned all the way up, possessed of the same eyes as the man who is clearly her father. They're standing in front of a carousel at a state fair.

The man's sadness permeates everything around him. The chain of the swing set, his hair, the air. His grief is a palpable void, with a gravity all its own. Something inside me tears. I feel for this man and his child, who I know is dead.

"Her name was Mari." He clears his throat. "Marigold. Like the flower."

The air gusts. A smattering of ice crystals tickles my cheeks, reminding me that this place is imagined. A holographic lucid dream shared by two people, where only one has any choice in being there. "What happened to her?"

The man looks out to the horizon where a patch of orange flowers quiver, then fade to black, before turning yellow then orange again. "A little over a year back. She got up this chinaberry tree. Until that point, she'd tried and tried but never done it. The weather looked like this." He pushes himself gently back and forth with the tips of his shoes. His fingers are white around the picture frame. His eyes go wet and his face brightens a measure. "You know, it's so instantaneous. The shock of it. One moment that child is everything in the world – not just to you, her parents, but to herself. At that age, death is a rumor. The future goes on forever. To the horizon in every direction, a million arrows pointing everywhere. A million choices she had yet to make. If I'd had the power to give my own life to put her back at the base of that tree, to stop her and say, 'Not today, kiddo,' I would. One simple mistake erased a whole future and all those infinite choices." He swallows hard. "We've been waiting for her to choose a new ... um ... mother, since the first attempt didn't take."

Another gust of wind. The chains on the swing turn cold in my hands. I notice there's no sun in the sky, even though it's bright out. "Didn't take?"

"Doctor Edevane says that if miracles were easy they wouldn't be called miracles." He makes a furtive glance in my direction, like to see if I'm following. "I know, it sounds like a bad cliché, but it's so far proven to be true. For us and so many other families. She's shown us the results. We've spoken to the others. The success stories. The first woman who accepted Marigold's insinuation... Well, it didn't work out. Doctor Edevane explained that it's akin to guiding someone along a journey off the trail through a forest in the dark. Sometimes you get separated."

I stare at him like a puzzle in the community room. Pieces strewn about the table but converging inward to make a picture. But there are pieces still missing.

He's still going. "In the woods you can hold hands to keep close, and even then, a lot has to go right to get through. With insinuation, nobody is holding anyone's hand. You ... produce the seed and the Earth plants it. After that, it's up to the spirit and the" –his voice drops out– "to be on the same vibration."

"The *what* has to be on the same vibration? I didn't hear you."

"The..." he begins to say, but his voice goes away even as his mouth moves.

Seeing my struggle, his countenance collapses. I see his hope beginning to fade. He gathers himself. He tries again, determined and earnest. My ears go warm as I feel hands forming cups over them, like my mother when she didn't want me to hear words meant for grown-ups. Only now it's Charlotte. And though in the scene of our hallucination, my ears are naked, I am deaf to the man's explanation. He speaks and Charlotte presses harder, making sure that nothing gets through. He stops talking and looks at me, his face searching mine for a response.

"I still can't...."

He says something else. He repeats it. I don't hear.

"Nothing–" My voice goes out like a switch is thrown.

The man shifts on the swing. His lips move. He begins to fade.

The blue eyes disappear last. There is the wind in the grass. The prairie goes black and the sky follows.

Alone in the cabinet, my breath is the only sound. But now, I think I know. This isn't a haunting by the ghosts of Hollyhock's past. It's something far worse.

THIRTY-SEVEN

The door opens and the hallway light washes the floor. I feel my weight again, like gravity has returned. Our restraints are released and the cowls lifted. Mamie puts us in line.

I follow in a daze, moving in slow motion toward the community room. Hettie is there as usual with a platter of smoothies. Approaching for my suppertime communion, I am adrift. I don't know anything anymore. I could pretend it was just another breed of torture, but there was a difference. It was the thing we are waiting for. Hettie puts a tumbler into my hand. The smell is oversweet and cloying. I allow it to slip away. A geyser shoots red and frothy through the straw on impact with the floor.

I turn from the line and walk. Behind me, they call out. Then I'm running. The end of the corridor approaches. I know my way out – it's not even hard. The stairs, the underground passage to the main building, a door that locks from the inside, then the big entry hall and a gateway to freedom. I'm well fed. Uninjured. I could run forever. Farther, certainly, than Hadleigh.

With echoes at my back, I leap down the steps and sprint through the dim tunnel, then up the second set of stairs two at a time. I shoulder the door before trying the latch. The wood complains but doesn't give. Mamie cries out behind me. Her footsteps drum the ancient floor. I fumble for the latch, and flip it, then barrel out. Racing down the short hall and turning into the main corridor, I stumble and somersault, quickly right myself and I'm up again, gaining steam, sprinting faster than I've ever run, and I know that I can keep going forever, or at least until Hollyhock is out of sight. Mamie roars and I swear the bear inside of her has burst from the skin. My socked feet strike the long burgundy rug that marks the final distance between myself and freedom.

I slam into the door. The bars are locked. I go for a metal bin sitting at the foot of the stairs, lift it overhead, and launch. Glass rains down. The bracing night rushes in.

Then I can only describe it as being hit by a locomotive. Mamie flattens me to the floor beneath her, crushing me, smearing me, filling my ear with animal breath. She is unemotional as she pushes up and stands. Seizing an ankle in her massive paw, she drags me back down the corridor. I claw the floor. The nail pops from my middle finger, catching the light like a bloody fish's scale. Exhaustion overcomes the initial rush of adrenaline, and I guess I black out.

The room is butter tiles with me at the center, shrieking through the mouthpiece. Hettie looks down, grimacing. "We won't let you deprive yourself of the gifts," she says, pressing the plunger on an intravenous line.

A layer of me falls away. Just like the first time, Charlotte knows what's coming and makes herself absent. In this moment I realize how much she truly weighs.

The bones of my spine blaze like Christmas lights under surge, the muscles of my back pulling them taut as veins sparkle hot to my periphery. There's an element of sadism in the power and flow of this session that wasn't present in the last. The sedation is mild, the current is high.

I plummet from the sky and hit the ground, but continue through it, past layers of earth and stone, then through the roof of a house and the ceiling of a room. I am back in the child's bed. Things have changed since last time. The paint is white instead of light blue. The pictures on the wall to either side of the opened door are still kid-themed, though they contain different images and occupy new spots. The sheets are altered, too. A scene of cartoon robots in battle this time, rather than horses running wild. The child moves and as before, I am inside him, watching.

He picks up a small sketchpad and props it on his knees beneath the comforter. He draws a rectangle with a pencil. Then two more smaller rectangles nearby. A faithful rendering of his view of the room. He draws a circle for the doorknob, then scribbles in the door. He flips the page and draws it again. Just the same. The door shut and filled in black. In his version of the room, the door is emphatically closed, barred, and covered with locks.

A shadow darkens the hall. He slams the sketchbook closed, stuffing it beneath the sheets. In comes the woman with her tray.

She sets it down. The boy's veins flood with adrenaline and cortisol. I feel it as he does. She takes up a vial and syringe.

The scene fades, only to be replaced by another. The same room. Different paint, different pictures, different sheets on the bed. The moment of the boy hiding his drawings as his mother enters.

Again and again and again. The details always changing, but the big parts are the same. A boy in bed, terrified of his mother.

She sits and fills the syringe in front of him. Tenderly, she strokes his forehead. "Medicine," she says.

The boy tenses like he always does. She leans her weight over his legs and smothers his movement before he can struggle, then brings the needle to the divot at his arm's bend.

SPD INTERVIEW RECORD
EXCERPT OF TRANSCRIPTION

GASTRELL: Charlotte mentioned that another patient had tried communicating with "the boy who lives in the electricity." Did you ever see him again?

WITNESS: I don't know. Can't remember as I sit here. Was the other patient getting electroshock?

GASTRELL: She stuck a hairpin into an outlet.

WITNESS: Oh my God.

GASTRELL: Yeah. Any idea who he is?

WITNESS: Gasper.

GASTRELL: Well, I mean-

WITNESS: Gasper is a ghost. And the scene I kept being shown was from right before that child becomes one.

GASTRELL: That's... uh. That's a lot. You think the mother was murdering her child?

WITNESS: That's how it felt. I think I saw his death.

GASTRELL: You don't think it was just a vision from the cabinet?

WITNESS: I don't think so. Didn't feel the same.

GASTRELL: Speaking of the cabinet, we found your cat. Dr. Bentham has her.

WITNESS: Are you serious?

GASTRELL: Yes.

WITNESS: Oh, Jesus, thank you. Have you not found Darius?

GASTRELL: No. Nothing yet. Sorry.

WITNESS: Yeah.

GASTRELL: Hey, write down the feeding schedule and all that stuff on here. I'll get it to her.

WITNESS: She's okay?

GASTRELL: Yeah, the only problem you'll have is getting her back. Bentham is a full-on cat lady.

WITNESS: Me too.

THIRTY-EIGHT

My eyes crack open to the electroshock room. I'm strapped into a wheelchair. My face hurts and my shoulder aches like it's been run through with rebar. A dry migraine punishes my brain and crackles like the storm raging outside. I wonder if the brain can be a capacitor for electricity left behind, and if the dose from last night's shock is still firing out from my temples and forehead.

The Elizabeth collar is around my neck. Hettie stands before me. She says she will leave me here if I can't behave. I don't answer at first, hoping for a return to my cabinet. When it fails to come, I promise to be good.

Rhoda is returned to us that afternoon, met at the entryway to the community room by the other women, including Honora. They huddle and fawn over her, asking her about her time away. I move closer as well, trying to make sense of their quiet exchanges. They speak vaguely in the language of the recordings, which I don't understand, but I know how women act when one of them announces that she's pregnant.

Rhoda hasn't said anything blatant, of course, but the truth is written all over her. Wearing her hair down, she is aglow, a hand held absently over her stomach.

Insinuation.

Rhoda hadn't been pregnant before Mamie had come to get her from bed, not at least that I knew. A clear picture coalesces, the puzzle pieces in my mind sealing themselves into place. Was this Hadleigh's past? Iva's future? Honora's? Mine?

"Hey," I say, pushing through the scrum. She blithely considers me. "You're pregnant now? Is that it?"

Her smile disappears and the other women recoil like I've blasphemed in church. "What is the matter with you all? How is it possible that you're..." I gesture to her belly.

Rhoda's face is disbelief, like the answer is obvious. But then she seems to take pity on my ignorance. "Given a mouth, the Earth speaks with its breath. Lashing with its tongue the seed that brings about the new flesh of old life."

Honora places a hand on my shoulder. "The spirits perennial."

I pull away. "And what? They keep you here for nine months?"

"In such time as the hairstreak pupates," says Beryl.

"It's nearly springtime," says Honora, drawing her hand across an invisible landscape. "Lambing season."

TEXT RECORD, PHONE NUMBER

(814) ***-**58

Hadleigh?
Hadleigh?

Please pick up.

I'm so sorry. Call me.

I'm so so so sorry.

Please call me.

I have to talk to you.

I have to tell you the truth.

You deserve the truth.

You will never forgive
me and I don't deserve
it. But you have to know.

You were right.

TEXT RECORD, PHONE NUMBER

(814) ***-**58

> Hadleigh?
> I need to talk to you.
> Please pick up.

Morgan?

> OMG I thought something
> happened to you.

This is Clayden.

> Why do you have her
> phone?

She's not here anymore.

> You told her, then?
> Good. It's about time.

No. Of course not. We
agreed it was a one
time mistake. That YOU
instigated.

> Where is she, Clayden?

A few weeks ago, she got
mad and flipped out.

No shit! Just like anybody
would have. Tell me what
happened to her. Where
is she?

Pulled all my stuff out of the
house. She lit the kitchen
trash on fire. Smashed all the
plates we got at the wedding.

Where the fuck
is she, Clayden?

She took the car to
the sanctuary and drove it
into the marsh.

What! Is she hurt?

Physically, she's fine. No
injuries... but there was a
court ordered mental eval.
I found a place – a good
place. She's being looked after
now.

What the fuck does that
mean? Looked after?
Where is she? Is she in
the hospital? I'm flying
out there.

You've done enough
I think.

> I've done enough? What
> about you?

I didn't come wandering into
your room. You wandered
into mine. I was hardly
conscious.

> Not the way I remember it.

Fuck you.

> Tell me where she's being
> treated.

It's not a place you can
really visit.

> You piece of shit. Tell me
> right now. You know I'll
> find her. I'll call the cops
> and file a missing person's
> report.

The police are who found her
when she crashed. She's not
missing. I know where she is.
Goodbye, Morgan.

TEXT RECORD, PHONE NUMBER

(814) ***-**58

SHE'S DEAD!?

Not delivered (!)

SPD INTERVIEW RECORD
EXCERPT OF TRANSCRIPTION

GASTRELL: What?

WITNESS: I can see it on your face.

GASTRELL: See what?

WITNESS: Astonishment. Disbelief. How could someone do what I did, right?

GASTRELL: Not really. I see people every day who do things even though they know with every fiber of their being that it's wrong, that their bad choices will put them in the lockup. Crazy, outrageous, insane shit. You slept with your sister's fiancé. People do worse than that all the time. If I'm shocked, I guess it's that you don't really seem the type. Not that I especially know what that type is. But I guess you had your reasons.

WITNESS: I didn't have reasons. I wish I did. I wish Hadleigh had been an awful person and that I could tell myself it was an act of revenge. But she was innocent! I was just high as hell. And you know ... looking back, I was always going to fuck up her life. It was just a matter of time. Set in motion since childhood. For a little while it looked like we'd all escape it.

GASTRELL: It's okay, just–

WITNESS: It's not okay! I didn't even have the decency to be sober when I came for that first visit. I was going to see my successful sister whose life was taking off, and I got back on the kick so I could cope the fact that I was a failure. I was coasting on rimmies when I stepped off the plane. The worst part is that I wonder if I meant to do it. To take what was hers. I wonder if deep down beneath the haze I knew exactly what I was doing. Did I do it to fuck up her life so she'd have a taste of mine? The irony is that the one time I got clean – like all the way clean – was after she died. Sober as a nun and too fucking late. She'd sent me to rehab. Paid for it herself. She'd checked on me. Written me every day while I was there when my parents couldn't be bothered. And in the end, what it took for me to get sober was her being dead.

THIRTY-NINE

In the next days I am visited, reset, tormented anew. Between living nightmares, I am transported to the swing set, where broken people tell me that I have been selected by their deceased loved ones to ferry their spirits to the corporeal world. I ask them to explain how this works, and every time Charlotte takes my voice. They look at me with saccharine pity; a woman suffering with domestic psychosis, who should be thankful for the opportunity to mend families beyond the walls of Hollyhock but who is too disturbed even for that.

They blubber and squeal, tell me through snot and tears of their loved ones, thrusting family portraits and school photos in my face. All I see is that chimerical thing I pulled from the can of cranberry sauce.

Eventually, I quit. Sitting slack in the strip of rubber, eyes blurring as the landscape changes, as the seasons leap, as night becomes morning becomes afternoon, then night once more, I hear their voices. As the sun burns away the dew or is hidden behind clouds. As fog rolls, as storms explode, as it all succumbs to blizzard. They come, they beg me. I sit. They go away.

The only surprise is that Charlotte doesn't intercede. I take this to mean that she is being selective, waiting for the right spirit to ferry back across the river Styx.

Afterward, we always return to the community room and receive our smoothies from Hettie. It comes to my turn. I refuse.

"You have to eat, Charlotte."

I sneer openly, showing my teeth.

"That's fine. There are other ways of getting food into you. You'll be hungrier in the morning."

I'm already walking away.

"Charlotte?"

I spin. "What!"

She digs in her pocket. "Doctor Edevane asked me to ask you if you know who this belongs to."

I step closer and my heart lurches. "How?"

"How what?" says Hettie. "Do you know whose ring it is?"

I study her face and see that she doesn't know. Edevane gave her the ring just to show me she had it. Darius had received the signal and returned. Then... Then what? What did she do to him? I slump down the wall. How many times can the world break?

That night, when everyone is sleeping, I rise from my mattress and go into the bathroom, numb with the knowledge that this folly has led to another death. It could be Edevane playing games, but I feel it in the air – his absence. I pushed Hadleigh to her death, and now Darius has followed me to his. *For I am a machine of death.*

The toilet closest to the wall is out of view of the ward. My best guess is that Charlotte sleeps mostly at night. Breathing easy, I try not to wake her, leaving my mind as clear as one can in such a moment. Behind the bowl I find the knitting needle I'd earlier stashed, and drive it into my neck.

The pain is a revelation. Glorious proof of my autonomy and the most amazing high I've ever felt. My entire body tingles with delight as I exult in the freedom. I'm thrilled, shocked Charlotte didn't stop me. It's when I try jamming the needle sideways, that my arm doesn't obey.

She growls, fighting me as I watch my fingers release the needle still embedded in the meat of my neck.

Thankfully, you missed the important vessels.

She pushes me away until I am a mere observer. My body stands from the toilet and moves quickly from the ward into the short hallway to the community room. She knocks softly on a door, saying, "Aunt Mom? Sorry about the hour." Mamie swings the door wide and gasps at the needle sticking from my neck like a stray arrow.

I try to recapture myself. Charlotte senses it and clamps down, pushing me into the well of inexistence. The last thing I see is Mamie picking me up and rushing me away.

When I wake, there is a bandage on my neck. I push a finger underneath and press into the pain. There's a small butterfly strip stuck to my skin. That's it. I stabbed myself in the neck and did enough damage to warrant a Band-Aid.

It's morning, but the ward is empty. I lay slack on the bed, feeling like something that is both hollowed to the point of weightlessness and too heavy to lift. I wiggle my fingertip against a spare thread that juts out of the sheets. I'm controlling it, but it looks like someone else's. Feels like someone else's.

Charlotte phases into view in the distance, blurry in my eyes. Still wearing her nightgown, she's on the toilet with both hands in the water, scrubbing. Water splashes out of the bowl and onto the floor. She levels her gaze. "Go eat your breakfast."

"No."

She stops splashing and huffs in exasperation. "Stop being petulant. We need to eat. It's almost time."

"Time for what?"

She stands slowly, exposing a rope of tissue hanging between her legs, sloshing in the bowl. She speaks the answer with an earthquaking voice. "Motherhood."

FORTY

I am slumped at the table when the coughing starts. Honora heaves from her seat and bows over, mouth wide, gagging like a cat on a hairball. Strings of phlegm leap from her throat like a spray of frogs' tongues and anchor on the table. I quickly slide around the table, trying to shield her from view. When that fails, I offer the excuse that she's caught a cold, and try pulling her toward the ward.

But the other women are programmed to the sound. They flow to us, all anticipating, wide-eyed and smiling, cooing and happy. I can't hold them at bay. Honora gags once, then all the air is choked. Face slack, her mouth hangs open as a bolus of flesh pushes up from her throat. It emerges in its yellow flan pocket and drops wetly to the table. I slam the puzzle box over it and pull her from her seat. She seems catatonic as I convey her across the room, reminding her in feverish tones what this means, and what is going to happen. I tell her to deny that she coughed up the spirit seed – Mamie didn't witness it, and maybe Honora could deny, sow enough doubt to stave off the Calming Room. She stares blankly as I recount the hasty plan, but my words don't scratch the surface of her serene affect. Her responses are oblique, fashioned after the pseudo-religious jargon of the recordings. As with the others, she appears to welcome what is coming. When Mamie rushes into the room, Honora leaves my side. "No," I mutter as she pulls away and is swallowed into a swarm of adulation.

Mamie shushes the group and clears them away so she can inspect the regurgitation beneath the puzzle box. I stare through the wired-glass window in the door to the outside world, imagining that the sky and ground are melting together, with me in between. I hear her fingers in the plug of flesh. It sounds like wet pasta.

She makes her proclamation. Honora has produced.

That afternoon, when we are placed in line, I situate myself last behind Honora, and whisper a string of anxious ravings over her shoulder. "It will be hours, maybe, until you are contacted. You'll have nightmares over and over. It will be terrible, but you'll always come back. But then, there will be others. It comes as a cold chill at first – you'll hear the sound of sand pouring. And then a swing set. You'll see them there. What they want is… Honora, they want you to be like Rhoda. They want you to be a surrogate for someone else. Someone dead. Honora? Can you hear me?"

"Yes, Charlotte," she says, passive, placating.

"You can prevent being picked just by refusing. It's the one choice you still have. If they pick you, just say you don't want to. They'll move on. Someone else will come in. It will give us time to figure something out. Are you listening?"

She nods slightly. "Harmonization."

"Look – I know you've got some idea in your head from the recordings. Give me your hand," I say. "Give me your hand, Honora."

She half turns and I stuff the locket into her palm and squeeze her fingers over it. "Remember who you are. Remember your real child, Isobel. She is your baby. No one else is. Honora, do you hear–"

"Charlotte," calls Mamie from the front of the line. "Why don't you go in first? Get yourself buckled."

I give Honora's hand another squeeze. "Don't forget. Don't

forget. Remember. You have to remember her. Remember *who you are* to her."

Mamie smiles beside the door. Inside, I hover, hoping to get myself into a cabinet near to Honora. Mamie sees me lingering and directs me into a chair on the edge of the room. We sit. Straps pull tight. The boxes come down.

FORTY-ONE

That night my eyes are like rolling window shades that refuse to stay down. Exhaustion is its own type of energy. Like antimatter. Charlotte keeps me awake, I know it. Sleep deprivation as control, maybe also as punishment.

Rhoda, back in the ward now, stirs. "Rhoda?" I whisper, but she doesn't respond. She tosses side to side in her bed, whimpers and calls out, sometimes loudly. A bad dream – no shortage of those here. Strain accents her noises. Eventually she goes quiet. Time is syrup. Maybe I doze, but it's fitful.

I crawl out of bed and go to the bathroom where I gulp water from the sink. Turning to the room, the center aisle between the beds forms a continuous line out through the hall to the community room and past that door into the distant corridor where CALMING is located. In the dark it seems to go on forever, which it shouldn't, because the farthest door is usually shut.

More Charlotte games. I feel a sneer warp my face. I'm over fearing her. If anything, I yearn for confrontation rather than existing in the shapeless vacuum of her interstitium. I walk the aisle purposefully, down the short hall and into the community room. The long corridor beyond is snow-light and shadow. I search the slanting bars made by the walls between windows and the spaces where doorframes create narrow columns of black. In a triangle of shadow where the stairs enter from the underground passage to the North Wing, is a figure.

I wonder if it is her, but they are distant and no more than a smudge nestled within a pocket of darkness.

"Charlotte?"

They move some, twisting. Their dress flows slowly, submerged beneath invisible waters. The shadow where it is concealed begins to lengthen, stretching down the corridor to where I stand at the threshold to the community room. It envelopes my feet and chills my toes.

The figure bursts from the corner. Running, dress flaring, hair streaming. At halfway, she raises her arms skyward and I see her face – her wide, fearful eyes. Hadleigh's eyes. She leaps forward onto her hands and does a cartwheel. I lunge aside as she flies past, cartwheeling across the community room, the ward, and through the wall in the bathroom.

It's a wet sound, a repetitive slapping like a child playing in mud. I roll over. Rhoda is on her bed, sitting cross-legged, humming then talking to herself, arms and hands working furiously.

"It's all wrong," she says. "Mmm-mmmmm. Yes. Insinuant and spirit. Harmonization, but no. Mmm-mmmm. Was a discordant breath that quickened the flesh, left the life behind. No. It's all wrong. A sour-tongued lick, oh yes. Do over. Do over. Lick, lick, lick. Sour sour. Hmmmmm-mmm."

"Rhoda?"

She turns her head without interrupting her desperate monologue. "... flesh without breath turns the vessel septic, yes it does... Do over... All wrong... Mmmm-mm, mmm."

I slide from my bed and go over, switch on her bedside lamp.

Her mattress is a wake of blood. At first, her hands seem severed at the wrists, the stumps pressed against the skin of her pendulous stomach. "Rhoda!" I yell, grabbing one of her arms. Her hand appears, then, pulled out from a gaping hole in her belly. Lumps of viscera lay tossed over her legs. Strings of it tangle her fingers, and I think about what comes out of a pumpkin when you scrape its guts. Dirt spills from her mouth.

I pull on her other arm, but she's strong. I can see the outline of her hand digging under the flesh. The others awaken and gather around the bed, long-necked and curious, but without any sign of alarm. "What's the matter with you! Go get Mamie!" I yell. I rip the sheets from the side of the bed, thinking I'll staunch the bleeding, but her stomach is a cavern. Flaps of skin hang loose where once there was fat and muscle and organs. I see her liver on the bed. How can human hands rend living flesh without a tool?

Mamie rushes in as Rhoda toils at her middle. Her eyes wander and her hands go languid. I seize the chance to push her onto her back and wrap the sheet across her body. Her humming ceases, her rant grows weak.

"... *sharpened and honed into the machines of life, and that without the miracle of creation made flesh from stardust, all life desiccates and the Earth is rendered–"*

"Help me get her on her side," says Mamie. I obey as the others attend like spectators to a car crash. Mamie wraps the sheet over Rhoda's feet, using the twisted end to pull her to the edge of the bed. I see the flash of a tiny body no bigger than a squab – pterodactyl arms and shriveled legs – before the blanket obscures it. Hettie storms in. Rhoda's eyes focus on me as the sheet covers her face. Then, as if she was already dead, they carry her out, with one at either end.

I swivel to the other women, speechless, exasperated by their passivity.

Decima meets my glare. "The spirit and the Earth and the mouth each play their part," she says, matter-of-fact. "Without harmony, the tongue wets an empty seed. Rhoda understands that."

I find Honora, search her face for a kernel of the person now glamoured by Hollyhock's spell. She looks at me with pity in her eyes. "The body has a way of rejecting what is wrong." She draws a finger through the blood and rubs it thoughtfully against her thumb. "It's beautiful in that way."

"She was hemorrhaging!" I'm losing my breath. "She disemboweled herself!"

"She will deliver the Earth or become it." Honora tastes her fingers, then looks back to me, her head tilted sympathetically. "Don't cry."

EXCERPT OF
"HOLLYHOCK RESEARCH"

Taken from Personal Computer belonging to Morgan
Bright aka Charlotte Turner
(Evidence Tag #N402, Shelf G4)

Category: Historical Accounts, excerpt taken from *The Final
Days of the High Plains Fur Trade* by H. Charles Instadt, 1919.

"This curious piece of land to which I have alluded above, meanders
across the Nebraska counties of Dawes, Box Butte, and Sioux. It is by
all measure fertile land, the quality of its soils no different than that on
which Nebraska farmers have long grown their corn, soybeans, and
sorghum. But accounts of those familiar with the landscape during the
tail end of the trapping era say that it was markedly different from any
other section of the American high plains, though not in appearance,
for it was, like the rest of the region, an expanse of tall grass prairie
which stretched in all directions horizonward. This land was different,
they wrote, because it was, to use their word, "antagonistic". The type
of place a man falls off his horse for no reason.

I have located two bits of information that elucidate, however
dimly, these accounts.

The United States Government began drawing reservation maps
for the territory that would become Nebraska as early as the mid-
1830s. Over the next decades, the region's Indian populations ceded
their land for nominal prices and accepted relocation to one of eight
reservations. There were plans for a ninth, its boundaries set to capture
portions of this particular plot, but it was never established. The tribes
made it clear they would not set foot upon it.

The French fur traders, who had long shared their entrepreneurship with the tribes, understood why. I have interviewed a cadre of those who were last to abandon the trade, hunting and trapping the region until it was inarguably barren. They warrant without hesitation that the area's Indians considered these lands off limits. They would not venture upon it for any reason, not for water or to pursue game. Nor would they cross over it, even to reach distant hunting grounds. They had their own descriptors explaining why, spoken in their native tongues, which the French trappers approximated thusly: *Mauvais Fruits*. Bad Fruits.

The tribal leaders interviewed for this book were forthcoming in helping me to understand all aspects of the trade, but have declined to discuss anything touching upon these strange acres."

SPD INTERVIEW RECORD
EXCERPT OF TRANSCRIPTION

GASTRELL: Morgan?

WITNESS: Where are we?

GASTRELL: We had to move you.

WITNESS: Where?

GASTRELL: Saint Luke's Hospital.

WITNESS: I told you I wouldn't consent to hospitalization.

GASTRELL: This isn't a psychiatric hospital. You're not required to stay here.

WITNESS: Fine. I'm leaving. I can't be in a hospital.

BENTHAM: Tell her.

WITNESS: What?

GASTRELL: Yeah, okay. It seems like we found Honora.

WITNESS: Where? Where was she? Why didn't you tell me?

GASTRELL: Slow down. We weren't sure at first, but we've confirmed it.

WITNESS: Where was she?

GASTRELL: I only have what the survey teams send back, okay? The whole place is reconstituted as something new. Except for a few square feet that were left entirely untouched. It was like what tornados sometimes do. Those big hydrotherapy tubs were ripped right out of the floor. Some tossed as far as Crawford. All but one, and Honora was inside it.

WITNESS: Don't tell me anything else unless she's alive.

BENTHAM: Oh, she's alive.

GASTRELL: Right. And so is the infant they found with her. They're both here in the hospital downstairs. A bit rough for the going, but okay. It's a miracle. And I mean that when I say it. That entire place was annihilated. You've seen the pictures. Only two things were left untouched. That tub with Honora, and you.

WITNESS: What does she look like? The baby? Normal?

BENTHAM: Just like Isobel.

WITNESS: How do you know?

BENTHAM: Honora still had the locket you gave her.

WITNESS: But ... how did she give birth to her dead child?

GASTRELL: We thought you might be able to clear that one up.

FORTY-TWO

Hadleigh and Clayden's place is nice. That's the only thought in my head as they take me around the house and the yard, then cook me dinner in their gleaming modern kitchen. This place is so nice. How do people get enough money to have a faucet over their stovetop just for filling pots with water? I can't even believe this life that Hadleigh has made. I'm overjoyed for her.

I don't belong in a place like this. It's too nice. Too clean.

Dinner is so ridiculously good, it feels like a joke. Spaghetti with little neck clams flown in from the West Coast. *Flown in.* I know she's putting it all on for me since it's my first visit, but who would even think to go find food that has to be flown in? Back when I gave a shit, I might vacuum the carpet in my apartment if someone was coming over. Now, I don't have anyone coming over that would even notice the color, much less whether it was clean.

I can't handle it.

Between the entrée and dessert, I go to the bathroom and load another parachute full of dream hammers. I tear off a square of toilet paper. It's so thick and soft that I worry for a second if I'll be able to swallow it. Anyway, I peel the plies apart and lay one onto the raw stone countertop. Into that I use a ceramic soap dish to crush up the pills, then dump the crumbles onto the square of white. Twist it all together and *voilà! Morgan's anxiety reliever for the evening.* I fill a glass with tap water, shove the parachute in my mouth and down the hatch. Smile big in the mirror. Flush the toilet. Run water again for fake hand-washing. And on to the crème brûlée, or whatever delicacy Hadleigh plans to summon in her kitchen.

It's a scratch blackberry crumble with vanilla ice cream. So *easy* and *simple*, and truly fantastic that I want to strangle her. It's so delicious I literally beg for more.

Over the course of the evening, Clayden drinks maybe a six-pack of fancy beer while Hadleigh and I have enough white wine to bench our mother's tennis team. We all stay up late talking, but it's really Hadleigh and I loud-talking and catching up. Clayden finishes his last beer and says goodnight.

A few hours later, Hadleigh is sleeping. Noisy fucking snorer she is. You'd never expect it. I'm still flying, so I figure I'll go wander around this fancy house and see what's what. I arrive in the kitchen in a kind of haze, my mind twitching and burning like it does when I'm kicking. I drink more wine right from the bottle, thinking it's fine because I'll just finish it and no one will know. In the moment, I can't remember if this is a rental place that we got just for the meet up, or what. And the truth is, I don't even know who we're all here with. It was Hadleigh and some other people. A party, maybe? Beer guy. Where did the beer guy go?

So, I do what I always do. Being a bit of an adventurer, I start opening doors. It would be cool if I could find a way to get some music going. But anyway. It's a little chilly and I want to get warm. And I'm thinking beer guy looked pretty warm. So I open doors until I find him. He doesn't say anything when I crawl under the covers, but he's awake, I can tell. I kick off my pajama bottoms. His hands come alive. I search him for warm places. They're easy to find.

He rolls on top and we get warm.

Out on the couch, Hadleigh stirs, calls for me, then falls back to sleep.

It's dark beneath the covers. Then there are no covers. Just the cabinet.

FORTY-THREE

Gasper had shown me the truth in the pantry, only I'd not understood what it meant then: Insinuation gone bad. The miscarried thing in the cranberry sauce was identical to what Rhoda had excised from herself. *Mauvais Fruits*. I try to break through to the other women, but they are their own brick walls. They accept – they welcome – this consequence as a cost they are happy to pay if it means a chance to *sing upon the breath of the Earth*. Even Honora, who goes with Mamie one day and doesn't come back.

I cannot leave. I cannot die. I can only continue to refuse.

Whenever a match is made inside Calming, both Mamie and Hettie radiate the joy of new grandmothers. There is no escaping for me, I am trapped in this building as much as my own body. I continue my cold recalcitrance as the loved ones of tortured ghosts beg for me to carry them back to the living. If it's to be my penance to die on that swing set, then I will. I won't become Rhoda.

The cabinet comes down. Whispers of sand. A breath of the dead, and it is springtime. The swing beside me squeaks.

"Hello, *Morgan*."

The transmission of Althea Edevane fades in and out, the preternatural colors of the prairie dripping down her face and arms, over her chest.

"You're wondering how I know," she says, removing one

finger from her grip around the chain to point it at me. I don't react. She gazes back out over the prairie. "I was already curious by the time you gave up your implant. Your behavior, while by no means unusual for a place like this, has a different character to it. Your deviations aren't especially remarkable. It's these other periods of behavior that raised my interest, the times when you're a model patient. Right at the start, I wondered. And I've been wondering. But when we discovered the transmitter you'd brought along, I sat and thought long and hard. I went over your profile again and again. And then, one afternoon a few days ago, while studying your photo, it came to me like revelation. I knew who you were.

"We still have Hadleigh's file, of course. I checked that first. And there it was: one sister listed. *Morgan Bright. Benezette, Pennsylvania.* Right under my nose. I was so excited when I saw it. A mystery for me to solve. I dug a little further. Your digital footprint is small, inconspicuous, mostly scrubbed, but I still found you. A college dropout. A steady, if unremarkable, criminal history flagged by all the hallmarks of drug addiction. Was this just a coincidence? Did you uproot yourself and move to Hay Springs to live in the shadow of your dead sister, only to then suffer a psychotic break necessitating institutionalization? No, no, I don't think so. The real explanation, easily deduced, was that you had decided to take the laboring oar on solving the mystery of your sister's death. *The Snow Walker*, a new modern legend of the high plains. I'm guessing you weren't doing it out of pure curiosity, either. Having oneself institutionalized is a big move even for those enduring the deepest survivor's guilt. You did it because you feel responsible in some way. Something in your drug-addled past, maybe."

I shake my head, trying to rid it of the imagery that won't go away. "Why are you doing this?"

"You think *I* am doing something? After everything you've seen, you think I'm the lynchpin here? The Earth expresses herself whether or not Althea Edevane plays a role. I'm her acolyte, her facilitator."

"You did this to Hadleigh, didn't you? She sat right here, didn't she?"

"Hmm."

"How? Why? Why did you pick her?"

Edevane looks at me without focusing, like the question has caught her off guard. "Why is anyone picked? I don't pretend to know the ways of the spirits perennial. Just like you, she carried a heaviness that attracted them."

Honora had called it guilt. But what had Hadleigh done to regret anything, besides not cutting loose her deadbeat sister?

Edevane gestures to the dreamlike image of the asylum behind us. It shimmers bright like a building of ivory reflecting the sun. "This whole wing was going to be a museum, you know. There was some lip service about keeping it original. It was scheduled to be gutted and remodeled, with little bits left here and there to reaffirm Hollyhock's narrative as an innovator in mental healthcare – which we are. Less a museum and more a foyer with some display cases and placards."

"Why wasn't it?"

"Oh, I stopped it. Explained to the board that we could save money by running things out of the North Wing, with the option to expand if necessary. Let me say: if you ever need a corporation to look the other way, just dangle the prospect of cost savings." She gives me a conspiratorial grin, like this advice is somehow relevant to me. "Truth is, I'd happened across destiny, Morgan, accidentally discovered why someone built a state asylum in the middle of these endless plains. You feel the energy here, that's easy to see. I do as well. Not everyone does. A handful of those who walk upon it register the gift. Hollyhock sits in a special place … a spiritual hot spot, a nexus of some kind. Maybe it's ley lines. You've heard of those? Anyway, there's something down in the dirt. Call it what you will, a song composed by the universe, played on an accidental instrument. An entrance, an exit. A door, a mouth, a birthing canal. The fulcrum of life and death. I felt it in those first days before the hospital was up and running. Didn't know exactly what it was, but I knew it had to be preserved. And of course, the first time I lingered in a place where the plaster had fallen away, I was visited. Just like you."

"Who are they?"

"The summoned. Left-behinds. Spirits called away from the bed of death but unable to find it again."

"How do you know all of this?"

"Oh, some of us can hear them talking."

"Christmas."

"Yes, Christmas. And a woman before her and another before that."

"She's some kind of medium, is that what you're saying?"

"Sure, if you like. The parlance is immaterial. She's attuned to their frequency. A spiritual semaphore." Her eyes trace the horizon, then she turns and says plainly, "Brain damage."

"You keep her here to show you who to pick," I say, knowing that Honora was right again.

"The first spirits who visited me had been waiting near a century and a half – and possibly longer – from before the hospital was even constructed. For them, the land around the nexus, and later the building itself, was a prison. They'd been torn away from death and placed here, into this purgatory on the high plains. How, or by whom, I can only guess. But they were angry. It took some time, but I figured out how to return them to death. To die, you have to live, so that's what I do. I give them life."

"Insinuation."

"That's right."

I leap from the swing and turn to face her. "You're using living people to bring spirits back to life? You're actually doing that?"

"Spirits *are* life, Morgan. The breath of the Earth. But yes, the first were patients of mine, those who had been placed under my care by the State before the latest iteration of the hospital was up and running."

"And you experimented on them."

"Are you unfamiliar with how medicine works? I was solving a problem. Besides, these women were lost causes. They had no family. I delivered the spirits out of limbo and gave them new flesh. Their new mothers received the gift of family, and of purpose."

"How could you do this to other women?"

Her smile is loaded, hinting at events that only she is privy to. "You have no idea. The very first experiments were on men. That was in the early days, before I understood exactly what was going on. These were spirits, and so naturally I was thinking along the lines of inhabitation. Pregnancy hadn't even entered my mind."

"You mean possession? You were offering your own patients to be possessed?"

"Can you blame me for thinking that's what spirits were supposed to do? But I was mistaken. The tongue of the Earth is corporeal, not ethereal. It brought conception, not possession. Men could be insinuated but their bodies aren't built to carry life, are they? There was a quickening in their bellies, but the rest–" she waves her hand, "–not good for anyone. Broken bodies."

I'm beyond knowing how to react. I'm just numb. "You're sick."

"I understand you saying that. I do. Knowledge comes at a high cost – sacrifice. But what I learned, I never could have expected. Women are so much more than we realize." She points to herself and then to me. "Women, Morgan. We can birth the Universe. Men can only constrain it and then die trying. How can it be sick to accept what is offered by the Birthmother herself?" She nods to a large elm tree next to the powerhouse. I don't recognize it. It doesn't exist in the world beyond this illusion. "You see those birds?"

A trio of black dots shoot into the branches.

"Those are cowbirds. Do you know anything about cowbirds, Morgan?"

Maybe I shake my head.

"You've probably seen them thousands of times but never paid attention. Plain-looking things. They're ubiquitous, but you'd never find a cowbird nest because they don't make them. The females are brood parasites. They lay their own eggs in the nests of other birds. Then their young are raised together with those of other species. A sparrow, a cardinal, a robin."

I glare at her.

"I'm a cowbird of sorts, looking for a robin."

"A robin?"

"You, Morgan."

"Me? No. I refuse. You can keep me here forever and I'll never consent to that."

"You've known loss. I have, too." She tilts her head in a friendly way. "Surely you've seen the photographs of my son that I keep in my office. His name is Jonathan.

"I was really too old when I had him. We were fortunate, though, dodged all the complications that sometimes come with late pregnancies. The Earth gave me a perfectly healthy little boy. He was my little miracle. Six years later he was dead. I made a mistake. Let go of his hand in a parking lot. The people in the car didn't see him. The EMTs had to pull me away.

"People want to help. They want to be there for you. They love you. I was surrounded by family, because that's how it's supposed to work. That's how people say you're supposed to grieve. Know what I learned? None of that is true. That grief was mine and Jonathan's – mother and child. When you lost Hadleigh, did you want to be around others? I bet you didn't. You wanted to be alone to mourn. There's a reason for that. Grief is the only eulogy the dead ever hear. Not words, or flowers, or donations to charity. You don't see them, but they stay with you until they're ready. You want your loved ones to rest in peace? Sorrow is the lullaby that puts them to sleep. When the process is rushed or interrupted, no one rests."

She wipes her face. "Anyway. Afterward, I felt like a traitor to my child. My heart wanted to be alone with him. I should have sent those people away. I shouldn't have rushed back to work. It was my place to stand in the darkness of Jonathan's death until he was ready to leave. There's no clock or sign when the dead retire to sleep, but the living feel it. It's that moment when stepping into the light no longer feels like a betrayal. I didn't know that then. I do now. But it's too late. I stepped away before he was ready and neither of us ever found peace."

"Wait... So, you're trying to ... bring him back?"

She looks up, the ponds of her eyes deepening. "I have been trying, Morgan, yes. I called him here from his sleepless wanderings, summoned him to the doorsteps of the living. Eleven times the tongue of the Earth lashed the seed in my womb, and eleven times it failed to grow. I'd hoped menopause wouldn't be a barrier to spiritual insinuation, as it is corporeal pregnancy. But I was too old when I first had him and I've only gotten older since. I knew it the first and second and third time I tried. But the energy of this place was such that I willed my baby to come back alive. I was mad, obsessed. I was convinced that I could be Sarah and the Earth my Abraham. Seven, eight, nine times. Even with the brevity of insinuated gestation, the risks were too great. There was only blood and tissue."

I sit back in the swing. "Maybe you should have taken the hint."

"Yes," she says. "Maybe it took me longer than it should have. But a lost child is a lost child. Like you, I'm trying to right past wrongs."

I cough out a laugh, cruel and mocking. "I'm not trying to resurrect my dead kid through someone else's womb. You should have killed yourself like Rhoda did."

"Consider the lengths you've gone to in the name of your sister, Morgan. The outrageous charade you concocted and acted out. The spiritual nexus is no farce. Think about it from my point of view: I'd discovered a way to guide the dead back into the world of the living shortly after losing my child. It was hard not to see it as fate. A responsibility."

"And the fact that it wasn't working didn't persuade you that fate had nothing to do with it?"

"That's a narrow view. Fate is the destination, not the road taken. Others stepped in to accept insinuation on my behalf. For one reason or another, none have worked."

"*Patients*, you mean. You *brainwashed* patients and then *forced* them to carry your child."

"Brainwashed? No. I've told them the truth, and they are given to understand the nature of the Earth. How is it brainwashing to tell the truth? How many of these women act like they're being forced to do anything? And this isn't just about my own child. I'm sharing the gift with others, as you know. You've met them right here where I sit."

"Grieving parents and siblings and children of the dead whose loved ones you called back but couldn't get born."

"Insinuation is a tricky business. It rarely works on the first try. But it *does* work. I've reunited families, Morgan."

I stare out to the spot in the landscape where the flipping woman would be if she were still here, trying to make sense of it. She'd been stretched so long that the wind took her away. But it's ambiguous. Was she escaping or giving up? "Did you ever think that maybe your little boy doesn't want to be reborn, and that's the problem?"

"That's not how it works. The dead are drawn to the mouth by a token of séance. Something from their lifetime that pulls them in."

"So it's forced birth on both sides of the equation."

Edevane looks at me with genuine hurt on her face. "I would never force you to accept the gift, Morgan," she says. "Even if I wanted to, insinuation doesn't work without a willing surrogate."

"And I'm not. I don't listen to your sermons."

"No, that's right. You don't," she says, gazing to the flower-carpeted prairie and inhaling the fresh air. "But Charlotte does."

"Charlotte–"

"And no need to accuse me of brainwashing again. Charlotte needs no prodding. And Jonathan chose her to bring him back to me. It's a perfect match. A pure connection."

Maybe I block it out, or don't really hear the words. My mind goes hollow.

"You, Morgan Bright, do not acquiesce, but Charlotte Turner absolutely does. With every fiber of her being. She is what all these other women, including you and me, lack: perfection. Successful insinuation is like threading a needle, and there is something in our humanhood which *taints* the process and makes it difficult. Maybe it's the unfamiliarity, the strangeness of it all that gets in the way like a burr of steel in the gears. Hesitation. But Charlotte isn't exactly human, is she? She is a story given by the author an exquisite singularity of purpose that no actual human being possesses. Even the most obsessive among us have our reservations. We stop to consider. Take pause and evaluate our desires. Not Charlotte. She is the embodiment of pure, distilled drive. Every person is a gemstone, Morgan. But ask a jeweler and they'll tell you there's no such thing as 'flawless' in the natural world. Flawlessness only exists in the imagination. And that is where Charlotte was born."

There's a delay between the words and my hearing them before I comprehend. A defense mechanism, maybe, put up by my subconscious to dull reality. Maybe I mumble something. An objection. I hear the word 'no.' There's a sprinkling of ice like you see when a gust of wind pulls snow down from a roof. It peppers my skin and disappears. The sensation is of reality breaking.

I push off the swing and stand, looking as far away into the distance as I can see.

SPD INTERVIEW RECORD
EXCERPT OF TRANSCRIPTION

GASTRELL: Then what?

WITNESS: I... I don't remember anything else.

GASTRELL: And the breadcrumbs? What about them?

WITNESS: No more breadcrumbs at Hollyhock. The next thing I remember is the road. Running. I'd gotten out. Hollyhock was out of view, but something was happening behind me. A sound like an earthquake or a volcano. Howling. I just remember running until the police found me.

GASTRELL: So, you got out before.... insinuation?

WITNESS: Yes. Honora was the last person who I remember going with Mamie.

GASTRELL: There's nothing else?

WITNESS: There's not.

GASTRELL: Okay. Okay.

WITNESS: I'm sorry I don't remember more.

GASTRELL: None of that is your fault. Let's... uh... take a break and work on getting you situated. We've got calls placed to your family back East. Haven't heard anything yet.

WITNESS: I wouldn't expect them to rush to call you back.

GASTRELL: It's the police calling, though.

WITNESS: Yeah, they're used to that.

GASTRELL: Fair. Well, we'll keep trying. I'll ask Dr. Bentham for a referral for treatment.

WITNESS: She really killed Darius, didn't she?

GASTRELL: Nothing has turned up. I'm sorry.

WITNESS: Can I have a cigarette?

SPD INTERVIEW RECORD
EXCERPT OF TRANSCRIPTION

GASTRELL: It's colder out here than before. Let's make it quick. Here: there are a few more left.

WITNESS: No thank you, Detective. You know I don't smoke.

GASTRELL: Charlotte?

WITNESS: Hello.

GASTRELL: What's going on?

WITNESS: Do you ever notice how the sky and the ground melt together?

GASTRELL: Sure. Let's get inside if you're not going to smoke.

WITNESS: And they look like you could walk right from one into the other. That's how I feel right now. [Indicating] This right here is the top of the stairs. [Indicating] This is where you stand when you've taken all the steps and you become the next thing.

GASTRELL: We are standing on a sidewalk, one hundred feet from the front entrance of St. Luke's Hospital, out in the cold.

WITNESS: It's a metaphor, silly. I thought you'd understand.

GASTRELL: No, I get it. You've been taking the steps and now you're at the top. Okay. What does that mean?

WITNESS: My journey took longer than I'd hoped, and of course Dr. Edevane is nowhere in sight, so I can't thank her in person, but now seems

	as good a time as any to speak to you of the gifts.
GASTRELL:	Can we do it inside, please?
WITNESS:	To be honest, I'm a bit conflicted. I want to do the right thing, you know? For the sake of the State's investigation. And to be fair to Morgan, I did stash away some of her more painful memories. She's been through so much already. But I realize how important a full accounting of the facts is to your work. And now that everything is done, I suppose it's neither here nor there to me if she hears them.
GASTRELL:	Why don't you just tell me?
WITNESS:	Well, that wouldn't be right, Detective. They're her memories, after all, not mine. You should hear it from her.
GASTRELL:	Why are you smiling like that?

FORTY-FOUR

"There's nowhere out there for you to go," Edevane says. "We're meeting at the confluence of spiritual pathways. I don't know what happens if you get too far from the swing set."

I don't answer. I don't care. Anything is better than returning to Hollyhock. Maybe oblivion is what happens if I go too far. That's not so bad. At least it's a place I know.

I march across the yard to the chain-link fence and take hold, running my fingers over the loops of steel along the top. The land beyond seems real enough. The breeze moves over the grasses, rolling the prairie like an ocean. A gang of cowbirds crosses low through my line of sight and settles into a tree. They pluck berries and swallow them, then sit, watching. I could disappear here.

I look back to the woman on the swing, watching, her face inscrutable.

Braced on the fence, I slip a toe into the mesh and hop over. The grasses are thick and stiff; they poke my bare feet, but I ignore it. It feels right. The air is full of springtime smells, some light and sweet, others cloying, the mixture of blooms calling out to pollinators. They dart from one splotch of color to the next, indiscriminate in their fervor of collection and passive fertilization.

I come to a trot, the muscles in my legs working and burning pleasurably from the movement. It's life. It fills the air. My lungs are drunk on it. Then I am running, sprinting through the landscape, cutting across flotillas of wild quinine and blue vervain. Grasses and flowers whip my legs, my hands, scratching, even cutting them. I barely feel any of it; my entire attention is given to becoming part of this world, stretching and finally snapping the connection with my past and my guilt, Hollyhock House and Althea Edevane. My legs carry me faster than I ever knew they could, and I bound gazelle-like across the prairie, yards at a time, over a rise and into a shallow trough where blazing star and rose gentian have emerged bright from winter slumber. I am her. I am the woman who breaks the pattern. I am the woman who refuses to give herself to the world.

Away, away, be away.

There's a pull on my arms, and my momentum stalls. Lengths of white string trail behind from each elbow, growing longer as I run. Looking over my shoulder, they extend over the rise, back toward the yard and the swings. Feverish to break Hollyhock's grip, I run even faster.

The strings go taut. I turn to see.

Charlotte shoots up from the grass, thrust into the sky like a kite as I pull. Arms out, legs straight, she throws her head back and roars. Vast paper patterns billow from her body, giving lift and carrying her higher. I twist and stumble, try to break the line, but she and I are inseparable. The strings wind around my arms as she reels herself in.

We collide on the crest of a swale, with our momentum carrying us over the land and into the mirror surface of a small pond hidden by tallgrass.

Charlotte is there now, submerged, nestled within a bed of algae and *Hydrilla* inches from my face. She opens her eyes and embraces me, pulling me below and squeezing me against her body. I struggle like a minnow in the mouth of a predator, but her strength is overwhelming. As the weaker animal, I sense my doom, drowning here in the murky waters of death's dream. Then, she lets go.

I burst from the pond and scramble onto the bank. Charlotte breaches the surface with a smile, bobbing like Ophelia in the disturbance of my exit. My sopping hair brings a shiver. A cowbird whistles somewhere overhead.

Charlotte hovers up, water streaming, skin draped in loops of pondweed, and travels over the surface. Arms wide, she tilts to standing like a vampire awakened. I feel the immensity of her presence, emanating from her skin in pulsing waves. A rainbow of emotions casts the prairie in the spectrum of jubilance and self-actualization. She considers me with indifference. I am an object to her, a tool suited to a purpose, of no value if not employed to the task I was designed for. She opens her mouth, releasing a gout of pond water, and in a beastly voice speaks from her unmoving lips. "We are the machine of life."

I feel the weight of her dominion as she floats closer, heavy-lidded and serene. I lay paralyzed in the grass as she comes.

Her toes brush mine. She shuts her eyes and angles slowly forward until she is floating directly horizontally above, blocking the sun, casting shadow across my face. "We are the juncture," she rumbles. "Angels of the afterworld." She descends then, falling slowly into my skin and bone, a ghost assuming flesh. My flesh.

We stand. *She* stands. I strain to push her out. She is implacable as I am impotent, an annoyance, at most, to this parasite of my own making. But she doesn't hide me away. She lets me watch.

I see the clouds and imagine the flipping woman getting farther away, leaving me behind.

Charlotte, blissful, in control, leaps gracefully to the highest point of the swale and locates the swing set in the distance, where Edevane waits. She bounds through the flowers and grasses. Touching earth, she plucks a stalk of primrose before levitating over the chain-link fence. Her feet settle into the rut of dirt below the occupied swing.

"Charlotte?" says Edevane.

Charlotte offers her the lemon-yellow flower. The director lowers her head and weeps. Charlotte stands tall, taking the other woman's head against her breast.

SPD INTERVIEW RECORD
EXCERPT OF TRANSCRIPTION

WITNESS: For laying beneath the anonymous fields of wheatgrass and sideoats grama, the Ear Muhly and little bluestem, where man and beast tread oblivious through the saltbush and winterfat, run Earth's silent channels of connection to all those creatures who ever did crawl, fly, swim, or walk upon and through it, and know that here is a place seated at the crossroads of the ley line compass rose, demarcated by ancient stone so placed among the glacial moraine, the icy till of God, and left in waiting to be seen by that which sings in the frequency of Pluto, that below this soil lies the fecund womb of Hades and the birthing canal of spirits perennial, which upon the offer of a token of séance are summoned, need only taste the mortal flesh to seed it for renewal, and in such time as the hairstreak pupates, the new flesh of old life shall emerge once more, wide-eyed and washed of sin from the mouth of the Earth, sublime.

FORTY-FIVE

The door to Calming opens. Purple light from the windows in the hall paint the floor beneath the box in a haze. Buckles are undone and the straps removed. The cabinet hinges open. Mamie stands silhouetted against the door. She radiates joy. "Charlotte," she says. "Althea gave us the happy news."

Charlotte answers, not me. Her voice is liquid, warm as mother's milk. "I want to breathe the Earth's breath."

Mamie holds me out of the line as the others make their way to the community room. I throw myself against Charlotte's interior, but she smothers me like cold wraps. I perceive my surroundings through her senses, I just can't control my body. It is no longer mine, and all I want is to disappear. I know my future now.

Mamie smiles and shows Charlotte a photograph from Edevane's wall.

"Jonathan," says Charlotte. "Can I hold him?"

"I hope you will," says Mamie, giving it over.

Charlotte presses it to her chest. "Andrew and I will have a child of our own someday."

"I'm sure of it," says Mamie. "Are you ready?"

Waves of anticipation course through Charlotte's blood – my blood – like adrenaline. "Yes."

"Come then, Charlotte."

With the sun taking its leave of the winter sky, we walk the hall, retracing the steps I'd taken on my first day in the South Wing. Charlotte remains impenetrable, stifling my efforts with such ease that I feel planted beneath the soil of her subconscious, leaving her free to be herself completely; unbothered by my dwindling protestations.

We descend the steps into the subterranean passage that leads to the North Wing and stop halfway. Mamie bends down and locates a metal ring embedded in the floor and lifts it, revealing a cellar door with stairs going down. She motions Charlotte inside and throws a switch.

Old bulbs hum down the length of a tunnel that goes on forever, with every surface covered in infinite, butter-colored tiles. In some places, they've fallen away and shattered into small piles, hastily pushed to the walls. Exposed patches reveal uneven courses of hand-made brick and mortar so old it disintegrates before my eyes. It is the place Edevane had found.

Running along the center of the floor is a gap in the tile revealing a deep and narrow channel. Charlotte glances into it. The light doesn't reach the bottom but there's water inside; I can hear it. We walk far enough that we must be somewhere beneath the back end of the main building, or even the powerhouse. We come to a confluence where two additional passages cross the tunnel. Each escorts a fissure cut into its foundation. I've seen this portrayed in my cabinet dreams. The six-way river.

But it isn't just a product of my subconscious. Others have been here. It is the place that so many years before had driven patients to escape the asylum and beg for death rather than be returned to it. *Rivers of ash that hide the Devil's finger.*

"*And know that here is a place seated at the crossroads of the ley line compass rose,*" says Charlotte aloud, but I feel it's directed at me.

"That's right," says Mamie. "Can you feel it?"

"I haven't stopped feeling it, Aunt Mom."

I feel it, too. The atmosphere is thick and vibrating. Like the air around Christmas's head whenever she spoke to me of those who spoke to her.

Steps descend into the void where the channels meet. Charlotte doesn't look inside and so I can't see where they go. Only the lapping of water reaches my ears.

"Charlotte." Althea Edevane's voice echoes out from another passage before she emerges in a simple white gown. Her wet hair blooms with sprigs of clove and thyme.

"Doctor," says Charlotte.

"I am so proud of the journey you've taken with us. What a model patient you have become."

Charlotte goes warm inside. She clutches the photograph and nods humbly. "Thank you."

"Charlotte, you are the mouth of the Earth, chosen by the spirits perennial to bear the flesh of Jonathan Edevane as if he were a child of your own. Do you invite his spirit to take root, so the Earth might breathe him into the world?"

"I do."

I tumble and roar in silence.

"For the lash to find seed, you must be as you were upon your birth."

Charlotte begins to disrobe. I fight my own body to disobey the will of this nonexistent person I created, this … demon. Charlotte, though, brushes me aside as she unbuttons the bodice, pulls it off my shoulders, and pushes down the dress and leggings. My skin prickles in the cold. She undoes the bra, then rolls the panties to her feet. Mamie dutifully gathers up the clothes.

Edevane tenderly loosens the tie from my hair, freeing it to fall across my shoulders. "You won't have any more need for this. They lose interest once the seed is planted." She reaches into her pocket and brings out her fist. Ash streams from between her fingers. She tosses it into the channel and presses her palm flat to my sternum, drawing a heavy black line all the way down past my stomach. "Anointed as such, you are the intermediary of séance."

"*The birthing canal of spirits perennial, which need only taste the mortal flesh to seed it for renewal,*" says Charlotte.

"Good," says Edevane. "Aunt Mom? Do you have the seed?"

Mamie lifts a vial to the light. I already know what's inside. The thing … the pearl I'd regurgitated. She hands it to Edevane, who takes my hand. "Let me guide you." She gestures to the steps. Charlotte descends.

There is a sound, deep and slow, pulsing below.

Concrete foundations give way to a layer of stone and mortar, and below that, what seems like dry stone and dirt or clay. It is *ancient* – something excavated rather than built. By the time we reach the bottom, the walls tower over our heads.

My destination rests partially submerged in water, its wooden frame and slats rising up. The final resting place of Eleanor and Olive, open and waiting. I see them fresh in my mind, their bodies fused, their milk-crusted mouths agape, eyes straining blindly toward salvation that would never come.

Standing at the bottom step, Edevane unscrews the vial and dips it into the water. Holding it to the light, she whispers something, then offers it. "Only the water, not the seed," she says.

Charlotte accepts the vial. I rage, but all I can do is bring a tremor to her hand.

"Don't be nervous," says Edevane.

"I'm not," answers Charlotte, sounding contemptuous at the assumption. She tips the vial and drinks down the contents, leaving the pearl.

Edevane rolls the pearl into her palm, then tosses it into the crib. It bounces on a slat and is lost to the water, which bubbles after it. "May it find you again."

"And the token of séance for the summoning?" says Charlotte.

"Yes, of course."

Edevane slides a small notebook with a black cover from her other pocket, and hands it to Charlotte. Charlotte flips through the pages. They are crinkled and water-damaged, but every image is the same: a rudimentary drawing of a door in a wall.

It's like a lightning strike to the sternum.

Charlotte! I scream it, but my voice – whatever it is I use to speak – falters. The closed door. The boy. The mother. The tray. The injection. *Charlotte! Listen!*

"The token is strong," says Edevane. "It contains the markings of his own hand, and such will be its strength that he will flow to the seed. Hold it to your heart and welcome him home."

"I will."

Charlotte! But she's not listening. *It's a lie! Charlotte! Charlotte! Charlotte! She's going to ki–*

There is a buzzing in the mind of me. Static. And I know she has switched me off, deafening herself to my warnings.

Charlotte presses Jonathan's notepad to her chest and steps over the side of the crib into water at the base of it. She accepts the cold even as I am pierced by it, turns and sits, then lies fully on her back. The water, roiling now, nearly covers my body. It fills my ears, splashes across my mouth and nose. Edevane peers in from above, eyes agleam, then lowers the slatted lid on its rusted hinges, pinning us inside. I see the gouges in the wood, clawed there by desperate sisters who would die inside it. Edevane throws the latch and tears away a sprig of cloves tied there with a ribbon.

The channels pulse with dim illumination. The same inner light I have witnessed over and again during my time at Hollyhock, and I know that at this moment, streaks of it present themselves throughout the asylum to a few cursed women, as they have to me. Even as my ears swamp, the sound of spirits coursing through voids between frame and lathe, the skin and bone of Hollyhock, fills me.

The light bulb on the ceiling dances in the waves of refraction made by the gathering of weary apparitions. Flurries of ash form and fall in their wakes.

Charlotte is calm. The water takes on my shape, caressing the expanse of my skin. The spirits' touch is light, but insistent, the full extent of whatever force they can still exert in the physical world.

Droplets splash my lips tasting of ash, and I am given a glimpse of their lives. Some who lived long and died old, as well as those whose lives were cut short. Many are tired and quiet, wishing only for a return to the eternal black of death, while others rage incandescent at being wrenched from it, shrieking their desolation in the tongue of the dead. There are others who move in a frequency almost lost beneath the rest, who bubble with the helplessness and fear of those who died before they ever understood that they existed. For them there is only confusion and eternal searching.

The crib shifts and the water drains through the slats. The churn of spirits sinks away.

The walls drop, but I realize that this is a trick of perception. It is the crib that moves. Carried upon the heavy air, ascending from the water, it lifts high above the vault where the channels meet. Somewhere below, Mamie and Edevane vocalize their gospel.

The crib turns upright so that I am effectively standing, and spins slowly in place. And I see the words painted on the placard inside the entrance to Hollyhock: *You Will Twirl With Us*. I am on display in this penultimate moment, a presentation of a home, a vessel, to be assessed and occupied and used. The twirling stops and the crib angles forward to the channel so I am belly down. Suspended there, with gravity pressing me to the slats, I feel the momentum of inevitability. It is the moment before the moment. The reckoning for my part in dooming my sister. Reciprocity. Justice. It was supposed to feel right, but it doesn't.

A thing emerges from the water. A dark and serpentine shape, fat at the base and festooned in squirming branches, the rest of it drawn long and thin, smooth like a muscle. Farther down the channel, the middle length draws up from the surface, rising, pulling with it a slender tip, tapered and coiled upon itself like a scorpion's tail.

It ascends from the water, past the ancient layers of rock, brick and cement, twisting gracefully, looping back and forth across itself as it grows longer and thinner, a whip seeking a place to lay its lash.

It centers beneath the crib, and the slender point blooms like an iris. My pearl appears, set upon the curve of stamen.

Charlotte squeezes the sketchpad, exulting. Hers is a different reality, but it is the only one that could have resulted from how I made her: a two-dimensional façade built with a singular purpose: to have a child. Her chest heaves with pride. She's taken the steps. Her mind is healed. And now she will reap the reward she was programmed to pursue.

Curving around the pearl and swallowing it, the needle point breaches the slats of the crib. It pushes into my stomach, puncturing the skin, piercing the muscle and the organ within. I understand everything. The seed will implant. A fetus will grow. I will carry a child I did not ask for. I will give birth to the wish of a psychopath.

A bead of light follows the seed through the ashen tongue.

It withdraws from my flesh, basted in blood, then disintegrates into the water.

FORTY-SIX

The crib settles into the channel. The air remains thick, saturated by spirits who must continue to wait.

Showering Charlotte with praise, Edevane opens the lid and pulls her from the water. Up the steps, Mamie wraps her in a large, soft towel. They fawn, cradling her cheeks in their hands, pushing her soaking hair away from her face. Charlotte is quietly aglow, tranquil, as Mamie presses a bandage over the puncture in her abdomen and helps her into her clothing.

I want to die. I want to sink into the darkness of Charlotte's void and drown. But even as numbness comes – a familiar numbness I've felt every time I wanted to escape my reality – I am distracted by Charlotte's. The static is gone. I wonder if she can hear me.

Charlotte, I whisper. *I need you to listen.*

Meanwhile, Mamie goes into the vault and ties a fresh bundle of herbs onto the crib. Edevane takes the notepad from Charlotte.

I speak quickly, afraid of being shut out. *You need to understand something. You are not building a family. Doctor Edevane is not interested in the welfare of her child. She's not bringing him back because she is some grieving mother.*

Charlotte doesn't answer, but she doesn't put me away.

During those times when you left me alone, I was visited by one of the spirits here. Gasper. But Charlotte, it was Jonathan. The boy who lives in the electricity. During electroshock, he showed me his life. His lives. And how they ended.

Outside of me, Charlotte is passive. Edevane and Mamie dress her as attendants would a monarch.

I keep talking, fearful that I will lose the ability if I pause. *Something happened to Althea Edevane after her son died. I don't know what it was – she's broken, obsessive about getting it perfect or something. She's brought him back before. Many times. The pictures on her wall? You've done individual sessions. The row where he's under that same tree? Dressed in different ways? All about the same age.*

I know them, Charlotte answers. My heart skips.

Those aren't the same boy. Or what I mean is: they're not the same body. Most of these women are doing insinuation for other people. These sad, sad people. But she's using some of them – including you and me – to resurrect her own son, and when he reaches a certain age, Charlotte... He showed me what she does. You're giving Doctor Edevane her boy back so that she can do it all over again.

She tells him that he's sick and gives him an injection. Then the vision ends. At some point in his childhood, which he has relived over and over, he realizes she is going to hurt him. He drew the doors in the notebook. You've seen that. It's the source of his fear. Her, coming in. He's shown me his death, Charlotte. And he's suffered it again and again.

Mamie fastens the buttons on Charlotte's bodice.

He's just another creature that she can bring back as often as she likes. Another butterfly. A hairstreak.

Flanking Charlotte, Mamie and Edevane turn and escort her down the long passage.

You're going to hand over this child and she's going to kill him again.

Charlotte shuffles to a stop. The others are a few paces ahead before they notice. They spin around, and Charlotte strips away the bundles of herbs stuffed into their braids and buns. Their faces are stricken, like they've been given a death sentence. Which, I realize, they have.

Veils of quivering atmosphere obscure them. Their hair pulls long and taut, haloing faces emptied of blood. Edevane leaves the ground, her back arched over an invisible wheel. Her arms stretch wide and she releases the first notes of her final sound.

Her centerline erupts. Balled-up organs spill into orbit on tethers of omentum while the red wet of her forms a great rooster tail, then settles through the air and onto the ground as rust-stained ash, drained of all moisture.

The halves of her spatchcock open, then split and fall away. And I see the moment in her eyes when she registers that she is in two pieces. They flop to the ground, her bisected abdomen a cavern, hollowed of all viscera, which now lays in a mound on the tile like a deflated parachute.

Even suspended in a whirlwind of ghosts, Mamie lurches, strong and quick, but her movement is interrupted. She is frozen like a video paused, the very image of her a quivering mirage. For a split second, I marvel. The herbs. The fucking herbs. Were they a ward of some kind? Did Charlotte know? Had she planned this all along? And the only answer I can give is *yes* – and it couldn't have gone any other way. She was always going to try and keep the child.

The tunnel quakes. Tiles clatter and smash to the floor. Charlotte races past as Mamie is carried behind us through the air. Her visage ripples. Her voice stutters and skips. She tears down her middle and a spray of her begins, just as the walls crash in from the sides, sparing her the worst of what Edevane got. I glimpse her emulsification amid gargantuan crystals that erupt from the foundations.

We sprint for the steps. The tunnel collapses. Charlotte punches up through the cellar door right as it splinters. Chased by a brume of ash, she runs for the South Wing.

North Wing! I shout, knowing there's no way out of the south. A quake sends her stumbling into the wall. She rights herself and rushes toward the community room.

Sabina, says Charlotte, rocketing down the corridor.

What?

The orderly. That's how I knew about the herbs. Sabina's cloves came out when she fell and that's when she was attacked. No one else figured it out but I did.

Then why didn't they kill us the same way?

Maybe because we're trapped like they are.

We dart through the community room and into the ward. Charlotte skids to a stop when she sees the other women suspended high above the beds on shimmering currents of swarming spirits. They spin and sing, a choir of paper dolls. Charlotte takes hold of Decima's stockinged foot and makes a half-hearted attempt to pull her down. Decima laughs. "Twirl with us!"

Crashes echo. Paint flakes from the ceiling. Charlotte hefts an end table and tries throwing it into the window. The glass fractures, but the wire holds.

Hettie rushes in with Enid close behind. Their faces swirl with confusion. Enid shrieks, "What's happening?"

Charlotte collapses to the ground, crying out, "I am the mouth! The Rose of Jericho! I carry the boy!"

The two orderlies rush up, working their shoulders beneath her arms. Charlotte doesn't wait. She rips the botanicals from Enid's hair and ducks away.

I don't know why she spared Hettie. But behind us is a snapping, wet, sucking sound that means there is no more Enid.

Back in the kitchen beside the community room, Charlotte tries the door that leads to the path and the swing set. It's locked. The small window is more reinforced glass. In the ward behind us, the women sing as the roof crumbles in.

SPD INTERVIEW RECORD
EXCERPT OF TRANSCRIPTION

GASTRELL: How did you escape?

WITNESS: Through the oven. Morgan said that Jonathan had shown her in the dollhouse. The one in the kitchen wasn't even working. I pulled it out from the wall. It was covering a vent hole. There was plywood on the other side. So I kicked it out.

GASTRELL: What happened to the other women?

WITNESS: Absorbed by the Earth. Where is Dr. Bentham?

GASTRELL: She just stepped out. Tell me where Morgan is.

WITNESS: She's in Special Therapies.

FORTY-SEVEN

It's a hydrotherapy room. An imagined one. Not my imagination. Charlotte enters through a door on the far side of the room. She locks it; it disappears. Rows upon rows of gargantuan tubs stand between us. I call out, ask her why we are here.

"I'm going to give you what you came for," she says, stepping into a shaft of light. Her gown is barely visible beneath all the sewing patterns she's pinned to herself.

I don't know what I thought I would achieve coming here. I know the truth. I suppose that's what I'd wanted. But it doesn't feel like any triumph. Hadleigh is still dead, and I suspect I'll soon follow her. My mind is lit with an anxious fever. I imagine my womb. A skewed infant quickening inside. But after everything, I don't feel any different. Is it possible I'd imagined what I'd seen beneath Hollyhock? Had Charlotte made that up, too? Have I been inside the serenity cabinet this whole time, fed this experience by a malevolent ghost? Because I know what I would want if the insinuation really happened. I glare across at my creation. "What did I come for, then?"

"To end your suffering."

"You're going to purge me from my own body?"

"Don't sound like that," she says. "You know you don't want to live anymore."

"I do," I say, though I feel unsure of it. "But not while you're here."

"I wouldn't trust you to carry the baby. He's mine. I am the mouth of the Earth, not you."

"You don't know that you're pregnant."

"I do, Morgan. I can feel him." She lays her hands across her belly and steps around a tub. The patterns crinkle as she moves. I shift my weight instinctively, as if to run. But this is her world. There's nowhere to go. "That doctor up there," she says. "Heeda Bentham? She already suspects I'm with child, she just hasn't said anything yet. But she'll show you." She steps into one of the tubs, sloshing water out of it, then continues over the back edge and onto the floor. Every tub is full to the brim. "I can't wait to tell Andrew."

"There is no fucking Andrew!"

"Andrew Turner, of Hay Springs, Nebraska. He sells tools that people use to make other tools."

"That's just the story I made up for you!"

Charlotte floats over another tub. Her wet feet pound the tiles. "You're jealous."

SPD INTERVIEW RECORD
EXCERPT OF TRANSCRIPTION

BENTHAM: She's been like this since I left?

GASTRELL: Yeah. I called the nurse. She's just sleeping. Exhaustion, maybe.

BENTHAM: Hmm-mm. Might be something more than that. Here, look.

GASTRELL: Morgan's blood tests. Okay. Sorry, unless it's blood alcohol, I'm not really one for interpreting–

BENTHAM: Right here. This line. Her hCG, see it? Off the charts.

GASTRELL: Want to fill me in?

BENTHAM: It's a hormone. Human chorionic gonadotropin. She's pregnant, Abram.

GASTRELL: How? No. I don't care what she said about that place, this is too much. She ... Honora ... must have been pregnant when they showed up at Hollyhock. Same with Charlotte ... er, Morgan.

BENTHAM: What of the negative tests on admission? They don't take pregnant women for a reason, Detective. Stop denying what is in front of your face.

GASTRELL: It's a mistake. All just a mistake.

BENTHAM: No. No. All intentional. You're the detective. Did you ever question that insane diet they were fed? The why of it?

GASTRELL: I mean, it was an upscale place.

BENTHAM: Jesus, man, it was a fertility diet.

GASTRELL: How do you know that?

BENTHAM: I know what women eat when they're trying to get pregnant. A folate-rich diet. Anyone who's tried would know. Buried in those onerous daily medical exams were temperature checks. They were tracking their fertility cycles. They were groomed for pregnancy from the moment they showed up. If it wasn't really happening, then why were they investing so much effort into it?

GASTRELL: I need a cigarette.

BENTHAM: Think about it. Since you've been interviewing her, she's passed out, no doubt because of dips in blood sugar, vomited – morning sickness, for God's sake. She's had nosebleeds and rapidly shifting food preferences. Increased body temp on top of all that.

GASTRELL: Oh my God.

BENTHAM: Yeah.

GASTRELL: Okay, okay. But, look at her.

BENTHAM: Right. The only thing missing is that she isn't showing yet. I can't believe I'm saying this, but it's consistent with all that nonsense Charlotte has been regurgitating. What Edevane told Morgan. "In such time as the hairstreak pupates." I looked it up. That's a one- or two-week gestation. That's it. And Rhoda? Plus, the ... whatever it was Morgan claimed to see in the pantry? Some sort of disproportioned infant.

GASTRELL: I was hoping that was a hallucination.

BENTHAM: The physical evidence matches the story. Honora is with her child downstairs right now.

GASTRELL: How is it looking?

BENTHAM: Yeah ... different. But the first Isobel died young. So, the proportions aren't way off. It's not like it's trying to age up, like Edevane's little boy will.

GASTRELL: This... This test could be a false positive.

BENTHAM: I've ordered an ultrasound to be sure.

GASTRELL: Shit, I've been letting her smoke.

BENTHAM: I wouldn't worry about a few cigarettes at this point.

FORTY-EIGHT

Charlotte continues forward, then stops and holds her belly with both hands. It's grown from just seconds before. She points to it. "See? And my milk is coming in." Her gown darkens wet at her breasts.

Slipping to the side, I rush into the corner of the room, angling for anything I might use to defend myself. I grab the hose for a showerhead and rip it from the wall. It turns into a limp length of red yarn in my hand.

"You don't even want to be a mother," says Charlotte. She raises her hands, prompting all of the faucets to begin running. The huge tubs become waterfalls.

"No, I don't. Give me my body back."

"Oh dear, Morgan, no! I can only envision what you'd do. *Illegal* things. And we know the law has never been a barrier for you." She shakes her chin and flutters her hands helplessly. "It's out of the question."

Water rushes under the tubs and swamps my feet. With my hands on a porcelain edge, I move around as Charlotte closes in, talking calmly as she goes. "I know that he was Jonathan to the Doctor, but I intend to give him a new name to go with a brand-new start in life, just as I've been afforded. William Grant Turner. What do you think?"

My heel loses purchase on the slick floor and I slip to the ground, striking my hip. I pull myself up by the lip of another overflowing tub and limp away, nearly tripping again on the strange gown she's put me in. What am running for? There's no way out. Is this going to come down to a fight? She is only an idea. An idea can be defeated.

"Not if the dream is stronger than the dreamer," she says, having eavesdropped on my thoughts.

Then she's at my side, a hand around my neck. She lifts me effortlessly from the floor and vaults me across the room into a distant tub. She's there in an instant, pushing me along the bottom, then up the side beneath the running faucet. "Look at you. You're like a wisp. Was there ever anything more to you?"

She pushes me under. Chunks of something float in the water like orange jellyfish, waterlogged and ragged. She rips me back to the surface. Any notion of being able to fight her has flown.

"How did someone like *you* make *me*?" she says, lifting me by the collar of my gown and inspecting my face. "You didn't, did you? You're just a liar. I quickened on my own. *I arose, immaculate.* Spawned by the Birthmother, no doubt." She stands, hands on hips, mouth downturned.

She looks to her shoulder and removes a sewing pin, moaning pleasurably as it slips from the skin. The pattern droops, rolling down across her chest. She moves to the pin at her sternum. It looks embedded in the bone beneath her clavicle. It comes out and the paper lolls. She plucks the pins at her waist and hip until the pattern is free.

She considers me through gauzy eyes. I sip timid breaths, wondering what she's doing. She bends over and fishes around in the water, then stands, having grabbed a bright ball of pulp, and shoves it into her mouth. Her jaws crush it, sending a spray of juice and seed down her chin.

Then she lunges into the water, pressing the pattern onto my chest, and stabs the first pin into my neck.

SPD INTERVIEW RECORD
EXCERPT OF TRANSCRIPTION

[ALBERTA ZHANG, Sonographer, enters the room.]

BENTHAM: This is Alberta. Alberta, this is Detective Gastrell.

ZHANG: Hi. I just need to get set up.

GASTRELL: We can take a quick break.

[Break taken from 5:02 pm–5:08 pm]

ZHANG: Okay, here we go. It'll all come up on my monitor right here. Yep. There's baby right there. I see an arm, and here's a foot.

GASTRELL: Oh my God.

ZHANG: Looks to be about eight, nine weeks–

GASTRELL: That's impossible. She wasn't even there that long.

ZHANG: Is everything okay?

BENTHAM: Yes. Please go on.

ZHANG: There's baby's heart. I'll zoom in for a tracing now. Steady. That's normal – 162 beats per minutes. Perfect. There's baby's spine, tailbone. Bringing a hand up to the face, right here. Oh my.

GASTRELL: What?

ZHANG: Oh, it's probably nothing. The arms are further along in their development than I usually see, but it's all a bell curve. Otherwise, baby is quite active. Moving around. What a little dancer. Fetal environment is good. There's plenty of amnio. The patient has a full bladder. That actually makes this easier for me to see, funny as that sounds.

FORTY-NINE

Charlotte stabs me with the pins, jamming them deep and repeatedly when I try to pull them out. My palms and fingers stream red into the tub, punctured in defense of myself. My arms and shoulders burn, the muscles moving ever more languid beneath her relentless attack. Between shocking moments when my head is shoved beneath the water, with lungs starved for air, Charlotte transfers the sewing patterns from her body to mine.

The idea of her isn't just strong, it's invincible.

While my body fights, my mind is elsewhere. It stands in the landscape of my adulthood. It shows me, like the Ghost of Christmas Past, how I had taken Hadleigh for granted, treated her like a crutch, and allowed myself to stop growing, to stop trying. Somewhere I gag on water, surfacing from the deep of a hydrotherapy tub, sputtering breath. And I know that the idea is winning. She assumes flesh as I become the two-dimensional pet of the monster I've created, who is – I now realize – just a paper doll of the monster I already was. In this slice of a second it is clear to me that all of this was inevitable.

SPD INTERVIEW RECORD
EXCERPT OF TRANSCRIPTION

BENTHAM: And?

ZHANG: I don't understand this, Doctor. Three days ago, the fetus was nine or so weeks. The patient wasn't even showing. Now the baby is the size I'd expect at around thirty weeks.

WITNESS: Insinuated gestation whisks the spirit to fruition! It is the nature of the Birthmother!

ZHANG: What?

WITNESS: It's all in the recordings, nurse.

ZHANG: Excuse me? What is she talking about?

BENTHAM: Just... Sorry – just tell us, based on the progression, when will she deliver?

ZHANG: Days. Tomorrow? The next day? I'm going to order an amniocentesis.

WITNESS: The mouth of the Earth opens to speak and all shall see and rejoice.

BENTHAM: I'll talk to labor and delivery. Let's move her now.

FIFTY

Charlotte releases my neck and allows me to bob on the surface. My chest heaves. "Out there, the baby's coming," she says. "I thought you'd like to know."

I have no sense of time. It feels like she's been drowning me for minutes, but it must be days, or longer. There are no windows. There is no time. It is hollow, but it is familiar – the oblivion I'd been addicted to for so many years, returned. I'm glad Charlotte hasn't let me see what is really happening. I never want to see.

I think about the woman who became the kite, endlessly flipping in place until the one day she'd stopped. When she'd stretched long in the wind and flown away into the sky, I'd seen it as her escape, and celebrated it as a triumph. But it wasn't an escape at all, was it? It was just a different kind of defeat. There was no destination sitting veiled behind the clouds, no salvation. Just endlessness. It was proof that the world had more than one way to beat you. The flipping woman wasn't escaping, she was giving up.

And I wonder. Why is it that fighting must always be the choice? It depends on what you're fighting for, I suppose, and what winning – should you prevail – actually means. Sometimes the end sneaks up and surprises you. That's probably how it works for most people. Though now I realize there's another way, where you're conscious of your timeline's end. You see it coming.

I can't see Charlotte through the water when she holds me

down, so cloudy it is with the stain of my blood floating in clouds and ribbons. She pulls me up and dunks me, again and again, saying whatever she's going to say. I think she wants me to fight more than I am. What's the point? To give over every bit of strength and not take any of it with me, wherever it is I'm going?

The calmness of peace expands through my core upon realization of my own truth. That fighting for the sake of fighting is for people who don't stop to look around. Sometimes not fighting is the answer.

Or maybe I'm in the cabinet. Maybe darkness is set to return. That is where I hang my hope.

I release my limbs to the onslaught, which stops as soon as Charlotte sees my surrender. Her face, predictably, is that of disgust. In giving up, I cheapen her victory. Roaring, she punches me in the center of the chest with such force that it sends me bouncing off the floor of the tub. When I surface again, she is zipping the long canvas cover used to keep patients inside.

"You stay," she says. "My baby is here. I won't miss it." She snaps the zipper into a small metal device that I couldn't reach if I wanted, leaving only the circle of my face exposed to the air. I whisper, "Don't leave. Finish."

"You can watch."

Then it unfolds: a reflection on the surfaces of my eyes, a scene no person should witness. And even as I watch it happen, Charlotte holds me there so I can't escape. And I have no eyes to close. I can only think that if I'd fought harder, she would have finished the job and I wouldn't have to bear witness as my body, this machine of life, betrayed me.

SPD INTERVIEW RECORD
EXCERPT OF TRANSCRIPTION

[DETECTIVE ABRAM GASTRELL enters labor and delivery]

GASTRELL: Baby's here?

BENTHAM: Just now. Nurse has him.

WITNESS: There he is! There he is! Bring him to me!

NURSE: Hold on one second, just completing the Apgar score.

WITNESS: Oh, my tiny one. Hewn and ground. The fruit which swaddles the seeds of spirits perennial. If only Althea could see you. She'd take you up in her arms. What a reunion it would be. But she is gone, claimed by the Earth herself. I will tell you of her deeds, and then her memory will be ash to you. For you deserve your own life!

NURSE: What?

GASTRELL: Psychiatric patient. You can ignore all that.

WITNESS: Andrew? Let us discuss a name.

GASTRELL: Charlotte, I'm Detective Gastrell, remember? I'm not Andrew. Andrew doesn't exist.

WITNESS: Oh, nurse? Is it true that the husbands get baby-brain too? You'd think it was Andrew who just went through nearly an hour of labor. Men!

NURSE: I'm sorry?

GASTRELL: Dr. Bentham? Thoughts?

BENTHAM: There's no need to do anything rash just
            yet. Observation for them both, then
            management and care for Morgan–

WITNESS: You can decide this moment to stop calling
            me that. You say Andrew doesn't exist?
            Well, neither does Morgan. She's gone.

GASTRELL: Sure. Observation. I'm trying to get her
            parents here. A blood relative. We'll talk
            more outside.

WITNESS: Oh, and Andrew? I've decided on a name.
            I hope you don't mind, it's just time passes
            so quickly for the spirits perennial and they
            should feel a sense of identity from the
            start. Don't you agree?

GASTRELL: I'm not Andrew.

WITNESS: The child will be William Grant. I know,
            I know. That's been the name ever since I
            imagined him. But it will be the name of a
            great man.

NURSE: Apgar is stellar. But... I couldn't help but
            overhear. The baby... The baby–

WITNESS: William Grant Turner.

NURSE: The baby ... is not a boy.

WITNESS: What? Let me see him. Let me see him!

BENTHAM: Careful.

NURSE: Here you are. She's absolutely stunning.

WITNESS: Get this off! [indistinct]

BENTHAM: Whoa, careful, careful. Be careful, Charlotte.
            Oh, my–

WITNESS: This is not my child! There's been a mix-up
            in the nursery. Take it away. I do not know
            this baby. I rescind the naming!

NURSE: She never went to the nursery.

WITNESS: Get it away from me!

NURSE: What is happening?

BENTHAM: I'll take her. Here. I got her. Charlotte, please stop screaming.

NURSE: I'll call the attending.

GASTRELL: Charlotte! Charlotte! Stop, please!

WITNESS: [Indistinct]

GASTRELL: Charlotte, careful! Put that down!

WITNESS: But how did you do it, you cruel, you selfish whore? How did you supplant the token of séance? You tangled the finger strings of Pluto, you did, placing a lie upon the altar of the ley line compass rose, corrupting the mouth of the Earth with the filth of deception, filling its teeth with the stinking offal of your vile designs!

GASTRELL: Get back in the bed, Charlotte.

WITNESS: I defy your infection! No! I will not wear the mantle of wretched usurper to the deserving dead.

BENTHAM: Nurse, bring some midazolam, please.

NURSE: It's already going in.

GASTRELL: Here, help me get her back into the bed – yeah, just take her feet.

NURSE: She shouldn't have been up. Her BP tanked.

BENTHAM: It's recovering.

GASTRELL: Here, can you hold the baby up?

BENTHAM: What are you doing?

GASTRELL: Just ... hold her up like that for a second. I'm checking something. Doc: look at this.

BENTHAM: [Indistinct]

GASTRELL: The inside of the ankle. See it?

BENTHAM: What is that, a birthmark?

GASTRELL: For her it is.

BENTHAM: Oh my God. Is that a wolf?

GASTRELL: This baby already has a name.

FIFTY-ONE

There is movement between my feet, a mass. Fleshy and slick. It grows and pushes my knees wide until they touch the sides of the hydro tub. Fingers curl over the canvas edge at the far end and pull it to the sides, forcing the zipper to open. Charlotte's florid face presses through as her form congeals. She rises from the opposite end of the tub and opens her eyes. A mouth cuts across the skin of her face and then growls. "You rotten, scheming witch!"

"I... I don't understand. I saw the baby born. You pushed me down after that. What happened?" My heart flutters. I think I know.

Charlotte screams, "How? How did you do it?"

"Do what? Tell me what happened!"

"You took away my baby. You stole him away and put *her* in his place! How did you do it?"

And now I know that in the world just beyond the prison of Charlotte's brain, Hadleigh lives again. I don't want to think about it – my body building her, pushing her out. It's a nightmare. But now, sitting across from the demon who took my autonomy and made the nightmare real, a new energy suffuses my blood and I burrow into Charlotte's eyes. "Open the cover and I'll show you."

Sneering, Charlotte draws a knee to her chest and hooks her big toe into the zipper between the halves of the tarp, then pushes it the length of her leg. I snatch her ankle before she can pull it away. "That!" I say, pointing to the tattoo just above the bone. I lift my leg from the water and rest it on the edge beside Charlotte's face, so that she sees the mirror image of Hadleigh's bird up close. "We both have one. Token of séance."

I hadn't known what Gasper – *Jonathan* – meant when he told me that I had the token. But down in the tunnels, just before the Utica Crib, Charlotte and Edevane used a phrase: *token of séance* – something personal to the spirit that would draw them in. For Jonathan, it had been his sketchbook. For Isobel, it was her portrait in Honora's locket. For Hadleigh, it was the very ink she'd placed with needles into my skin. There could be no stronger draw on the dead than a mark they'd placed upon the surrogate while living. And Jonathan knew it.

Charlotte comprehends and screams inside her throat, then stops abruptly and scrubs her face in her hands. When she pulls them away, her eyes are raw with fury. She launches across the water. I shoot out my arm and catch her by the neck, surprising us both.

Charlotte fights then, punching and scratching like a cat as I push myself upright. I thrust her away and she topples backwards, slamming her head into the porcelain. Rose-tinged bathwater sloshes onto the floor.

She looks up at me, her eyes strangely focused. There's realization in them. An awareness she was incapable of having before this, the understanding that she was only an idea. Having failed to get what she'd been made for, her purpose is gone, and with it, her strength. Even though she is whole, I can sense the pit growing within. A guttural sound turns in her chest and she smiles through her tears. Her voice goes deep and beastly. "You and that baby deserve each other."

I pull her from the side of the tub, ready to slam her head a final time. "What does that mean?"

She coughs, speckling her chin with bloody saliva, and smiles bloody teeth. "I found something, Morgan. Down where I lurk in the darkness of you. Where you've buried so much of yourself. Do you want to see it?"

"No."

"Please," she says in baby talk. "A little something before I go. A gift from Auntie Charlotte to mother and baby. The ungerminated seed of a memory, buried in the soil of years."

"I don't want any more memories–"

She gives them to me anyway.

A scene opens on the swing set behind our childhood home. The memory I've always had plays out: me swinging too high and falling to the ground, the pain that shook my tiny body. My parents rushing from the house in response to my cries.

The colors bleed away, the sounds fade, and it starts anew. Charlotte speaks as it renders. "Did you never wonder how you got so high, swinging alone by yourself at not even five years old? High enough to fall and break your arm?"

The water goes cold.

In the memory, a child swings higher and higher, terrified. The child – me. I scream for it to stop. With every swing, hands punch my back, sending me up so high that the chain slackens at the apex and I can barely hold on. And then, another push, and I lose the chain. My heart slips up my throat and I fall backward. I see the sky receding. Hear the bone snapping, my screaming. See our parents running over.

Glimpse Hadleigh's bare feet rounding the side of the house.

There in the tub, I feel the injury fresh. The stinging bolt. The childhood fear that such an injury meant death. But the real pain is deeper than that.

It. Was. Hadleigh.

The scene plays again, a gratuitous offering from Charlotte to make sure I feel its impact. I do, and my perception of my entire life carried on from that moment is cast in new light.

I remember now how fervently she talked to me whenever the accident came up, each time editing herself from the story until she was no longer a part of it. She'd come at it from different angles, adding layers to her innocence. *The next time you shouldn't swing so high,* or, *I was never able to swing like that at your age,* or, *Still, you should get me if you want to try something scary,* or, *Morgan, you remember how hard you were swinging that day?* When strangers asked about the cast on my arm, it was Hadleigh who interjected with the answer. *She went too high on the swings!*

So, she lied. Kids lie all the time for all kinds of reasons, mostly to avoid getting in trouble. But when the days turned into weeks, she held to it. Months became years, and she kept the truth to herself, allowing the lie to be reaffirmed over and over, to become history. Whenever I was hurt and couldn't play with the other kids, during doctors' visits, and even when I became addicted to pills, she let the lie live and it set like concrete around the sunken truth. She went off to college and a few years later I followed. She graduated early and went to grad school, while I was kicked out after my sophomore year. She watched as my life fell apart, and still said nothing. It would have been easy for her to confess the mistake then, as an adult, to admit the fear and cowardice of a child who didn't want to get in trouble, who wanted to cling to her image, but she never did. Through addiction and arrests and solitude and loathing, she let me think that I'd done it to myself. All for the sake of a trivial lie. And why? To maintain her flawless persona, her status as family favorite? Had she really been so callous?

I see our history together at once, like life flashing before my eyes, only it's the two of us, our lives. Every moment, every laugh, jape, inside joke, every time we covered for each other with our parents, or cried together on Hadleigh's bed as we shared the pain of a broken heart. Every accomplishment of hers that I celebrated – the pride I felt that people knew *I* was her little sister. I adored her. Worshiped her. Acted like an idiot for her attention. Looked up to her, tried to be her. Judged myself through the lens of her. Hadleigh formed who I was, whether she intended to or not. And yet, the whole time – the whole *fucking time* – she knew. She let me adore her – the curated version of the real thing.

I thought I was jaded enough, but this revelation is perhaps the worst of all. Because it wasn't just childhood. Hadleigh had become the beacon that saw me through the turmoil of my adulthood. She was something I aspired to, even though the perfection that she represented to me was unrealistic. There was Hadleigh, and there was the idea of Hadleigh, no longer the same thing.

I try telling myself that maybe she'd simply forgotten, just to hear how it sounds – or even that she'd come to believe the lie was really the truth.

But no. *No.* She'd remembered. It was guilt – not some saintly altruism – that drove her to prop me up with loans, rehab, bail. Absent her own regret, the spirits of Hollyhock wouldn't have singled her out to Christmas, and she wouldn't have ended up inside the Utica Crib.

Now, with the truth revealed, I wonder if I'd always known it, deep down. Looking back, my own actions read different in this new light. Maybe I'd been on autopilot, driven by a subconscious sense of revenge when I'd left the couch and found Clayden sleeping in his room.

I come back to myself in the realm of Charlotte's mind. "Why did you show this to me?"

"You wanted the truth, didn't you? Isn't that what all this hubbub was about? Well, now you have it. All of it. And you know who your sister really is."

"She held onto a stupid lie and it killed her," I say. And hearing the words aloud, I register the simple truth in it. Hadleigh *died* for what she did. My anger gutters. I'm baffled. Confused. I don't understand why she did what she did for so long, but I have no energy for rage. I'm just … tired. "I want to … forgive her."

"Forgive? Neither of you deserves forgiveness." She growls and lurches again, swipes at me, but I catch her and push her back down.

Persimmons bob on the surface. I grab one and cram it into her mouth. When she screams into the fruit, I push harder and she goes under. The water bubbles as her lungs empty, and she stops moving. The tub begins to drain. The room gyres and disintegrates. Walls and ceiling tear apart in long paper strips, exposing the inky nothingness beyond. Propped on my knees, I reach down, churning the water as she melts through my grasp, but soon the water is gone, and Charlotte Turner with it. Yellow-topped sewing pins collect in the wet around the drain.

SPD INTERVIEW RECORD
EXCERPT OF TRANSCRIPTION

GASTRELL: Morgan? Morgan? What's the matter with her?

NURSE: All her vitals are fine.

BENTHAM: It looks like she's sleeping. Dreaming.

GASTRELL: How long will she stay this way?

BENTHAM: Till she wakes up.

NURSE: Well, she's been able to nurse. Baby has a strong latch.

BENTHAM: Yeah, and growing fast.

NURSE: I meant to ask: have you noticed her arms? I haven't seen anything like it before.

GASTRELL: Uh...

BENTHAM: We think it could be a variant of Marfan's or another kind of arachnodactyly. I've got calls in to some specialists. Um, nurse, can you give us a minute?

NURSE: Sure.

[Nurse Langdon exits room 6:16 pm]

GASTRELL: Is there any way to stop it?

BENTHAM: I don't think so. Isobel is already physiologically back to her death age. It only took six days. How old was Hadleigh when she died?

GASTRELL: Thirty-five.

BENTHAM: Oh God.

GASTRELL: What do we do?

BENTHAM: Keep it quiet. Protect her from prying eyes as long as we can. Which is gonna be hard.

This case just keeps getting stranger. Here.

GASTRELL: What's this?

BENTHAM: The results of the amnio.

GASTRELL: I don't know how to read this. It's all over the place.

BENTHAM: Hm-mm. See this one? Hemocyanin?

GASTRELL: That's a blood thing?

BENTHAM: A component of hemolymph. Basically, insect blood. Butterflies.

GASTRELL: Why is that in this report?

BENTHAM: Because what they drew out of her womb wasn't exactly amniotic fluid.

TEXT RECORD, PHONE NUMBER
(814) ***-**58

Morgan u there?

> Hmm-mm.

Don't be mad at me, please.

> Not mad. Just upset.
> You're going away.
> I know it's my fault.

I swear to you it isn't.

> Tired of babysitting me.

That's not true at all. I would
take care of you every day
for the rest of my life if you
needed it. I'd spoon feed you,
change your diapers!
But you don't need that!
You've been doing so well
This time around.

I'll say it again: this
move is about ME. You know
I've always wanted to go

somewhere like this. Wide
open. Beautiful. Air.

But Nebraska? There's
nothing but grass.

That's kind of the point, lol.

I mean I'd understand if it
was Colorado or Idaho
or Wyoming or a place
like that.

I don't know. There's
something amazing about
being able to stand in one
place and see for a million
miles in every direction.

It's something.

Isn't Nebraska one
of those states that's
passed all those
terrible laws?

The job is there, so.

There are other jobs.

Can we not?

Fine.
When do you leave?

Move in two weeks. Job
starts the next Monday.

I'm worried. Okay, scared.

You will be fine! It's
not like I was physically
holding your hand.

Something about just
knowing you were near,
that's all. I still need my sister.

I'll be able to help you
out – whatever comes up.

It's not about money!

I know – I'm just saying.
You don't have to worry
about it.

I'm not going to need the
money.

You don't have to say that
because it doesn't matter
to me. You're like five
weeks clean anyway, right?

Four weeks and five days.

That's the longest you've
gone in a while.

Yeah. In a while.

I feel like it's a breakthrough,
Morgan. At six months you
need to come visit and we
can celebrate together.

Oh, I don't know.

Yes. We're doing this.

You can bring me out into
the endless grass and
show me how interesting
it is.

It will be spring by then and
everything will be in full bloom.
You'll eat your words.

Leave me one of your
moving boxes. Something
that actually takes some
work to unpack.

I will.

THE NACREOUS HOME

A woman stands alone in a darkened nursery. Exhausted, she has wept until her eyes click dry. Inside the crib, her newborn coos and grunts, flails its arms and legs, which have quickly grown disproportionate to the rest of its body. She gazes down, feeling adrift from the world, and wishes for the cabinet's black.

AFTERWORD

I suppose many authors who decide to provide an afterword struggle with the decision. Including an afterword presumes you think you have something more to say after a reader has already committed their time to read your book. It presumes that what you want to say should be said at all and that anyone wants to hear it.

In some cases, though, I don't think there's any such thing as saying too much. When the rights of vulnerable groups are under attack, you can only say too little. What I tried to say with THE REDEMPTION OF MORGAN BRIGHT cannot be said enough, *especially* by people like me—someone whose body is *not* the subject of discussion in state legislatures, governors' mansions, and courtrooms.

Roe v. Wade was overturned as I was planning this story, a disastrous decision that handed the issue of reproductive rights to the States, many of which wasted no time putting women's reproductive rights to the torch—including Nebraska, and Texas, where I live with my family. At the time, I knew I was going to write a ghost story set in an asylum, but the death of *Roe* changed the trajectory entirely. There was no other way for me to write the book.

Forced birth *is horror*. It is traumatic and dangerous and dehumanizing. Anyone can see that if they care to. More people should see that. And not just the ones suddenly cognizant of the issue because they have a daughter and start doing the math.

I had people tell me that a future like the one I painted in this novel is unrealistic, as women's rights have come so far, and this to me is the most terrifying aspect of our current situation. Yes, it is true that I resurrected an old law allowing husbands to have their wives institutionalized. But just because it is hard to conceive of something happening again doesn't mean it won't. There is a belief, apparently held by some, that once rights are recognized, they can't be taken away. A quick look around the globe shows this not to be so. And it's obviously already happened in the U.S. with *Roe*. Governors and legislators speak openly about plans to close state borders to restrict travel for reproductive healthcare. Some towns and municipalities are *already doing it*. Nebraska, Texas, and other states have proposed laws on the books to end no-fault divorce.

Rights are at their most vulnerable when they are taken for granted.

There are ways to fight back. Many countries have robust court systems with avenues for challenging laws that affect reproductive autonomy. The non-profit Center for Reproductive Rights carries the fight across five continents and has claimed legal victories advancing the cause in over sixty countries. I hope you will consider lending your support to them or another group that defends reproductive freedom.

– Chris Panatier

ACKNOWLEDGMENTS

As with many of my stories, the seed of this one began with something my (at the time) four-year-old daughter said. Just a few words. But it was creepy enough (kids, huh?) to get my mind turning. So, thanks, kiddo: not just for the kernel that became this story, but for reminding us every day what happiness looks like.

I knew early on that this was going to be an asylum story. Naturally, I learned about Elizabeth Jane Cochrane aka Nellie Bly and her audacious voluntary commitment into New York State's infamous Women's Lunatic Asylum on Blackwell Island at age twenty-three so that she might report on the patients' conditions. I needed a way to get Morgan into Hollyhock and Bly had already laid the blueprint. Bly's account is entitled *Ten Days in a Mad-House*, and it is widely available for those who would like to learn more.

Though the time period of *Morgan Bright* isn't precise, I wanted to create the feel of an institutional scheme reminiscent of the United States in the 1950s insofar as current events have pushed things backward in that direction. To that end, Carol A. B. Warren's book *Madwives: Schizophrenic Women in the 1950s* was tremendously educational. Warren's work inspired how I came to envision Hollyhock, with its group sessions, Home Skills and Housework. Additionally, I spent many hours listening to and watching old clinical interviews of women from the 1940s and 1950s. The thing that struck me from both Warren's book and the interviews was the extent to which the "sick" women repeatedly quashed their own doubt about their diagnoses because learned people (men, in the interviews I watched) were telling them they were sick. It's exactly what happened to Bly, who, upon revealing she had faked her symptoms, was told by hospital doctors that she was, in fact, "positively demented". What a coincidence.

To Courtney, thank you for being my most trusted reader— always helping me navigate what's good for the story and what isn't. You hold me up. As always, my father reads everything I write even though genre fiction isn't really his thing and none to date have featured any account of the French Revolution. Thanks Dad. My agent, Sara Megibow is a relentless champion of her authors (it is known) and I am so grateful to have you in my corner. You sold this project in record time and kept me from spiraling in author limbo. Thanks to all of those who read early drafts and gave feedback: Jessica Hagemann Bross, Bonnie Jo Stufflebeam, Michael Carter, Sam Rebelein, and Gabriela Houston.

This is the third novel I have shaped with my editor Gemma Creffield. As usual, she understood exactly what I was trying to do and helped me get the story where it needed to be. I am so grateful. I appreciate so fully the efforts of copy editor Steve O'Gorman, publicist extraordinaire Caroline Lambe, campaigns executive Amy Portsmouth, and Sarah O'Flaherty, who designed the toothsome cover. *Nom nom*. Further thanks to everyone at Angry Robot Books who push the books out and then boost them.

I'd also like to express my gratitude to all of those in the horror community who have welcomed me. So many of you have made me feel a part of this special place. To Gemma Amor, you've been so willing and available to give me advice and guidance when I've needed it. You are an absolute gem, an artful potty mouth, and a human being I am thrilled to call my friend.

To the reader, it means so much to me that you spent your

valuable time with this story. That's everything an author can wish for – to share the experience with those on the other side of the page.

And lastly, I can't forget metal, music's horror genre. Here are some bands I listened to while writing this novel: Spirit Adrift, Ghost, Aara, MGLA, Grima, Faidra, Asagraum, Power Trip, Witch Ripper, Blut aus Nord, Alterbeast, Skeletonwitch, Ringworm, Crypta, Blackbraid, Escuela Grind, Lifecrusher, Tool, Stagnater, Sepultura, Totem Skin, Between the Buried and Me, Hail Spirit Noir, Russian Circles, Tides From Nebula, Zhrine, Gojira, and the Neighbor's Fucking Leafblower. \m/

ANGRY
ROBOT

BURROWED
MARY BAADER KALEY

DEEP DIVE
RON WALTERS

We are Angry Robot

THE CIRCUS INFINITE
KHAN WONG

THE HOLLOWS
DANIEL CHURCH
A Storm is Coming...

HIM
GEOFF RYMAN

angryrobotbooks.com

Joshua David Bellin

MYRIAD
Time travel is murder

Captain Moxley
AND THE
EMBERS OF THE EMPIRE
DAN HANKS

SILVER QUEENDOM
DAN KOBOLDT